Fairlyden

Gwen Kirkwood

First published in 1991 by Headline Book Publishing PLC

This edition published in 2016 by Endeavour Press Ltd.

One

Alexander Logan turned and looked back down the sloping hillside, making a conscious effort to relax his tense muscles. The funeral was over at last. Everything appeared to have gone smoothly but an uneasy prickle crept up the back of his neck. He recalled Jacob Reevil's beady eyes surveying the greening fields around Nethertannoch's neat farmsteading, the clean, cosy parlour - and Mattie.

Dear Mattie. He had watched her clench her small, work-roughened hands within the folds of her black skirts, he had seen her teeth fasten upon her lower lip during the Reverend Lowe's interminably long prayers, but she had maintained her composure. Indeed she had conducted herself with all the grace and dignity of a young queen, despite the sorrow in her heart and the ordeal of facing so many grim-faced, black-clad mourners.

'There's no reason to be feeling edgy now,' he muttered to himself. Almost every family in the glen had been represented. Even the laird had been present in person. Usually Duncan Blair, the estate factor, represented the Castle, especially at the funeral of an ordinary tenant. Sandy sensed that Sir Douglas Irving's austere presence had caused Mattie more apprehension than reassurance.

Matthew Cameron's death had ended the security of the Camerons' three-life lease of Nethertannoch, but Mr. Blair had understood the old man's anxiety concerning the future of his only child. The factor had given his assurance that Matthew Cameron's wishes would be granted, his years of toil rewarded. The tenancy of Nethertannoch would be secured in the name of Alexander Logan. Sandy felt a glow of pride. He would ask Mattie to be his bride, when she was ready. The knowledge had brought comfort to her father in his last hours.

'Ye'll tak care o' ma bairn, Sandy?' The words, whispered so faintly, echoed clearly in Sandy's mind. Mattie is no longer a bairn, he had wanted to say. She's almost a woman grown - with a mind o' her own. Aye, and pride too! She's beautiful with her crown of thick, brown hair and her dark eyes.

'You know I'll always look after Mattie - always!' he had replied.

'Aye.' The word had been no more than a gentle sigh, then a brief burst of strength had returned. 'Ye dinna mind that Mattie canna hear, I ken that, Sandy. You've aye been guid tae ma lassie.'

'Aye, but no more than she deserves. I was thirteen when I came to Nethertannoch; the world seemed a bleak, dark place then. She was but a wee maid, eight years old, but I shall never forget the way she slipped her hand into mine and shared her secrets so trustingly; she roused me frae my misery with her merry smile. I shall never forget the sound of her lilting voice, her silvery laughter. Even my own mother found comfort from Mattie.' He knew it gave the old man pleasure to talk of his daughter, and indeed he liked to talk of her himself.

'Aye. That was before the fever though. She could hea then.' Matthew Cameron had fallen silent, as though sleeping. When his eyes opened, his gaze was clear and earnest.

'Ye're a grand farmer, laddie, just as Mr. Blair said. Ye've been a son tae me in a' but name. I offered your mither that tae once, when she agreed tae make her hame with us, an' brought your faither's stock frae the mill. She took guid care o' me an' Mattie.' He sighed.

Sandy watched sadly as the clock ticked away the silent hours of the night. Matthew Cameron had indeed been a second father and the best friend he could have wished.

'I would hae liked ... to see you and Mattie wed, Sandy.' In the dawn light the old man's face had turned an alarming shade of grey; pain seemed to rob him of each shallow breath. 'It's a few weeks before she's age tae marry without consent.' He began to gasp. His words were faint. Sandy strained closer. 'Ye have - ma blessing, laddie. Ye'll aye dae what's best - whatever's best for ma bairn ?'

'I will always do whatever is best for Mattie. I need her even more than she needs me.' He had squeezed the withered fingers comfortingly in his warm, strong clasp.

'The bible? Hev ye found...?' Matthew Cameron had fallen back against his pillows for the last time, his thoughts on the book that had guided him day by day throughout his life.

Sandy welcomed the breeze which dried a shaming tear as he vividly recalled Matthew Cameron's last hours. He wished with all his heart that he could have shared the old man's unshakeable faith in the Almighty, but his own faith had been shattered by the cruel events of his youth and the grief he had witnessed on his mother's face when they had been forced to leave their home and the bustle of the Caoranne mill. Nevertheless, when he returned to the house, he resolved to open the small parcel which had been Matthew Cameron's last gift to him some weeks ago. It was wrapped in grey linen and securely bound with thread but Sandy knew in his heart that it contained a bible.

He bent to push a bunch of thorns firmly into a gap in the hedge. The April day had been warm and still, a blessed calm after the incessant raging of March's icy winds and lashing rain. Tomorrow he must begin to plough the five-acre field. It was time to sow the corn, to keep his promises to Mattie's father. First he had to be sure Reevil's hungry cattle could not penetrate the Nethertannoch boundaries and devour the precious grass. Jacob Reevil had the largest farm on Caoranne estate but he made no effort to prevent his hungry animals from marauding over his neighbours' land. During the winter it had been impossible to plough the iron-hard earth but Sandy had spent every minute he could spare doggedly repairing the grey stone walls and layering Nethertannoch's hedges, using all the skills which Matthew Cameron had taught him.

It was more than six months since Mattie's father had had a bitter quarrel with Reevil over his straying, disease-ridden cattle. A few hours later he had suffered the seizure which had rendered him a frail and dependent invalid. It had been a long winter, and a harsh one. The bad weather had started early, long before the year of eighteen hundred and fifty-six had drawn to a close. Snow had begun to fall on the twenty-fifth of November, but it had not lessened the frost's iron grip - indeed more snow had added to the rigorous conditions. Before the week was out the cold was intense and its effect had been increased by a keen north-west wind. In the town of Dumfries, some thirty miles or more to the east, curlers had been out on the River Nith. Reevil had left his farm, and his starving cattle, and travelled for days to join in the festive sports. It was said that a frost of such severity had not visited the district for twenty years or more. The bitter cold had taken its toll on both men and beasts, and for many, including Reevil's own workers, the failure of another potato crop had added to the burden of survival.

Meanwhile Matthew Cameron had clung tenaciously to life. He had endured the short dark days huddled in a corner of the oak settle beside the open peat fire. He had slept fitfully in the box bed through bleak unending nights - only to succumb at dawn on an unexpectedly bright morning when the world seemed to have been reborn at last.

'Sandy! Sa-andy!' Startled, he turned instantly from his contemplation of the surrounding fields. Mattie rarely raised her voice from the carefully controlled tone which Mistress Lowe, the minister's wife, had painstakingly encouraged when she first began to supervise Mattie's education. He saw her scanning the surrounding hills and waved his arm. She saw him and turned, pointing towards the track leading up from the glen. Sandy's heart filled with unexpected tenderness. Mattie's neat, black-clad figure looked so small, so alone, silhouetted against the sturdy grey farmhouse. Yet she had more courage than anyone he knew. He shaded his eyes against the fleeting glare of early April sunshine. Most of the track was hidden from his own view by the fold of the hill, but he knew Mattie's sharp eyes seldom made a mistake. He listened carefully.

The faint jingle of harness carried on the quiet air. He frowned. Surely that was the sound of wheels scraping the flinty stones at the sides of the track? Except for a weekly call from Jem Wright, the carrier, few vehicles ventured as far as Nethertannoch. Besides, no one would be likely to call so soon after the funeral. Mistress Lowe had left less than an hour ago and she was the only one from the glen who bothered to call on Mattie as a friend. He lifted his arm in a second salute. Mattie acknowledged it and returned to the house.

She had been on her way to feed the hens when she spotted the carriage far below on the twisting track. She was almost sure it was the laird. Her brow puckered. Why should he return for the second time in a single day? Could he be intending to reassure them about the lease perhaps? Mattie's frown deepened. Somehow she could not visualise the laird putting anyone's mind at ease.

Sir Douglas had been a soldier until his elder brother had died during the fever epidemic; it had taken so many of the glen's young men and women, Mattie reflected sadly, including her own mother and twin brothers - and Sandy's father and elder brother. Sir Joshua Irving had been alive then. He was old, but he had possessed a steely determination when it came to the survival of the Irvings of Glen Caoranne. He had summoned his remaining son home from the army. Sir Douglas Irving had no interest in the remote Scottish glen with its small farms, tenant farmers, and traditions. He used military strategy, without humanity.

Ruthlessly he had dismissed Sandy and his mother from their home at the prosperous little mill although there had been Logans there for four generations. Mattie shuddered involuntarily. She felt very vulnerable; the house seemed empty and forlorn without her father's presence. She bent and hugged Buff, the little dog who was her constant companion.

Mattie knew that her handicap embarrassed most of the glen folk, despite the unrelenting efforts she made to lip-read.

'If only people would face me. If they would speak with a little care,' she murmured against Buff's silky head. She grimaced sadly. 'Even a smile would suffice.'

Sandy's mother had saved her life with the help of her healing herbs, but it was Sandy who had encouraged her to watch his lips and his hands and willed her to understand - to communicate again. How patient he had been. How unfailingly kind. She sighed. She had learned to laugh again with Sandy. She had been so desperate to learn. Most of all she had longed to be able to read the book which her mother had once read to her each evening before she said her prayers. She treasured it still - German Popular Stories, written by two brothers named Grimm and translated into English. It had taken her a long, long time before she had managed to read the book for herself. Yet how eagerly she had returned to the little school in the glen, her young heart filled with childish hope.

Mattie shivered and tried to banish the memories which came flooding back with frightening clarity. The sight of Dominie Butler's tall gaunt figure at her father's funeral had recalled the hours of terror and misery.

'His eyes are still cold and hard, his lips so thin they are almost invisible.' Buff raised her intelligent brown eyes as though she agreed and Mattie rested her cheek briefly on the dog's soft head. Still she could not dispel the uncomfortable feeling that the dominie had eyed her with the same disapproval in every line of his long, harsh face. She had seen the tight-lipped glance of the laird and she had known the two men were discussing her. As far as Sir Douglas Irving was concerned she might have been a horse that he was assessing, to be bought or sold. She shivered again and chided herself for being fanciful. It was almost time to feed the animals and start the milking but she would do nothing until the laird had made his visit.

'Dear God help me to understand him!' she prayed fervently. Again her thoughts returned to Dominie Butler. He had rarely spoken to her directly in all the time she had spent in his schoolroom. He had shown neither patience nor compassion. Whenever she had misunderstood his instructions - which had been often, since he always mumbled and frequently turned his back on her - then he had beaten her and she had seen a peculiar satisfaction in his eyes and on his grim face.

'He wanted to punish me,' she told Buff, 'I never knew why.' Every morning she had trudged the four miles to the school with new hope in her heart; this would be the day she would learn to read or to add up the figures on her slate as the other children did. Dominie Butler had callously accepted her father's precious pennies, then ridiculed all her efforts. Usually he had not even bothered to wait for her answers and sometimes he had made her so nervous and confused that she had not known whether her voice was a whisper or a shout. Gradually the children had followed his example, either making fun of her or simply ignoring her. Sometimes she had almost despaired of learning anything as she faced another long day in her own silent world, yet she had been determined not to give in or to complain. Sickened and bewildered though she had been, her desire to learn had remained paramount and she had suffered the beatings in silence and without complaint, unaware that her pale face and dark, fear-filled eyes betrayed her unhappiness and caused Sandy's mother a great deal of anxiety.

Mary Logan had discovered something of Mattie's ordeals while delivering one of her herbal remedies to the home of a sick child.

'Then Mattie must never enter Dominie Butler's school again!' her father had declared with rare anger and bitterness. She remembered how hurt and angry she had felt at first. She had been convinced she must be a failure, even an idiot. Now she knew this was certainly not the case, but today Dominie's cold stare had succeeded in shaking her hard won confidence.

It was Mistress Lowe who had searched out ways to help her overcome her handicap, after a discussion with Sandy's mother; the two women had been friends since girlhood. The minister's wife had promptly written to a distant kinswoman for advice and Mattie knew she would be eternally grateful for the new world which had opened up to her as a result. Slowly, painstakingly, Mistress Lowe drew pictures, made shapes with her mouth, counted and wrote down numbers. Mattie watched intently. Gradually she began to understand, then to read herself.

Sometimes Mistress Lowe rewarded her efforts with a book of her own. Mattie had inherited her father's love of reading and books became her most treasured possessions. Once she had learned to read and write there was nothing she would not attempt. Sandy's mother had encouraged her thirst for knowledge, passing on many of the herbal recipes which she had inherited from her own father, a highly respected apothecary. She had learned to cook and to make butter and to keep account of everything that happened in the house and dairy.

'Ye're a richt clever lassie, indeed ye are!' Jem Wright had declared in amazement when Sandy's mother had died so suddenly three years ago and Mattie had taken over the house and dairy.

Mattie tried hard to bolster her self-confidence now as she awaited the arrival of the carriage, but she was relieved to see Sandy's tall figure come swinging through the farmyard, sending the hens scattering with protesting squawks.

Sandy noticed that her eyes seemed even darker and larger than usual in the pale oval of her face and he felt an almost overwhelming urge to gather her slender figure into his arms and protect her, though from what he did not know. Instead he took her hands between his warm, work-roughened palms and squeezed them reassuringly, as he had done so many times in their long friendship. Mattie smiled tremulously but she could not quite hide her apprehension.

'It is the laird's coach!' The words burst from her involuntarily. 'He is coming back. So - so soon!'

'You must not worry, Mattie.' Sandy spoke with the slow, precise speech he had learned to use with her. 'The laird will grant us the tenancy as Mr Blair promised.' Her eyes followed his lips with earnest concentration and he was rewarded by her nod of understanding but lines of anxiety still creased her brow. 'I made a promise to your father. Please trust me, Mattie. I will always look after you.' She nodded again. Encouraged he went on impulsively, 'It was his wish, and it is my wish also, that we should be mar—' His voice trailed to a halt for her eyes had been distracted from his face; she was already gazing intently over his shoulder and he felt her hands tremble. He sighed and turned his head.

Sir Douglas Irving gathered up his long coat, grasped his silver-topped cane and descended regally from his coach. They watched tensely as he came striding up the narrow path from the head of the track. He picked his way fastidiously through the farmyard, scattering the protesting hens once more. Mattie bobbed a curtsy and led the way indoors. Sandy started to follow. Sir Douglas Irving turned his head briefly, fixing him with a cool, grey-eyed stare. For the first time, Sandy felt like an intruder at Nethertannoch, although it was his home.

In the small parlour the laird looked around for the second time that day. He had been surprised to find the place so clean and comfortable. Small tenant farmers had little money to spend on comfort. Mattie had painted the walls with a wash of white lime which reflected the pale shafts of April sunshine streaming through the small-paned window. The smell was fresh and clean and the room looked larger now that it was emptied of black-coated men. The peat fire lent a cheerful glow, as did the bunch of spring flowers which Mattie had gathered and placed in a blue bowl on top of the oak press. She had found a few late snowdrops, her father's favourite flowers. 'Harbingers of spring,' he had called them, believing they brought the promise and purity of new life, and hope for the future.

As Sandy watched the laird's erect figure and stern face he prayed that the man who had been the friend and guide of his formative years would be proved correct once more, but already the frail flowers were fading, their span of glory almost over - at least for another year.

The laird inspected the room slowly, his gaze resting briefly on the unusual silver-framed picture of Mattie's mother, before settling almost reluctantly on the girl herself. He noted her neat, though drab, appearance. She might have been a raw recruit in the regiment, instead of a young girl mourning the loss of her beloved father, Sandy thought indignantly.

Mattie felt all her earlier apprehension return. She tried desperately to remember the advice Mistress Lowe had repeated so patiently when she was a child; keep calm watch the mouth but it was impossible to follow the rapid movements of the laird's thin lips as he paced, to and fro, across the small room. Even Buff, her faithful little dog, crouched uneasily against her feet. All the anxieties she had pushed aside since her father's illness now gathered together and swelled in Mattie's brain. Her carefully controlled voice, her precise speech, deserted her, and of course she could not hear the pitch of her voice. She scarcely knew whether she was shouting or whispering.

Sir Douglas turned to Sandy impatiently. 'I believe you can communicate with the girl?'

'Mattie can communicate herself, Sir. If she could see your lips.' The laird frowned irritably and carried on as though Sandy had not spoken. Mattie watched intently and the strain on her pale face wrung Sandy's heart. Then, to his profound relief, it seemed his fleeting prayers had been answered.

'You may tell her,' The laird cast another frowning glance at the silver-framed picture, trying to ignore the sweet, soft mouth, so ready to smile - so like the girl's. He turned away abruptly. 'Tell the girl, Nethertannoch will remain her home!'

As the laird's words sank in, Sandy's face was transformed with relief. He turned to Mattie and gripped her shoulders.

'Everything is all right! Do you understand, Mattie? We can go on farming at Nethertannoch just as your father wanted!'

Behind him he heard the laird's swiftly indrawn breath, but he was intent on watching the tension melt away from Mattie's wide brown eyes as understanding dawned. A smile illuminated her pale face. She walked past him and stood before Sir Douglas Irving, a picture of youthful grace and dignity.

'Thank you, Sir,' she said clearly. 'We shall work hard to be good tenants. Mr Blair says Sandy is one of the best farmers in the glen!' Her colour deepened and she gave a quaint little bob.

The laird's only response was a frown. His grey eyes met Sandy's blue ones, then slid away. His expression was cold and remote. He bent and stepped hurriedly through the low doorway. A terse jerk of his aristocratic head ordered Sandy to follow.

Sandy smiled quickly at Mattie, though he was puzzled by the laird's attitude. Sir Douglas Irving did not halt until they were some distance from the house. Then he turned on Sandy abruptly, fixing him with that cold, unnerving stare which had reduced men of considerable rank to stuttering boys.

'You deliberately misled the girl!'

'I-I misled Mattie?' A perplexed frown creased Sandy's earnest face. His heart began to thud.

'Jacob Reevil will take over the tenancy of Nethertannoch. The girl may stay. As Provost I shall take it upon myself to attend to her needs since she has no family of her own, and considering her affliction. Marriage to Reevil's son will provide a suitable solution. I shall arrange it immediately.'

Sandy reeled with shock. The colour had drained from his ruddy face. He groped for words. None came. His brain felt numb.

'The usual period of mourning will be waived in the circumstances,' the laird continued. 'The Reverend Lowe leaves for a meeting with his fellow Ministers tomorrow. He will hold a simple ceremony as soon as he returns. You may tell Miss Cameron to prepare herself. It will be a mere formality since she cannot hear.' In accordance with Jacob Reevil's demands, he added silently, loathing himself for his compliance.

'No!' Sandy found his voice at last, a strangled croak. 'Ye canna' do that! Mattie is but a lassie.'

'She has the makings of a woman beneath those shapeless black drapes.' The laird found himself echoing Jacob Reevil's words before he had collected himself. 'The match will be entirely suitable. Tam Reevil is but a boy.'

'Tam Reevil is an idiot! He canna read or write. He canna even...'

'My dear fellow, most of the labouring population in England cannot read or write,' Sir Douglas interrupted curtly. 'Few of them get the opportunities given to the people on this estate - an opportunity which this girl spurned! Dominie Butler informs me she is unteachable.' His tone held condemnation, but he could not help recalling Mattie's amazingly clear speech and dignified manner when she had thanked him. 'Absolutely unteachable,' he reiterated.

'The dominie lies! Mattie Cameron can read as well as any man or woman in the glen. Aye, and she can write and keep accounts!' Sir Douglas's disbelief was genuine and Sandy rushed on, 'Mistress Lowe taught her. Jem Wright will tell you.'

'The girl cannot hear,' the laird snapped impatiently. 'How could Mistress Lowe teach her anything? The dominie himself despaired of her.' Sandy's blue eyes met the laird's disbelieving grey ones. His gaze did not waver. He had great respect for Mistress Lowe, even though he despised the man she had married.

'Mistress Lowe is a fine teacher. Mattie had learned most of her letters and numbers before the fever made her deaf. More than anything else she wanted to learn to read. Dominie Butler failed to help her, but Mistress

Lowe had a kinswoman, Mistress Munro, who was governess to the children of the Earl of Strathtod. Mistress Munro sent many letters of advice; she also wrote of a school in Glasgow, specially for deaf children. Mr Cameron hadna' money to send Mattie there, but Mistress Lowe helped her well enough. She has books of her own. She reads her bible, aye, and all the books and news sheets Mistress Lowe brings. She has a slate for writing.' Sandy was unaware of the pride in his eyes and in his voice, but the laird of Caoranne Castle was not.

'If the girl is as skilled in her letters as you say, she will make Tam Reevil a good wife,' he declared coldly, trying unsuccessfully to dispel the memory of a pair of remarkable brown eyes, and a high, intelligent brow.

He thought of Jacob Reevil. All his soldier's pride rebelled against the rogue's ceaseless extortion! Sir Douglas Irving had never had his wife's love. Their marriage had been arranged by their respective parents, but after the death of his elder brother and his return to the glen the respect of his wife and the love of Charles, their only child, had become very important to him.

Reevil's silence must be bought with the tenancy of Nethertannoch and a bride, supposedly for his idiot son. The laird of Caoranne avoided Sandy's frank blue gaze. The marriage must be arranged immediately. He was doing the Cameron girl a service. After all, she was deaf. Who would want a deaf wife? She was alone and unteachable. The dominie had assured him of that, despite Logan's protestations. She would have a home of her own, and a husband, even if Reevil's son was a half-wit.

'No one would give the girl work,' he announced, as much to himself as to Sandy. 'She could not hear a word of command. She would be a burden on the parish.' Then, with shattering finality, 'Her marriage to Tam Reevil will take place after the Sabbath services.'

Two

In his consternation for Mattie, Sandy forgot his own precarious position, his earnest desire to become the laird's tenant.

'Ye canna do such a thing! Mattie will never be a burden - not to the parish or anyone else! I will take care of her. We ...'

'You!' The laird's eyes sparked with anger at Sandy's outburst, yet he could not deny a flicker of admiration for the fellow's courage. He would have made a fine soldier.

'We shall work hard. We have the cattle and pigs. My mare is in foal, and to one of the best stallions in the country. I...'

'Your mare?' The laird's attention was jerked back to Sandy's serious face. Reevil had made particular mention of a mare at Nethertannoch. Duncan Blair had mentioned it too, a fine Lanarkshire-type - a Clydesdale. Taking over all the Nethertannoch stock, along with the girl, had been part of Reevil's bargain. 'What proof have you that the mare is yours? You have letters from Matthew Cameron?'

'I-I have no letters but the mare is mine - bought frae Lanark with every penny I had! And it was Mr Cameron's dying wish that I should take care of Mattie. He gave us his blessing. He - he thought that we should marry.'

'Aah!' There was a wealth of suspicion in Sir Douglas Irving's brief exclamation and Sandy flushed. 'You have only the words of a dead man. Words the girl could not even hear.' Sandy was dismayed. He had never told an untruth in his life. 'No doubt you have the impudence to think you could take on the tenancy of Nethertannoch?'

'Yes.' Sandy held the laird's gaze steadily. 'I am a good farmer.' He spoke without conceit. 'Matthew Cameron taught me all he knew - and he knew more than most of the tenants on the estate. He read the Farmers' Journal, and he learned from his uncle - a drover who travelled through England, before the railways began. Nethertannoch has proper rotations; the drains and ditches are in good repair. Our cattle are healthy.' He waved his arm in a wide arc. 'You must see!' he cried despairingly. 'Mattie and I...' He was silenced by Sir Douglas's icy glare. The laird had no wish to recall his factor's excellent report on Nethertannoch and its occupants. Duncan Blair would be displeased to learn that Reevil was taking over Nethertannoch, but the thing was done. He had made a bargain - Nethertannoch and the girl for Reevil's silence.

Sandy sensed the laird's withdrawal. 'Tam Reevil is a fiend - a cruel fiend!' he almost shouted in his desperation.

Sir Douglas frowned angrily. He clearly recalled Tam's boyish face, the snub nose and long gold-tipped eyelashes, so like Emilia's, so like their mother's. Then he remembered the vacant grin and the eyes, close-set like Reevil's. It was said the boy's brain had been damaged by the prolonged birth. The doctor had warned Reevil, begged him even, to spare the mother's life and sacrifice the infant - but Reevil had refused to listen. He had wanted a son - and he had allowed Emmy to die.

Sandy glimpsed the flicker of uncertainty on the laird's grim face and pressed his advantage, praying that he had said enough.

'Mattie is as skilled as any matron about the house and in the dairy but she kens nothing o' the world away frae Nethertannoch. She's a modest maid. She canna hear Tam's cackle or his gabble, but she can feel!' He shuddered at the thought of Tam's long bony fingers. 'She's as innocent o' a man's doings as a daisy wi' the dew on it.'

'You plead the girl's cause well, Logan,' Sir Douglas said tightly. 'No doubt Reevil will need an extra hand. You could ask him for work, here at Nethertannoch.'

'Work for Reevil? I would never work for him! I would rather starve!'

The laird shrugged his black-clad shoulders and turned away.

'Ye've got tae listen!' In his anxiety Sandy grabbed his arm.

'Unhand me at once, you insolent whelp!'

Sandy felt the sharp sting of Sir Douglas Irving's cane, but he had gone too far to stop now.

'There's a family in the glen, the Mackays. The oldest lassie is thirteen. A wee scrap of a thing. Her father found her in the woods. It was last November. She was naked. Bleeding. She had been whipped! But there's more, Sir. She hasna' been outside her father's cottage since. She is with child. A bairn herself!' There was both pain and contempt on Sandy's face. 'She hasna' spoken, save once - when Wull Mackay carried her home, more dead than alive. "Reevil" was the only word she uttered.'

Sir Douglas Irving stared for several seconds in shocked silence. Then he bellowed, 'You lie, Logan! I have listened too long to your insolence.'

'But it's the truth!'

'You blacken the boy's character for your own gain. If this - this fable had been true, the girl's father would have come to me for justice. I would see a man hang if I found him guilty of such a crime.'

'The Mackays live in Reevil's cottage,' Sandy stated simply. 'They work for him. They have seven other children. Reevil is an elder of the kirk. Which man would you believe, Sir?'

Sandy had given only the barest facts of the story which had horrified every God-fearing man and woman in the village and the surrounding cottages. Wull Mackay had pleaded with Joe Kerr, the blacksmith, begging him not to interfere, not to go to the Minister or to the laird. It was believed that Reevil had already threatened Wull. Reevil himself had escaped justice more than once. Already he was trying to ingratiate himself with the newly appointed constable for the glen. Everybody had reluctantly respected Wull Mackay's wishes. Sandy would not have flouted them either, except for Mattie. It gained him nothing.

'I have given my word. Reevil is to be tenant of Nethertannoch.'

'Give him the lease then! But I beg of you, Sir, dinna ask Mattie tae wed Tam Reevil.'

'As to that, I shall look into the matter. As one of his flock, the Reverend Lowe must be aware of the condition of the Mackay child. If Tam Reevil has committed the terrible crime of which you - and only you, Logan - have accused him, then the Minister would not sanction the marriage. Tam Reevil would have to pay the penalty for his evil crime.' He muttered the last few words with dismay. He squared his shoulders instinctively. Such a thing could not be allowed to happen. Reevil would use every weapon in his power! The scandal would be unbearable!

Sir Douglas Irving turned from Sandy abruptly and strode to his carriage without a backward glance.

Sandy remained staring at the distant hills with unseeing eyes. He thought of the Minister, but his mouth curled with contempt. He could not be relied upon to help. He had always resented the time Mistress Lowe had spent helping Mattie. The Reverend Lowe was a weak man, an ambitious, frustrated hypocrite. He had entered the church only for power and position. He was under Reevil's influence. He would never have the courage to speak out against Tam Reevil.

There was so little time! Even if he could persuade Mattie to be his wife tonight, they could not marry until she reached her sixteenth birthday - and that was not until the middle of May.

Only one thing was clear in Sandy's mind: he could not tell Mattie of the laird's intention to marry her to Tam Reevil. He must find a solution and quickly!

Sandy was glad to rise before dawn the following morning. He had spent a sleepless night. No amount of washing in the ice cold water, or rubbing with the rough towel could ease his troubled mind. Already he was missing Matthew Cameron's presence and the old man's wisdom. Anxiety gnawed at his insides like the teeth of a trapped animal. Had he the right to withhold the truth from Mattie? Yet he could not add to her burden so soon after her father's death. How could the laird contemplate such actions at this time?

Ploughing had been a source of pleasure to him ever since Matthew Cameron had laid his calloused hand over his own, when he was thirteen years old. He had revelled in the powerful strength of the horses and the satisfaction of a straight, well-turned furrow of shining soil. Today he had no heart for it, yet to delay would arouse Mattie's suspicions. So his mind grappled constantly with every possible, and impossible, solution as he walked steadily behind the horses.

Mattie was too observant not to realise that Sandy was troubled. She felt hurt by his failure to confide in her; they had always been so close, despite the barrier of her deafness. As she churned the butter her thoughts returned to the long winter evenings they had spent together at her father's bedside. She trusted him implicitly. She knew he would not allow any harm to befall her but - now the colour burned in her cheeks - what if Sandy had begun to suspect the new, secret feelings which had entered her heart of late? When his hands rested upon her shoulders, when he looked into her face and smiled, so tenderly her heart seemed to skip with a new rhythm. She no longer saw the boyish companion who had shared all her childish secrets. She saw a man with tanned skin roughened by wind and weather, she saw crinkles at the corners of his blue eyes when he laughed, and her blood surged like a tidal wave when he threw back his russet-coloured head and his fine white teeth gleamed in a big spontaneous laugh. How she longed to hear the sound of it. She could not bear it if Sandy considered her a burden because he had made a promise to a dying man. She wished passionately that her father had not extracted such a promise!

At mid-day Sandy sat down beneath the hedgerow with the bread and cheese and a stone bottle of butter-milk which Mattie had prepared for him. The food lay untouched. His thoughts were with her, down at the lonely farmstead. He had a clear view of the yard through the bare thorn branches. He was startled when he saw two horses tethered beside the water trough. His pulse quickened. Visitors were rare at Nethertannoch since his mother's death. His own horses were content to enjoy their rest. Sandy knew he could safely leave them a while. Seconds later he was loping across the field below, back to the steading. Even before he reached the open door of the house he was amazed, and extremely relieved, to hear laughter. Buff lay contentedly across the threshold, but she rose to greet him with a wag of her tail. Mattie saw the dog and looked up, her bright eyes warming in welcome. A girl was writing on a slate. Mattie scanned it swiftly and a mischievous smile lit her dark eyes.

'The butter is a good colour, even in winter, because I tie a scrubbed carrot in a cloth and hang it in the milk,' she explained promptly. The girl clapped her hands, clearly delighted that she could communicate with Mattie so easily.

Sandy had already recognised Charles Irving, the laird's son. He had often seen him riding round the estate with the factor; it was well known amongst the tenants that he had inherited his grandfather's love of Glen Caoranne and its people. He thought the girl must be a relative for she had the same shining brown hair and clear grey eyes as Charles Irving himself, and she was fashionably dressed in a green velvet riding habit. They had no chaperon. He felt a pang of dismay when Mattie announced, 'Sandy, this is Miss Reevil.'

'I came to offer Miss Cameron my sympathy,' the girl supplied gently when Sandy stiffened with suspicion. He had to admit that Miss Reevil was a lovely young lady - yes, lady. She bore no resemblance to her father, in looks or in manner. Indeed she had an extraordinary air of purity. It was the only word he could find to describe the perfection of Emilia Reevil's face, and the innocence and sweetness which seemed to be part of her.

'Miss Cameron has refreshed us with buttermilk and her excellent oatcakes and butter,' Emilia began pleasantly, but Charles Irving had inherited a little of his father's imperious manner.

'I would like to speak with you, Logan - outside.'

Sandy's mouth tightened. He accompanied the laird's son into the yard.

'Miss Reevil wished to meet her brother's bride-to-be.'

'Tam Reevil isna fit to marry Mattie!' Sandy began angrily.

'Be quiet,' Charles Irving hissed. 'I will not have Miss Reevil distressed by your malicious gossip about her brother.'

'It is the truth.'

'Tam is slow-witted but he is not evil. Why, he would do anything for Emilia. He has followed her around like a devoted hound-dog since she returned from France. I will not have her hurt.'

'I have no wish to hurt Miss Reevil,' Sandy's blue eyes held Charles Irving's grey ones fearlessly, 'but I cannot allow Mattie to be hurt either. Her father trusted me. It was his wish that we should marry.'

Like his father, Charles Irving was impressed by Sandy's bearing and forthright manner, the determined thrust to his square chin.

'As the laird, my father considers himself responsible for Miss Cameron now that she has no kin of her own. She is deaf. She cannot have expectations of a normal marriage.'

'Sir Douglas knows I want to marry her!' Sandy protested, but Charles Irving hurried on.

'Jacob Reevil led us to believe that Miss Cameron was - er - a simple maid, entirely suited to Tam.'

'Mattie is not suited to Tam at all!' Sandy protested furiously.

'No.' Charles frowned thoughtfully. 'She certainly seems sensitive and intelligent even though she cannot hear. While Tam, well he can never be more than a boy, in every sense. Every possible sense,' he repeated sternly. 'Do you understand my meaning, Logan? Miss Reevil would be extremely disturbed if she were to hear your fictitious and evil accounts of her brother. She knows nothing of life in the glen. She has lived all her life in a convent. She obeyed her father's summons to return because she thought he was gravely ill. Obviously she misunderstood.' Suddenly Charles Irving gave a disarming smile which took Sandy by surprise. 'I know Tarn could not have used the Mackay child so,' he declared with conviction. 'Look, Logan, Lady Irving, my mother, is very fond of

Emilia, even though she is the daughter of one of our own tenants. Now if Tam were to marry a sweet, respectable girl like Miss Cameron…'

'No! Mattie must never be forced into marriage!' Sandy insisted vehemently.

'Ah!' Charles stared speculatively. 'You love Miss Mattie Cameron? So that is the reason you wish to marry her - not just to get Nethertannoch.' The grey eyes warmed and Sandy wondered how he could ever have thought Charles Irving resembled his cold-eyed sire. 'Well, then, I must persuade my father to withdraw his consent for the marriage between Tam and Miss Cameron,' he declared with beguiling confidence. 'I ask only one thing '

Sandy waited tensely.

'You must promise that you will never repeat any gossip concerning Miss Reevil's family.'

'You have my word,' Sandy agreed.

The laird's son nodded, and glanced around the tidy little steading and the greening fields beyond. Sandy saw the approval in his grey eyes and felt a glow of pleasure. Here at last was someone who would appreciate his efforts - and Mattie's. But the glow was dimmed by Charles Irving's next words, spoken with obvious reluctance.

'I cannot promise you the lease of Nethertannoch. But I shall do my best for you - and for Miss Cameron.'

'There is not much time. The Minister will return in time for the Sabbath and…'

'I shall speak to my father without delay.'

The laird's son was young and impetuous - and he fancied himself in love. Therefore he felt the urge to champion the cause of all young lovers, whether lords or labourers. Moreover he had been impressed by conditions at Nethertannoch, and by Alexander Logan and Mattie Cameron. The landowner in him told him they would make excellent tenants. He spoke to Duncan Blair and the factor agreed instantly.

He lost no time in seeking out his father and telling him of his visit to Nethertannoch. He did not mention his companion but he did describe Mattie's hospitality, her intelligence and her sensitivity. He remarked upon the neatness of her house and dairy.

'She must marry Reevil's son! My decision is final! Anyway the girl is deaf.' To Charles's surprise his father had slammed out of the room in an undignified scurry, totally unlike his usual measured habit.

Cheerfully undaunted, understanding nothing of the threats currently hanging over his family, Charles made his way to Westertannoch to win Jacob Reevil's support. He went as a friend but was greeted with open hostility. Jacob Reevil had already interrogated Emilia on every detail of her morning ride with Charles. She was too innocent, and far too nervous of the man who called himself her father, to dissemble.

Charles was immediately conscious of Jacob Reevil's insolent manner, as well as his conviction that all his demands would be met. Charles was astounded by his arrogance, especially considering the fact that his son was an imbecile, and he a most disreputable and unworthy tenant. Even if he had not seen the neglect and decay for himself, Duncan Blair had left him in no doubt of his low opinion of Westertannoch and its tenant. On his way up the track Charles had been forcibly reminded of some of the factor's criticisms. He had passed a young bullock, bloated in death, its eyes and entrails picked out by crows or foxes. It had clearly been dead for several days yet no effort had been made to bury the unfortunate beast and it was a sickening sight to all who passed. He agonised over the effects of such a spectacle on Emilia's tender heart. The whole place was a picture of slovenliness and waste - a disgrace to Caoranne estate.

Charles made no effort to hide his contempt of Jacob Reevil. He found it difficult to believe that so coarse an individual could sire a daughter as gentle and sweet as Emilia. He longed to be able to take her away. If only he could win his father's support He shuddered to think of Mattie Cameron being in the power of such a man, for Tam would be no more than a puppet, blindly obeying his father's commands. Little Miss Cameron would become a drudge - or maybe even worse! She was pretty, she had the freshness of youth and innocence.

'Sir, you misled my father as to the character and ability of Miss Cameron of Nethertannoch,' he addressed Jacob Reevil coldly. 'She is intelligent and far too sensitive to be a suitable wife for poor Tam.'

'The marriage is arranged, and 'twill be none o' your business!'

'Everybody in the glen knows Tam is not fit to marry! As to Nethertannoch, it is my business, or it will be in less than three years' time. I shall be twenty-five, the age when my grandfather deemed the

Caoranne Trust should be put into my care. I intend to take a more active part in the affairs of the estate and its tenants than my father has done.' He looked around Reevil's filthy, broken-down steading in disgust. 'Already Miss Cameron and Alexander Logan have proved excellent tenants, as well as taking care of Matthew Cameron during his illness. I will not stand aside and allow her to be destroyed by you!' He had not intended to antagonise Jacob Reevil but there was something about the man's sneering face and piggy eyes which irritated him intensely. It was difficult to remember he was Emilia's father.

Reevil was fully aware of Charles Irving's revulsion and it angered him. Even more important, he suspected that Charles's loyalty to his father would remain unshaken by the facts surrounding Emilia's birth. The young fool would probably accept her as a sister, once he recovered from the initial shock. He might even take her to live at Caoranne Castle! His own power over Sir Douglas was dwindling. Only the threat to Lady Irving carried weight.

He was also incensed by the idea that Logan and the Cameron chit had gained Charles Irving's attention. He recalled the girl's slender figure, her dignity and self-control. He would teach her not to be so cool and aloof with him! The desire to corrupt Mattie's innocence suddenly took on the force of an obsession. He intended to have her - one way or another - and Nethertannoch, and the stock. He would make sure of her! The tenancy would be securely in his name long before Charles Irving took over the estate. And as for Logan and that frosty-faced factor, they could go to hell!

Charles's interference and contempt had fuelled Reevil's spiteful nature, but he was too sly to retaliate openly.

'We'll leave the matter o' Tam's wedding to the laird. Ye'll be wanting to see Emilia now that ye're here, eh? Just gang up to the hoose. She'll be pleased tae see ye - even if it is only a few hours since ye were riding together.'

Charles was taken aback by Reevil's sudden conciliatory tone and obsequious manner. It was true, he did want to assure himself that Emilia was surviving in such terrible surroundings.

Sir Douglas Irving had barely finished his dinner that evening when the footman presented him with a note from Reevil, demanding a meeting - immediately.

Jacob Reevil wasted no time in informing the laird of Charles and Emilia's morning ride together and the fact that Charles could not even wait for another day to dawn, but had called at Westertannoch in the afternoon – 'for the sole purpose of seeing her again'. He did not hesitate to add a few nods, winks and hints from his own evil imagination. The laird's consternation grew. He had no reason to suppose that his son was any less impulsive and headstrong than he himself had been in his youth; Charles was a normal young man with a healthy appetite for food and for physical sport - so why not for women too? But not Emilia! Never Emilia!

The laird personally ushered Reevil out of the Castle, but he had no thought of returning to the excellent port he had left. His mind was already busy making and rejecting plans with all the speed of a soldier involved in active combat - plans which would immediately remove his only son from the glen, and away from temptation.

Three

Like the fickle April weather Sandy's spirits were alternately bright with hope and dark with despair as he walked doggedly behind the plough, impatient for the news he hoped Charles Irving would bring.

Standing on the knoll behind his house, Jacob Reevil observed Sandy at the ploughing and his eyes gleamed. He called for Tam to ride with him. Tam gabbled an incoherent protest; he was nervous of horses and equally nervous of his father. Dim-witted though he was, he recognised the sadistic glint in his sire's beady eyes. In the end he assembled his gangling limbs on his horse's sturdy back and followed his father up the track towards Nethertannoch.

A particularly heavy shower had sent Mattie scurrying indoors. She filled the heavy iron kettle and pushed the swee over the fire. She needed boiling water to scald the vegetable peelings to make a tasty mash for her hens. The memory of Sandy's troubled face occupied her thoughts. Her lack of hearing frustrated her more than it had ever done before. Why was Sandy so withdrawn? Did he consider her deafness more of a burden when they were alone? Or did he think she would not be able to help him enough, now that Nethertannoch was their responsibility? It was true she did not take her eggs and butter to market as other women did. Her father had been reluctant to let her leave the farm after he learned of the dominie's cruelty; but she was a woman now and Jem Wright assured her she made the best butter in the glen. He always claimed that he obtained the best prices on her behalf. She trusted Jem. It was he who had brought her Buff, and the little dog had been her companion, and her 'ears' throughout her father's illness.

She was less alert to Buff's canine signals now that her father no longer needed her attention. As she waited for the kettle to boil she was too preoccupied with thoughts of Sandy to see Buff prick her little pointed ears. She could not hear the dog's uneasy whine. Even when Buff rubbed at her ankles, Mattie merely bent and stroked her absently; she did not notice the two riders who had dismounted and were leading their horses surreptitiously into the empty stable.

The sunlight emerged from behind the clouds and came streaming through the open door once more. Mattie lifted the kettle from its hook. Suddenly the sunlight dimmed. She turned, frowning, the kettle grasped in her hand. Her eyes widened. She recognised the stocky figure of Jacob Reevil instantly. He had been at her father's funeral. She remembered his eyes: small, bulging like glass balls, staring at her. Her heart began to thud.

In his hands Reevil held a whip - yet there was no sign of his horse tethered to the iron ring beside the water trough. An inexplicable dread crystallised in Mattie's chest, like a great, hard rock. Mattie had learned, long ago, at the hands of Dominie Butler, never to show fear.

'You wished to shelter?' She willed her voice to be steady, her words to be clear.

'Shelter, ugh!' Reevil sneered. 'It isna' shelter we're wantin'!'

Mattie stared intently, trying desperately to decipher the words fumbling from his thick lips. Jacob Reevil was not a clear speaker at any time. Now his words were slurred like those of a man intoxicated. It was not liquor which made his blood run with fire.

Behind him Tam alternately grinned and gabbled fatuously. They stood between Mattie and the bucket of peelings outside the open door. Instinct warned her not to move nearer to Jacob Reevil. Innocent though she was, her flesh crawled uncomfortably beneath his hot stare. She turned away to set the kettle back on its hook beside the fire.

'You deaf idiot, ye dinna understand a word!' Reevil grabbed her arm. Mattie jerked involuntarily. Some of the water bubbled from the long iron spout on to Reevil's trouser leg. The water was hot, but the quantity was far too small to scald him through the thick material. Even so shock triggered his swift temper. He raised the whip. Mattie recoiled instantly, dropping the kettle. Its boiling contents spewed out. Mattie jumped back instinctively, but Reevil was less agile.

He grabbed frantically at his outer garments, tearing them off. Tam cackled insanely, but Mattie's eyes widened. A new terror gripped her, impossible to hide. Unhampered by his wet clothes, Reevil seized his whip and moved towards her, menace in every line of his bloated face and bull neck.

Buff's low growls became a frenzied bark. She sprang at Reevil in a desperate attempt to defend her mistress. Mattie was light and fleet of foot, despite her wooden clogs. Terror lent her speed. She darted round the heavy wooden table. Reevil kicked the little dog ruthlessly, bringing a gasp to Mattie's white lips. But she pushed the gaping Tarn roughly aside and rushed towards the open door.

One of the few skills Reevil had acquired in a misspent youth, frequenting taverns, cockfights, bear-baiting and gambling dens, was that of wielding a whip. This he had learned from a group of gypsies with whom he had taken refuge - until they too, had found him to be a cheat and a liar, unable to pay his debts.

Reevil used his skill now, with cruel effect. The thin lash snaked around Mattie's knees, bringing her to the floor with a crash. Reevil sprang at her instantly. Buff darted between them, her loyalty undaunted by the cruel kick. Mattie scrambled swiftly to her feet, her breath coming in sobbing gasps. Reevil heaved the dog effortlessly through the open door and slammed it shut, simultaneously imprisoning Mattie in the iron circle of his arm. She kicked frantically, wildly. To submit meekly was not part of the Cameron character. Her resistance surprised Reevil - and it pleased him. His cold, pale eyes gleamed. Mattie saw them. She screwed her own eyes tightly shut, uttering a silent plea: 'Please God, help me!'

Reevil showed no mercy. The strength of his arm was squeezing the very life out of her. He pushed her roughly against the wall, and held her there. She opened her eyes and stared into his broad face, horribly close to her own.

'I'll teach ye a lesson! Ye'll be an obedient wife by the time I'm done wi' ye!'

'Lesson?' Mattie's brow puckered. 'Wife?' she repeated more sharply.

'Aye, "wife",' he spat, and nodded his head contemptuously towards Tam.

'No! I...' She flinched as Reevil slapped her face and pushed his great head even closer. His hot, stale breath made her stomach heave.

'You have no choice. The laird agrees. Understand?'

Mattie stared back at him in horror. The laird had said she could remain at Nethertannoch. Surely not with the Reevils? In a flash she understood Sandy's strange behaviour. But why had he not warned her?

'I will not stay here!' It was the nearest Mattie had ever come to hysteria and her voice was like the sound of an animal in distress. Reevil was unmoved, his eyes fixed on the agitated rise and fall of her firm young breasts beneath the tight bodice of her dress. The girl had more spirit than he had expected. He liked a woman with spirit - not like that limp pink and white doll he'd married. Still, he'd got what he wanted - land as well as money - through Emma and her noble laird! He looked into Mattie's face again.

'Ye'll be his "wife". Ye'll be my "woman"! My woman. Understand that!'

Mattie struggled to understand Reevil's meaning, but when his heavy hand seized her breast her eyes glazed with fear and humiliation. No man had ever touched her like that! She writhed helplessly but his fingers groped even more insistently. Anger outweighed humiliation and pain. Mattie lashed out. Her wooden clog caught Reevil squarely on his shins.

Retribution was swift and terrible.

He swung her around like a puppet, flinging her furiously face down over the table. The thrust knocked the breath out of her body - but Reevil was not done yet. Frenziedly he hauled her petticoats up, above her waist, above her head! One after the other. She fought like a wild woman but Reevil was strong and he was enjoying her torment. In seconds she was utterly constrained in a suffocating cocoon of muslin and red flannel. Still Mattie fought frantically, shamed beyond all imagining, gasping for breath beneath innumerable layers of material. No one, but no one, had seen her in her drawers!

Humiliation was not the only punishment Jacob Reevil had in mind. It was not the first time he had derived satisfaction from seeing a fellow human being writhe in pain - pain which he himself inflicted. When the writhing body was that of a woman - especially a proud and spirited young woman - he savoured his sadistic pleasure to the full. Even Tam no longer grinned. His wide mouth gobbled still, but silently now. He dared not disobey his father's order to grasp the shroud of petticoats, stretched across the big wooden table, but he flinched each time the whip lash curled, for he had felt its deadly sting. The more Mattie struggled the swifter came the lashes, but her lungs were bursting in the dark, airless shroud. Desperately she gasped for breath, scarcely aware of the relentless pain of Reevil's whip as the terrible darkness claimed her. She was falling… falling.

When the heavens opened for the second time that afternoon, instead of taking temporary shelter beneath the hedgerow, as was his habit, Sandy turned the horses' heads for home. He knew the rain would soon pass, but his heart was not in his work. He was uneasy, anxious for news from Charles Irving. The Reverend Lowe would return from his meeting in Castle Douglas in time for the Sabbath services, and today was Friday. There was so little time!

Dark Lucy, the mare, was now heavily in foal. She welcomed the prospect of returning to the stable. Sandy frowned and his own footsteps quickened instinctively at the sound of Buff's frenzied barking as they neared the farmsteading. The horses pricked their ears; Flick side-stepped nervously at the dog's extraordinary noise.

They approached the yard through the narrow opening between the stable and the byre. Sandy was surprised to see Buff jumping up at the door of the house. It was closed. That surprised him too. The rain had passed. Mattie rarely shut out the daylight. She never barred Buff from the house. The little dog rarely left her side. Swiftly Sandy tied the horses to the ring beside the watering trough. It was dry. Mattie always drew water from the well in readiness for the horses.

Buff did not halt her assault on the closed door until Sandy threw it open. The tableau within burned instantly into his brain, as the little dog shot between his legs.

'Do as I say, you fool! I showed you once b—' The words died on Jacob Reevil's ugly lips at Sandy's bellow of rage. He lifted a defensive arm as the dog hurled herself at him with a snarl. In his hand was the whip which had held Mattie pinned to the floor, her head still smothered in her own voluminous skirts. It was from this tightly trussed bundle that a muffled, half-human scream emerged as Tam Reevil's groping fingers tightened tentatively on the soft flesh of her thigh. He leaned over her, his broad head tilted, a vacant grin on his large, flat face. Although his coat had been cast carelessly aside, the rest of his clothes were intact despite his father's urging.

Apparently fascinated by Mattie's writhing figure he bent closer, at the precise moment that Sandy hauled Jacob Reevil furiously away from her. Mattie kicked out with the strength of a terrified colt. In her silent world, confused by the suffocating darkness, she was still unaware of Sandy's return. Her flailing heel caught Tam Reevil squarely in the groin. He reeled beneath the blow, powerless to prevent himself from falling. His head hit the corner of the oak press with a sickening thud. He lay there, still.

Jacob Reevil was no longer a young man but he was thick-set and strong, and he fought with any means at his disposal. Sandy could not avoid several sharp lashes from his whip but most of them had little effect through the thick, rough cloth of his coat, until an unexpectedly deft manoeuvre raised the skin from his cheek bone. Rage and pain, added to Mattie's distress, removed any lingering inhibitions Sandy might have had about striking a man old enough to be his father. He gave Reevil no room to strike again but sent his heavy body crashing across the room.

Only then could he turn his full attention to Mattie. She was unable to free herself from the petticoats which Reevil had formed into a sack and tied over her head, effectively imprisoning her arms as well as blindfolding her. She could not hear Buff's soft, comforting whimper, or the ensuing fight. Her legs continued flailing in a desperate bid to prevent anyone from getting near her. Sandy had some difficulty in releasing her. When her head emerged at last, her breath came in harsh, gasping sobs. She stared at him with wide, terror-filled eyes, utterly devoid of recognition, and he realised with a pang that she would have fought him too.

Behind him Reevil rolled to his feet.

'A spirited filly needs a lesson!' he sneered. 'Ye're too soft, Logan, an' slow.' He raised his arm. 'I'll give her another taste o' this.'

Hastily Sandy bent to shield Mattie as she struggled with her skirts. He stared down in horror at the blood and the angry crimson weals clearly visible on her tender buttocks. His face whitened. His earlier anger was nothing to the murderous rage which consumed him now. He turned in time to grip Reevil's upraised arm. He twisted it viciously and saw the lust in Reevil's eyes turn to pain and frustration. He squirmed impotently. Sandy was pitiless.

'It was you! You whipped the Mackay bairn - aye, and had your way with her! I know it now.'

'You ken naething!' Reevil's denial turned to a groan of agony as Sandy tightened his grip.

'Sir Douglas Irving said he would see a man hang by the neck for such a crime.'

He saw Reevil's florid face whiten, but the man blustered: 'Ye've nae proof.'

'I have proof o' your evil deeds this day!' Sandy's tone was bitter. 'I'll be awa' to see the laird before...'

'The laird willna' listen tae that deaf wild cat!' Reevil interrupted viciously, struggling to free himself from Sandy's painful grip. 'Anyway, the laird's awa'! Aye, an' yon arrogant young fool o' a son. Gone tae say farewell tae Lady Clare, afore he gangs tae be a soldier.'

'A soldier? But he loves the glen, the estate, the...'

'Aye, weel, this'll teach him a lesson!' Reevil announced with venom. 'An' the laird'll teach you a lesson tae, if ye gang spreading nasty tales about his friends. I am his friend - dinna ye be forgetting that.'

'We'll see about that when he returns,' Sandy muttered in disgust, but some of the fire had gone out of him. He did not doubt the truth of Reevil's statement. He propelled him to the open door and hurled him head first into the yard, muddy now after the recent shower. He landed heavily. Winded by the fall, he lay where he had fallen, his flabby jowls wallowing helplessly in the mud, like the swine he was. Sandy gathered up his clothes and threw them after him.

Tam Reevil rose unsteadily to his feet, like a man wakening from a deep sleep; he ambled after his father. Sandy was too concerned by Mattie's shocked face and pain-glazed eyes to pay attention to him, until the sound of his inane cackle made him glance outside. He saw Tam dancing gleefully around the ludicrous figure of his spluttering father. The lad's long, uncoordinated limbs were like those of a prancing colt. He seemed oblivious to the mud his great feet were splattering over his prostrate parent.

Tam was still cackling, triumphant as an old hen who had laid a dozen eggs, as they rode away, apparently unaware that his idiotic laughter was whipping his father's smouldering anger into insane fury.

Sandy refilled the kettle from the wooden pail and swung it over the fire. He looked around him at the littered floor and saw the treasured tea box which had once belonged to Mattie's mother. He picked it up. The hinged lid was broken and the mother of pearl bird had been chipped. Mattie watched him through a haze of pain, bewilderment and shock. He made tea, hot and sweet. It was the only comfort he could think of. Innocent young girls had been known to become mentally unhinged after such an ordeal. It was said the Mackay bairn would neither see, nor speak, to any man - even her own father.

In truth Mattie could scarcely believe that Sandy had really come, or that she was safe - for a time at least. She felt numb, yet her bones ached. She felt hot with pain, and shame, yet she could not control the violent shivers which shook her whole body. Sandy placed the cup in her trembling hands and guided it to her lips, but after a few gulps of the comforting brew she pushed it away and wrapped her arms tightly around her slender body. She could not look at Sandy. She could not bear him to look at her. Sandy sensed her withdrawal. He felt chilled. He reached out to take her hand but she flinched away from him.

'Don't touch me!' she insisted. Her voice was unnaturally loud. 'Leave me!'

'But, Mattie, you can't be afraid of me!' He realised she did not even know he had spoken.

'I will not marry th-that m-man, wh-whatever the laird th-thinks! You knew, Sandy!'

'Mattie! I did not want to…'

'I had a right to know too! I will not! I will not do it! Oh, if only I could hear!'

Sandy had never seen Mattie so distraught; he felt helpless and guilty. He had promised Matthew Cameron he would take care of her and already he had failed. He should have warned her. He should have guessed Reevil wanted more than the land and the stock. He was vile and immoral.

Mattie began to shudder convulsively. 'I must wash! I must wash myself! Everywhere!' She jumped to her feet, muttering urgently.

If only water could wash away the memory of this day's evil work, Sandy thought miserably as he went to bring more water from the well. He had never felt more helpless. When he returned Mattie had dragged out the wooden tub she used for washing clothes and was emptying the big iron kettle into it. Her white face remained stiff and remote, as though he was a stranger. He set down the pail of water and took the kettle from her. Then he grasped her gently by the shoulders, turning her bruised face towards him. She cringed but Sandy ignored her trembling. He raised her chin tenderly; she had to look at him.

'I am going outside now, Mattie.' Momentary terror filled her eyes. His face softened. '1 shall not leave you alone again, I promise. Open the door when you are ready. Do you understand, Mattie?' She nodded, shivering, but not with cold. Never before had Sandy considered Mattie's deafness to be such a terrible barrier as he did now. He did not know how to comfort her. He wanted to take her in his arms and gently hold her but he sensed her rejection, her withdrawal, and his hands fell helplessly to his sides. As he reached the door, she called his name.

'I will not marry Tam Reevil! I shall go away! Now! Tonight!' Sandy was at her side in a flash.

'Hush, hush, Mattie lass.' His voice was gruff. He tried to take hold of her but she stepped back and looked into his face. He realised with a shock that she suddenly seemed unnaturally composed. There was a steely determination in her brown eyes.

'You cannot protect me from the Reevils, Sandy. No one can!' Her face crumpled, then hardened. 'Reevil said the laird has agreed. But I will not marry Tam Reevil. Never! I shall leave Nethertannoch. I shall go before dawn.'

'But, Mattie, you canna go! You know no one beyond the glen! Everything we have is here, at Nethertannoch - the cattle and horses. We have nothing else. No money '

'I must go!'

'This is your home, Mattie.' He gripped her shoulders now. 'I promised your father '

'I would rather die than s-see Reevil again!' A shudder passed over her. 'I must b-bathe! Please, Sandy, l-leave me.'

He went reluctantly. His heart was heavy as he closed the door behind him.

Four

Mattie scrubbed herself from head to foot, despite the stinging wounds of Reevil's whip; then she bathed again; still she could not wash away the memory of Reevil's bulging eyes, his thick, probing fingers. She shuddered and bundled together her torn clothes, burning them ruthlessly, one by one. It was a desperate bid to root out the shame and humiliation she felt. Yet deep in her heart was the thought that Sandy had known of the laird's plans, and he had not warned her. Had he agreed to them? Her mind was in a turmoil. She felt dreadfully alone, and uncertain about so many things.

Reevil had touched her. Could he have given her a child? She did not want anything that would remind her of that vile man! Not even an innocent babe, and Mattie loved all young things.

Her handicap, coupled with Nethertannoch's natural isolation, had deprived her of the company of other girls and women. Even the breeding of the animals had been shrouded in secrecy. Bessie and the other cows were taken away to the bull at Benlochy farm. Ten months ago a stallion, a very special stallion, had come to the glen and now Dark Lucy was to have a foal, but Mattie had only the vaguest notion of what had transpired to bring about that state of affairs. Several farmers in the glen brought their sows to visit the Nethertannoch boar, but Mattie was never there when they met. It was all so frustrating - and frightening.

Jacob Reevil's shadow seemed to leap out at her from the very walls of the home she had loved. What could she do? She was not afraid to work but she had no money. Almost everything her father had possessed had been tied up in the cattle and pigs, seeds and lime; half of the animals belonged to Sandy, brought by his mother from Caoranne mill. Everything they could spare had been spent on improving Nethertannoch - building for the future. She shuddered convulsively. She must leave it all! She would never return - not while Jacob Reevil lived. He would come again, she knew he would. She had seen the look in his eyes - like an animal.

Mattie's soft mouth hardened. She pushed the memories to the deeper recesses of her mind and forced herself to concentrate on the present and her own immediate future. If only she knew more of the world beyond the glen! She would need food for the journey. There was the money for her father's funeral and the little she had saved from the sale of the butter and eggs. She must take her book of herbal receipts, and the little medicine chest containing the pestle and mortar which Sandy's mother had given her. Her own precious books must be left behind. The thought grieved her. It was a daunting prospect to leave everything that was known and loved; she felt a surge of doubt at the very thought of venturing alone into the silent, unfamiliar world beyond Nethertannoch, a solitary world where people like Dominie Butler would regard her as an imbecile. She trembled, but then she clenched her small fists and lifted her chin. She would not allow herself to think of the future - or her parting with Sandy. She would rather die than be in Reevil's power. She looked down and saw the bewildered eyes of her dog. She bent and stroked her gently where Reevil's vicious boot had bruised her side.

'You are my only friend, dear Buff.' She choked back a sob. 'You will go with me.'

Sandy's mind was also seething with questions as he fed and watered, cleaned and milked. The cows sensed his preoccupation and fidgeted beneath his distracted touch. It would break Mattie's heart to leave them, Sandy reflected, especially old Bessie. Surely the laird could not agree to her marriage when he knew what Reevil had done this day? He would visit Caoranne Castle as soon as Sir Douglas and his son returned.

He had finished all the afternoon's chores except the pigs. He was mixing meal for them when a familiar voice startled him. He spun round.

'Mistress Lowe!' Relief washed over his lean, strained face. Had he been a devout Christian he would have thought the Lord had answered his sub-conscious prayers. 'I will attend to your pony and trap,' he said quickly. 'Mattie needs you, more than she has ever needed you before.'

'I came on foot, over the moor. I judged it wiser to let no one know of my visit,' Agnes Lowe panted breathlessly. 'Jacob Reevil means to see you hang if Tam dies! Why did you hurt him so? Why, Sandy?'

Sandy's bewildered face whitened. 'I have done Tam no harm!' His heart was pounding. 'Mattie…'

'Sandy, you must listen to me!' Mistress Lowe insisted urgently. 'Reevil intends to see you pay for your wickedness!'

'But l didna hurt Tam!'

'His throat is cut! There is a terrible bruise on the side of his poor head. Reevil says you meant to kill the laddie ... He brought him to the manse. I have seen him with my own eyes! Indeed, I tended the poor boy with my own hands. His wounds are ugly indeed.' She suppressed a shudder. Sandy shook his head mutely, staring at her in dismay.

'Tarn gabbled on about hitting his head while he was at Nethertannoch, but he is almost incoherent. It is his poor throat slashed almost from ear to ear, and probably poisoned by the look of the filth. How?'

'Slashed?' Sandy echoed sharply. He was remembering Tarn's inane cackle at the sight of his father sprawling in the mud. 'Slashed like this?' He moved his head and a shaft of pale sunlight fell on the raw wound inflicted on his own cheek by Reevil's whip. Agnes Lowe gasped in horror.

'Jacob Reevil is an expert with a whip,' Sandy muttered grimly.

'He did that? But surely he would not whip his own son? No one would believe such a thing.' Her voice quavered. 'He - he brought Tarn to the manse. He called Mary, my maid. He brought her from the kitchen. He called old Billie from the garden too. "You are witnesses," he said, "to Logan's evil deeds!" Oh Sandy!'

His mouth tightened. Reevil was a devil, a cunning, loathsome villain. He wanted Sandy out of the way, rotting in some evil jail no doubt - so that Mattie would be alone, in his power. This was more than revenge for being flung into the muck like the filthy swine he was. Tam had laughed at the sight of him - and the poor lad had paid already! But Mistress Lowe was right - who would believe a man would deliberately wound his own son? Reevil was an elder of the kirk, the glen's largest tenant farmer. Sandy struggled to hide his growing dismay. If Reevil's plan worked, he would never even see the laird - except at some farcical trial - and Mattie would be entirely at Reevil's mercy. It would be the end of freedom for them both. And supposing Tam Reevil died? Supposing his wounds had been poisoned deliberately? Sandy shuddered. Then he lifted his chin.

'I have done no wrong. I willna run away like a coward!' Then, more quietly, 'But Mattie is right, there is no safety for her here, nor anywhere in the glen while Reevil is around. I thank you for coming, Mistress Lowe. You will take some refreshment? Mattie needs a woman. Reevil whipped her cruelly.'

Mistress Lowe stared at Sandy, the colour ebbing and flowing in her cheeks alarmingly.

'Reevil whipped Mattie? I-I cannot believe it!'

'It is true. And - and maybe worse ' His voice trailed off hoarsely at the question burning in his tortured mind.

'My poor, poor child! But no Mattie is no longer a child,' she muttered almost to herself. 'I saw it, that look in Reevil's eyes, at her dear father's funeral.' Mistress Lowe looked up then and her mouth firmed, her tone became brisk. 'Now I understand why he wants you locked away and left to rot.' Sandy flinched involuntarily. 'Those were his words. I pray Sir Douglas Irving will return soon to see that justice is done. And yet Reevil has great influence with the laird '

'Justice!' Sandy echoed bitterly. 'What justice allows a man to steal up on an innocent girl in her own home and use her so?' He took a deep breath, striving for control. 'Mistress Lowe, I swear to you, I have committed no crime against Tam Reevil. But I gave Matthew Cameron my word; I will not break it. If Mattie leaves Nethertannoch, I shall go with her. If she stays, then I shall remain also - and take my chance with the laird and his justice.'

'It will be your word against Reevil's - the boy's own father. He is clever, that one. There are many things you do not know, Sandy.' He was surprised at the bitterness in her tone. The minister's wife was the gentlest and most loyal of women. 'Reevil has sent more than one innocent man to prison for the flimsiest of reasons. He has planned witnesses against you already,' she insisted urgently.

Sandy sighed heavily, but he remained silent. The only witness he had was Mattie. Would she even understand the laird's questions - and the searching questions of strangers? Men -.their prying eyes? How could he even ask her to face Reevil again?

'Ach, Sandy!' Agnes Lowe shook her head to and fro in growing agitation. Wisps of grey hair had escaped from the confines of her muslin cap and Sandy saw how tired and anxious she looked. She needed rest and refreshment. He took her arm and led her towards the house, but before he opened the door for her he spoke, his voice quiet but firm.

'The decision will be Mattie's, but she must know nothing of Tam's injuries - or his father's threats. Do I have your word, Mistress Lowe?' Agnes Lowe looked at him anxiously, but she saw the determined set of his jaw. She nodded slowly.

Agnes Lowe loved all children but she had been blessed with none of her own. Sandy's mother had been her closest friend. She had bounced him on her knee when he was a child; he would always have a special place in her heart. Mattie had needed her help as no other human being had ever needed her. Together they had fought to overcome the solitary world of silence. It was small wonder then that she wept at the sight of the wounds left by Reevil's whip, and enfolded Mattie in her motherly arms.

Mattie remained adamant about leaving, but she was reluctant to let Sandy accompany her. There was no time, or opportunity, to sell their cattle and pigs; she feared the sacrifice of leaving everything they possessed might prove too great; he might resent the encumbrance she had become. Nethertannoch was his life, it was his home too.

Sandy was equally determined that he would follow her if she left without him. Despite her doubts Mattie's heart surged with relief and gratitude. Silently she vowed she would never become a burden to him; one day, somehow, she would repay him.

Agnes Lowe gave them two gold sovereigns which she had brought with her. Sandy accepted the money reluctantly. He guessed it was probably the last of a precious hoard, preserved from Mistress Lowe's miserly husband since her wedding day.

'I have saved nearly ten shillings towards Dark Lucy's foal fees. We will take that too. I will send the money to the owner of the stallion as soon as I can find work. If only we knew where we should be safe - at least until Mattie attains her sixteenth birth-day.' He turned to Agnes Lowe. 'And until we hear news of Tam.' Mattie misunderstood their anxious expressions.

'Surely we could take the horses? We cannot leave Darkie with th-that man - and his wh-whip! They could carry meal and - and some of our possessions. We cannot leave them, Sandy!'

His eyes rested thoughtfully on her white face. 'I could fix baskets to Flick's saddle,' he said slowly, then with growing enthusiasm, 'We could take two of the young pigs as well. They are ready to wean now.'

'Then you cannot go by the glen road!'

Sandy frowned and glanced towards the bleak moors. He could never ask Mattie to make such a journey, especially with the bruises and wounds Reevil had inflicted. Mattie guessed his thoughts.

'We must travel over the moors. Tonight. I shall prepare food now, for the journey.' There was a determined set to her soft mouth.

'Yes, you must cross the military road and find a safe hiding place before daybreak,' Agnes Lowe agreed. 'Then the searchers will not know whether to proceed westwards to Ireland or eastwards to England, unless you are seen. ' Her gaze rested fondly on Mattie's pale face. Her speech was almost perfect in tone, except when she was upset, or excited, and her understanding had improved tremendously since those early lessons.

'The lessons! Of course!' she cried suddenly. 'You would be safe with my kinsman, Daniel Munro! For sure, the Lord does work in mysterious ways!' She spoke with a note of wonder. Sandy frowned. He was in no mood to believe in miracles.

'Who is Daniel Munro? Where does he dwell?'

'It was Daniel's mother, my cousin Sarah, who sent advice when I was helping Mattie. Daniel lives at Fairlyden,' she turned to face Mattie. 'Fair-lee-den,' she enunciated carefully. 'It is a farm on the edge of Strathtod Estate, some miles east of the town of Dumfries.'

'His mother was the governess to the Earl of Strathtod's children?'

'Yes.' Agnes Lowe's face flushed. She seemed flustered, but she raised her chin almost defiantly. 'The Earl was Daniel's father.'

'His father!' Sandy exclaimed involuntarily.

'Sarah was not a wicked woman. She was not a harlot as Mr Lowe declares. She loved Lord Jonathan's children dearly - or at least the two little girls. Their brother, Gordon, was older; he was difficult - mean and moody, greedy too, even then. His Lordship was overcome with grief when the Countess died. The children looked upon Sarah as a mother, especially Lucy, the youngest. She was very delicate - like her mama. The Earl visited the nursery every single day. As Lucy grew weaker, and later, when she died. I-I think Sarah comforted him. Lord Jonathan's son resented his father's friendship with a governess, or indeed with anyone except himself, but Sarah had promised Lady Fairly that she would remain at Strathtod Tower until Lady Elizabeth was old enough to go away to school. The Earl did not want Sarah to go away, especially after

Daniel was born. He built her a house, and gave her land. He called it Fairly's Den. He visited every day and sent his own men to do the work.'

'Yet you think we should be safe there?'

'Oh, yes. Daniel is alone at Fairlyden now. Since his stepbrother became the Earl, no one from the estate dares to help him. Apparently Lord Gordon has threatened to evict anyone who goes near Fairlyden. He hoped Daniel would leave the area so that his father's "indiscretions" could then be forgotten. But Daniel loves Fairlyden, and he did not need help. However, I received a letter recently from the Reverend Robert Mackenzie. Daniel is suffering from an aching and swelling of the joints; he is becoming crippled by it. The Reverend Mackenzie wrote to inform me of Daniel's plight. He is Minister of the Free Church - a circumstance which aroused Mr Lowe's acute displeasure. He forbade me to offer any assistance or even to reply. The matter has troubled me sorely.'

'You think your kinsman would give us work and a safe refuge at Fairlyden?' Sandy asked slowly.

'Yes. My prayers would be answered if only you can help each other. Daniel has never taken a wife so he has no children to inherit the lease of Fairlyden. It must be returned to the Strathtod Estate when the Munro line dies out - and Lord Gordon can scarcely wait for that to happen, although he already owns two thousand acres of his own. Fairlyden is Daniel's only source of income, I'm afraid.'

'Ah!' Sandy nodded bleakly. Now he understood the real reason why the Reverend Peter Lowe had forbidden his wife to communicate with her ailing kinsman. Daniel Munro was not only a bastard, he was an invalid and he had little money! The Reverend Lowe was no Good Samaritan, however much he thumped and thundered and exhorted his flock.

While Sandy went outside, Mattie counted the money from the small green tea pot which contained everything she possessed. She pushed it towards Mistress Lowe.

'Would you pay Mr McKie for my father's funeral please, Mistress Lowe? Also, we ordered a new rim for the cart wheel from Mr Kerr.' Her brow furrowed anxiously.

'Bless you, lassie!' Agnes Lowe murmured hoarsely.

'It is time to leave if we are to cross the moor before daybreak,' Sandy said, reappearing at the open door. 'I have put two of the best pigs in the baskets.'

'The pigs!' Mistress Lowe exclaimed, and her lips firmed. 'Why should Jacob Reevil be left with Nethertannoch's fine stock? Here, Mattie, take back your money.' She swept the little pile of coins from the table and pushed them into Mattie's reticule. 'It is little enough, and you will be needing it for the journey. I shall tell Joe Kerr you left a pig in payment for the rim; Master McKie can collect a cow to pay for the funeral.' She caught Sandy's look of alarm. 'Hugh McKie will not breathe a whisper out of place to any man, least of all Jacob Reevil. And I shall not tell him more than he needs to know - for his own sake. He will send young Iain up before dawn to collect his "payment" and attend to the rest of the animals before Jacob Reevil discovers you have gone.' Her voice choked a little.

She grasped Sandy's hand tightly in farewell, then pulled Mattie into her arms and hugged her fiercely. Mattie bit her lower lip in an effort to stop it trembling. Her eyes were bright with tears but she would not let them fall.

'I shall write to you,' she promised.

'No. Perhaps it would be better not to write for a while, my dear.' Agnes Lowe turned to Sandy with anxious eyes. 'No laird or law would protect her from Reevil until she is married!' And maybe not even then, she thought to herself. 'There is the business with Tam too. I shall write to the Reverend Mackenzie if - that is, when he recovers,' she amended firmly.

Sandy nodded, but his blue eyes were troubled. Mattie had already turned away, her own eyes bright with tears she refused to shed. Mistress Lowe was her dearest, her only, friend except for Sandy; her spirit almost failed as she contemplated the future, the loneliness she would be forced to endure in a world of silent, uncommunicative strangers.

Side by side they watched as Agnes Lowe hurried down the track - back to the glen, and the familiar lamp-lit manse. Then Sandy turned the horses' heads towards the open moorland beyond Nethertannoch's northern boundary. His face was pale and taut in the fading light. Mattie gave one last yearning look at the dear, familiar objects which had made up her home -the oak settle beside the fireside where her father had spent his last months, the oak press, the tiny child's chair made especially for her by her father's hands, the broken tea box. So many, many cherished possessions.

She swallowed the knot of tears in her throat with a struggle and called Buff to her side. For the last time she closed the door on the only home she had known.

Five

A chill wind had risen, whistling eerily between the rocks and heather as Sandy and Mattie approached the higher peaks. Sandy felt his leaden spirits dragging at each step which took them away from the familiar glen and Nethertannoch. A little way behind, Mattie trudged on uncomplaining. He thought of her bruised body, and felt ashamed of his own weakness.

Mistress Lowe had thrust her own woollen cloak around Mattie's shoulders. It was too long for her slight figure and added to the weight of her numerous petticoats, which were now wet with dew. Her progress was sorely hindered but she was grateful for its ample folds and cosy hood since a lingering frost had sharpened the piercing fingers of the wind. Even Buff trotted quietly at her side, instead of making sudden forays into the heather after real and imaginary quarry.

At last dawn began to break over the hills of Galloway, painting the sky with every shade from vermilion to palest rose, from aquamarine to gold, in a glory of ethereal splendour. Although they had not yet reached the military road, Sandy felt his heart lighten at the sight of so much beauty spreading over the eastern sky. The fingers of light seemed to beckon them onward, promising new hope. This was a new day, the start of a new life, his and Mattie's. In spite of his lack of religious faith, the words of one of Matthew Cameron's favourite psalms sprang unbid-den into his mind:

"I to the hills will lift mine eyes, From whence doth come mine aid. My safety cometh from the Lord, Who heav'n and earth hath made."

Mattie shared her father's faith implicitly. Sandy knew she found hope and courage from her reading of the scriptures. He set his jaw with new determination. He must never let her down. He knew she had put her father's unopened parcel in one of the panniers. When they stopped to rest he would unwrap the grey linen. Together they would read a few lines from the bible he was sure he would find within.

'It would have been so much easier and quicker if we could have travelled along the public roads,' Mattie sighed as they descended the last rough stretch.

'Aye.' Sandy turned to look at her anxiously. 'But with two laden horses, a dog and two squealing piglets, the keepers at the toll gates would certainly have remembered our passing.'

He wondered if Jacob Reevil had already alerted the constable and sent out a search party. He shuddered at the prospects before them if they were caught now, running away like criminals in the night; he apparently abducting an innocent girl to whom the laird had deemed it his duty to offer protection. Some protection, giving her to Tam Reevil as a bride, Sandy reflected grimly. Tam Reevil! What if he died of poison from his infected wounds? Sandy thrust aside this unwelcome thought.

Jacob Reevil savoured the prospect of revenge for the humiliation he had suffered, grovelling in the mud while his idiot son cackled his head off. He had been almost insane with anger when he attacked Tam, but he would have the sympathy of the glen folk and the newly appointed constable, when his only son died of fever from his ugly wounds. Their wrath against Logan would be stirred. He decided to wait until after the Sabbath to give Tam's fever time to develop. Then he would approach the constable with a demand for Sandy's arrest. Since his visit to Nethertannoch he had been unable to get Mattie out of his thoughts. Once Logan was safely locked up in gaol, he would soon make sure she gave him another son, maybe several sons

Reevil was disconcerted when he met Mistress Lowe at the door of the kirk. Instead of developing a fever, she reported that Tam's health was improving; even more alarming, she declared that the boy's habitual gabble was becoming almost intelligible now that she was getting used to him and winning his confidence.

Logan's arrest could be delayed no longer! But another unpleasant surprise awaited him when he arrived at Nethertannoch with the constable. The place was deserted. The cattle had been loosed to drink water from the burn. The stable was empty. The Nethertannoch mare had gone, as had the girl. Jacob Reevil knew they must have had warning of his plan. He was furious.

The constable was new to the glen, appointed under the 1856 Police Act. He had taken an instinctive dislike to Reevil; his own position was secure, and independent; he had found no difficulty in resisting Reevil's bribes. Now he had been brought to the top of the glen on a wild goose chase. He had met Sandy Logan once at the smiddy and he had thought him a pleasant, honest fellow. The smiddy was the hub of the glen and the place to hear gossip and opinions. He had heard no ill of Logan. He looked about him at the neat steading and the healthy cattle. Why, he asked himself, had Reevil not reported the alleged attack on his son immediately? Contempt showed in his expression and Jacob Reevil fumed inwardly.

'The girl is not yet sixteen. Logan has abducted her!'

'Abducted a girl?'

'The laird is the Provost, as ye ken. The Cameron girl has neither kith nor kin o' her ain. Sir Douglas is responsible for her. Logan has taken her away like a thief in the night!'

'So, Master Reevil,' the constable's eyes narrowed, 'it is the girl who concerns you then? Not Logan's attack on your son?' Reevil flushed angrily.

'I am an elder o' the kirk and it is the kirk's duty tae tak care o' the young an' innocent i' the parish,' he announced piously. 'A search party must be sent oot afore Sir Douglas Irving returns. Tis his duty tae keep the law i' these pairts. Ye'll remember his word has a powerfu' influence in mony a quarter,' he added malevolently. The constable seethed at the barely concealed threat behind Reevil's words. He knew his job, and he would prove it.

'I shall organise a search party at once,' he informed Reevil coldly.

Jacob Reevil was incensed that Logan had made a fool of him again; had deprived him of his pleasure with that spirited little deaf brat too. He could think of only one person who had cause, and the courage, to betray him. She had aroused the old raging passions in him ever since she arrived from France - and now she must assuage them.

Mistress Lowe, the mild, middle-aged wife of Caoranne's spineless minister, was the last person Reevil suspected of betraying him.

It was five nights since Sandy and Mattie had set out from Nethertannoch. They had avoided the roads by day and their progress had been slower in consequence. They were stiff and tired. Even so they both felt a flutter of anticipation as they crossed the bridge over the River

Nith into the town of Dumfries for the first time on that Wednesday morning in early April.

'I never dreamed I would ever see so many people!' Mattie breathed in awe. Cattle, sheep, pigs and horses were gathered beside the river.

'It is market day,' Sandy said with a frown. He hoped they would not meet anyone who might recognise them.

Drovers and dealers were bargaining vociferously. Mattie's dark eyes darted back and forth watching the changing expressions, the rapidly moving lips pouring forth a profusion of words. It was a little frightening. It reminded her of Dominie Butler and the children in the school at Caoranne; so many mouths to watch - and the sensation of humming bees and dark muffling velvet. She shook her head irritably from side to side, as frustrated now as she had been then.

Sandy grabbed her, pulling her roughly against him. Flick jibbed nervously. A pair of horses clattered by. The heavy, iron-rimmed wheels of their wagon rang loudly on the granite cobbles, but not in Mattie's ears.

'Oh!' she gasped with shock. Death had missed her by a hair's breadth. Only Sandy's lightning action had saved her. She began to tremble. He squeezed her arm reassuringly but when she looked up she was amazed to see that all the colour had drained from his ruddy face. He guided her hurriedly away from the main bustle of the town. Even then there was danger. Flick began to dance nervously and it took all Sandy's strength to hold the gelding as a strange rumbling sound filled the air. It was followed by a great hissing. Mattie looked around, wondering what had frightened the horse. She saw great white plumes shooting into the air.

'Look! Look, Sandy! It must be a railroad! A steam engine?'

When he had calmed the horses they moved further along the road until they could see the long black and steel engine. It was Sandy who stared in awe now. It was as high as a man standing on a horse's back and it had so many iron wheels that there seemed scarcely space for them to turn. Suddenly the monster gave a great belch, sending up a column of dirty black smoke into the sky. Flick fidgeted uneasily and Sandy moved on; secretly he wondered if the great black-bellied monster was going to explode.

Neither of them noticed the pale-faced young woman who had been making urgent inquiries for a train to London - and ultimately to France.

Emilia Reevil swiftly averted her bruised face behind a black veil and willed her torn and ravaged body to hasten back to the anonymity of a shabby closed cab.

The sun was well past its zenith when Sandy and Mattie at last found themselves on the road to Strathtod and the April day was changing fast. Yet in spite of the lowering skies their spirits lightened as they followed the narrow winding road which had brought them to a valley where the River Annan wended its leisurely way in wide loops and curves towards the Solway Firth. It was the most green and fertile stretch of land either of them had seen. Most of the fields were bordered by thick thorn and beech hedges, many of them guarding flocks of sheep. Already young lambs frolicked; newly sprouted corn carpeted some of the fields with emerald shoots. The season seemed more advanced than it had been on the rocks and bogs of Nethertannoch, despite Matthew Cameron's years of effort to improve his land.

Before they reached the long track which would take them up the incline to Fairlyden, darkness was falling fast, and with it came gusts of wind and the first squall of rain. The pigs were squealing for food, the horses walked wearily, heads bent, and Buff sidled along with her tail between her legs. Mattie huddled inside her cloak, thankful that they were nearing the end of their journey at last. Although the weals left by Reevil's whip were healing, she still felt the pain and stiffness, and her shoulder was badly bruised. She longed for a warm straw pallet to sleep on again and a glowing peat fire, with hot broth and crisp, fresh oatcakes.

Sandy's spirits, which had risen so readily at the sight of the green fields, plummeted as they neared the end of the deserted track. The fields suddenly seemed forlorn and empty. Through the deepening gloom he could see gaping holes in the overgrown hedges and tufts of long, dried up grass waved eerily as they passed. No sheep grazed here. No fat black cattle loomed out of the thickening mist. They passed no humble cottage, and no glimmer of candle light shone out of the darkness to welcome them.

Another anxiety had plagued him for the last few miles. Every instinct warned him of a certain uneasiness in Darkie. Yet there was no waxing at the end of her teats to warn of imminent foaling. He tried to shrug away his fears. Many mares carried their foals for a full twelve months, especially a first foal, and it was only ten months since the stallion had called at Nethertannoch. Perhaps Darkie was feeling the effects of the long trek and the meagre rations. So many of his dreams for their future rested on Darkie's foal. He had long had an ambition to become a breeder of fine, strong horses - the kind the waggoneers were demanding to move their goods from the ever increasing railway stations to the factories, and to other towns and villages where the iron monsters could not reach.

Suddenly the track curved almost at right angles, taking them around a small hill. There before them was a dark huddle of buildings. A stone wall, broken and uneven now, had once divided the open field from the rickyard. As they approached they saw a half open gate swinging precariously on its broken hinge with each gust of wind.

Mattie soothed the fretful horses while Sandy lifted the gate wider. The steading seemed completely deserted but they moved forward cautiously. A narrow opening in the dark mass of stone buildings allowed them to pass into an inner yard. Suddenly, out of the shadows, a large shape came ambling towards them.

'A cow!' Mattie gasped in relief.

The animal appeared to have been foraging for food, or seeking shelter from the rising wind and the rain which was now falling steadily. For an instant they were both painfully reminded of the animals they had left behind, especially Bessie, the cow Mattie had reared from a weakling calf.

On the opposite side of the rectangular steading one building stood taller than the rest. They guessed it was the dwelling house, though it also seemed deserted. There was no glimmer of light, no sign of human habitation; nothing but the whistle of the wind, the flip-flap of a broken door, the increasing drum of rain on an old cart. Silently Mattie took charge of the horses. She was too tired and hungry to feel any apprehension as she watched Sandy stride towards the house. She leaned her head against Darkie's wet neck and the mare blew a friendly snort of warm breath.

Sandy knocked loudly. There was no reply; he pushed at the door. It opened with a protesting creak and he found himself in a chilly, stone-flagged passage.

'Go away! Get out of my house, whoever you are!' He was startled by the voice; clipped, cultured - but distinctly querulous.

He moved forward undeterred. A cobweb clung to his cheek and he brushed it aside as he groped his way to a door at the end of the passage, the direction from which the voice had come. He knocked briefly. There was no response. He waited, frowning, then he pushed that door open also. Immediately he was almost overcome by the fetid smell which seemed to leap at him. He felt his stomach heave. It took all his control not to slam the door and hurry away. Slowly he forced himself to go further into the shadowy room. It was lit only by the smouldering embers of a fire in an iron grate which did little to dispel the damp chill.

Slowly his eyes became accustomed to the gloom and his gaze fell on the hunched figure sitting in a high-backed chair, his twisted fingers fixed to its wooden arms like the claws of a great bird. Even his bony knees seemed to project at odd angles. A grubby blanket was flung around his shoulders. Sandy gaped in dismay. Neither the man nor his filthy surroundings could have any connection with Mistress Lowe.

'I - er - perhaps we have come to the wrong place.' The only response was an irritable snort. 'We are searching for Mr Munro - Mr Daniel Munro of Fairlyden.'

'I am Daniel Munro. What business have you, coming into my house? I heard horses. I'll have no gypsies here! I have told your leader before! Get out! Get...

'We are not gypsies! We come as friends.'

'I have no friends! Get out, I tell you!' He tried to rise from his chair. He would have fallen had Sandy not rushed forward to support him. As he did so he could not suppress a gasp at the overpoweringly foul smell which seemed to come from a small chest of drawers in the corner where the man was sitting.

'My name is Alexander Logan. Your kinswoman, Mistress Lowe... '

'I have no kin, nor need of any!' Although the man was brusque to the point of incivility, his voice was firm and deep, his words beautifully rounded, completely at odds with his lined face and decrepit surroundings. Indeed, his voice was probably the only beautiful thing about Daniel Munro, Sandy thought cynically, but they were in desperate need of shelter from the rain, and of rest and food.

'Mistress Lowe received a letter some months ago, from a Reverend Mackenzie of the parish of Muircumwell,' he persisted patiently. 'She was unable to reply. Her husband is the Minister at Glen Caoranne '

'Minister!' He uttered a harsh laugh. 'That dried up, soulless hypocrite who dares to call himself a Christian!'

Sandy could not argue with Daniel Munro's description of the Reverend Peter Lowe, but he was growing concerned. Mattie was waiting with the horses in heavy rain.

'Please can you give us food and shelter for the night? Do you have empty stalls for the horses?'

'Empty stalls!' Daniel Munro echoed bitterly. 'The whole place is empty; except for Constance, and a few flea-ridden hens - if the fox hasn't taken them. And the devil take you, whoever you are! Go away, get out. I don't want you here!'

Sandy stared in dismay. 'My companion is cold and wet. She has walked many miles.'

'She? A woman! I don't want any gossiping woman in my house! Poking her nose into my affairs!'

'Mattie is deaf, completely deaf. She does not gossip. Your mother would have helped her. Indeed, she has already helped her once through Mistress Lowe.' Sandy's voice was cold; he was exasperated by the man's truculence.

'A deaf mute! Ah, I might have known the Reverend Lowe would send one of his charity brats!' he declared bitterly. 'Well, I have no money. No money for any of the waifs from his miserable parish - or anywhere else.'

'Mattie is not a waif. Nor is she a charity case. We will pay for a night's lodging, and stabling for the horses. We shall move on in the morning. But we have a mare; she is heavily in foal. We need hay and bran.' He held out some of their precious coins, knowing that tomorrow they must find work urgently, any kind of work, if they and the horses were not to starve.

Daniel Munro looked at him sharply. 'A mare, eh? In foal, you say? We-ell, you're certainly persistent! Go on then! Bring the girl in - just for tonight! There's no food until the Reverend Mackenzie brings me some of his own holy crumbs tomorrow, or the next day, or the next.' His mouth twisted. Daniel Munro hated being dependent on any man, even a man of God who did far more than his calling demanded, willingly and without complaint.

He made no effort to rise. The effort of moving even the few paces from his chair to the box bed cost Daniel Munro more effort than Sandy would expend on a hard day's work. Then there was the excruciating pain which had recently accompanied the slightest movement. Yet when Sandy lit the taper he had indicated he was amazed to see that the man's hair was as black as any boy's, and all the life in the rest of his twisted, wasted body seemed to be concentrated in the depths of his watchful dark eyes.

Daniel Munro of Fairlyden was not an old man. He was in fact only eleven years older than Sandy himself and he had been just as strong and fit and full of vigour - until the rheumatism had taken him in its strangling grip. One aim had sustained Daniel since adversity struck. It was a resolve to survive as long as possible, to thwart his half-brother's greed; ever since he was a small boy he had been aware of Gordon Fairly's jealousy and his ambition to restore Fairlyden to Strathtod Estate. Strathtod - the very name meant 'valley of the fox'. Gordon was as sly as any fox and he longed to rid his family of the taint of the Munros.

That night Sandy made the mistake which other men had made before him. He underestimated Daniel Munro's stamina, his perception, his intelligence -and above all his unreasoning desire to maintain the name of Munro at Fairlyden as long as humanly possible, preferably for as long as his half-brother lived.

Mattie groped her way through the darkness to a small room festooned with dusty cobwebs. As she huddled in her damp cloak on an even damper straw pallet she felt she had never been so miserable in her life. In the darkness she had been unable to see Sandy's face so it had been impossible to communicate with him. She was cold, wet, hungry, and weary to the point of exhaustion. She gritted her teeth in an effort to still their chattering. She could scarcely believe that this house belonged to any kinsman of Mistress Lowe. Yet however cold, however inhospitable, however unwelcoming Fairlyden appeared, she reminded herself that it was infinitely preferable to sharing the comfort of Nethertannoch with Tam Reevil and his bestial father. The fustiness of the straw now mingled with the overpowering smell, which she had recognised immediately as human excreta. The gnawing pangs of hunger were replaced by a tendency to retch. Buff sensed something of her misery and homesickness and curled at her feet. Mattie was grateful for the little dog's warmth and comfort. She delivered to herself a silent lecture. It was a habit to which she had resorted often during the long, lonely days in Dominie Butler's schoolroom when her courage had almost failed her.

You are no longer a child, Mattie Cameron! You decided to leave the glen. You caused Sandy to leave it too. There will be no returning, no tears, no giving in. Mr Munro needs you. He cannot harm you. He is helpless - even if he does look like a devil without horns, with those black brows arched in that horrid frown. Remember, his mother helped Mistress Lowe to give you one of your greatest pleasures. Now you must pay your debt; keep your promise; help if you can.

Then she said her prayers, repeating her plea: 'Please God, give me strength and knowledge to bring comfort to Mr Munro in his sickness and pain. Please do not let me be a burden to Sandy.' So Mattie spent her first night at Fairlyden.

'Well, what are you waiting for?' Daniel Munro taunted Sandy as soon as Mattie had left them alone. 'It is no use thinking you'll wait until I fall asleep then join her. Sleep is a luxury I rarely experience these days.'

Sandy flushed but his voice was quiet. 'I shall sleep with the horses.'

'As you please.' Daniel Munro shrugged. 'No doubt you have bedded her often enough before.' Sandy controlled his anger with an effort.

'Matthew Cameron trusted me with his daughter's safety, and her honour,' he said tightly. 'We travelled as brother and sister!'

'Then you're a fool!' Daniel declared cynically. 'Even a blind man could see you want the girl. Ach!' he scoffed aside Sandy's protest impatiently. 'Don't deny it. I've no time for liars - or cheats. Remember that, Logan, remember it well.'

'I am neither a liar nor a cheat,' Sandy declared angrily. 'I do not deny that I love Mattie, but I respect her. I cannot make her my wife. She is not yet sixteen and Sir Douglas Irving of Caoranne has taken her under his protection!' He was scarcely aware of the bitterness in his tone. 'Even if we can remain free until the fifteenth day of May, I canna ask her to be my wife until I can offer her a home.' Daniel Munro gave a sceptical snort. Then his dark eyes narrowed.

'And when will that be?' Suddenly there was a speculative gleam in the coal black depths, but Sandy was too engrossed in contemplation of his own grim prospects to notice. Subconsciously he had pinned his hopes on finding work here, at Fairlyden, with Mistress Lowe's kinsman. Maybe a home too. He had even hoped to keep his horses. All his dreams centred on Mattie, but their future now depended on his ability to find work.

'After the hiring fairs, God willing,' he muttered disconsolately.

'God!' Daniel scorned. 'He only helps men who can help themselves! Men like the Earl of Strathtod, my miserable half-brother. To him that hath shall more be given!' he added scathingly.

'You're a non-believer?' Sandy commented with some surprise, remembering Agnes Lowe's own unshakeable faith.

'Humph!' It was a contemptuous grunt, but Sandy saw the flicker of uncertainty in Daniel Munro's dark eyes. And something more - fear? Loneliness perhaps? He hesitated but Daniel's head had sunk on to his chest in a dismissive gesture.

Sandy spent an uncomfortable night in the cold, cheerless stable, bare of all but dust and the empty wooden meal chest. Even so he must have dozed. He woke to find the mare giving birth soundlessly, almost secretly.

Swiftly but silently he made sure the tough membrane was clear of the foal's nose and mouth. It was small but it looked perfect, just perfect. He stood for a moment gazing down at it with a prayer of thankfulness in his heart. Then he turned and ran eagerly to the house. He couldn't wait to share the news with Mattie.

Despite the previous night's fatigue Mattie was already up and standing at the open door, savouring the sweet freshness of the morning air. The previous night's rain was almost forgotten, especially when she saw the expression on Sandy's face.

'Darkie has had her foal, Mattie!' He hugged her exuberantly in his excitement, then looked down into her bright eyes. 'It's a filly.'

`I can't wait to see it!' Mattie laughed joyfully. Suddenly nothing, not even the dirty, smelly house, seemed so bad as she walked at Sandy's side to see the foal. As she peeped into the stable the foal was already struggling to get up on its gangling legs.

'Such long legs!' she chuckled in delight. 'It must be a good omen.'

Even Mr Munro seemed interested in the foal, Mattie decided when she saw him speaking earnestly to Sandy. She was shovelling up the piles of ashes which had clogged the grate and spread over the hearth, preventing the fire from burning, as well as making an awful mess. She wondered if his expression was always so grave.

The birth of the foal had aroused Daniel's interest more than he would have believed possible.

'Maybe the mare has no signs of milk because she has foaled early. A few decent feeds of bran might help bring it on.'

'Aye,' Sandy frowned. 'The foal is early right enough and Darkie hasna had a good feed since we left Nethertannoch. The foal is nuzzling so that should stimulate the milk, don't ye think?' He looked anxiously at Daniel Munro. The dark brows were drawn together thoughtfully and Sandy realised that the crabbit, crippled man was far more interested and concerned for the foal than he had been for himself and Mattie the previous evening.

Sandy had no way of knowing that Daniel Munro's ambition when young had been to study animal health and science at Edinburgh University. His father's health was already failing at the time and his mother had pleaded with him not to leave Fairlyden. He had contented himself with reading his books and his knowledge now formed a fragile bond between him and Sandy, despite his sharp tongue and abrupt manner.

Mattie's attention was taken up with finding food for themselves. She was dismayed to discover there was barely enough oatmeal in the house to make even the thinnest brose. The flour chest was empty; there was not even a potato or barley to make broth, and certainly no scrap of bacon or mutton. Once there had been a garden, now it was a mass of weeds, as was the farm yard and the surrounding fields. Sandy had been equally shocked when daylight showed him the full extent of the decay and neglect; the stench and filth from the overflowing midden at the back of the house was overpowering. Yet it was evident that the buildings had been carefully planned, and constructed of the best stone and slate. The house was twice as large as Nethertannoch, and there were proper bedroom windows sprouting out of the sloping roof at both the back and front.

Sandy decided his first priority must be to find the nearest mill and procure food for the animals as well as themselves.

'Strathtod mill is nearer,' Daniel informed him grimly, 'but you'll get nothing there when it is known you have come from Fairlyden. Follow the burn in the direction of Muircumwell. It is easy enough to cross into Muircumwell parish, except when the burn is in spate.'

Sandy followed his instructions and, with the help of some judiciously placed stones, reached Muircumwell without trespassing on the Earl of Strathtod's vast estate. On this particular April morning the water was tumbling merrily over the pebbles and Sandy wished he had brought Flick. Daniel Munro had not warned him that Muircumwell mill was a good four miles away. It would be impossible to carry enough meal for all their needs on his own back. As well as Dark Lucy, the pigs needed food. Sandy frowned; some of Daniel Munro's concern for the little filly had affected him. He had watched it carefully before he set off, but although it nuzzled it seemed incapable of grasping the teat and actually suckling. Eventually it had given up and stretched out on the bare floor. Yet Sandy did not really believe that such a perfect foal could slip into the world so easily only to give up on life without a fight, as Daniel Munro had warned. All his hopes for the future rested upon its survival. He must get bran to help Dark Lucy produce milk without delay, even if it needed most of their precious money. He would have to look for work.

His stomach churned emptily as he reached the mill. A plump, pimply-faced youth sullenly inquired his business. Sandy's small order elicited a scornful curl of thick lips. The youth disappeared into the depths of the mill and Sandy waited with growing impatience. Edward Slater returned at last carrying a small bag of oatmeal and a larger one of bran. The sum he asked was exorbitant and Sandy scowled.

'Take it or leave it!' the lad declared insolently. 'Ye're a stranger in these parts. Ye'll no' find meal anywhere else in this parish - but ye can try at Strathtod, if ye've a mind.' Sandy saw the sly gleam in his small, deep-set eyes. He could not know that from his vantage point on the top floor of the mill, the fellow had watched him cross the Strathtod burn from Fairlyden. He looked into the bags. The oatmeal was indeed of the finest quality. Even so the youth had grossly overcharged him, but his need was great and he paid the price reluctantly.

Hunger was gnawing at Sandy's stomach by the time he returned to Fairlyden. He was looking forward to a bowl of thick porridge. He handed Mattie the bag of oatmeal, and crossed the yard towards the stable intending to mix a bran mash as soon as possible. Mattie's anguished cry halted his footsteps. She was still standing in the doorway.

As soon as he saw the meal trickling through her fingers he knew the youth at the mill had played a mean trick, a trick which Mattie had suspected when she felt the weight of the bag. Only a few inches at the top of the bag were best oatmeal. The rest was little more than husks, barely fit for the pigs.

Six

Time and time again Sandy patiently guided the foal to the mare, but without the slightest success. It simply could not suckle. As the day wore on his spirits sank.

He was leaving the stable for the umpteenth time late that afternoon when he saw the tall, slim figure of a man approaching along the burnside, from the direction of Muircumwell. He was leading a laden horse. As he drew nearer the man smiled warmly, and Sandy found himself looking into a pair of shrewd but kindly grey eyes. The man extended a hand in greeting and Sandy was taken aback to learn that he was the Minister of the Muircumwell Free Church.

'So I was not misinformed!' the Reverend Robert Mackenzie exclaimed. 'Only this morning I received a letter preparing me for your arrival.'

'A letter?' Sandy echoed faintly. Frae - frae Mistress Lowe?' The colour ebbed and flowed beneath his ruddy skin. 'Did she - did she send news?' he asked tensely.

Robert Mackenzie frowned. It had been abundantly clear that Mistress Lowe had written the letter in haste, but he had sensed distress behind the staccato sentences.

'Did she mention Tam Reevil?' Sandy could not hide his anxiety.

'Mistress Lowe mentioned a boy who had been in her care.'

'Had?' Sandy's face paled.

'Yes. His father removed him from the Caoranne manse. His sister too.'

'Miss Emilia must have been helping to care for Tam at the manse then. He - he must have recovered, if Reevil took him away! Thank God for that!' Sandy breathed with relief.

'I do. Every morning and every evening, and many times betwixt - thank my Maker, I mean,' the Minister murmured drily. Sandy was surprised to see the wry gleam in his fine grey eyes. He was totally unlike the pompous Minister at Glen Caoranne. When he looked up again, however, the Reverend Mackenzie was frowning.

'Mistress Lowe asked me to use my influence to keep you and your companion at Fairlyden. She also insists that you must not write to her until she contacts me again. She seems deeply concerned for Miss Cameron's safety.'

'We canna stay at Fairlyden! Mistress Lowe understands little of her kinsman's present circumstances. I must provide a home for Mattie, and food. I must get work!'

'Mistress Lowe assures me of your integrity and loyalty, Alexander Logan, and she explained a little of the events which forced you to leave. She begged me to persuade Miss Cameron to remain at Fairlyden. She said there had been "unspeakable happenings", as soon as her absence was discovered.'

'Happenings?' Sandy echoed sharply.

'Yes. Mistress Lowe's letter reflects distress. A girl was ravaged and beaten. She escaped from her own bedroom by climbing down an ivy stem. Mistress Lowe found her on the door step of the manse. She had crawled there for help. The Reverend Lowe was shocked by her story. Apparently she had spent most of her life in a French convent. She pleaded with him to help her get away from the glen. He hired a carriage and gave her money.'

Sandy was dismayed. Surely the girl could not have been Emilia Reevil? Yet who else from the glen had lived in a French convent? He recalled the purity of her face, the sweetness of her manner. No one would attack a girl as innocent as that - unless he was insane.

'The Reverend Lowe must have been truly shocked if he gave her money.'

'Yes. He was absent while Mistress Lowe was writing the letter. He had expressed his intention of discovering the truth. Mistress Lowe seemed extremely disturbed because her husband had not returned by the time she had finished the letter, although the hour was late. Unless Mistress Lowe sends better news, I shall be failing in my duty if I do not try to keep you and Miss Cameron at Fairlyden.'

'Whatever happens we shall never return to Caoranne while Reevil is there. He is a sly fiend! Even Sir Douglas Irving could not have protected Mattie from him.' Yet even Reevil would not attack his own daughter, would he?

They entered the kitchen at Fairlyden together and for the first time Sandy saw an expression approaching warmth in Daniel Munro's dark eyes, though his tone was as brusque as ever. Robert Mackenzie's own eyes softened as he talked to Mattie. Throughout his visit he did his best to include her in the conversation, and Sandy warmed to him. He was proud of Mattie's intelligent responses. Her brown eyes sparkled at the challenge as she became accustomed to the careful movements of the Minister's lips.

It was Daniel who mentioned the mean trick Edward Slater had played on Sandy. The light died from Robert Mackenzie's eyes and his expression was grave.

'Joseph's family have been millers at Muircumwell almost since time began, hence his surname - Miller. He is scrupulously honest. It would grieve him to hear that Edward has dealt so meanly with a stranger. The mill has kept its trade because Joseph has a reputation for honesty and fair dealing.' The Reverend Mackenzie sighed. 'Unfortunately he has no son of his own to help him. He does have a very pretty daughter though,' he added with a smile at Sandy. 'Jeannie Miller is the apple of her father's eye.'

'The fellow Slater then? He is a labourer at the mill?' Sandy inquired.

'The Millers try to treat him as a son. Joseph's sister was his aunt by marriage. Edward has no relatives of his own - but I fear he has proved a sullen, ungrateful wretch.'

'Well, I shall certainly keep an eye on him if ever I return to the mill,' Sandy declared grimly. 'We have little enough money to spare, especially until I find work.'

'Do you wish to leave Fairlyden, Miss Cameron?'

'We cannot leave. Not yet. Mr Munro needs help.' She could not hear Daniel Munro's sharp denial.

'I must leave. We need money to buy food, Mattie.' Sandy looked into her troubled eyes and his heart sank as he saw her soft mouth firm.

'I must stay. We promised Mistress Lowe that we would help her kinsman.'

Daniel Munro glowered fiercely but he had yet to learn how determined Mattie could be when a person, or an animal, was sick or in need.

'It is possible to produce more food at Fairlyden than you could ever use, so long as a man has health and strength to cultivate the land and tend his animals and crops,' the Reverend Mackenzie remarked. 'Is that not so, my friend?' he looked at Daniel.

'If a man is not afraid of hard work, and challenge and making enemies!' came the uncompromising reply.

'The land is fertile. The old Earl selected the best fields on the estate for Daniel's mother,' the Minister persisted. Then he looked up, and his eyes met and held Sandy's. 'The name "den" means "a narrow valley with trees" - but it also means "a lair" - a safe place to stay. It was Lord Jonathan Fairly who named it "Fairly's Den". Truly there is no place more beautiful in spring, in summer, even in winter. Soon there will be an abundance of grass in the meadows, neglected though they are. As for the house...' He shrugged helplessly as he looked around the room at the tidy hearth, the cheery fire, the floor and furniture now free from dust. Even the commode, discreetly hidden in the shape of the small chest of drawers, had received Mattie's attention. 'You have done more for Daniel in a single day than I can do for him in a month.' He spoke clearly and slowly, his grey eyes never leaving Mattie's face. She shook her head and smiled.

'I have only cleaned. You have brought food.' She turned to Sandy. 'A mutton pie with carrots and potatoes; cheese and a piece of bacon, as well as a bannock and fresh meal.'

'Tomorrow I shall send vegetables - leeks and potatoes, kale and carrots and turnips.'

'We cannot live on charity!' Sandy declared indignantly. 'It is almost a wilderness here. I must earn money to buy food!'

The Minister glanced at Mattie, and his eyes filled with compassion, but it was to Sandy he spoke.

'The manse garden is large; the glebe is productive too. I have no family so the needs of the manse are small. I shall send seeds for Mattie to plant in the garden here. A new season has begun, a time of change.' Again Sandy began to protest but the Reverend Mackenzie went on quietly: 'It is not charity. It is my duty to help - as a Christian. People - men especially - would take advantage of Mattie. There are many who would believe - or pretend to believe -that she is half-witted because she cannot hear. They would use it as an excuse for poor payment, however hard she worked.' His eyes held Sandy's. 'Even if you find work together, she may be no better than a slave.' Robert Mackenzie spoke with the clarity which befitted his calling and Mattie was watching intently. She understood the gist of his words with disconcerting accuracy.

'I am deaf - but I can cook and clean, milk the cows and churn the butter.' She broke off and shuddered. Sir Douglas Irving himself had thought she was an idiot, suited only to be mated like an animal with another idiot.

Daniel Munro reached out and touched her hand. He looked steadily into her clouded dark eyes.

'I have no money to offer, but you may stay here if you wish; there would be no one to give you orders, or to use you ill. This was a beautiful house once.' He turned to Sandy. 'It would be hard work and little reward, but she would be safe with me.' He grimaced. 'Can you protect her at all times, against all men?' Mattie could not see his lips and the old frustration rose up in her. Was he pleading?

'I shall stay here, if that is your wish.'

'But Mattie!' Sandy crossed the floor and stared into her face in consternation. 'Mr Munro cannot afford to buy food, even for himself!'

'I will make butter to sell as I did at Nethertannoch. It is springtime, Sandy. The grass will grow soon, and the hens will lay again.' Mattie knew life at Fairlyden would be hard, very hard, but she wanted to help Mr Munro if only to repay Mistress Lowe and her kinswoman for the help they had given her.

'I can set eggs to rear more chickens. Next year we shall have younger hens and more eggs. The pigs will grow. Mr Mackenzie has promised seeds for the garden.' She stopped, as amazed as Sandy at her lengthy speech. He looked down into her flushed face and thought he had never seen her look so lovely, despite the faint bruise which still coloured her temple. His own eyes were tender.

'You cannot make butter. We have no cows,' he reminded her. There would be no eggs either from what he had seen of the bedraggled hens pecking around the empty rickyard.

'There is Constance,' Daniel Munro said drily.

'Constance?' Sandy turned to him.

'My only remaining cow. I reared her with great difficulty. She was a twin. Constance often wanders, but she always returns - hence the name.'

'I see,' Sandy muttered slowly.

'No, you don't!' Daniel Munro snapped bitterly. 'One by one my cattle and sheep disappeared; gaps have appeared in the hedges overnight since I became a cripple! I sold the few animals which remained. This year even Constance must go - unless Mattie stays to milk her when her calf is born. Anyway, she is getting too old to forage for herself in winter, and I can no longer make hay or grow turnips. A younger man - a man unafraid of hard work - could grow the best crops of corn and turnips in the area - in a year or two.' Sandy knew it was a challenge.

'I am not afraid of work, but I canna accept charity - even frae a minister!'

'I believe you mentioned horses?' the Reverend Mackenzie inquired.

Sandy nodded. 'A gelding and a mare.'

'Then I think Joseph Miller would give you work at the mill for a few weeks, if you would use one of your own horses. He delivers flour and meal to the outlying farms, and carts corn back to the mill. His own mare is due to foal any time now. He could use a temporary carter.'

Sandy hesitated. Matthew Cameron had taught him all he knew about the land and animals. He was a farmer now, a good ploughman. He loved the land, the ploughing - and above all his horses. But he loved Mattie more! He turned to Daniel Munro.

'If I can get work at the mill, would you keep Darkie at Fairlyden until she has reared her foal? I could work here in return, when I am free. I want to breed horses - the kind the waggoners need,' he declared impulsively. 'But it will be many months before I can sell the foal.'

'If the foal lives,' Daniel reminded him with more than a trace of regret in his own dark eyes. Sandy's heart sank. It would be years before he could make his fortune from breeding and selling horses. He could not even afford the stallion's fees for Darkie to have another foal. A whole year would be wasted. Even if he saved enough for the service fees next year, it would be two years before Darkie had another foal. He needed work urgently - any work!

A little while later Sandy listened to the evening song of the birds and watched the Reverend Mackenzie ride away into the purple shadows. It was such a peaceful valley, almost hidden from the world. There was no money but there was challenge in the neglected land, the dilapidated fences, the sheds full to overflowing with rotting manure. In his heart Sandy knew he could be happy here at Fairlyden, just so long as Mattie remained at his side. They had the pigs, and they would breed more - good ones too; he had the horses to plough the land; Mattie was thrifty. Perhaps in time they could buy another cow, more hens, maybe even sheep too - if he could earn enough money at the mill.

Joseph Miller rode up to Fairlyden early the next morning, bringing with him a bag of finest quality, newly ground oatmeal.

'I hear ye're needing work,' he remarked as soon as he had apologised for Edward Slater's mean trick.

'Aye,' Sandy answered warily, realising the miller had come in person to make his own judgement.

'And ye have a gelding, as weel as the mare an' foal?' Sandy nodded.

'If ye're willing to use him to cart to and frae the mill, I could give ye work for a few months - just three days a week though - to save my ain mare.'

'We-ell,' Sandy frowned consideringly, 'I suppose that would earn us enough to eat. At least until the hiring fairs in May.'

'I can only pay ye two shillings a week in cash,' the miller declared hastily.

'Even wi' the use o' ma ain gelding?' Sandy asked in dismay. He began to shake his head.

'Ye wad have enough oatmeal and flour for the house, and meal to feed your two pigs forebye.' Like his ancestors, Joseph Miller still made most of his transactions in kind, swapping corn for a weaned piglet, a bag of flour for a pair of leather boots; his wife's hats and his daughter's dresses were all paid for in pounds of flour and stones of oatmeal. He rarely parted with the little money which came into his hands and trade had decreased ever since Edward Slater had begun to work in the mill.

Sandy was disappointed but he knew he had little choice in the present circumstances. Also he liked Joseph Miller's frank blue eyes and honest face.

'At least I shall have time to tidy up here a bit,' he said ruefully, glancing around him at the neglected cow byre and the dairy. Mattie would need help with that if she was to make any butter. 'Yes, I'll take the work ye're offering.' Joseph Miller's rosy face broke into a smile and he held out a work-roughened hand.

'I could let ye have a few oats for seed, if ye have a notion to plough an acre or two.'

Sandy brightened at the prospect of ploughing and cultivating some of Fairlyden's neglected acres.

'Aye,' he said, 'and maybe I could manage a few acres o' turnips for the winter. I wadna weary for want o' work.' He grinned. 'There's the midden and sheds to be emptied, an' the hedges needing attention.'

Not even Mattie's patient care and diligent attention could persuade Dark Lucy's filly foal to suckle. They watched despondently as the little animal gradually grew weaker. One morning less than a week after their arrival at Fairlyden it slipped out of the world as quietly as it had entered, taking with it Sandy's dream of rearing a fine filly to sell at the Lanark Fair. His hopes of asking Mattie to be his wife receded. He had nothing to offer her, not even a roof for shelter. Even Daniel Munro, crippled and penniless as he was, could offer that.

Sandy found the work at the mill strange, but he enjoyed visiting the farms and houses throughout the sprawling parish of Muircumwell. He met humble men and women from the farm towns, who worshipped the Reverend Mackenzie almost more than the God he represented. There were others, new traders and small merchants, men suddenly made wealthy by the spread of the new railways. Such men thought they owned the Minister, and his thoughts, because they contributed to his living and the Free Church. They resented his outspoken criticism of their shady businesses and their greed. They denounced his actions when he helped those to whom the charity of his elders and parishioners could not, or would not, extend - people such as Daniel Munro and Mattie Cameron.

Sandy found a new friend in Nicky Jamieson, the young horseman from a farm called Mains of Muir. He became familiar with several other cottagers who proudly trudged barefoot each Sunday, through sun and wind, rain and snow, to sit on rough wooden benches or even to stand, thankful just to be present in Robert Mackenzie's little church, and free to listen to his words. Even his sternest critics agreed he had a God-given gift of speaking from the heart, and many had cause to thank him for his wisdom, and his tolerance.

Mattie had cause to thank the Reverend Robert Mackenzie many times, especially when he supplemented their meagre diet with vegetables from his own garden and an occasional pie from the manse kitchen, unknown to his housekeeper, Mrs Simmons. He continued his weekly visits to Fairlyden, but now he had time for conversation with his old friend. Sandy had been amazed at the menial tasks the Minister was prepared to undertake in the name of friendship and Christianity. His own experience of ministers was confined to the Reverend Lowe, who would not have demeaned himself to call at Fairlyden, much less help its unfortunate occupant.

Daniel himself was taken aback by Mattie's acceptance of his human frailties. At first he had tried to resist some of her ministrations but she had either failed to understand him - or, as he frequently suspected, had simply ignored his protests and did what had to be done, calmly and efficiently. Young as she was, Mattie had attended to all her father's needs during the last year of his life and she accepted Daniel Munro's dependence philosophically. Gradually Daniel began to accept her help more gracefully. His temper improved along with his health, and both were greatly assisted by the warmth of a well-tended fire and the airing of the musty house, as well as by the herbal infusions which Mattie prepared to relieve his pain.

When the Reverend Mackenzie's seeds had been planted in the vegetable garden, she declared, 'Now I shall turn my attention to the herb garden. It must have been very well planned and stocked once?'

'Yes, my mother also had a fine knowledge of herbs.' Then, unexpectedly, Daniel found himself reaching for Mattie's hand. 'She would have been pleased to know you, Mattie, and grateful to you - as I am.' Mattie flushed with pleasure. She knew how much it cost a man as proud as Mr Munro to utter those few words. She went to work in the little herb garden with renewed vigour.

Sandy also discussed his plans with Daniel Munro.

'The South Meadow was always one of the earliest fields,' Daniel advised with a new glow of interest in his dark eyes. 'All the fields will be needing lime, I suppose. Aye, and muck from the sheds. But it should do well enough with oats and a few turnips, if you can plough it soon.'

So Sandy laboured long and hard at Fairlyden on the days he did not go to the mill, but he derived satisfaction from all the improvements he made.

Indoors Mattie had discovered several fine pieces of furniture beneath old covers and layers of dust. One afternoon she startled Daniel when she rushed through from the room which had once been his mother's best front parlour.

'See, I have found a whole cupboard full of books!' she declared with delight, holding up some of the leather-bound volumes. Her pleasure both amused and gratified Daniel Munro. His mother had treasured her books. He held out his hand and Mattie put one of the musty volumes on his lap. He smoothed back the thin, gold-edged pages with a gnarled finger.

'I read them all once.' He smiled. 'Perhaps we could read some of them together, Mattie?' So he began to find renewed pleasure between the musty pages of Scott's Lay of the Last Minstrel, Marmion, and The Lady of the Lake. Mattie was delighted to discover he shared her interest.

'Would you like to borrow my book of poems by Robert Burns?' she asked shyly one wet afternoon.' It is small and light enough for you to hold, I think, without bringing the pain to your fingers.'

Daniel read the poems with a new appreciation now that he could no longer see for himself the beauty and simplicity of the crimson-tipped daisy or the humble mouse; he smiled at the humour and wisdom of the poet's 'Address to the Deil'. He longed to be able to discuss the books more freely with Mattie as she plied her needle, mending and remaking innumerable garments and neglected linen. Unfortunately when her eyes were fixed upon her work she was oblivious to any utterance he made and he found himself envying the little dog which lay at her feet and drew her attention with no more than the touch of a silky white paw. Almost as though she sensed his scrutiny, Buff looked up at him inquiringly.

'Aye, you have no fine pedigree either, but your mistress loves you well for all that!' he said aloud, and grinned when Buff cocked one chocolate-coloured ear towards him and brushed the floor with an eager wag of her tail. Mattie saw the movement and raised her head.

'I was just talking to Buff,' Daniel explained. 'She always looks as though she is winking at me with that dark patch above one eye.'

Mattie laughed and fondled the little dog's ears affectionately. 'I don't know what I would do without her.'

Sandy knew he ought to be pleased that Mattie had found such unexpected pleasure and companionship but he was filled with a strange misgiving. Time was passing swiftly. Why had Mistress Lowe not written to them? Was Reevil still searching for Mattie? Sandy shuddered at the thought. In a few weeks she would be sixteen. How can I ask her to be my wife when I have not even a roof to offer her? He thought despondently. Soon his work at the mill would end. He would be forced to put himself up for hire at one of the local fairs. Mattie worked hard at Fairlyden for little reward, but she was her own mistress, and she was safe. It was true that her dark eyes were sometimes haunted by strange shadows, but she never complained and Sandy knew Daniel Munro enjoyed her company and did his best to make her happy. How can I uproot her again so soon? He pondered unhappily.

He had seen and learned a great many things since leaving Nethertannoch. Fairlyden was almost a palace in comparison to the hovels in which many labourers lived. Even the best of the cottages were small and dark and damp, with mud to the door. The lucky ones might have a pig in a shed in the garden, but that was all. He knew Mattie would make even the humblest place into a home but how could he ask her to live in such conditions when Matthew Cameron had had such bright hopes for her future at Nethertannoch? How can I ask ye to become a drudge, at the bidding of some sharp-eyed mistress from dawn to dusk, just for me, Mattie? He thought despondently.

Daniel's thoughts were remarkably similar to Sandy's. During the day, when Mattie was sweeping, ironing, dusting and polishing, his dark eyes followed her constantly. Sometimes they lit with involuntary amusement, such as when she wrestled with the flues of the 'new-fangled' fire. He missed her serene expression, her quiet presence, whenever she was away from the kitchen.

'Where have you been?' he demanded in alarm one afternoon after she had been absent longer than usual.

'I followed a duck up the burnside.' She was flushed with the success of finding three ducklings and several eggs on the point of hatching. Daniel knew she longed to have fresh eggs to add a little variety to their meals but he could not share her elation. Mattie guessed his thunderous scowl was no more than a camouflage for his relief.

'I would never leave Fairlyden without telling you,' she assured him gently.

Leave? The very word made Daniel shrink. He realised how much he had grown to appreciate her presence, and the cleanliness and comfort she had brought to his home again.

Mattie missed the Nethertannoch cattle more than she cared to admit - the milking, the routine of setting up the creaming bowls, the challenge of churning butter - and of course the selling of her eggs and butter to the packman, and the pleasure of ordering her own provisions. So she was delighted when Constance, Daniel's only surviving cow, at last showed signs of calving again. She looked forward to having fresh butter and buttermilk.

'Constance has had twins,' she announced a few mornings later. 'One is black from the tip of its tail to the points of its tiny cloven feet. The other is a bluish roan.' She wondered why Mr Munro looked so dismayed.

Constance had already lived through eight summers, and she had had a lean winter. The production of two sturdy offspring had taken its toll, as Daniel had surmised. All the milk she could produce was needed to rear her calves.

Mattie struggled to hide her disappointment, but Daniel was too perceptive not to notice. He had one last treasure - all that stood between him and a pauper's grave. Yet anything he could do to tempt Mattie to stay at Fairlyden would be worth the sacrifice. He resolved to discuss the matter with his old friend, Robert Mackenzie.

The opportunity came a few days later. Mattie was bending over the griddle attending to her oatcakes when he raised the subject.

'Sandy intends to put himself up for hire at the Annan Fair,' he announced glumly. 'There will not be enough work at the mill during the summer.' The Minister looked keenly at Daniel's furrowed brow. 'I can give him nothing, though he works constantly. I am afraid Mattie may want to go with him.'

'That would indeed be a pity!' Robert Mackenzie exclaimed. 'Your health as well as your temper have improved since Mattie Cameron came to Fairlyden, my friend.' He drew slowly on his pipe, discreetly observing Daniel, surprised at the anxiety he detected.

'She is happy here,' he remarked with more gravity.

'Yes, but she misses her dairy, her animals, the satisfaction of making her own butter - and selling it. We must have more cows if we are to make a living. Mattie has her pride too.' Daniel hesitated. 'I still have the diamond and emerald brooch.'

'No! You cannot sell the last, the most treasured, of your mother's jewellery, Daniel. You have always said nothing would give the Earl greater satisfaction than to see you in a pauper's grave.'

'It would please my beloved brother to see me in any grave. And the sooner the better!' Daniel grimaced. 'But I have no intention of giving him that satisfaction yet. I want you to sell the brooch and buy Mistress MacFarlane's cow for Mattie. The rest of the money I shall leave in your keeping - to be used when the time comes. I fear it would grieve our little Mattie as much as myself if I were to end my days in a pauper's grave.'

It is the least I can do, Daniel decided without regret after his old friend had gone and he looked around him at the changes Mattie had brought to his home in so short a time. Gone were the cobwebs and filth, the layers of dust, the sickening stench, the stale porridge on which he had existed between Robert's visits. Their meals were still simple; Fairlyden's garden and larder afforded little variation as yet, but Mattie made even a dish of brose taste better, hot and fresh and cleanly served, and her willow bark powder helped him to sleep and consequently improved his spirits.

The early summer sun danced on the limewashed walls and the shining surfaces of the mahogany chest, the table and the matching chairs. Daniel raised his face to its warmth and brightness and felt new hope in his heart. Even the fire seems to have a brighter glow, a greater warmth, since Mattie cleared away the piles of ash, he thought with a smile, recalling how studiously she had examined and poked out the assortment of flues and dampers which alternately fascinated and frustrated her. Daniel guessed she preferred the swee and a simple peat fire such as she had known at Nethertannoch. He longed to be able to talk to her, to ask about her old home, and her father; he wanted to tell her that his mother had shared her antipathy towards the elaborate range. His father had insisted on installing it, as well as the copper boiler in the scullery. Lord

Jonathan had believed them to be the very latest amenities, and he had been eager to provide them for the woman who had brought him happiness and companionship in his later years. It was this companionship which his brother had resented so bitterly, Daniel reflected. Yet he remembered his mother requesting, oh so gently, the return of her old swee. She had not craved grandeur or a position in society. The young Lord Gordon Fairly need not have been so jealous if only he had turned a deaf ear to maliciously wagging tongues.

As the weather became warmer Daniel even managed to hobble to the stone bench outside the door with the aid of two stout hazel sticks which Sandy had cut specially for him, patiently smoothing the rounded ends to suit his twisted hands.

'I never expected to see the outside world again,' he sighed happily one morning as he surveyed the fields and the distant wood, and the Strathtod Estate beyond. 'Could you bring your mare to the house, Sandy?'

'Aye, indeed I could!' He complied eagerly. He led Dark Lucy as close to the stone bench as he could get. Daniel stroked her smooth flanks and rippling muscles with sensuous pleasure.

'She is a fine animal, a beautiful mare. I never dreamed I would see the likes of her at Fairlyden.' His words brought a glow of satisfaction to Sandy's lean face.

Daniel slowly accepted that his pride could no longer blind him to his need, his utter dependence on other human beings. Pride and pain had seemed the only things left in his life. Pain remained, but even it was made bearable with Mattie's help. Serenity seemed to surround her like a cloak, despite her own adversity, while Sandy's dreams of horse breeding and his love of the land had reawakened Daniel's interest in his own birthright. I do need help, he admitted silently, but not just any help. I want Mattie. I want her to stay at Fairlyden - to be with me to the end.

Seven

Daniel was sitting in the open doorway of the kitchen, half dozing in the morning sun, when the skimmer flew from Mattie's nerveless fingers in the adjoining dairy. The cream bowl lay in pieces and a miniature river of precious milk trickled towards the dairy door. Mattie was oblivious to everything. Icy terror clutched at her heart. She was back in the glen. She was alone - always alone - but this time it was not part of her recurrent dream!

She had made a determined effort to put the past behind her. She had refused to trouble Sandy with the nightmares which made her heart pound with fear and bathed her in cold sweat. Now every detail of her last day at Nethertannoch returned with petrifying clarity as she stared through the dairy window - the only window facing the cool north-east. It was exactly one week before her sixteenth birthday.

She had seen two men on horseback riding up the track. They were temporarily hidden from view by the rising ground and the sheltering clump of trees, but she had seen them in the distance - one thick-set, older, the other slight, slim, the figure of a youth. No friendly visitors came to Fairlyden from the direction of Strathtod!

Daniel was dismayed when Mattie flung herself to her knees in front of him, her brown eyes dilated with the same fear he had once seen in the eyes of a young rabbit caught in a trap. It had died.

'Don't tell them!' she gasped. 'Don't tell them I am here! Sandy is at the mill! He did not make me run away. He came only to keep his promise to m-my f-father!'

Daniel was alarmed. Mattie - calm, self-possessed, little Mattie - was on the verge of hysteria! He reached out a soothing hand.

'Don't let them take me away!' She stared down at his crippled hands with a moan of despair. What could he do to protect her? He saw the words written in her wide eyes as clearly as if she had seared them across the sky with a burning brand.

'What? Who?' He began. She choked on a sob. Before he could make his lips frame the question, she was on her feet, fleeing towards the burn, her skirts gathered in her hands. Buff ran at her heels.

'Mattie! Come back! No one...' Of course she did not turn, she could not hear! Daniel cursed his helplessness. He stared into the sun, a frown deepening the lines of pain. Two horsemen rode slowly into view and as they drew nearer his lips tightened with anger.

The last time his beloved half-brother had called on Daniel he had been more dead than alive, prostrate in a cheerless room - cold and hungry amidst his own filth. The charming Earl of Strathtod had offered neither food nor warmth but looked down his supercilious nose.

'Do not expect me to pay for your funeral. You'll be buried where you belong - in a pauper's grave!' There had been malicious satisfaction in Gordon's pale eyes then. Yet what reason had Mattie to fear him?

Daniel watched silently as the pair made their way through the gate, which now opened easily on its hinges. Even from a distance he sensed the Earl's surprise and displeasure. The buildings had been solidly constructed of the best materials his father could locate. Sandy had cleared the accumulation of dung which had spilled out and prevented doors from shutting; windows, carts and gates had all been repaired. The whole place was neat and tidy. Daniel felt a glow of satisfaction.

Even Mattie's flight was temporarily forgotten as he watched his brother with sardonic amusement. He was peering over the half-door of the stable now, into the barn and the byre. His companion seemed uneasy. Aah, so it is Reginald, Gordon's eldest son, Daniel thought speculatively. But the Earl was within a few feet of the dairy now. Daniel could see his frown as he viewed the trail of milk spilling through the open door. Mistress MacFarlane's cow must be milking just as well as Robert Mackenzie forecast, he thought with unholy glee.

'Good morning to you, brother!' He could not resist the familiar greeting and was amply rewarded by his visitors' startled jump. Incredulity, suspicion and anger chased each other over the Earl of Strathtod's grim countenance, while Reginald strove in vain to hide his embarrassment. 'If you have called to inquire after my health,' Daniel drawled with an acid sweetness few could match, 'you will be pleased to learn that I am in excellent spirits - and improving daily!'

For a moment or two Daniel thought his half-brother might die of apoplexy; unfortunately he managed to regain a small measure of control.

'The devil take you, Munro!' he spat furiously. 'I came to inspect Strathtod land - land which you neglect shamefully, buildings which you allow to rot'

'But Sir,' Reggie protested mildly, 'things are...'

'Quiet!' his father thundered. Reggie glanced unhappily at Daniel. He wished passionately that his father could forget Fairlyden. The estate was big enough without it. He did not know his father had resented Daniel Munro since the day he had heard of his birth while eavesdropping on servants' gossip. To see him in his grave was becoming an obsession. Daniel read his thoughts with disconcerting accuracy.

'You'll have to wait a little longer before you can gloat at the pauper's funeral, and sweep the dust of our father's indiscretion into the past, dear brother!'

'You are a pauper, depending on that hypocrite of a minister for his crumbs! Letting some gypsy woman attend your every need!' the Earl sneered furiously.

Inwardly Daniel was seething, but he maintained his composure and the old, confident smile which had never failed to enrage his half-brother. When Lord Fairly saw that his taunts would not rouse Daniel's temper, he resorted to threats.

'If your henchman sets one foot on Strathtod, I shall have him hung for a thief! As to the woman...' he spluttered with impotent fury before he thought of some dire punishment, 'I shall have her beaten and thrown in prison as the whore that she is!' The Earl turned on his heel and strode back to his horse. Reggie threw Daniel a shamefaced glance and followed unhappily.

As Daniel watched his unwelcome visitors depart his face was dark with anger. He thought of Mattie's flight - her terror. Had his brother threatened her already? He had plenty of time to wonder for Mattie did not return - not even when the sun was high over-head and he had struggled indoors to his seat by the dying fire. His thoughts turned to Reggie. Daniel was sure his nephew would never be a party to the persecution of an innocent girl.

As a child Reggie had frequently accompanied his grandfather on his rides to Fairlyden - until Gordon found out. He had been a pleasant boy. Now he looked hollow-cheeked and his skin had an unhealthy pallor -yet Reggie still resembled Daniel more closely than his own father; they had both inherited the dark eyes and hair of Jonathan Fairly. Daniel had never seen William, the child born to Gordon's second wife a year before her death. He would be nine or ten years old now, Daniel mused. Doctor Murray had said he was also the image of his grandfather. Only Gordon's two middle sons had inherited his colourless grey eyes and sparse sandy hair; unfortunately they had also inherited Gordon's spiteful jealousy, and in addition James Fairly had displayed the greed and gambling habits of his maternal grandfather at an early age, according to Doctor Murray.

His father's old friend had defied Lord Gordon Fairly's threats and called at Fairlyden regularly. Since his death Daniel had heard little news of Strathtod. His replacement, a young fellow by the name of Baird, was a surly creature. In Daniel's opinion he had little ability either as a physician or as a horseman, yet strangely he had also called at Fairlyden. The last visit had been a few days after Sandy and Mattie arrived.

'I can afford neither your time nor your medicine!' Daniel had informed him bluntly. He had been amazed when Doctor Baird shrugged aside all mention of payment.

'I'll leave ye a good supply of laudanum. Ye'll need plenty to relieve the pain. It is sure to get worse.' He had left far more than Doctor Murray would have deemed wise, even for a man of Daniel's character. In truth, when the pain had been at its worst during the long dark days of winter, Daniel had been sorely tempted to seek total oblivion with the opiate. Only his strong will and the memory of his mother, kneeling in prayer, had stayed his hand. Yet he had been grateful for the relief which the laudanum brought, despite the deplorable stupor it induced and the almost insatiable craving for more.

Thanks to Mattie's herbal preparations he had reduced the laudanum dosage considerably recently, but he had stored away the liberal supply which Doctor Baird had insisted on leaving on his second visit, for there were still nights when the pain almost defeated him.

Daniel fretted helplessly when Mattie still hadn't returned by the time the fire had turned to ashes and the sun was sinking in a glory of crimson and gold over the western horizon. As the minutes dragged into hours he fumed at the painfully twisted limbs which had once been so strong and straight. Where was Sandy? Why didn't he return to search for her? Why was he so late?

At the mill Edward Slater had deliberately neglected the order of a load of meal for Mains of Muir, the largest farm in the parish.

'For goodness' sake, man,' Nicky Jamieson exclaimed in exasperation, 'this is the second time this week that ye've forgotten. Ye ken how angry Mr Sharpe gets if I'm late.'

'Ye can gang wi'oot the meal then!' Edward Slater shrugged insolently.

'An' lose ma job! Look, Slater, I ken fine ye dinna like me, or any ither body whae does a decent job o' work, but Mr Sharpe has already threatened tae tak his trade tae the new mill in Annan if he disna get a better deal than ye've bin giving him.'

'Why should I care if ye dinna come back! It wad be less work for me!' Slater jeered.

'Mr Miller disna deserve tae lose his business through your idleness, an' him treating ye like a son!'

'Load the sacks yersel' if ye want 'em! I've din enough.'

Sandy had driven Flick into the mill yard in time to hear this exchange. He had had a particularly busy day and he was tired and hungry. He saw Edward Slater's sly smirk as he turned his back on Nicky Jamieson. In a flash he had jumped from the shafts of the cart where he had ridden the last mile home. He strode towards Edward Slater and grabbed him by the shoulders. He wanted to shake the sneering fellow until his teeth chattered in his fat face. Instead he gritted his own teeth.

'Ye ken Joseph Miller ordered ye tae get that meal ready first thing this morning! Ye ken the Mains is his most valuable customer! Now get up to the top floor and lower the sacks. I'll help Nicky load them myself.' Edward Slater glowered furiously and for a moment Sandy thought he might refuse, but then he scowled and turned back into the mill.

It was their mutual dislike and distrust of Slater which had first formed a bond between Sandy and Nicky Jamieson. Now Nicky turned to his friend with a grin; gratitude replaced the consternation which had clouded his honest blue eyes.

'Thanks, Sandy, but Ye'll be late tae.' The grim set of Sandy's mouth relaxed a little.

'Aye, mebbe that was his intention.'

'I reckon he's a mite jealous o' ye. I've seen the way he watches ye, whenever Miss Jeannie comes near the mill!'

'Och, he has nae reason tae be jealous o' me! How's your own wee lassies, and what about Betty? Is she better?'

Nicky flushed and grinned sheepishly. 'We-ell, I was hoping I micht get a chance tae tell ye. It's another bairn, ye see,' he confided shyly. 'Betty's fine again noo. It'll be due in the autumn; we're baith hoping it'll be a laddie this time.'

'Och man, Nicky, that's grand news!' Sandy clapped him on the shoulder before he grasped the bag which Edward Slater had lowered clumsily on to the edge of the cart.

'As a matter o' fact ' Nicky said diffidently ' Betty an' me, well, we were wonderin' if ye wad come tae visit an' bring your Miss Cameron? But it wad hae tae be a Sunday afternoon. It's the only time Betty is free frae Mistress Sharpe's beady eyes. I'm sorry we canna offer ye a real meal.' His face reddened in embarrassment. 'Mistress Sharpe's gae mean wi' a' the maids. Betty is saving every farthing we hae tae pay the midwife, an' she's praying she'll no' need anything mair.'

'I wad be delighted tae meet your family, Nicky! An' I ken fine Mattie wad love tae see the bairnies. We wadna need anything else.'

'Och, Betty'll make a wee cup o' tea, and one o' her bannocks. Ye'll ask Miss Cameron then?'

Sandy nodded. He already knew that Betty had lived all her life at the Mains. She had taken over from her mother as head dairy maid, and had charge of thirty cows and the women who helped with the milking and butter making. Most of them were wives of other workers and lived in the Mains cottages, or helped in the house if they were single maids. Betty's parents and grandparents had been at Mains of Muir long before Abraham Sharpe married the daughter of a Lancashire mill owner who had bought the farm lock, stock and barrel.

They were just finishing loading the last sack when Edward Slater came clattering down the stairs at great speed. Seconds later Jeannie Miller appeared at the mill door.

'He must hae seen her coming frae up there!' Nicky whispered to Sandy with a knowing grin.

'Mother says will ye join us for a bite o' supper, Sandy?' She smiled coquettishly.

'He's moaning enough aboot being late already,' Slater informed her maliciously before Sandy could answer. 'His little Miss Cameron will be waitin' for him.'

'Oh, ye must come in, Sandy. Mother has made a mutton pie wi' carrots and onions, and there's potatoes and gravy, just as ye like it a'!' Nicky Jamieson rolled his eyes heavenward, his mouth watering as much as Sandy's.

'How can ye resist?' he teased, and Sandy knew he was not referring only to the food. Jeannie Miller was a very pretty young woman with her golden curls and blue eyes, her pretty blue dress in the latest fashion and crisp white apron.

'I hae made a special custard for ye, Sandy,' she wheedled now.

He could feel his stomach churning hungrily and Joseph Miller had proved himself more than generous with his hospitality, if not with his money. He enjoyed his meals at the mill and felt it must surely help Mattie's meagre larder to have one less mouth to feed. This was the second evening this week that Mistress Miller had sent Jeannie out to invite him to join them. He suspected Joseph Miller enjoyed the chat after the meal too.

Sandy did not realise that it was his hesitation, and his resistance to her pretty beguiling ways which proved such a fatal attraction to Jeannie Miller. She had had almost everything her heart desired since the day she was born. Sandy's quiet charm, his tolerant smile and polite manners, intrigued her. Slater glowered at them both. Sandy knew he did not welcome his presence at the miller's table; an imp of devilment made him accept.

'How can I resist the offer of such a meal? Thank you, Miss Jeannette.' He ignored Slater's sullen scowl as he bid Nicky cheerio and accompanied Jeannie into the mill house.

Even when the meal was over, Jeannie would have had him dally longer but Sandy knew he was already much later than usual. He hurried away without a backward glance, up the track to Fairlyden and Mattie.

As soon as he entered the kitchen Sandy realised something was wrong. Daniel's face was almost as grey as the cold ash in the fireplace.

'Why are you so late? Where have you been?' he demanded harshly. 'Dallying with the pretty miss at the mill while Mattie may be lying injured! Or even dead for all we know!'

'Dead? Mattie?' Sandy's face paled. 'Where is she? What happened? In God's name, man, tell me!' Rapidly Daniel recounted the morning's events and Mattie's uncharacteristic panic.

'Which way did she go?' Sandy interrupted abruptly, sensing Daniel's anger hid an anxiety almost as great as his own.

He followed the burn up to the higher fields in the direction Daniel had indicated, knowing that darkness would soon hamper his search, especially when Mattie could not hear his calls. As his eyes scanned the fields, the hedges, and the banks of the burn without success, he was filled with remorse for the time he had wasted when Mattie needed him, and tormented by pictures of her lying injured in some gully.

Buff heard Sandy's whistle long before he reached the copse on Fairlyden's northern boundary. The faithful little dog would not leave Mattie's side, but she guided Sandy with eager barks, welcoming him ecstatically into the thorny thicket where Mattie had spent the long day.

She was only vaguely aware of Sandy holding her tenderly in his arms, stroking the wild tendrils of hair from her pale face as she choked back her sobs of relief, but Sandy was increasingly conscious of the warmth and softness of her body pressed against his own. Only her profound distress kept him from telling her how deeply he loved her; it took a supreme effort to control his mounting desire but at last he held her away from him.

'The riders were the Earl of Strathtod and his son,' he explained.

Mattie stared in disbelief. Haltingly she told him of her nightmares, of her secret dread that Reevil would find her and force her to return to Glen Caoranne with him. Even with Sandy at her side, shepherding her through the peaceful dusk of the May evening, Mattie could not control her shivering. The long day crouched in the bushes, the fear that Reevil would take her unawares, had proved an intolerable strain. Her eyes swamped her pale face like pools of darkness and Sandy reluctantly acknowledged that she was far too drained and exhausted to discuss the idea tugging at the edges of his mind - a plan which must surely banish her fears, if only he could get enough work to support a wife and a cottage where she could make a home for them. If only...

'Why did the mere sight of my brother and his son fill Mattie with such fear?' Daniel demanded as soon as Mattie had sipped one of her own calming potions and retired to bed. ' Her eyes were wild with terror. Why, Sandy?'

He listened intently as Sandy related some of the events which had driven them from Nethertannoch.

'Jacob Reevil was in her mind and I suppose it was easy to jump to conclusions when she glimpsed two similar horsemen. Yet I had no idea she was haunted by such dreams! She seemed so serene.'

'Yes. It is difficult to remember Mattie is still so young, so innocent.' Daniel was silent for several minutes, then suddenly his questions became more searching.

Reluctantly Sandy described their last day at Nethertannoch in more detail. Daniel's dark eyes grew sombre. 'Is it possible that Mattie is haunted by another fear - a fear which triggers off her nightmares?' Sandy stared at him in bewilderment.

'Could she be carrying the child of this man Reevil?' Daniel demanded more sharply.

Sandy's face lost colour. It was a question he had asked himself many times in those first days when they travelled together. Later he had put it out of his mind when Mattie had appeared content at Fairlyden.

'I - I dinna ken! I couldna ask.'

'No-o.' Daniel stared pensively into the glowing embers of the fire. Sandy had no premonition of the plans crystallising in his mind - plans which had been only flights of fantasy, until now.

Supposing Mattie did have a reason for wanting to stay at Fairlyden? She must know he would never harm her; indeed, Mattie Cameron could almost have been his own daughter - in looks and in age. Yet if his plan was successful she would have protection from the man she feared, and she would have the security of a permanent home. Even the Earl of Strathtod could not put her out of Fairlyden - if she became Mistress Munro!

When Daniel looked up into Sandy Logan's open, honest face, and knew the heartache his plans must bring to a man who had come out of the night and proved himself a friend, even the Munro determination almost wavered. Then his lips firmed. If Sandy Logan truly loved Mattie, he would wait for her. One day Fairlyden would support them all, with Sandy's help; one day he and Mattie would reap their reward.

An inborn sense of honour compelled him to warn Sandy of the proposal he intended to put before Mattie in the morning, but first he asked him to draw forward the writing desk. It was imperative that Mattie should not misunderstand his proposal. He intended to spend the night hours forcing his aching fingers to write. He would grant her - and Sandy -exactly one week's grace. When she attained her sixteenth birthday, he would demand an answer.

'Tomorrow I shall ask Mattie to be my wife,' he announced abruptly when the desk was in position. Sandy stared at him incredulously. He began to laugh, but the laughter died in his throat as he looked into Daniel Munro's dark eyes.

'Ye canna mean it!' he croaked hoarsely.

'I have never been more serious.'

'But you're old enough to be her father! And you - you are...'

'A cripple.' Daniel inclined his head.

'I didna say that.'

'You thought it, and it is true.' Suddenly Daniel dropped the irony, and the defiance. 'Listen to me, Alexander Logan, I am telling you this because I believe you care deeply for Mattie.'

'You know I do.'

'Then listen. This would be no ordinary marriage.' Daniel looked down at his own twisted limbs with revulsion. ' Mattie is already a pretty girl - one day she will be a beautiful woman, in mind as well as in body.' He sighed. 'I shall offer her my name; nothing more. As my wife, no one can force her to leave Fairlyden - neither the Earl of Strathtod nor any other villain from Glen Caoranne. As a Munro she would have the right to live at Fairlyden, and to farm it free of rent for the rest of her life. I shall use what little money I have left to buy another cow. Mattie makes excellent butter, she is skilled in the garden - indeed, she is extraordinarily efficient and thrifty for one so young - but even she could not use all the Fairlyden acres without help. She will need those who consider themselves true friends.' His eyes searched Sandy's face. It had lost its usual ruddy glow as he stared unseeingly at the leaping flames, his jaw set.

'It will be Mattie's choice,' he muttered almost inaudibly.

'It must be,' Daniel agreed. 'I have learned that she has a mind of her own. You must consider well before you try to influence her, Sandy. Can you give her the security of a house such as this? Freedom? A home of her own, for the rest of her life? Or would you offer her a damp hovel, dependent on the whim of an employer? Can you give her land to keep even one cow? Or hens or a pig? Think well, then consider what is best for Mattie. If she bears a child then it will have my name also - another generation of Munros to farm Fairlyden.' He tapped the sheet of paper he had placed upon the desk. 'I shall make that absolutely clear.'

Sandy shuddered, but he made no reply. Could he take a child of Reevil's and care for it as his own? Could he give it the name Logan - willingly and with-out resentment? He lifted his head and looked around the firelit kitchen. His eye fell on the blue bowl on top of the polished mahogany chest. Mattie had brought it from Nethertannoch. He heard her father's words again, whispering his final plea: 'Ye'll aye dae what's best for ma bairn, Sandy.'

Eight

The day had started badly at the manse. Robert Mackenzie had slept little. Yesterday news of the trouble in India had reached even the local news sheets. He had never forgotten Elizabeth Fairly, the sweetheart of his youth, and all his instincts had warned him that she was in danger long before he read the announcement of her death in the paper. Her snobbish brother had made sure she was beyond reach as soon as he inherited the title. Despite her pleas he had married her off to a Major in the army and dispatched her to India without a second thought. His old anger against Lord Gordon Fairly resurfaced a thousandfold, despite his urgent prayers to the Almighty to cleanse his heart and soul of bitter and destructive thoughts.

As if Robert's own anguish was not enough to bear, Daniel had sent a message requesting him to visit Fairlyden to discuss a 'serious and urgent matter'. Daniel had loved his half-sister dearly and frequently assisted in their secret meetings. It was one of the reasons for the enduring friendship between himself and Robert, despite the differences in their ages, character and calling. Knowing nothing of Daniel's new plans for Mattie's future, Robert Mackenzie mistakenly assumed he was anxious for news of Elizabeth, and for the first time he was reluctant to visit Fairlyden. Elizabeth was dead; he could offer no comfort and had no heart for a discussion which would reopen old wounds.

Before he had reached any decision, or even begun to plan his day's work, another far more urgent summons banished Daniel, and even Elizabeth, from his mind. His presence was required at one of the farm cottages at Mains of Muir. A young man - a fine husband, a loving father -was even now facing his Maker. Two small girls called for their father; a young wife mourned. Nicky Jamieson was dead.

Nicky had displayed the courage which only true heroes possess. He had tried to stop a runaway horse and waggon and saved a boy's life at the expense of his own. The boy lay in pain, fighting against death's clutches, one leg broken, the other shattered. His widowed mother could not bring herself to tell him he would never again walk the fields and lanes he had loved. Sometimes Robert Mackenzie despaired of carrying out the work the Lord had set him to do.

Sandy was stunned by the news which awaited him that morning when he arrived at the mill. He could not believe that Nicky was dead! Nicky, who had been so full of life and hope - and love. His unborn child would never know a father's loving care. Would it even have a home?

The Jamiesons lived in a cottage at Mains of Muir. Betty had lived there all her life but she would have no man to labour for her now. Would she be forced to move out of her home to make way for another worker? Where would she go? How would she live?

In the face of so much grief and uncertainty Sandy's own problems seemed almost trivial, yet even then he knew he had no right to ask Mattie to be his wife, to deprive her of a secure home for the rest of her life. True, Daniel Munro had neither health nor wealth to support her, but he could give her land to earn her own living, and she was not afraid to toil.

Abraham Sharpe had sent an urgent message to the mill, asking for meal to be delivered to feed his cattle. Mains of Muir was four miles from the mill, in the opposite direction to Fairlyden.

'Could ye take it, Sandy?' Joseph Miller asked anxiously. 'I couldna trust Edward wi' your gelding anyway. But he can make the short deliveries to the village and get the rest o' the meal bagged ready for

Burnside and East Moss farms. The sacks'll be ready to load when ye return.'

Sandy nodded. Edward said nothing. He was too sly to argue, and he knew the miller would be too busy keeping the kiln going and grinding the corn which Sandy had brought in the day before to notice him.

Slater was nowhere to be seen when Sandy returned to the mill, and the same thing happened the third time and the fourth. Sandy had to unload the cart full of the corn he had just brought in before he could reload. He knew if he did not deliver the meal to Burnbank farm that evening, then Joseph would have to set out at dawn tomorrow. Slater was lounging on a bag of meal in the shadows of the mill when Sandy finally finished work that evening. Joseph Miller had gone to feed his pigs.

'Ye're a lazy, good for nothing fellow!' Sandy told Slater contemptuously. 'Ye ken fine the extra deliveries had tae be made tae the Mains if the mill is tae keep Abraham Sharpe's trade!'

'It isna my fault Jamieson wanted tae be a hero,' Slater shrugged carelessly.

'I do believe ye dinna care that a fine man has died so horribly! I don't suppose you care about the laddie either - lying there in pain when he should be full o' the joys o' youth!'

'Naw, I dinna care. Naebody ever cared about the joys o' my youth.'

'Why, you...' Sandy broke off abruptly as Jeannie Miller came round the corner.

'Supper's ready, Sandy,' she said softly. 'Mother says ye've had a bad day. Ye must eat afore ye walk back tae Fairlyden.'

Sandy bit his lip hard. He longed to be alone - to contemplate the terrible events. He knew Mistress Miller and Jeannie made a special effort to cook his favourite meals on the days he worked at the mill. Tonight he had no appetite even for Mistress Miller's excellent cooking. He would have preferred to return to the peace of Fairlyden and share the pot of broth he knew Mattie would have waiting for him, but Jeannie's smiling face and gentle urging towards the house was impossible to refuse without causing offence.

He would have had to be both blind and deaf to be unaware of Jeannie's bright eyes, her eagerness to fetch and carry anything she thought might please him. Edward Slater's jealousy and spite were equally obvious. Mistress Miller's kindly manner towards Sandy only aggravated him more.

Joseph Miller always liked to discuss the news of the countryside over a pipe of tobacco at the end of the day. Inevitably on this particular evening his mood was sombre, his thoughts returning again and again to Nicky Jamieson's death.

'Abraham Sharpe pays the best wages o' any man in these pairts,' Joseph Miller declared, 'but yon wife o' his is the hardest woman i' the parish!' He shook his head sadly. 'Puir Betty. She's aye bin a gran' worker - jist like her mither before her. She makes a fine bit o' butter and 'tis hersel' teaches the new maids tae milk and churn.' He sighed several times and stared moodily at the fire. 'Aye, aye, but I doot Mistress Sharpe willna be lettin' her bide in her wee hoose.'

'Och, Joseph! Even Mistress Sharpe wouldna turn Betty out!' Mistress Miller sounded shocked, yet such things happened regularly.

'Weel, Abraham Sharpe will need anither man, and he'll hae a hard job tae be findin' a horseman as guid as Nicky, puir laddie.' So the discussion went on.

As the hours passed and darkness fell Mattie had ceased to stare down the track for a glimpse of Sandy's returning figure. She had pulled the broth off the fire, but she had covered the newly baked bread and the yellow pat of butter with a snowy cloth - still hoping. She had waited restlessly. She felt a desperate need to talk to Sandy - to tell him of Mr Munro's astonishing proposal. She needed his reassurance; she wanted him to say, 'Mattie Cameron, you must marry me!' Yet as the minutes ticked into hours her heart grew heavy; her mind filled with doubts. Night after night he lingered at the mill house - and this night, when she needed him so badly, he lingered longer than usual. She could only suppose he preferred to dally in the company of the miller's pretty daughter.

Daniel Munro also felt a gnawing anxiety when Sandy had not returned by nine o'clock. His own conscience troubled him for he had seen the stricken look in Sandy's eyes. This morning he had seen the shadows and known that the young man had passed a sleepless night.

At last Sandy walked back to Fairlyden in the shy light of the young moon, but he was oblivious to the beauty of the night sky; even the wafting scent of the bluebells beneath the trees failed to stir his senses.

He moved slowly, almost too weary to walk; his heart was heavy with sorrow for the new friend he had lost, and for Nicky's young widow and her two small daughters.

When he reached Fairlyden the broth was cold; the bread was dry. The intricate pattern on the butter, so lovingly executed, had blurred with the warmth of the fire. In her own weariness and dejection Mattie was scarcely aware of Sandy's drawn face and shadowed eyes. News of Nicky Jamieson's tragic death had not yet penetrated the isolation of Fairlyden.

'Will you take the broth?' she asked, already pushing the pot over the fire. Sandy shook his head.

'You ate at the mill?' He nodded.

'Did you have meat?' Mattie asked wistfully, knowing her limited larder could not compete with that of the mill house.

Sandy summoned a smile and gripped her shoulders, intending to reassure her.

'Mistress Miller made my favourite stew, with meat and vegetables. Jeannie made a special apple dumpling. I am well fed. Do not worry about me.' Mattie twisted away from him abruptly.

'Then I need not have waited to attend to you. I will go to bed now.'

'Mattie.'

Naturally she did not hear him, but neither did she look back to bid him good-night with her usual warm, sweet smile.

'Leave her be. She was worried when you did not return,' Daniel said a trifle shortly.

Sandy nodded and sank on to a chair, wondering if he would make it to the large room above the kitchen where he had chosen to sleep, as far as possible from Mattie - from temptation. The stairs led directly from the kitchen because it had been the maids' quarters in the days when Sarah Munro lived at Fairlyden under the protection of her lord. Sandy looked at the wooden stairs as though at a mountain side. He closed his eyes. Slowly he began to tell Daniel of the accident at Mains of Muir.

As Mattie ladled the porridge for his breakfast the following morning Sandy noticed her pallor and the dark shadows around her eyes. She ate nothing herself. Daniel Munro's suggestion that she might be carrying Reevil's child haunted him afresh, yet he could not bring himself to question her. Neither would he add to her distress by telling her of the troubles of the Jamieson family. Indeed the desperate plight of Nicky's widow and children now prevented him from telling Mattie what was in his heart.

It was not until the day after Nicky Jamieson's funeral that the Reverend Mackenzie set out for Fairlyden. He welcomed the dewy freshness of the May morning as it revived his jaded spirits. Mattie was already churning the cream in the dairy when he arrived. Buff lay outside the door, guarding her mistress as usual. The little dog gave him a sniff of approval then allowed him to put his head round the door to exchange a smile.

He went on into the house. He was surprised to see Sandy still there. Tension hung in the air like a pall. He soon understood the reason.

'I have asked Mattie to marry me,' Daniel declared defiantly.

Although Sandy still felt compelled to remain silent about his feelings for Mattie, because he had nothing to offer her, he had secretly believed she would refuse to marry anyone else. At the very least he had expected her to discuss her plans with him. She had done neither. She had promised to give Daniel her answer the day after the Sabbath. Sandy was hurt and dismayed, and he blamed Daniel Munro.

'I did not ask Mattie to keep silent!' Daniel insisted vehemently. 'I hope you will remain our friend, whatever her decision.'

'Friend! You said you had no need of friends!' Sandy reminded him bitterly.

Daniel nodded. 'The need for friends is in every man, but when he believes he has none, he denies the need of them - even to himself. I have nothing to give Mattie except my name. As Mistress Munro she cannot be forced into marriage with another; she will also inherit Fairlyden. But, yes, it is true that I do not want to die alone! You are young, Sandy Logan, and in good health. You cannot know '

Yet Sandy did know. Even Matthew Cameron, for all his steadfast faith in the Almighty, had not wanted to die alone. Sandy knew he had to keep the promise he had made to a dying man. "Ye'll aye dae what's best for ma bairn." The words had haunted him, waking or sleeping, since he heard Daniel's intentions. Daniel Munro could give Mattie more than a roof. He could give her freedom to work in her own home, in her own way; not hounded and bewildered by commands she could not hear or understand, an underpaid drudge at the bidding of a sharp-eyed mistress.

Sandy loved Mattie, but what protection could he promise her in the harsh reality of the outside world where a man could be thrown from his cottage at the whim of his master?

The Reverend Robert Mackenzie looked keenly at Daniel.

'Am I to understand that Mattie's duties as your wife will be no more than those she already undertakes - in her daily care of you and your home, my friend?' He saw the wry twist of the lips, that familiar gleam in the magnificent dark eyes.

'That is so.' The answer was swift and firm. Then, with a glance at his twisted limbs and a wry grimace, 'It could be no other way - though I wish it were so. Yet there is a condition and I charge you both to hear it. If Mattie consents to be my wife, any child she bears - even nine months after my death - must bear the name Munro!' Daniel surveyed them fiercely.

'I entrust you both to see that such a child inherits Fairlyden, according to the wishes of my father, Jonathan Fairly, the late Earl of Strathtod. Everything must be done to ensure that the name Munro is carried on - and on - and on.' A small triumphant smile briefly erased the lines on his pain-ravaged face. Silence fell in the room.

It was broken by Sandy, and his tone reflected his unease. He felt that Daniel Munro had just taken a long look into a future which only he could foresee.

'I believe you want Mattie to bear a child.' He shuddered, thinking of Jacob Reevil.

Daniel Munro's eyes looked into his - dark, penetrating, and unwavering.

'If Mattie agrees to become my wife, if she stays with me to the end, that alone will make me a happier man than I had believed possible. Yet I say again, any child born to my wife must bear my name. You will remember?'

How could he forget? Sandy wondered, with those black eyes boring into his mind.

'And you, Robert, you will baptise the child? Daniel Jonathan Munro?'

'Ah, Daniel.'

'Your promise please?' he demanded peremptorily.

'The child, if there is a child, may be a girl.'

'Then you must baptise my daughter - Sarah. Yes, Sarah Munro.' He stared into the fire for a long time and neither of his companions could bring themselves to disturb his reverie. Suddenly he looked up and smiled, directly, charmingly, at Sandy. In that moment Sandy's heart was filled with compassion for the crippled man before him, and a deep, deep sadness for himself. Only his own selfish desires could prompt him to influence Mattie now. She must reach her decision alone - and whatever she decided, he must accept, graciously, without jealousy. He must keep his promise to Matthew Cameron, whatever the cost to himself.

Sandy was surprised when Mattie announced her intention of attending the Reverend Mackenzie's church the following morning. She had not ventured beyond Fairlyden's southern boundary since they arrived. The Reverend Mackenzie was an exceptionally clear speaker and he and Mattie had achieved considerable success at communicating with each other; but today the minister would be speaking to his congregation from the pulpit. Mattie would understand little. She knew no one at the church. Sandy was at a loss to understand the reason for her sudden desire to attend. Nevertheless, if she was going, he must accompany her. Mattie sensed his reluctance and put her own interpretation upon it.

She had brushed her best black dress in readiness, and pinned the jet brooch which had belonged to her mother at her throat. She coiled her shining hair neatly around her head before fastening on a small black bonnet. Her boots were clean, and if her heavy shawl was a trifle shabby there was nothing to be done about it. In one of the upstairs bedrooms at Fairlyden she had found two trunks carefully packed with all manner of dresses in silks and satins and in a glorious array of colours. Daniel had told her they had belonged to his mother, and he had given her permission to make them into gowns for herself, but Mattie would not be tempted, even by the brown figured silk, until she had mourned her beloved father with proper respect.

Daniel eyed her slender white neck and the delicate structure of her high cheek bones and firm young chin. He admired the neat curve of her dark eyebrows arching above her wide, expressive eyes; eyes almost as dark as his own. He would have been proud to own Mattie Cameron as his sister, or as his daughter, but she was surely too young and too lovely ever to be his wife.

Sandy was keenly aware of Mattie's appearance, and of Daniel's approval. His face darkened; his heart was a leaden weight. Consequently his usual cheerful smile was absent, his lips were tight. Mattie sensed the rare anger in him and her spirit almost failed her, but she lifted her head high and stepped out of the door with an air of determination. She would ask the Lord Jesus to give her guidance for the future - a sign.

The day which had begun so brightly had already clouded over before they reached the confluence of the streams which marked the boundary between the parishes of Muircumwell and Strathtod. Although Mattie lifted her skirts above her leather boots they were spattered with mud by the time she had struggled across the burn, even with Sandy's help. The stepping stones were more suited to a manly stride.

It was the first time Sandy had entered the little church and in spite of the stories he had heard of the Reverend Mackenzie's popularity, he was amazed to find it already filled. There were people in ragged clothes and bare-footed urchins wherever they could find a space. Many people were seated on wooden benches. The Reverend Mackenzie saw them arrive as he was crossing the grass from the manse. The warmth of his greeting did not go unobserved. Several people watched curiously.

'Joseph Miller is looking your way,' the minister whispered, 'I believe he is making room for you to join him. His pew is over there, beneath the window.'

Sandy flushed with embarrassment. No one could mistake the welcome in Mistress Miller's smile, nor in the bright eyes of her daughter. Jeannie's cheeks were flushed a becoming pink and she did not trouble to hide her curiosity regarding Mattie, despite the time and place. She made only the smallest pretence of preparing her mind and soul for sober worship on this, the Sabbath.

The Reverend Mackenzie did indeed have a great gift for oratory. Nevertheless Sandy found his mind dwelling on Mattie's clasped hands and bowed head. He wondered what thoughts were occupying the silence of her mind, what help did she hope to find here, in the house of God, when she could not hear his word? He could not believe she needed forgiveness. If she was in trouble then the sin was not hers.

Sandy would have been surprised to know how fervently Mattie was asking forgiveness for that most unenviable sin - jealousy. She had broken the tenth Commandment after only a single glimpse of the pretty miller's daughter. Often she had wondered, and worried, when Sandy returned late from the mill. Now she knew the reason; knew, and with a sickness in her heart, understood. The miller's daughter was wearing a wide crinoline, but it was not only her dress which made her so pretty; she had golden curls and a delightful smile, and there was a merry twinkle in her blue eyes when she looked at Sandy. She could understand all his words, she could laugh with him, discuss those things which men and women delighted in. If Mattie's spirits had been low before, they were even lower now. Yet she chided herself; she should be praising the Lord for delivering her from Jacob Reevil and leading her to Fairlyden, into the care of Mr Munro. He was ill and in pain. He needed her. She clasped her hands more tightly.

Jeannie Miller was also thanking God, but the blessings she chose were frivolous indeed. She had no need to fear that Alexander's affections might be stolen after all. Miss Cameron was such a pale, quiet mouse. How drab she looked. Surely she could have contrived just a small hoop, when the crinoline was the very height of fashion, even if she was still in mourning. Of course Alexander was just being kind because she was deaf. Jeannie had overheard him telling her own father how he had made a promise to Mr Cameron when he was dying. How silly she had been to think he could ever be attracted to little Miss Cameron. So Jeannie's light mind ran on and her spirits soared.

Then the service was over. The people were trooping out. Many of the poor were reluctant to leave, eager for one more word from their beloved minister. The wealthier members of the congregation were relieved that the minister's rebukes had not been too severe on this particular morning when he had focused their prayers and thoughts on the family of Nicky Jamieson and the young boy who was now crippled for life.

The plight of Nicky Jamieson's widow was certainly exercising the minds of two members of the congregation - Abraham Sharpe, farmer of Mains of Muir, and his 'lady' wife. Mistress Sharpe was adamant that Betty Jamieson and her brats must go. Abraham was wondering how he could turn the family out of their cottage, without incurring the censure of the minister and bringing the vengeance of a wrathful God upon his head; or how he could suffer the vengeance of his wrathful wife if he refused. It would soon be the hiring fair at Annan but he did not expect to find a horseman to match Nicky, born and bred to the land. As for Betty, she could milk the cows and make butter standing on her head. Good clean butter too! Give her a week in bed to have the bairn and she'd be back to work. Her mother and grandmother had milked the cows and made the butter and cheese at Mains of Muir long before he and Florrie came. No, Abraham didn't like the idea of putting Betty Jamieson off the place.

He thought Florrie was wrong for once - but he needed another man. And as Florrie said, a man would need a cottage - the Jamiesons' cottage.

The presence of Alexander Logan and Mattie Cameron also caused some speculation. Mistress Sharpe was trying to recall some talk she had heard about the girl managing to milk Mistress McFarlane's temperamental cow. And she had sent down some of her butter - a fine flavour and no straws or hairs in it, the blacksmith's widow had declared. Mistress McFarlane didn't give praise readily, especially when it came to making butter. The girl was supposed to be deaf, but she had looked clean enough in church and her hair was neat. She wouldn't expect much in wages - not when she couldn't hear! The man beside her looked healthy and strong, too, and he had worked well enough at the mill by all accounts.

Sandy saw several people with whom he had become acquainted while making deliveries. Many of them stopped to speak but most of them looked embarrassed and turned away when they discovered Mattie could not hear. Only Mistress Miller and Mistress McFarlane had a kindly smile for her. She guessed Mistress Miller was inviting them to the mill to share the mid-day meal, but Mattie knew she could not bear to watch Sandy in the company of Miss Jeannie Miller.

'I must hurry back to prepare Mr Munro's meal,' she declared abruptly before Sandy could turn to speak to her. He frowned and Mattie supposed he was displeased at being deprived of Miss Miller's company and her fine cooking. She stared miserably in front of her on the long walk back to Fairlyden. Sandy did not touch her arm, or turn her face to his.

Nine

The following morning Mattie faced Daniel Munro, outwardly composed, though her face was pale and there were shadows beneath her eyes which told him she had slept little the previous night. He waited tensely.

In the privacy of her room Mattie had wept into her pillow for the girlish dreams which must be cast aside. She knew Mr Munro had told Sandy of his proposal of marriage. The days had passed - four, five, six of them - and Sandy had not given her any sign that her future lay with him. She had gone to the Reverend Mackenzie's church to pray for guidance, and she had received it, but it had done nothing to soothe the craving in her heart. Unlike the saints in the bible she felt no serenity of spirit for the sacrifice she was about to make. On the contrary her heart was in a turmoil whenever she thought of Sandy in the sparkling company of Miss Miller. Every instinct told her that the miller's pretty daughter loved him - and she had so much, so very much more, to give.

Now she must stick to her resolve; she must release Sandy from the promise he had made to her father; she must never be a burden to him. Even so the words of acceptance did not come easily to her lips when she stood before Mr Munro. She found herself unexpectedly delaying her fate - offering herself for the position of housekeeper at Fairlyden as Mama Logan had done for her father.

'No!' Although she could not hear the single word she knew Daniel had shouted, she could see the frustration and disappointment clouding his dark eyes. Then he was beckoning her closer, his lips forming each word with meticulous care.

'I cannot pay you.'

'You have given me a home '

'No.' Daniel shook his head. 'You must have the protection of my name. You must have security at Fairlyden, when I am gone.'

'Please, do not think of death!' Mattie shivered, knowing that death had been staring him in the face only a few weeks ago. Each day he had improved a little, with warmth and food and care.

'Will - you - be - my - wife, Mattie Cameron?'

There was no avoiding the brilliant brown stare which held her own, willing her to comply.

'Yes.'

Mattie saw the blaze of triumph, relief, even joy, which filled those dark eyes. She controlled the sickening jolt of her heart with an effort.

She must look forward now. She must accept the life which God had planned for her.

That morning Sandy set out for his second visit to Mains of Muir. His heart was sore at the memory of Nicky Jamieson, and the harshness meted out by a supposedly merciful God, but he could not help admiring the farm, spread out before him, bathed in the mellow light of Maytime sunshine. On both sides of the narrow farm track the hedges were thick, neatly laid and trimmed. Milk cows lifted their heads from grazing to watch him pass. Soon they began to amble towards the gate into the farmsteading, forming a long line in their own order of precedence. It was almost milking time. Sandy watched the cattle as he walked. He had never seen so many, thirty at least, all on one farm.

Then he saw the gap in the hedge, the ravaged bushes, wheel scars slicing into the grassy bank and dark stains ... a scrap of material hanging on a thorn. Was it Nicky's smock perhaps, or the boy's? Sandy quickly averted his head. Bile rose in his gullet.

One of the Mains men had seen the accident, and Sandy recalled his account of it the night after the funeral. The man had been on his way to the Crown and Thistle hoping to dull his memory, but the inn was only a few hundred yards from the mill and the man had stopped at the mill yard. He had needed to talk.

'It was the mistress's lapdog. It ran at the horse. He was a young'n - new broken. Boss shouldna' hae made wee Bobby tak him! The laddie is but thirteen, just started work at Christmas. The dog ran at the horse's heels, yappity yapping. The puir beast wis afeard. He took off, cart load o' muck an' a'. Young Bobby should hae let him run! He hung on like a man!' The speaker's voice choked, but he had to get the story off his chest, including his bitterness and a great deal of blaspheming. 'Nicky saw. He ran tae help. The sleeve o' Bobby's smock caught on the cairt shaft, dragged the laddie. Mercy, 'twas terrible! The laddie's smock must hae torn an' set him free. He was flung under the wheel o' his ain cairt! He screamed awfu'. Wad ye wunner! Wi his young banes mangled 'neath the iron rim o' the wheel! The noise o' him just sent the horse clean oot o'his head! Mad, he wis! Didna even see Nicky - straight intae him, he went. Trampled Nicky intae the ground, n' him as fine a horseman as ever wis kenned!' The man had broken down and sobbed like a child. Joseph Miller's eyes had glistened too, but Edward Slater had listened unmoved - and smirked at the man's tears.

When Sandy reached the steading one of the men showed him where to unload the meal, watching in critical silence while he backed the cart through the door of the barn with only an inch to spare. Even when they reloaded the cart together, carrying the twelve stone bags of corn down the wooden steps from the loft above, the man remained dour and silent until the last bag was in place. Only then did he mumble: 'Ye're tae see Mr Sharpe at the hoose afore ye gang back tae the mill.'

'Why didn't ye tell me before I loaded the cart?' Sandy demanded with irritation. Flick would now have to wait with the shafts of the heavily laden cart resting on his back. The man shrugged and walked away.

As he crossed the farmyard towards the house Sandy saw four women heading in the direction of the byre, each carrying a piggin and a three-legged milking stool. One of the women walked with bent head. Two small girls clung to the ends of her long, white apron. Sandy guessed she was Nicky Jamieson's widow, on account of her gently rounded figure. He touched his cap. He would have liked to speak to her but she was with the other women, and he was a stranger. She looked pale and troubled.

Abraham Sharpe was waiting at the house. 'Step into the kitchen, Logan, I'll come straight to the point. I've heard Ye'll be putting a straw in yer hat at the hiring?' Sandy looked at him blankly.

'Ye're wanting work as a horseman, or so I heard. Ye'll ken I'm two men short so there's a place for ye here. You'll be ready to start straight away, eh? No need to wait 'til the term.'

Sandy was flabbergasted. 'I have promised to work at the mill until the end of May.'

'Ye'll not get another offer like this. Mains o' Muir is the best farm i' the parish - and with the best wages!'

Sandy frowned. He did not care for Abraham Sharpe's assumption that he would leave Joseph Miller in the lurch. It was true the mill orders were falling now that cattle were being turned out to pasture again, and soon his work at the mill would end - but the miller still needed Flick to replace his own mare for house and shop deliveries.

'I'll pay nineteen pounds and ten shillings for a year's work and ye can take half of it at the November term, six months from now. Ye'll have oatmeal and a quart o' buttermilk.'

Still Sandy remained silent, weighing up the situation. Seven shillings and sixpence a week did not seem such a lot of money, but he would be able to visit Mattie most Sundays.

Abraham Sharpe went on, 'I've heard ye can plough a straight furrow, aye, an' set up a guid turnip drill, but I'll no hae a man that lies abed. Ye'll start at five every morning and finish working in the field by six in the afternoon and Ye'll hae a pair o' horses to mind after that. I reckon ye'd tak guid care o' Nicky Jamieson's pair. I watched ye back the cart into the barn.'

'Mr Sharpe,' Sandy broke in stiffly, 'I promised Mr Miller. I need to consider.'

'Consider! There's no time to consider! Ye needna worry about Joseph Miller. I'm his best customer! I'll fix things with him. Besides, Ye'll have a cottage wi' two rooms, not just one like some o' the farms hereabouts mind! Two rooms and guid water frae the well - no more than eight or nine hundred yards awa'. Ye'll be able tae wed yon wee lassie we saw in church.' Suddenly Sandy was alert. A cottage? If he had a cottage he could offer Mattie a home. Just for a little while he forgot about Daniel's proposal to make her mistress of Fairlyden. Even if Reevil found them, he could not take her away once they were married.

'Of course, Mistress Sharpe would be expecting her to help wi' the milking,' Abraham Sharpe went on again. Suddenly he threw back his head and bellowed: 'Florrie! Are ye there, Florrie? He's here!'

The door was pushed open immediately and Sandy knew that Mistress Sharpe had been listening on the other side. She came in, a woman at least as tall as himself. Haughty, he decided as she frowned down at her husband.

'My name is Florence. When will you remember, Sharpe?'

Sandy looked at her thin pursed lips and the scraped-back, steel grey hair beneath her white cap. Mistress Sharpe was dressed in a day gown of brown silk, its skirt so wide she had to squeeze herself into the kitchen. There were so many buttons running from her long scrawny neck, and over her flat chest, down to her waist, that Sandy thought it must take her at least an hour to dress and undress. She reminded him of a bell on a withering stalk. It was obvious she did not help with the milking, as most farmers' wives had to do. He found her steely gaze fixed upon him. The vertical lines above her beak-shaped nose deepened.

'I understand the girl is deaf. I suppose she can scrub at least - though how I shall make her understand, I really do not know!' she sniffed. Sandy felt himself tense.

'I have not agreed to take the work yet, Mistress Sharpe. I shall have to discuss this with Miss Cameron.'

'Not agreed?' Abraham Sharpe muttered. The man had too much pride. It did no good to have a working man with pride like that. But he was good with horses an' no mistake.

'Discuss!' Mistress Sharpe snorted scorn-fully. 'How can you "discuss" with a deaf chit!'

'Mattie understands most things well enough. She has managed a house and dairy without instruction since she was thirteen. How much would you pay her, Mistress Sharpe?'

'Pay? Why, she would share the cottage with you. You will be able to keep a pig. That is enough for a maid who cannot understand a word, I say.'

'A pig?' Sandy stiffened. Nicky had said he lived in the end cottage in a row of four. His was the only one with a pig-sty. He had been proud of that. 'The Jamiesons' cottage?'

'Yes.'

'You would turn Nicky's widow, and mother, and children out of their home?'

'What else can we do?' Abraham Sharpe whined. 'Ye'll be needing the house if you wed your lassie.'

'Mattie wouldna want a house at such a price!'

'Oh, very well, she will receive three shillings a week,' Mistress Sharpe snapped, completely misunderstanding. 'She must be in the byre by four each morning or I shall make a deduction.'

Sandy groaned with anger and frustration. He could never ask Mattie to work here, for such a woman. Neither could he be responsible for turning Nicky's widow and children, and his ailing mother, into the road. But some other man would come.

'I would not ask Mattie to work in your dairy, Mistress Sharpe.' His mouth was tight. He turned to her husband. 'If you consider a single ploughman, I will ask Joseph Miller if he will hire my gelding and release me from my bond - but there is one condition.'

'Condition! I make the conditions at Mains of Muir!' Abraham Sharpe interrupted angrily. Sandy grimaced, his eyes travelling from Sharpe to his mean-mouthed wife. He nodded and turned to the door.

'Conditions! Discuss this, discuss that!' Mistress Sharpe screeched. 'My father always said no good would come of teaching labourers to read and write. None of the men in his factory in Bolton learned such things. They had to work to survive.'

Sandy paused, his hand on the door. He had heard rumours that Mistress Sharpe's father had paid her husband a handsome sum to relieve him of his daughter. He had thought it just spiteful gossip. Now he thought it could be true.

'Good day to you,' he said quietly.

'Just a minute,' Abraham Sharpe called urgently and followed him outside. He needed a man who could think for himself, whatever Florrie believed.

'What was this "condition" then?' he asked curiously. Sandy looked him in the eye.

'I would work for you, but only if you let Nicky Jamieson's family bide in their home. His widow needs the cottage and the work - and to be with the friends she has known all her life.'

Abraham chewed his lip thoughtfully. He liked Betty Jamieson. She was a good clean dairy worker. But there were turnips to hoe and sheds to be mucked. Soon it would be haytime, then the corn to harvest. He needed a reliable man, a man who could turn his hand to the scythe or the plough, a horse or a cow. He pulled thoughtfully on his earlobe. Abraham did not share his wife's views on education. Nearly every Scottish bairn learned to read and write and add up figures. Why, the lad Telford had been born but a few miles away, up there in the hills, in a humble shepherd's cottage, and he had built great canals and bridges everywhere. Aye, Mains of Muir was a big farm now, and it needed men who could think. Maybe Logan was a bit too proud, but there were rumours that he had a fine mare of his own, and ideas about breeding horses, as well as working them. There was a place for him, here at the Mains.

'I'll "discuss" the matter o' Betty Jamieson,' he announced at last, with an ironic grin. 'I'll come to the mill tomorrow - when I've considered.' Sandy saw the gleam in his eyes and an answering smile spread slowly over his tanned face. Maybe Mistress Sharpe didn't always get her own way after all.

During the evening meal at the mill Sandy told Joseph Miller all that had transpired at the Mains. The miller was genuinely sorry he could not employ Sandy permanently at the mill, but an opportunity to work at Mains of Muir was too good to be missed, despite Mistress Sharpe. He agreed to release Sandy and hire Flick, the gelding, for a few more weeks in return for oatmeal and flour for Fairlyden. The news set Jeannie in a flutter. Sandy had not seized the chance of taking the Mains cottage and marrying Miss Mattie Cameron, so clearly he felt no more than a sense of duty towards the deaf girl.

'You will come to visit us, Sandy, when you go to work for Mr Sharpe?' Jeannie dimpled prettily, ignoring Edward Slater's sullen glare.

'Yes, you are always welcome at the mill, Sandy,' her mother agreed with a warmth which dispelled a little of the gloom which had hovered over Sandy since Daniel Munro had proposed making Mattie Mistress Munro of Fairlyden.

Sandy was reluctant to agree to all the conditions which Abraham Sharpe sought to impose - not least that of committing himself for a whole year. However the Mains was only eight miles from Fairlyden and he knew he could end up in a far more inaccessible place if he took his chance at the hiring fairs. He guessed it was Mistress Sharpe who had insisted on his helping with the Sunday morning milkings if Betty Jamieson was to be retained as head dairy maid.

One thing brought him a measure of consolation. Abraham Sharpe had recently acquired a stallion and he offered to serve Sandy's mare on condition that he was given the first opportunity to buy Dark Lucy's foal when Sandy sold it - as sell it he must. Sandy knew it was the only way Darkie could have another foal until he could afford to pay the fees for a stallion of his own choice. The Mains stallion, Loudon Jock, lacked the quality and type of the Wigtownshire Vic-tor stallion. His eyes were small, his head too narrow and his bones finer than Sandy would have chosen. Abraham Sharpe was shrewd; he had heard of Dark Lucy's merits. If she produced a foal of good type, much of the credit would be given to the stallion; the reputation of Mains of Muir as a stud would become established and other mares would be brought. Unknown to his wife, Abraham Sharpe also offered to waive the service fees if Sandy worked for the agreed year.

Nicky Jamieson's widow, Betty, had learned of Sandy's part in persuading Mr Sharpe to allow her to stay at Mains of Muir and she sought him out on his second evening at the Mains. She persuaded him to accompany her to her cottage so that Nicky's mother could express her own heartfelt gratitude. After his visit Sandy had no doubt that Abraham Sharpe had been wise to keep Betty in charge of his dairy. Everything about her person, her home, and her two small daughters was clean and neat, despite their desperate plight.

Betty had unwittingly rescued him from a black depression, the likes of which he had never before experienced, even when he and Mattie had fled from Nethertannoch. He had discovered the less pleasant aspects of sharing a bothy, or at least the Mains bothy. He had slept little during his first night. He was expected to share not only the dank and cheerless building but also the bed, and with none other than the dour and stolid Alf Wood, the man who had directed him to the barn on his second visit to Mains of Muir. The mattress of the rickety iron bed was a mixture of horsehair and straw and it exuded a strong smell of ammonia. Sandy had been in bed for perhaps two hours, dozing uneasily, when he became aware of a strange warmth creeping up his skin. It was not only warm, it was wet! Alf had urinated up his back! Sandy uttered an oath and sprang out of bed, pulling off the thick flannel shirt which he also wore during the day, and almost simultaneously yanking on his breeches. It was a dark night, and chilly even for the end of May, but he hurried out to the yard pump, clutching his own piece of hessian towel. He sluiced himself in the icy water and rubbed himself dry, then he washed his shirt and hung it over the pump to dry. He did not return to bed. He spent the rest of the night on a heap of straw in the stable, emerging before five o'clock brought the arrival of the other workers to feed and groom their horses. He found himself the butt of some ribald jokes. Apparently they were all aware of Alf's habit, especially with new workers. Later they informed him that Mistress Sharpe had ordered the maid to remove the second bed, supposedly to economise on the blankets.

It was Betty Jamieson who told him that others had suffered the same fate. Those who could not thole Alf's filthy habit used a pile of hay for a mattress. She warned him that the maid would probably complain to Mistress Sharpe, who in turn would complain to the master. Sandy found the idea of a bed of sweet-smelling hay infinitely more appealing than the stinking mattress, wet or dry, especially when shared with Alf's lumpish, sweating body.

The young maid, who was new and no more than twelve or thirteen, had no thought of complaining to the mistress. Her only aim in life was to struggle through her day's unending tasks and avoid the she-dragon of the Mains, if at all possible. Nevertheless Mistress Sharpe discovered the hay-strewn floor, and realising she would get no satisfaction from complaining to Sharpe himself about his new protégé, she attacked Sandy directly.

'Mistress Sharpe!' The precise pronunciation Sandy had learned for Mattie's benefit allowed no possibility of her misunderstanding him. 'Since you begrudge me a clean, dry bed ' He watched the sharp jaw rise and thrust forward. He could see the pulse beating furiously in the hollows of her scrawny neck. Her frosty gaze narrowed. 'I shall continue to sleep on hay, in the bothy.'

'Not in my bothy!'

Sandy's blue eyes held her grey ones. 'You are throwing me out? Then I trust you will inform your husband that our agreement is broken, Ma'am!' The frost turned to grey ice. Her thin lips became a colourless line across her angular features.

`I shall tell Mr Sharpe no such thing! You will remove that hay at once!'

'Not unless you provide another mattress,' Sandy declared quietly. Had Mistress Sharpe been a reasonable woman, a person he could respect, the conversation might have ended there, but she was not, and never would be. Sandy felt the stirrings of some devilish imp in his brain as Mistress Sharpe repeated furiously:

'I shall do no such thing!'

'And I, Ma'am, will not sleep in a bed with another man pissing up my back!' His tone was so calm, so even, that for a moment his words did not register in Mistress Sharpe's less than agile brain. When they did she opened and shut her mouth soundlessly, like a beached fish in a desert. Sandy left her - stranded. War had been declared.

Even Mistress Sharpe's mean and petty aggravations could not make Sandy as unhappy as the prospect of Mattie's approaching marriage to Daniel. He longed to ask her to wait for him but his promise to her father kept him silent. He was continually reminded of the plight of Nicky Jamieson's widow. He knew she had to suffer Mistress Sharpe's constant carping for the sake of her children. Their poverty and insecurity convinced him that he would not be doing his best for Matthew Cameron's bairn, if he begged her to break her promise to Daniel. Beside he had nothing to offer her in exchange - nothing but his love. Why has Mistress Lowe never written with news of Glen Caoranne? he asked himself. Was Reevil still searching for Mattie? Maybe the laird had refused to grant him the lease of Nethertannoch and its stock unless he provided for her? Soon she would be sixteen. Her destiny would be settled. Reevil had little time left.

'And neither have I,' he muttered glumly. 'Soon Mattie will make her vows - to love, honour and obey - to be the wife of Daniel Munro.' Sandy could scarcely bear the thought of it. If only they had enough cattle to support themselves at Fairlyden.

When the Reverend Mackenzie had received Mistress Lowe's first letter telling them Tam Reevil was not going to die, relief had flooded over Sandy. At least he could not be hung for murder. Recently relief had been replaced by resentment. The only crime he had committed was in helping Mattie escape from the whim of Sir Douglas Irving. The laird had used marriage as a means of discharging his responsibility towards the deaf daughter of one of the estate's oldest tenants, but surely the laird could not have been aware of Reevil's lust? It was Reevil who had forced them to flee - to leave the stock and their possessions behind. If they had the Nethertannoch stock now they could make a good living at Fairlyden; he and Mattie could be together. As soon as his year at Mains of Muir was finished he could ask her to be his wife. They could take care of Daniel Munro together; they would pay him a rent for his land.

The more Sandy thought about it, the more desperate he became. He pushed aside Mistress Lowe's warnings. That very night he wrote a letter to the laird at Caoranne Castle. He begged Sir Douglas Irving's pardon for taking Mattie away against his wishes. Then he appealed for recompense for the animals they had left behind, and concluded with a promise to care for Mattie all the days of her life. Finally he added a plea for an urgent reply.

Ten

Mattie was still in mourning for her father and Daniel Munro was incapable of making the journey to the church, but he insisted that all the formalities must be observed. He was adamant that Sandy should be one of the witnesses. Mistress McFarlane, the blacksmith's widow, was to be the other.

On the morning of the wedding the minister drove Mistress McFarlane to Fairlyden in his trap, all the way round by the road, through Strathtod village. As they approached the track to Fairlyden a slim, red-haired youth suddenly appeared almost out of the grassy bank. He waved eagerly and his thin foxy face split in a grin.

'It is uncanny how young Rory O'Connor seems to know what we are about,' the minister marvelled. 'He appears remarkably pleased.'

'Aye, I dinna ken the O'Connors maze. This is the first time I've left ma ain parish,' Mistress McFarlane mused, 'but I've heard it said the laddie wanders for miles in a' kinds o' weather, an' there's nought much he disna' ken - for all he wadna gang tae school.'

Rory had not been so happy with the encounter he had had an hour earlier as he viewed the world from his perch in the old oak tree on the other side of Strathtod. He had watched the stranger, a short thick-set man, as he approached the fork in the road. Without warning he had pulled his horse to a halt with a vicious jerk which had made Rory cringe with pity. The horse had reared on his hind legs in his effort to respond to his master's sudden decision. In no time at all horse and rider had returned. Amazingly Rory had abandoned his usual vanishing act and stepped into the road, determined to prevent the man repeating his cruel treatment.

'Hey, fellow!' the stranger bellowed. 'Show me the track tae Fairlyden. I hae business there.' His beady eyes gleamed malevolently. 'Urgent business!'

Rory hesitated. He did not like the man's smug sneer.

'There's a deaf chit there. Can ye no answer, you stupid fellow? Which road is't?'

Rory's eyes and hands twitched uneasily. Every instinct told him the stranger would not be welcome at Fairlyden. Rapidly he pointed and gabbled, and after a series of urgent gestures the rider galloped away.

The indomitable courage which had seen Mattie through the trauma of sudden deafness, and through her days in Dominie Butler's school, almost deserted her as the Reverend Mackenzie waited for her to make her marriage vows. The previous day she had scrubbed and cleaned everywhere. She had polished the large black range until it shone. She had filled her mother's blue bowl with flowers. At last she had crept wearily to bed, only to find sleep elusive. At dawn she had risen and attended her chores as usual. Then she had dressed with care in her best black dress. Now she stood beside Mr Munro in his chair beside the fire. She was wearing the jet brooch which had belonged to her mother. On her head she wore a square of black lace which she had found in Sarah Munro's trunk. Everything about the scene in the Fairlyden kitchen was familiar. Yet to Mattie her whole world suddenly seemed unreal. She gazed imploringly at Sandy, desperately needing his support, a smile of approval. But Sandy continued to study the rag rug and the cracks in the flagged floor.

It was Mr Munro's compelling dark eyes which drew Mattie's attention, his smile which gave her the courage to go on. 'in sickness and in health; and forsaking all other, keep thee only unto him so long as ye both shall live ' Mattie had little recollection of the vows and promises she spoke but she must have made the responses. Mr Munro needed her in a way that Sandy would never need her. As his wife she would be safe from Jacob Reevil, free from the fear which haunted her. So her thoughts went round and round until the Reverend Mackenzie pronounced her to be Mistress Munro of Fairlyden. Mattie knew life would be hard, and especially so without Sandy's help, but she had given her word to Mr Munro and now she would keep it; she had carried out her resolve to free Sandy from the promise he had made to her father. She would be a burden to him no longer. He was free.

Sandy had expressed his reluctance to be a spectator at the ceremony which would bind the woman he loved to another man, but Daniel had made sure he had no excuse to absent himself. The day had been chosen specially. The men and maids at Mains of Muir enjoyed a rare holiday to attend the fair which followed the term hirings.

Mattie was almost overwhelmed when everyone presented her with a wedding gift. Sandy had ordered a tea box to be made by the local carpenter. He had pledged part of his wages in order to have it suitably decorated with mother of pearl in an attempt to replace the one which had belonged to Mattie's mother.

Mistress McFarlane had brought a broody hen with eleven fluffy yellow chickens. The Reverend Robert Mackenzie produced two ewes and their lambs, and Mistress Miller had sent a cooked chicken, well stuffed with onions and thyme, and a large plum cake rich with fruits.

Buff had done her canine best to add to the celebration with an offering of a rabbit the previous day. Mattie had promptly made it into a pie, more to mark Sandy's longed for return than to celebrate her own wedding day. It was the first time they had been apart since she was a child; she missed him dreadfully. She had also prepared a large custard and a bowl of tender pink rhubarb as well as a pot of his favourite broth and crusty bread.

Daniel had no intention of being left out. He had instructed the Reverend Mackenzie to use the rest of the money from the sale of his mother's brooch - the money which stood between him and a pauper's grave. The minister had bought a set of new scotch hands to work the butter and a special butter stamp as well as a newly calved cow and calf. Mattie was astonished and elated.

Sandy heaved a sigh of relief as soon as the little celebration was over. He did not wait to help Mattie with the pigs and cows as he would once have done.

'There's room for you in the trap,' the Reverend Mackenzie offered, noting his unusual pallor.

'No! I, er, no thanks. The evening air will do me good.'

Robert Mackenzie nodded. He sensed Sandy's need to be alone.

Sometime later Sandy reached the boundary. He stepped across the burn. Suddenly he halted. This was Mattie's wedding night. His feet refused to turn towards the south end of the parish and Mains of Muir. The prospect of the cheerless bothy and an evening spent in the sullen company of Alf Wood filled him with despair. He stood beneath the great expanse of the evening sky. Empty fields surrounded him. He had wanted to be silent; to be alone. But his thoughts promised no comfort to his tormented soul.

On an impulse he turned his steps towards the mill. As he passed the Crown and Thistle he heard sounds of revelry within. Although the railway was beginning to attract many travellers, the little inn was still a favourite resting place for stagecoach passengers and horsemen. Joseph Miller frequently passed an evening in its mellow warmth, listening to the news of people passing through. Sandy felt a desperate need for congenial surroundings and cheerful company tonight.

Joseph Miller was not at the inn when Sandy entered but he ordered a tankard of ale and found a seat beside the fire. It was warm and comfortable. There were more men than usual since many of them were on their way home from the Fair, reluctant to end their precious holiday. Some of them nodded a greeting, recognising him as Joseph Miller's man. Anything was better than sitting in the bothy, listening to Alf Wood's heavy breathing punctuated by the odd grunt or at best a sarcastic remark.

Like himself, few of the men had much money to spend on ale, but this was Fair Day and there was a festive atmosphere. Tomorrow they would all return to long days of sacrifice and toil. Another man came into the inn. His sister was one of the maids at the Mains and he worked at the neighbouring farm. Sandy had never met him before but the man had apparently heard of his confrontation with the Mains's Dragon. He began to tell the others how Sandy had helped Nicky Jamieson's widow and children to keep a roof over their heads. Tonight was a night for celebrating. What better to celebrate than a good man in their midst!

Despite Sandy's protests that he had no money to buy more ale, his tankard was kept full. The effects of the warm fire, the ale and the friendly faces, all worked upon him. The ice around his heart began to thaw; he found himself relaxing, even joining in some of the songs, though he couldn't remember offering to stand up and sing

Neither could he remember seeing the officer of the King's Own Borderers before. Yet the man who had just entered the inn was staring at him and his face seemed familiar. Sandy looked at the scarlet jacket and blue trousers with their distinctive red stripe but his usually clear gaze was somewhat blurred. He was astonished when the officer strode towards him and seized his hands.

'Why, it is you, Alexander Logan! I thought I would never find you! Where is Miss Cameron? I trust she is well?'

Sandy's brain cleared. He recognised the voice and the face now - Charles Irving of Caoranne Castle. Thinner, paler, but it was the laird's son. Sandy's blood chilled despite the ale he had consumed. The laird had not answered his letter. He had sent his son instead to take them back.

'Ye're too late! Ye canna take her back ' His tongue felt like cotton wool and Sandy was not even sure whether he had spoken the words aloud or whether they were still swirling around inside his confused brain.

The other occupants of the inn were agog with curiosity, especially when the young officer insisted that Sandy must join him in the back parlour of the inn where the landlord's wife was about to serve his meal, along with a glass or two of best French brandy.

Sandy stared at him, bemused, but did not resist when Captain Irving took his arm and led him through to the other room where a table was being set for a solitary meal. The pretty maid smiled seductively at Sandy and swayed her rounded hips invitingly each time she passed his chair. The room was cooler, although a fire had recently been lit. The atmosphere was free from the thick fog of tobacco smoke and various other evil-smelling products with which poorer men packed their pipes. Sandy's thoughts cleared a little, but Charles Irving was too wrapped in his own melancholy to realise that his unexpected appearance had set Sandy's heart thudding. Already Irving was homesick for his native glen, although he had not yet crossed the border into England. Alexander Logan suddenly represented everything that was beloved of Caoranne. He was no longer a poor farmer from his father's estate but a 'kenned face' - a friend in an alien land - and he might have news of Emilia

'Join me,' he pleaded, 'I need company tonight.' Sandy blinked uncertainly.

'You are -you have come frae - from the glen?' Charles nodded and rumpled his brown hair with restless fingers. He looked pale and strained.

'I have been on furlough. Four days, four miserable days to search for Emilia! I did not even see my father. He is in France - been gone four weeks or more - searching for somebody or other. And now I must rejoin my regiment in Manchester. I do not want to go back!' He groaned. 'In July we leave for Dover. I shall be further away than ever, and there is talk that we shall be posted to Gibraltar. I shall never find her!' He raised his glass and drank deeply. 'I never wanted to join the army.' He looked suddenly young and bewildered and very unhappy.

Sandy's fear slowly evaporated. The laird had not received his letter after all then? That was the reason he had not replied and now it was too late.

'Did ye speak with Mistress Lowe?'

Charles sighed and absently refilled his glass, his thoughts in the glen he had left behind.

'Mistress Lowe was indisposed. She could not see me. The poor woman is still suffering from the shock of her husband's death. She...'

'Death! The Reverend Lowe is dead?' Sandy echoed incredulously.

'Yes. He was thrown from his horse.'

'Thrown? But the minister was an excellent rider!' It was one of the few qualities Sandy had found to admire about the Reverend Peter Lowe.

'It was late, and a dark night. The minister had been making an urgent visit to Jacob Reevil. The horse returned to the stable in a great lather. Joe Kerr, the blacksmith, said the saddle was loose and nearly round his belly. One of the leathers had broken. They found the minister the next morning by the side of Westertannoch wood, just below Reevil's farm. Reevil blamed Tam for frightening the horse.'

'Why wad Tam do such a thing?'

'Joe Kerr thinks it was Reevil himself, though he could furnish no proof. There was no good reason. The minister was Reevil's friend.'

Sandy blinked and tried to clear his head. His senses were not so clear as usual on account of the quantity of ale he had consumed. He had always believed that Emilia Reevil was the girl whose fate had so distressed Mistress Lowe and prompted her to write to the Reverend Mackenzie, pleading with him to keep Mattie at Fairlyden. Reevil would have reason enough to fear the minister if he had ravaged his own daughter. And if the Reverend Lowe had indeed discovered the truth which he had set out to find that night. Where was Emilia Reevil now? He frowned.

'Did ye see Tam?'

'Och, I saw Tam, poor fellow. I visited him in Dumfries, at a special place built at the Crichton Institution. It is set upon a hill, and quite beautiful. But Tam talked more nonsense than ever! He just babbled about Emilia flying like a bird on the branch of a tree!'

Sandy gasped. In her letter Mistress Lowe had mentioned the girl escaping down a stem of ivy. Perhaps Tam's babblings were not all the wild imaginings of an idiot? But Sandy could not bring himself to tell Charles Irving what he knew - or thought he knew.

'So Mistress Lowe is a widow!' he mused aloud. It was not surprising that the poor woman had not written again. He must tell Mattie the news. Mattie or Mistress Munro as she was now. He groaned silently as memories came flooding back. He reached for the brandy which Charles Irving had poured for him. He took a large gulp. He had never tasted the spirit before. It burned all the way down his throat and made him cough. Charles laughed aloud and refilled both their glasses.

The landlord's wife bustled in carrying several covered dishes of steaming food. The interruption drew Charles Irving temporarily out of his dejection. Mistress Nellie Bryson was a pleasant, buxom woman and Charles asked her to set an extra place for his friend. Sandy began to feel quite mellow as he became more closely acquainted with the brandy. The food smelled delicious. There was a tureen of spring soup, boiled salmon and butter sauce, lamb cutlets, roast pigeon and a platter of vegetables. When Mistress Bryson returned with the young maid to set the extra place at the table she brought a dish of blancmange and a fruit compote as well as a platter of cheeses.

'Joseph Miller said ye were no' ordinary body,' she murmured in an aside, giving Sandy a broad wink.

He had eaten sparsely at Fairlyden, too sick at heart to enjoy the food Mattie had prepared for her wedding day, but the ale and wine had tempered the fine edge of his despondency and he enjoyed the feast. Charles Irving ate with little interest and seemed more intent on refilling their glasses. As soon as they were alone he returned to the subject which seemed to occupy his thoughts exclusively - Emilia Reevil. Sandy tried to divert him. Indeed, now that his earlier apprehension of a man in uniform had receded, he longed for news of the glen folk.

'Is M-Mistress Lowe still at the m-manse? Mattie will write.' Charles Irving drained his glass and refilled it absently.

'My mother has given her rooms at the Castle until she recovers.' Sandy was about to inquire for Jem Wright who had always been a good friend to Mattie, but Captain Charles Irving went on. 'There was a letter...' he frowned in concentration. 'To my father about you, no it was about Nethertannoch stock, I think. Mother commanded Reevil to make payment.'

Sandy sat up straighter and shook his fuzzy head trying to clear his brain.

'I heard nought!' He slumped back. Then he began to laugh drunkenly. 'Reevil? L-Lady Irving c-commanded him!'

'I called at Westertannoch. Jacob Reevil was not there. I wanted news of Emilia.' Charles looked down at his blue and scarlet uniform in distaste, his own words becoming more and more slurred. 'I had no wish to be a soldier in the Queen's army!' He grimaced bitterly and stared broodingly at the bottle of brandy on the table, stretched out a long arm and proceeded to recharge both their glasses.

'Nethertannoch is sad, neglected, unloved ... I am unloved' He hiccoughed several times then gave an ungentlemanly belch. His head, and his speech, seemed clearer and he went on: 'Reevil has taken his revenge!' He swirled his glass and stared into it. His face looked strangely young and vulnerable in the flickering light of the lamp.

Sandy shared his unhappiness. He drained his own brandy glass for the second time. It made him feel delightfully warm. He could almost forget this was Mattie's wedding day.

Charles looked up and his eyes were feverishly bright. 'When I return again to Caoranne, you will return also.' He waved his arm widely. 'I shall grant you a lease of all Reevil's land. I shall banish him from the glen.' His words slurred again and he blinked owlishly at Sandy across the table. Then he lurched forward and refilled their glasses once more. 'When I get out of this damned uniform I shall search for Emilia. She will marry me. And you, and Miss Cameron, will be our best, our biggest tenants.' He nodded vigorously at Sandy. 'Have you made her your wife, yet? You must, my man! Make that sweet girl an honourable woman, what-oh!' The alcohol was having its effect.

Sandy did not answer. His face crumpled as though he might burst into tears, like a girl. He had drunk more ale and wine in this one evening than in the whole of his life before - not to mention the brandy. It loosened his control - and his tongue. Discretion flew up the chimney.

'I couldna' marry her! We ran away like murderers i' the night. 'Twas Reevil's fault! We had no money had to leave everything 'cept the horses and twae wee pigs ' He broke off with a sound resembling a sob and a hiccough.

Charles Irving stared at him blearily, trying hard to focus his eyes on Sandy's face.

'Sure 'tis monstrous! Who did you murder, my friend?'

Sandy frowned, trying to remember what they were talking about, struggling to assemble his thoughts, lifting his brandy once more. He liked the warmth it sent coursing through his veins.

'I didna hurt puir Tam!' he muttered. 'It was his ain father wi' yon whip o' his. He tried to take her -to take my Mattie.' He began to sing: ' "Her as pure as the dawn ... the dawn. I brought her awa' frae the glen - the glen ... I hae no money ... to tak a wife

The maid came in to mend the fire and he grinned at her stupidly. Her face swam before his eyes but she gave his shoulder a suggestive squeeze as she passed.

'It is all my fault!' Charles Irving cried. 'I don't know why but it's my fault! My father said it was, so it is so. I must pay the price! What price? Here, take this, my man.' He pulled out his purse and counted out five golden sovereigns. He pushed them across the table to Sandy. He stared at the money, and for a moment his mind cleared.

'Take it back. I dinna want your money. It is too late!' he choked. 'She's married to another!' He pushed the money back across to Charles, who picked it up and struggled to his feet, lurching unsteadily round the table. He stuffed the money deep into the pocket of Sandy's vest.

'Now we'll drink to it!' he chortled happily. They finished the brandy and called for another bottle.

Sandy had no recollection of falling asleep, slumped over the inn table. He had even less recollection of Joseph Miller and his companion assisting him to the mill house, half singing, half sobbing.

'I love her, I'll never forget her! Mattie's th-the only maid for me '

'Whischt lad, Ye'll waken the dead!' Joseph Miller urged.

'Dead - aye, I wish I was dead,' Sandy hiccoughed noisily. 'I love Mattie, I tell ye all.'

Joseph and his friend grasped his arms more tightly and half dragged, half carried, him to the mill house. Joseph felt sorry for Sandy's lovesick misery, but in his heart he was glad little Miss Cameron had married another man. Sandy would forget her, in time. Then Jeannie's turn would come, if she was patient -maybe in about a year. Joseph had never been able to deny his golden-haired Jeannie anything, and he liked Sandy Logan himself, he liked him well.

Once in the mill house Joseph removed Sandy's boots and most of his clothes and put him into bed like a bairn, in a small room off the kitchen. Sandy, who had never tasted such wine or brandy in his life, was lost in a delightful golden haze where dreams and reality intermingled and it was impossible to distinguish between the two. There were pretty faces and soft hands all about him - Mattie's smiling dark eyes and Jeannie Miller's golden curls, the smooth rounded hips of the maid from the Inn. Even to his dying day, vague memories of that night lingered in his mind.

Jeannie Miller had heard the knock which had summoned her father to the inn at an unusually late hour. Her own small bedroom was directly above the mill house door and she slept with her window open, for the simple reason that its swollen wooden frame refused to shut. There were always a few who celebrated after the hiring fair, but the sound of Sandy Logan's name sent her scurrying out of bed to kneel against the low window.

She had not expected Sandy to be celebrating - and with an officer of the Queen's Army no less! This was the day Miss Cameron had wed the master of Fairlyden. They must have been drinking to the health of the couple. Jeannie's heart sang. Clearly Sandy was happy to be free of his burden; free of Miss Cameron; free to look where he fancied

Jeannie had already learned that Sandy Logan was proud, and excessively independent. He would not pay court to a girl until he felt he was worthy of her. Jeannie had never waited patiently for anything in her young, relatively untroubled life. Her parents had lost two babies before she was born. Consequently she had been doubly cherished and indulged. Now, at seventeen, she was decidedly pretty with her golden curls and blue eyes, and a mischievous dimple lurking at the corner of her small red mouth. She had an appealing manner when occasion demanded it, and most people granted her wishes.

When Jeannie was eight years old Grandfather Miller had still been alive, but almost overnight he had changed into a querulous old man, tied to his bed by his infirmity and demanding all her mother's attention. During the few weeks he had survived Jeannie had frequently sought refuge in the mill with her father. It was on one such day that she had climbed to the upper floor and settled herself happily on a sack of corn to await his return with the horse and cart.

The peace had been disturbed by a scuffling sound, followed by girlish giggles. When Jeannie peered through the crack of the trap door to the floor below she had been surprised to see Millie, their maid, rolling in the arms of a young man who helped with the pigs. Jeannie had stared, round-eyed, astonished!

Instinct warned her not to make a sound - never to breathe a word of the scene she witnessed that day -and she never had. But she had never forgotten. She had not fully understood the intimate groping and stroking, the giggles and grunts and heavy breathing. When the time came round for the hiring fair the couple had left the mill and taken a job at Cotter's Farm, where they could have a cottage and declare themselves man and wife. Now Millie had seven children - but the roll on the mill floor had got her the man she wanted.

Sandy Logan was sound asleep. The mill house was once more dark and silent. Jeannie knew every creaking step, every uneven flagstone. She did not light her candle as she groped her way silently down the stairs and through the parlour to the room where Sandy lay. She had no hesitation, no thought of rejection as she crept in beside him, eager for the warmth of his body. Yet she scarcely knew what she expected. He lay on his back, snoring gently, his arms spread-eagled across the mattress. He did not stir. Jeannie snuggled against him, her head close beside his on the feather bolster. His arm curved around her in sleep. She felt the hardness of his muscles against the softness of her own body and excitement shot through her. Her hands began to explore - like a child opening a surprise parcel - almost unwilling to discover the gift inside, savouring each step wanting, and yet not wanting, the ultimate thrill.

Sandy was by nature a gentle man, but the effects of alcohol had lessened his normal sensitivity. He was young and virile. All his waking thoughts throughout that day, and for days and nights before that, had been of Mattie. He had struggled valiantly to hide his deep and terrible yearning for her and he had welcomed the effects of the liquor which dulled his pain - and his senses. Jeannie's eager, experimental touch penetrated the alcohol-induced stupor; she aroused his latent desire with alarming speed! She was there, at his side, a willing partner in the blackness of the night. He took everything she offered and after the first shock, the brief initial pain, Jeannie offered much for she wanted Sandy Logan more than she had ever wanted anything or anyone in her short life.

So the shock was doubly severe when Sandy rolled away from her and she heard the words he murmured through the mists of intoxicated sleep: 'Aah, Mattie, I thought I had lost ye '

'Sandy!' Jeannie uttered his name. It was a cry of pain, like a wounded animal's.

'I aye loved ye. Only you ' He turned towards her in sleep, his arms outstretched, welcoming `ma 'ain wee Mattie'.

Ice filled Jeannie's veins. She evaded his clasp, lying rigid on the hard edge of the bed. Sandy lay still, snoring steadily again. Shivering violently, Jeannie edged silently out of the bed. For a moment she stood still, staring down at Sandy's recumbent figure. She could see little in the darkness but she heard him sigh, then the sound of his even breathing as deep sleep claimed him once more.

Stifling her sobs, Jeannie crept back to her room on trembling limbs, overcome with shame and humiliation - and anger. She would never, never speak to Sandy Logan again!

She was unaware of Edward Slater lurking in the deep shadow of the parlour wall. He had been at the Fair. He had scoffed at the gypsy woman who had told his fortune; yet he had not scorned the other pleasures she had offered. She had kept him longer than he had expected and he had had to hurry to reach the mill before dawn. He moved curiously to the door of the small room from which Jeannie had emerged in her flowing white nightgown.

Already the darkness of night was becoming less intense and he could discern the mound beneath the blanket on the bed. He crept closer. His eyes rounded incredulously. He lit the candle stub on the wash stand and held it nearer. He was right! It was Logan! And there was another dent on the bolster beside his head

So, the precocious Jeannie had also had a secret lover tonight! What would Mistress Miller and her bible-preaching friends have to say about that? Indeed what would Joseph Miller himself have to say? Oh, what indeed! He almost worshipped his golden-haired bairn. But Joseph Miller valued his good name, his Christian principles. Edward almost spat as he recalled the lectures he had sullenly endured, especially when he had substituted Logan's oatmeal with husks.

'Now dinna cheat the customers, Edward.' and 'Never tell a lie, Edward.'

He held the candle closer to the bed. Sandy did not stir. The rhythm of his breathing and the intermittent snores never faltered. Edward smelled liquor. Logan was drunk. Had he been too drunk for Jeannie to arouse him? Was that why she had slunk away looking so rejected? Edward touched Sandy's cheek. His head turned slightly on the pillow. 'Mattie?' The word was no more than a slurred murmur, but Edward Slater heard. His eyes narrowed. Logan was too drunk to know where he was! Or what he had done -or who had been his woman. Jeannie might just as well have been the buxom young maid from the Crown and Thistle for all Logan would remember. And Jeannie had offered herself like a common whore!

Edward expelled a long breath. It was enough to make the old man put her out of the house when he heard this - daughter or no daughter! His eyes glittered malevolently. He was almost at the door when he remembered the gypsy's words. He half turned and stared back at Sandy. Maybe the gypsy had been wiser than she knew? Maybe he wouldn't tell the miller -yet.

'Show a little brotherly love and you will reap great rewards.' Aye, those had been the very words. He had snorted in derision. When had anyone ever shown him brotherly love? Even his mother had died and left him the day after he was born. His grandmother had told him often enough that he was a burden. She had died when he was four. His father had coughed up his lungs and followed her within a year. Brotherly love! Still, things had improved a bit then. Uncle Fred, his father's brother, had taken him to live with him and Aunt Mary. They lived in a dark, stinking little vennel in the town, but it had been near the river, and the house had been clean inside; Aunt Mary had made him clothes out of Uncle Fred's that very first week, and he had nearly always had enough to eat until he was nine.

There had been an accident at the woollen mill where Uncle Fred worked. Something had flown through the air and hit him on the head.

His temper had been terrible after that and in the two years he had lingered on Edward had earned a pittance carrying messages for old ladies and delivering groceries and vegetables for the shopkeepers who lived in the vennel. He had learned to pit his sly wits against the other boys who wanted work; he had learned to lie and cheat, stealing a pie here or a farthing there. Aunt Mary had been too ill to do anything about it by the time Uncle Fred had died. That's why she had sent for her brother - and Joseph Miller had promised to treat him like a son. A son!

Maybe he would do well to consider the gypsy's words. She had certainly kept her first promise! She had shown him the delights which only a woman could; she had whetted his appetite for more, but she would soon be gone from this area

Eleven

Although Mattie's world was one of silence she felt the quiet stillness was almost tangible at Fairlyden when everyone had departed after the wedding ceremony. She had never been so conscious of being alone before, but she could not forget that Mr Munro was now her husband. It was true he had set out the conditions for their marriage in his black crab-like handwriting, but would he also observe them? Or would he expect more of her? She shivered nervously and lingered as long as she could over the milking, the feeding of the hens and the two pigs.

Oh, Sandy, her heart cried, if only you could have loved me and made me your wife. I would never have been afraid. She wandered slowly down to the meadow where Darkie was grazing. She caressed the mare's strong, shining neck and let her nuzzle her soft mouth against the palm of her hand. She returned restlessly to the farmyard with Buff, her ever present shadow, trotting at her heels. The sun was sinking behind the hills, the hens were beginning to roost in their little hut. She shut the tiny door to keep them safe until morning. The shadows lengthened and disappeared but still Mattie could not bring herself to enter the house. At last there were no more tasks and the early summer evening had grown chilly. She must mend the fire. Mr Munro suffered badly when the nights were cold.

Daniel had guessed something of Mattie's thoughts and fears but he had begun to worry when she was so late in returning to the house. He was relieved to see her at last, and his smile was warm, reflecting all his concern for her. Mattie looked anxiously into his dark eyes, but all she saw there was tender affection, as a father might feel for a cherished child. There was nothing of the lust and ugly desire she had seen in Reevil's eyes. She moved slowly towards the hearth and held out her hands to the glowing embers behind the black iron ribs. Daniel reached forward unexpectedly and took one of her hands in his. She felt the knobbly hardness of his twisted fingers, felt him drawing her to her feet to stand beside his chair. She began to tremble. Daniel shook his head reprovingly.

'You read my letter of agreement, my promise to you, Mattie. Trust me, my dear. I shall keep my word. You are my wife. I shall respect you, always.' Mattie looked down at him with troubled eyes as dark as his own. He smiled and there was no doubting the new kindliness in him, the softness he took such pains to hide from the world. 'I shall never hurt you, Mattie.' She found herself smiling back at him involuntarily. She returned the pressure of his gnarled fingers and nodded.

'Yes, I trust you, Mr Munro.' Mattie knew she could never bring herself to use her husband's God-given name, but a new understanding had opened up between them, an affection and warmth born of mutual need, mutual respect, and companionship.

'You must be tired, Mattie, as I am,' Daniel sighed. He felt unutterably weary; not at all a suitable bridegroom for an innocent young bride. 'Mend up the fire, my dear, then we can both go to sleep.'

A little while later Mattie knelt beside the big bed. She looked young and innocent with her dark hair hanging down to her waist and her prim white night-gown buttoned to the neck. Down below Daniel Munro lay in his wooden box bed beside the fire.

'Thank you dear God, for giving me a good, kind husband,' Mattie murmured fervently at the end of her prayers. She tried not to think of Sandy as she climbed into the big bed to lie alone on her wedding night.

The spring weather had ensured ample grazing for the mare and the three cows, even in Fairlyden's rank, neglected meadows. At last Mattie could make enough butter to sell, but no carrier's cart came to Fairlyden as it had to Nethertannoch. Doubts assailed her as she prepared to visit the village store alone. She also needed to visit the mill to collect meal for the pigs as well as oatmeal and flour for the house. The thought of dealing with so many strangers filled her with trepidation.

She coaxed Darkie from the meadow and harnessed her to the cart. In the pocket of her clean white apron she carried a pencil and a small slate although she had already written a list of her few requirements. She was determined there would be no misunderstandings, and no sly tricks from Master Edward Slater. He must understand that she was not stupid, just because she could not hear. Buff had had a thorn in her paw which Daniel had removed with some difficulty and for once the little dog seemed content to be left behind.

Although the burn was low, the cart lurched precariously as one wheel sank in a patch of soft sand. Darkie strained at the harness and pulled the cart up the shallow bank on the opposite side without much difficulty, but Mattie feared that even a small load of meal might make the cart sink dangerously low on their return journey. She bid the obedient Darkie stand still while she collected a pile of small stones, spreading them across the bed of the burn, knowing that the first heavy rain would wash them away. When she had finished her boots were wet, her skirt was hemmed in mud and her fresh white apron was splashed and stained. She had taken particular care with her appearance for her first visit to Muircumwell village, and she had not seen the Millers since the Sunday she had gone to church with Sandy. After her strenuous efforts she felt hot, tired and dejected. She longed for Sandy's company as well as his strength and help. She was unaware of the thin, wiry figure hidden in a clump of bushes just over the Strathtod boundary. A pair of grey eyes stared intently out of a lean, foxy face, watching, waiting for her to move on. Although the sun shone on a head of spikey red hair Rory O'Connor was well practised in the art of concealment and even Mattie's keen eyes did not detect him.

She drove the cart to the village store. Mr Jardine was clearly surprised to see her, and a little embarrassed. He knew she could not hear. How could he talk to her? She showed him her butter.

'It is the best quality and flavour,' she assured him earnestly. 'Will you buy it, and what will you pay?'

Charlie Jardine eyed the butter, then he gave Mattie a speculative stare. He held up ten fingers.

'Ten pennies?' Mattie gasped. 'I understood you were a fair man!' Charlie Jardine flushed uncomfortably. 'Fairlyden butter is worth twice that,' Mattie insisted. Eventually she succeeded in negotiating a price of one shilling and five pence for her two pounds of butter. She knew the grocer had underpaid her by a penny or even a penny ha'penny a pound, but it was a start.

'Now I would like to buy two ounces of tea, a pound of sugar, a small block of salt and a piece of fish, if you please, Mr Jardine. I am told the fish is caught in the Solway?'

'Aye, it is that, Ma'am! Fresh every day.' Mr Jardine had answered almost before he knew it and because he was facing her Mattie was pleased to be able to understand the gist of his conversation. 'I would like a copy of the Standard newspaper while I am waiting, if you please.'

Mr Jardine goggled. 'You can read, Mistress Munro? B-but I thought...'

'I am deaf, but I can read. I believe that leaves me one penny change?'

'Aye, aye, indeed it does!' Mr Jardine agreed in astonishment. Even so he did not dream that she could, or would, study the prices of the butter and eggs being sold in the town. Mattie was confident that her butter was as good as any in quality. She always carried fresh cold water from the spring to ensure the separation of the tiny golden grains.

Mattie was too preoccupied with her plans for the future of Fairlyden to pay much attention to the gypsy women who were selling their wooden pegs and wares at the doors of the cottages. Neither did she notice the two young gypsy men questioning the blacksmith about all the horses in the area.

Joseph Miller was absent from the mill when she arrived but Jeannie was speaking to Edward Slater in the cobbled yard. Jeannie's face expressed surprise, swiftly followed by resentment at the sight of Mattie, while Edward Slater gaped in amazement. Mattie was shocked by Jeannie's pale face; no smile lifted her drooping lips today. Indeed her blue eyes smouldered with an emotion which Mattie could only define as dislike. Mattie shivered and wondered what she had done to incur such displeasure.

Edward glanced at Jeannie's sulky face, then he turned to Mattie and exerted the charm he had been practising ever since his visit to the gypsy. Mattie had steeled herself to do battle with this young man, but now she responded with a smile of relief.

'I have come to collect the meal and flour, Master Slater, but I would also like to buy a small bag of sweepings, to make a mash for my hens.'

Edward smiled obsequiously. He could not resist another glance at Jeannie. The miller's daughter flounced away round the side of the mill. He loaded Mattie's cart with rare generosity, but without thought for her homeward journey across the burn. Mattie bit her lip anxiously, unwilling to offend the young man who had proved himself an unexpected friend. When she reached the burn there was no sign of the stones she had gathered so painstakingly; then to her amazement she realised they were hidden by a large, flat slab. Two other large stones had also been positioned to wedge the whole lot securely; with care, she could drive Darkie and the cart through the water, keeping both wheels on the stone tracks. She was jubilant.

Behind the bushes, where he had hastened just in time to escape detection, Rory O'Connor smiled his rare and most beautiful smile. His thin, foxy face was transformed, but it was a transformation few people were ever privileged to witness. Rory was the youngest of a family of twelve children. He had already reached his full height although he had not attained his thirteenth birthday, yet his wiry limbs were strong, and his untutored brain occasionally demonstrated remarkable ingenuity. He could neither read nor write and, except for a few words to his mother, Rory seldom spoke. His head was too full of the things he had seen or discovered during his wanderings; words were totally inadequate to express all he thought and felt. There was little about the countryside and the lore of the wild which Rory did not understand. He alone had witnessed the arrival of Alexander Logan, Mattie Cameron, two horses, two piglets, and a dog; but there was one rule which Rory's indulgent family insisted upon: he must never venture on to the land beyond the burn. Fairly's Den had been forbidden territory ever since the death of the old Earl, and to help a Munro would incur the wrath of the present Earl, on whom the whole of the O'Connor family depended.

Until Mattie's arrival Rory had obeyed willingly, but the girl who listened with her eyes drew him like a magnet to its pole. Twice he had witnessed the joy which lit her face when she believed Buff had brought a rabbit to her doorstep at dawn. Yesterday all his primitive instincts had warned him that she was in danger. He had deliberately directed the lone horse rider towards the Solway, and by the most circuitous tracks imaginable. He was sure the stranger would return. Today his self-appointed vigil had been delayed by the delivery of two pigeon eggs to the home of a sick child. So now, from the shelter of the thicket, Rory silently shared Mattie's relief as the horse and cart crossed the burn without mishap. Fairlyden was the deaf girl's home now. Soon she would reach it. Rory knew of no place safer than home.

Mattie entered the stone-flagged passage at Fairlyden clutching her few provisions in her arms. She felt elated with the success of her foray into the world of strangers and her pleasure was reflected in her sparkling dark eyes and parted lips as she entered the kitchen. She could not hear the voices raised in anger, or Buff scratching frenziedly at the locked door of the scullery.

The sight of the figure bending over Mr Munro drove the blood from her face. She thrust out her arms instinctively. Jacob Reevil! The devil who had haunted her dreams! He was here! He was threatening Mr Munro, the man who sought to give her protection.

She was oblivious to the little twist of tea, her precious sugar, the fish. They scattered at her feet amidst the shattered block of salt. Time stood still. She was back at Nethertannoch. She was utterly at Reevil's mercy.

'Sandy! Oh, Sandy,' she moaned silently. She retreated instinctively as Reevil turned and fixed her with his small malevolent eyes. She felt the cold stone of the wall at her back. She could not drag her eyes from Reevil's face.

'Lady Irving got the letter,' he drawled. 'She thinks I should gie ye my urgent attention. So here I am ' He leered at Mattie and she felt her flesh crawl. 'Pity I arrived too late for the wedding.' He glanced mockingly at Daniel Munro's crippled body. 'But I reckon I'll enjoy the initiation o' the bride, eh?'

Mattie could not understand but she sensed Mr Munro's agitation as he tried to rise from his chair.

'Leave my wife alone, I tell you!' he raged helplessly. For the first time he really understood why Mattie had run away from her home, why fear still haunted her, why Sandy had left everything he possessed to get her away from this lecher. It was not the law of the land they feared, nor the laird of Caoranne Glen - it was the devil in disguise!

Mattie could only see Reevil's sneer and watch his thick lips mockingly forming the word 'Wife!'

'I cannot be your wife - or your son's!' The words burst from Mattie as she almost pressed herself into the thick wall behind her. 'You cannot take me away!'

'Naw, I canna take ye awa, you bitch! But, by God, I'll take ye this time!'

Mattie saw the lustful glitter in his eyes as he lurched at her. She moved just in time, flinging herself away from him, to Mr Munro - her husband. She saw Daniel's dark eyes dart to the table. She saw the whip there. Her heart quailed at the memory of its stinging lashes. It lay across the corner of the table. She grabbed it blindly. Daniel held out his twisted fingers. Her eyes widened but he gave a brief, insistent nod. Before Reevil's slow wits grasped her intention Mattie had placed the whip in her husband's hand and pressed his crooked fingers around it. She knew the effort it took to lift his arm but she saw the whip snake out and streak unerringly across Reevil's broad, pasty face. He screamed in pain. Blood began to trickle from his brow, blurring his eyesight. Daniel lifted his arm again, but Mattie knew the effort it cost him, she knew he could never hold out against a strength and fury such as Reevil's. Even as he sprang at her she knew they would both pay dearly for their defiance.

*

The gypsy caravans were almost ready to begin the journey into Cumberland. They had done some satisfactory trading. There were some excellent horses in the area and the younger men were reluctant to move out until they had explored every possible deal. Two Romanies, more adventurous than their fellows, approached the Strathtod burn as the fellow at the mill had directed. They began to argue. Our leader has forbidden this place!' the elder declared. 'It belongs to the man with the eagle's eyes and clawed hands. He has no horses.'

'The fellow at the mill said he had the best mare for miles around!' the gypsy youth argued. 'Perhaps you are a coward, eh?' Such a challenge could not be ignored. The two set off across the fields to confront the eagle in his eyrie. They were still some distance from the house when Buff's agitated yapping reached their ears. They hesitated, half turning. They had been warned. The dog's barking increased to a frenzied pitch. The two exchanged a single glance. No gypsy dog barked like that unless there was trouble - and a dog was a dog.

They moved forward warily. The door of the house was open and they could hear voices now. One was raised in anger - the other mocking, sneering threatening. The elder of the two gypsies stiffened.

'That voice. I have heard it before.' He frowned, trying to remember; he moved silently into the stone-flagged passage, bidding his young companion wait outside. Suddenly he stopped and his eyes widened incredulously. He returned swiftly.

'It is the whip-man!' he hissed. 'I remember him! He cheated Dathi…'

'The white whip-man? You have seen him? You could not…'

'Yes! I was young. Five summers. No more. But I remember well. He burned the vardo. Dathi's wife died. I do not forget.'

'What shall we do?' whispered the young gypsy fearfully.

'We must take him! Take him to Dathi's son.'

'Across the water?' The youth's brown eyes widened.

'Across the water. We shall be rewarded. There will be a Romany Court! Dathi's son will take his revenge. Come.' He put a finger against his lips. Together they crept silently along the passage.

In the kitchen Jacob Reevil was holding Mattie against the far wall. He was enjoying watching the revulsion in her eyes whenever he lowered his bloody face to hers. It gave him a sadistic satisfaction to prolong the suspense, to watch Daniel Munro's anger and frustration as he struggled helplessly against the thong of the whip which now bound him to his chair. Mattie knew her husband was helpless. Reevil wanted him to witness her agony, to add to her humiliation.

The two gypsies hesitated and in that moment Daniel Munro saw them. He opened his mouth. Slowly he closed it again without uttering a sound, but there was desperation in his dark eyes - desperation for Mattie.

'The eagle man welcomes us!' the older gypsy whispered softly.

Reevil was taken by surprise. The sibilant hiss: 'White whip-man!' seemed to paralyse him with fear.

Mattie's dark eyes which had been wide with terror now stared incredulously as the two swarthy-skinned gypsies bundled Reevil effortlessly on to the floor. He stood no chance against their supple strength and his feet and hands were swiftly bound with their neckerchiefs. Tears of gratitude and relief shimmered in her eyes. The gypsies' white teeth flashed in a smile. Then the elder of the two turned to Daniel.

'Next year you will welcome us?'

Daniel nodded and his own face creased in a rare smile. There was inexpressible gratitude in his heart and it was reflected in his magnificent black eyes.

'Next year we shall buy your horses?'

'If we ever have horses enough to sell,' Daniel replied honestly.

'This year we have a better prize than horses. Our Leader will be full of praise.' The gypsy grinned.

'What will happen to him?' Daniel nodded towards Reevil squirming on the floor.

'He is the Evil One! 'The gypsy's face grew grim. 'He must face the Romany Elders.' Reevil began to whine, pleading urgently, offering bribes - money, his horse, the girl. The gypsy's lip curled in contempt. He raised his eyes and looked at Daniel, then at Mattie. 'He will not trouble you - or any other woman - ever again. He must pay! He will never return to this land.'

Sandy returned to Fairlyden on the first Sabbath after the wedding, and he stared at Daniel incredulously as he listened to the account of Reevil's visit. He dare not contemplate what Mattie's fate might have been if the gypsies had not chanced to call at Fairlyden. In dismay he realised that his own letter to Caoranne must have led Reevil to Mattie.

He went to look for her and found her cleaning the six stalls in the byre. Mattie turned in surprise at his appearance. The warmth of her smile, and the light which flared in her lovely eyes, filled Sandy's heart with yearning, but he had to tell her that it was he who had led Reevil to Fairlyden, however unintentionally.

'So you see I am to blame,' he said bitterly. 'I hoped the laird might send us the money for the Nethertannoch stock. I wanted to ask you to wait for me to finish my work at Mains of Muir, even though I knew you had promised to marry Daniel. I am sorry, Mattie.' Sandy bowed his head and shrugged helplessly, then he looked up again and his eyes met hers. 'I am truly thankful you are unharmed. Nothing else matters to me except your safety, and your happiness, my dear.'

Mattie had watched his lips intently, scarcely able to believe that Sandy had written to Sir Douglas Irving. Now her heart leapt with joy. He had not wanted to be free from his promise to her father after all. He would have made her his wife. Her dark eyes glowed as she realised the truth.

Sandy had the greatest difficulty in restraining his urge to gather her into his arms and hold her close to his heart.

Mattie's self-confidence increased as her trade with Mr Jardine's store continued, and when Sandy chose to spend his precious Sunday leisure at Fairlyden, instead of with Miss Jeannie Miller, she felt her happiness was almost complete. Together they planted the overgrown garden with vegetables and sowed several acres of oats and some turnips in preparation for the winter. Mattie had more work both indoors and out than she could ever complete, yet as the summer days lengthened her old serenity returned. She no longer dreamed of Reevil. She trusted the gypsies. He would not trouble her again. Sometimes she glimpsed the Solway Firth, gleaming like a silver carpet in the distance, gracefully unfurling over the golden sands as the tide came in. Beyond it lay the hills of Galloway, but her heart no longer yearned for the home she had known in Caoranne glen, though she often thought of her father, lying in the lonely little kirkyard on the side of the hill, and she longed for a letter from Mistress Lowe. Daniel was aware of her isolation and he made every effort to talk, and to share her interest in her books. Mattie was grateful, though in her heart she knew she could never think of him as her husband.

' "Six days shalt thou labour," ' the Reverend Mackenzie chided sternly when he chanced to meet Sandy on his way back to the Mains one Sunday evening; yet looking into Sandy's lean and tired face he had found it difficult to reconcile the word of God with the needs of men and women.

The minister was not the only person who had noticed Sandy's absence. At the mill house Joseph Miller missed his company and his conversation; Ruth Miller missed his mannerly appreciation; only Edward Slater was delighted by his failure to return and he continued playing his role of a reformed character with even greater zeal. He controlled his gluttony at the table, he went out of his way to please the customers at the mill, he even offered to help Joseph with the pigs, a task he had always shirked. Most noticeable of all was his attitude to Jeannie. He no longer provoked her at every opportunity, despite his longing to taunt her with his knowledge when she exercised her sharp tongue. He schooled himself to patience, knowing he would reap his reward.

Jeannie had waited tensely for Sandy's first visit. She was almost sure he had been too drunk to distinguish between dreams and reality on that awful night after Miss Cameron's wedding. She had heard her father struggling to waken him, sluicing his head with water from the mill stream in an effort to bring sense to his clouded brain, before setting him along the road to Mains of Muir.

In fact Sandy had so little recollection of that night's events that he might have been persuaded the whole affair had been a fantasy, but for an extremely painful head and Charles Irving's gift of five gold sovereigns jingling in his vest pocket. It was true that he had had a hazy feeling of spent passions but this, he supposed, must be due to the attentions of the flirtatious maid from the Crown and Thistle. He shuddered at the mere thought of such a drunken orgy. Yet it never occurred to Jeannie that Alexander Logan would be ashamed, and therefore reluctant to face the friends whose respect he had valued. She was too absorbed with her own shame and humiliation. Yet when two Sundays passed, and then a third, and still Sandy did not visit the mill house, Jeannie grew resentful. But another emotion was beginning to destroy her composure .

Edward Slater waited. He had chanced to witness Jeannie dashing to the closet at the bottom of the garden three mornings in succession. On the third morning she did not reach the little building in time. He watched as she spewed her breakfast over the lavender bed; his small eyes gleamed malevolently.

So June passed into July and Sandy scythed the first meadow at Fairlyden and prayed that the weather would stay dry so that he and Mattie could make, and gather, a good crop of hay for the winter. His brief leisure allowed so little time for all he wanted to do at Fairlyden and for Mattie.

Meanwhile Jeannie's fears increased. Her former good health had deserted her. She was wretchedly sick and it sapped both her energy and her determination. Ruth Miller grew increasingly concerned about her only child's unusual lethargy and pallor. Jeannie knew it would be impossible to hide her secret much longer, and although her parents loved her dearly, she knew there were some things they would not forgive. She trembled fearfully. How could she confess she had acted like a common slut - and with Sandy Logan of all men? Sandy himself would probably deny all knowledge and her father would believe him; she knew that instinctively. Her pale cheeks grew hot with humiliation. Then her drooping mouth tightened into a stubborn line. He was the father of her child. She wanted him for her husband. She must prepare him for her father's questions. She quailed at the prospect and her stomach gave another sickening lurch.

A few days later Edward Slater stood silently in the shadow of the mill; he had seen Jeannie waylay the Mains of Muir carter. He heard her questioning the man and saw him grin.

'Sandy Logan canna wait for day to break on Sundays afore he's headin' awa' tae Fairlyden.'

Jeannie barely stayed long enough to thank the man. Her mouth set. The deaf girl was married. Why did Sandy Logan still persist in looking after her?

Desperation left no room for pride. Jeannie was confident that Sandy would marry her and she made up her mind to waylay him. Not for a moment did she consider he might have reason to doubt her word.

The following Sunday she rose very early. It was becoming more and more difficult to parry her mother's searching questions and avoid her anxious eyes. Her stomach lurched abominably, a forcible reminder of her plight. She forced herself to sip a cup of cold water, then she washed her hands and face in the rose-patterned bowl. Everything was such an effort. Never in her life had Jeannie been ill and now she almost wanted to die. Nevertheless she dressed with care in a gown of fine green wool, trimmed with velvet ribbons. She brushed her hair, but even her curls lacked their usual bounce and lustre. Impatiently she pulled on her newest bonnet with its silk rose, then she made her way quietly down the stairs, out of the creaking old door and along the track towards the church. There was no one abroad at such an early hour and she skirted the high wall of the glebe and hurried up the track towards the Strathtod Burn. She hid behind the bushes and settled down to wait for Sandy.

Sandy was particularly impatient to get to Fairlyden. He knew Mattie would have spent every spare minute turning and returning the swathes of grass he had scythed the previous week. She would probably have piled it into heaps ready to cart, but their toil would be wasted if it rained before it was safely gathered in, and spells of dry weather rarely lasted longer than a week so near the Solway Firth.

Everything seemed to conspire against him. He had risen before four to attend to his horses, only to find that the cows had broken through the hedge and had clearly spent most of the night rampaging through the adjoining crop of corn. He needed help to gather them together ready for milking. Alf Wood was even more uncooperative than usual. The cows galloped wildly, evidently enjoying their adventure in the fresh field. Abraham Sharpe was furious and Sandy was dispatched to repair the hedge before he could attend to his own work. To make matters worse, the cows remained skittish and the women had a struggle coaxing them into the shed for milking. The youngest maid was still nervous and in the excitement she forgot to tie one of the cows in its stall. No one noticed until the woman who was milking was suddenly propelled into the gutter as the beast calmly turned around and walked out of the shed. The maid shrieked with shock, the milk spilled from her piggin, and the commotion set the rest on edge. The loose cow suddenly decided to make the most of her freedom; she took to her heels and careered round the yard, coming to a halt only when all four feet and most of her body became firmly embedded in the stinking midden.

It took Sandy and Alf Wood, as well as two other men, to heave her out with the help of two stout ropes. Before they could begin the laborious task of washing the chastened cow, Mistress Sharpe came into the yard to rage at the unfortunate women. The cow swished her tail. A trail of green, evil-smelling slime landed neatly on Mistress Sharpe's cheek and trickled slowly down the front of her gown. One of the maids tittered. Even Alf Wood began to choke with some suppressed emotion approaching laughter. Sandy, too, might have been amused, but he was impatient to finish his chores and be on his way to Fairlyden. Even so he paid the same penalty as the rest when they entered the kitchen for breakfast. Mistress Sharpe had indulged in petty revenge. Even the lumpy glutinous mixture she chose to call gruel was eaten with relish when a man had done several hours hard labour on an already empty stomach. That morning their plates were empty.

Sandy's mouth clamped in a tight line as he turned away from the spiteful triumph in Mistress Sharpe's cold eyes. She was dressed for church now and would undoubtedly expect the Lord to pardon her revenge. His stomach growled emptily as he strode across the fields towards Muircumwell village. He paused to scoop a drink of water from the burn, and hoped that Mattie would find him a crust and a lump of cheese before they started the long day's work ahead of them.

Twelve

Edward Slater had seen Jeannie leave the house early that Sunday morning and he guessed the reason. But there was no hurry. He helped Joseph Slater feed the pigs. He enjoyed an excellent breakfast and listened to Ruth Miller fretting over her daughter's absence from the table and her recent listlessness.

'Jeannie's needing tae be married,' he remarked calmly.

'She's jist a lassie!' Jeannie's mother retorted more sharply than she had intended. She tried to stifle her premonition of impending disaster. It had troubled her several times recently. The sudden improvement in Edward also troubled her. She could not understand it. Joseph was too preoccupied with his work to notice such things, she decided.

Now he was frowning. Maybe Edward is right for once, he thought. He had noticed the change in Jeannie since Sandy Logan stopped working at the mill. He knew how hard she had tried to win his attention, and had learned the reason why even his own bonnie bairn had failed to attract Sandy Logan. I wonder if he kens how the drink loosened his tongue, the nicht o' Miss Cameron's wedding? he pondered. Jeannie'll need tae be patient a while. Give Sandy time to forget. Joseph sighed. Jeannie had never waited patiently for anything.

'Jeannie's seventeen and ripe for marriage,' Edward drawled. Then, 'I want tae marry her.' Ruth's face paled. Joseph's eyes widened. His air of preoccupation had gone. He looked at Edward Slater as though seeing him for the first time. So that was why the lad was taking more care of his appearance. His work, his manner, everything had improved recently. In fact, the change had seemed too good to be true. It was amazing what love for a good woman could do but not his Jeannie! Never Jeannie

Edward could almost read his thoughts. 'Ye did tell Aunt Mary ye wad treat me as a son,' he reminded the miller slyly, but it was on Ruth he fixed his small, watchful eyes. She shuddered involuntarily. Joseph frowned and reddened. He had not found it easy to treat the unlikeable Edward as a son; the memory of his promise to his dead sister made him feel guilty - as Edward intended.

'Aye, we-ell but marriage! To Jeannie!'

'Wad make me a real son,' Edward supplied. He was enjoying the miller's discomfiture.

'I wad never make Jeannie marry against her will!' Joseph declared indignantly. Ruth gave an unconscious sigh of relief.

'Ye'll gie us your blessing though,' Edward paused deliberately, 'when Jeannie agrees tae marry me?'

'When Jeannie herself wants tae wed,' Joseph smiled, 'then of course I wad gie the lassie my blessing.' He thought fleetingly of Sandy Logan. 'And the man who wins her consent,' he added warmly.

Joseph failed to see the triumphant gleam in Edward's eye as he pushed his chair back and rose from the table, but Ruth had seen it. Her heart filled with a terrible foreboding, even before Edward halted at the door.

'I've nae doubt Jeannie will be relieved. I tried tae tell her ye'd want your ain grandbairn tae be born i' wedlock,' he lied smoothly, 'when ye're baith for the kirk an' sic like.'

Jeannie had almost given up hope of seeing Sandy. She had risen extra early to get out of the house without encountering her mother's watchful eye. She felt faint and hollow, but her stomach invariably rejected food, especially in the mornings. As the minutes ticked into an hour, and then into two, her earlier determination drained away. She had a terrible desire to lie down and die. Two huge tears gathered in her blue eyes and rolled down her cheeks.

Then suddenly she saw Sandy coming at last. He was striding up the track, only a few yards from the bushes. He looked tall and strong, but his face was set. Jeannie's heart began to hammer. Then he was level with her. Indeed, he had almost passed, he was striding so fast.

'Sandy!' Jeannie's voice was breathless and unusually nervous as she stepped on to the path just behind him. She had hastily scrubbed the tears from her cheeks and the friction had reddened them temporarily, but Sandy's steps scarcely slowed as he bid her a brief, ' 'morning, Jeannie.' After the frustrating delay at Mains of Muir, and with hunger gnawing at his stomach, his haste to reach Fairlyden was genuine.

'Sandy, I-I need to talk tae ye!' Jeannie almost wailed in desperation. He turned then, but he could not disguise his impatience. Only inherent good manners and his debt to Jeannie's parents made him pause. 'I-I'm in trouble, Sandy. I-I'

Sandy looked down at her reddened cheeks and her neat green gown with its velvet ribbons. He sighed. Jeannie loved to dramatise even the smallest crisis.

'You are looking well, whatever the great trouble, ' he retorted wryly. 'How are your parents?'

'They're in good health.' Already he was edging away. It was beyond her to blurt out the bald fact that she was expecting a child! Especially his child! 'Come with me now, please, Sandy. They would like to see you again.'

'Would they?' He raised disbelieving eyebrows and colour suffused his ruddy cheeks.' I doubt if that's true, Jeannie, after...'

'They would. Oh, I know they would!' Jeannie insisted. 'I-I have some n-news, I-I have to t-tell them. Please, Sandy, come with me.' Her voice softened. She was the same persistent Jeannie he remembered. 'You know Mama loves cooking for you.' The thought of Mistress Miller's thick creamy porridge, as well as bacon and eggs, tempted Sandy - until he remembered Mattie turning the swathes of hay, alone; feeding pigs; milking the cows; cooking and churning. Jeannie was almost a lady in comparison.

'I will call when the hay is finished. Goodbye, Jeannie.'

'No!' Jeannie tried to summon a winning smile.

'You must help me, Sandy. I'm going to...' Oh God, how could she tell him? It was clear he had no recollection of anything that had happened between them. She made a brave effort to flutter her eyelashes as she had so often done. 'I want you to marry me!' She clutched his arm.

'Stop it, Jeannie!' Sandy's face went white. Jeannie had never seen him look so grim. She saw the muscle pulsing tensely in his jaw.' I've had enough o' your play acting! I suppose your father told you I made a fool o' myself the last time I was at the mill house? Well, drunk or sober, I love her, do you hear? I love her and it isna kind, or funny, to mock your friends!' Jeannie shrank as he glared down at her. 'One day you will care for someone and...'

'Oh, Jeannie cares all right!' Edward Slater stepped on to the path from behind a grassy knoll only a few feet away. The remaining colour drained from Jeannie's face.

'You were listening!'

'Aye.' He glanced at Sandy and he could not suppress the triumph he felt as he moved between them, forcing Jeannie to meet his eyes. 'There's nae need to seek Logan's help. I told your faither about the bairn this morning. He's given us his blessing.' His voice was calm as though the question of marriage had already been accepted between them. 'Ye've only tae name the day when ye want tae marry me.'

Sandy stared from one to the other.

'I don't want to marry you,' Jeannie whispered hoarsely. Edward put an arm around her as she swayed. He had every appearance of a caring lover. Jeannie clung desperately to her senses. Slowly she pulled herself upright but her head was swimming. Edward must have known about the baby! Why was he pretending it was his? Sandy would never believe her now. Even her father must have believed Edward. She felt as though she had fallen into a long, long tunnel and everything was closing in on her. She was trapped. She had no strength; no will to fight.

'I willna marry you! I willna!' she cried hysterically.

Sandy gave her a pitying glance. Jeannie had played her little games once too often. He frowned. So she really had wanted to marry him. Jeannie looked up then. She saw the mixture of pity and contempt on his expressive face and her heart filled with black despair. The whole world became a swirl of blackness. She groped wildly towards Sandy, but it was Edward who caught her as she fainted.

When Jeannie's senses returned, Sandy had already obeyed Edward's instructions. He had no desire to upset her further with his presence. She struggled to sit up and she saw his long-legged stride carrying him rapidly towards the burn and Fairlyden - and the deaf girl. She gathered the shreds of her pride around her like a cloak. She did not need Sandy Logan's pity. If he would not marry her, he would never know the child was his. Never! She turned to Edward and her voice shook a little.

'Was my father very angry?'

Sandy never mentioned his encounter with Jeannie and Edward Slater to anyone, but his heart was filled with compassion for Joseph Miller and his wife. They had doted on their only child and Jeannie's fall from grace would be a sad blow to them, even without Edward Slater as a son.

Jeannie almost wished her father had shouted his anger from the top of the mill. Instead he was silent; his eyes looked hurt and sad and she knew he was utterly bewildered by the changes taking place in their secure little circle. Ruth Miller simply could not believe Jeannie wanted to marry Edward. She was forced to the conclusion that her wayward daughter had acted in a fit of pique because Sandy Logan had not responded to her girlish adulation. She knew in her own heart that she could never welcome Edward as a son, not in the way she would have welcomed Sandy, but even worse was the deep anxiety she felt at committing her erring child into Edward's care. Despite the shame a fatherless child would have brought to them all, Ruth Miller's instincts as a mother prompted her to influence Jeannie against marriage - or at least marriage to Edward Slater. Jeannie, still physically sick and drained of energy, and even more sick at heart, refused to discuss the sordid affair and for the first time a coolness entered their relationship.

Edward sensed Mistress Miller's disapproval. If ever she suspected the truth, he knew she would persuade her husband to go to Sandy Logan, and despite his doubts Logan might be influenced into marrying Jeannie, especially if Joseph offered him a partnership in the mill. That was the last thing Edward wanted. The mill must be his! So Ruth Miller was further dismayed when Edward asked - nay, almost demanded - to be made a partner in the mill. Jeannie, in a flash of defiance, and with a warped idea that she was spiting Sandy Logan in some way, unexpectedly added her support. Joseph had never been able to refuse Jeannie anything she wanted. He would have given his life to restore her bright smile and make her happy again. So Edward Slater became a partner at the mill.

At Fairlyden Mattie knew nothing of the upheavals at the Mill, or the part she and Sandy had unwittingly played in Jeannie's destiny.

Throughout the summer her small supply of butter had been in demand. Mr Jardine had soon discovered it kept sweet, even in the hottest weather, while that from some farms was rancid almost before it reached his store. The money enabled Mattie to add to her meagre store cupboard. She bought sugar and she scoured the hedgerows for wild raspberries, brambles, bilberries and nuts, and filled her shelves with jams and jellies and winter cordials, herbal remedies and vegetables from the garden. When the cows went dry, and the hens stopped laying, as she had known they would with the approach of winter, a small taste of summer's bounty brightened their simple diet of vegetable broth, potatoes, porridge, barley bannock and oatcakes.

Towards the end of her first winter at Fairlyden, in the year eighteen hundred and fifty eight, Mattie feared the threatening snowstorm would block the way to Muircumwell. She braved the keening wind and led Darkie over the iron-hard earth, down to the mill for a stock of meal and flour. She felt chilled to her bones by the time she reached the village. Edward Slater seized the opportunity to show her his daughter. He flung open the door of the mill house with an air of triumph.

'You must be very proud of her,' Mattie said with a smile, but as soon as she stepped over the threshold she sensed tension in the atmosphere. Jeannie was feeding the three-week-old baby. She glared sullenly at her husband, making no effort to hide her resentment at the intrusion. Marriage to Edward had proved worse than anything she could have envisaged. She had survived the birth of her child reluctantly. Now the nightmare would continue, and it was all due to this simple deaf girl!

'I will load up the cairt while ye warm yersel',' Edward announced and went out, closing the door firmly behind him. Mattie stood uncertainly, looking down at Jeannie's bowed head, but her attention was drawn to the tiny babe in her arms.

'She's beautiful!' she breathed in genuine delight. Jeannie glanced up then and saw the tenderness on Mattie's face, the unconsciously wistful smile. Jeannie's bitter heart softened a little. At least I have Sandy's bairn, she thought with a brief sense of pleasure.

'Here, wad ye like to hold her?' She stood up and placed the baby gently in Mattie's eager arms. Jeannie eyed Mattie curiously. How can she take so much pleasure in another woman's bairn? she wondered. Would she look at her wi' sic kindliness if she kenned Alexander Logan was her father?

'I'll ladle ye a bowl o' hot soup,' she offered, extending a rare hand of friendship, only to withdraw it the moment Edward put his head round the door.

A month later, at a quiet ceremony in the front parlour of the millhouse, the baby was christened Beatrice Victoria Alexandra Slater.

So a year had passed since Mattie and Sandy left Nethertannoch. Once more spring brought new life, and fresh hopes. Daniel Munro knew he owed his survival to Mattie's care. She had struggled to eke out their meagre supplies in those last long weeks of winter; she had done her best to keep him warm, to hold the crippling rheumatism at bay. Left alone in the grip of pain, he knew he would have been tempted to seek oblivion with the aid of the laudanum - but he was not ready to die yet.

Mattie could not hear the birds singing but she had seen the blackbirds building their nest in the garden hedge; the swallows had returned to their little mud caves in the eaves of the stable and spent the days gliding and swooping in and out of the half door. A cock pheasant strutted proudly beside the little wood, showing off the beauty of his iridescent plumage. Whins clothed every bank and gully in a blaze of pure gold, and beneath the trees bluebells scented the morning air. Mattie was young and healthy and spring was all around her, bursting with new life and new energy after the winter's rest. When she saw Jeannie in the millyard, with her baby bundled in her shawl, she gazed at the soft, rose petal cheeks and wide, wondering blue eyes and tried to stifle the sudden yearning which filled her heart. Jeannie displayed her baby with an odd reluctance which Mattie could not understand, for the child was beautiful. Her tiny, perfect head was covered with reddish-gold down, and with her fair skin, she bore no resemblance to the broad-featured, swarthy Edward.

The pullets which Mattie had reared herself had begun to lay. It was a relief to be able to milk and churn again, to have produce to sell, to be a little independent.

Darkie was showing definite signs of producing another foal, and this time her condition was excellent. Mattie felt it was a time for thanksgiving. God, in his mercy, had given them health and strength and fine weather to carry out their tasks. It was time to seek His forgiveness. They had used the Sabbath days for their own work instead of His. Sandy accompanied her to the Reverend Mackenzie's little church once more.

Mattie had set aside her mourning; she looked truly beautiful in the green and lemon silk dress she had made from one of Sarah Munro's gowns and Daniel guessed she would set a few tongues wagging with Sandy Logan escorting her to the church. They made a handsome couple and the sight of them together gave him a certain satisfaction. He was quite familiar with malicious gossip himself and Mattie would not hear it. If she felt the need for spiritual sustenance, then she should have it.

Sandy was less prepared. Doubting Thomas though he was, he could scarcely believe the malicious words being uttered within the shadow of the kirk, and so soon after joining the minister in his earnest prayers for the forgiveness of sins.

' Her husband is a cripple. She only married him for his money!'

'They say Mr Munro hasna any money '

'Ach, he has some of the best land in the county! The old Earl saw to that. Munro was his mother's name. He's a...' The harsh whine was lowered, then raised almost immediately. 'Now she's lusting after a navvy!'

'Och, Mistress Sharpe! Yon laddie's no' a navvy! Why, Mr Miller says...'

'He's a common labourer! Now I know why he hurries from the Mains at the crack of dawn every Sunday.'

Sandy bent his head, looking intently into Mattie's face.

'I wish to speak to someone,' he mouthed silently, 'I will catch up with you.' Mattie smiled up at him serenely, nodding her bright head. The ribbons on her hat bobbed merrily and Sandy was thankful she could not hear Mistress Sharpe's venomous tongue. His own face burned with anger as he lifted his head and encountered her baleful stare fixed upon him. His blue eyes glittered dangerously and the peace and gratitude which had entered his own heart during the minister's inspired sermon evaporated. Mistress Sharpe's companion moved hastily away as he covered the ground between them in two purposeful strides.

'I'll thank you, ma'am, to keep a civil tongue when you speak of Mistress Munro!' Florence Sharpe's eyes popped like colourless glass marbles. She drew up her narrow chest, and her hooked nose curled even more than usual; she glared furiously at Sandy.

'Why, you impudent lout! Civil tongue indeed! How dare you speak to me like that? Have you forgotten I am your employer?'

'You are not my employer, madam! Your husband is.' The next words seemed to spring involuntarily from Sandy's lips. 'But not for much longer.'

For a moment Mistress Sharpe was torn between anger and envy as she encountered Sandy's steady gaze, as blue as the summer sky. But his eyes were filled with contempt for her. She gave him her fiercest glare but his gaze did not waver and she flounced away with such speed that she almost collided with Joseph Miller.

'Weel now, and what has ruffled Florrie Sharpe's old feathers?' he exclaimed, staring in surprise at the gaunt retreating figure.

'I did,' Sandy answered grimly. The miller blinked.

'Och, no! Abraham Sharpe was only telling me a few minutes ago that he hoped ye wadna' be going tae the hiring at the end o' the month. If ye stick wi' him he'll make ye a better offer, mark my words. But Ye'll need tae be begging Mistress Sharpe's pardon.' Sandy snorted, but Joseph went on, 'Abraham thinks the Mains is big enough for a grieve! It's you he has in mind, Sandy. Now that wad please Her Ladyship! Only the lairds have a grieve in this airt.'

Sandy shook his head. 'Mr Sharpe maybe wears the breeches at the Mains but his wife makes the decisions. She has never forgiven me for depriving her of a cheap slave, especially after Mr Jardine told her Mattie made the best butter in the parish. Besides,' he grimaced, 'she was casting evil aspersions. I told her to keep a civil tongue.'

'Ye did what?' The miller stared at Sandy aghast. 'Eh, laddie, news travels fast - and far! Mistress Sharpe will make a bad enemy, mark my words. Ye'll no' get anither place, even at the hirings, if ye leave the Mains in disgrace. Surely ye can mak yer peace? There she is, getting into the Mains trap. Dinna waste time.' But Sandy was looking beyond the trap to Mattie's solitary figure, already beyond the groups of chattering people.

'No, I've had enough o' Mistress Sharpe.' He frowned and looked thoughtfully at his old friend. 'Daniel Munro was remarking only this morning that there is too much work for Mattie but it'll be a long time before there's money to spare tae hire a man at Fairlyden. I have my year's wages and I wad have some satisfaction for my labours. There wad certainly be more to eat at Mattie's table,' he added darkly. Even as he was speaking, his mind was made up. He bid Joseph a hasty farewell and hurried after Mattie.

He had been wary of accepting Daniel Munro's suggestion earlier - although in his heart he knew it was what he wanted; it was the feelings in his heart which troubled him. Daniel was right though, there was too much work for Mattie on her own and who better to help her than himself? He still had four of Captain Charles Irving's five guineas, and with his wages from the Mains, they could buy more cows.

When Mattie went to bring the cows from the meadow for the afternoon milking she saw a tall slim figure bending over Constance's prostrate form. The cow was writhing in agony. Mattie ran back to the house for Sandy but by the time they reached the meadow again Rory O'Connor had already given assistance and was hurrying home across the burn. Constance had given birth to a large blue-roan bull calf. It was alive, but only just, and they both knew it was thanks to the red-haired youth. Sandy bent closer, massaging its wet sides with rough circling movements, willing it to breathe. Suddenly the calf seemed to make up his mind. He lifted his head, looked around, then lolled back on to the soft grass, gathering strength to sit himself up properly.

'He'll do,' Sandy murmured with a final pat, but Mattie's concern was for Constance. She lay quiet, stretched unnaturally flat, her nostrils flaring, her breathing laboured. She was no longer young and the fine bull calf had taken its toll. Mattie had grown fond of the docile, ugly animal and it saddened her to realise that Constance had reached the end of her particular road; never again would she amble through the meadows.

The meal that evening was a sombre affair and Daniel knew that Mattie was anxious as well as sad. Constance's death would deal a severe blow to Fairlyden's fragile economy, and more so since the heifer, which the Reverend Mackenzie had bought with Daniel's remaining savings, had proved a failure. Mattie wondered how she would ever buy enough coal and provisions for the winter when there would be so little butter to sell.

While she washed the dishes from their meal, in the little scullery which connected the kitchen and the dairy, Sandy told Daniel Munro of his confrontation with Mistress Sharpe.

'I shall leave the Mains in two weeks' time. So 1 have considered your suggestion. I shall work at Fairlyden - but only on one condition.' Daniel's dark brows rose expectantly but he hid his secret jubilation. 'I shall use the money I have earned at the Mains to buy cows,' Sandy declared.

'No! I cannot allow it.'

'Can ye afford to refuse, especially without Constance? I can see her death has troubled Mattie. Anyway, I have my ain pride,' Sandy added quietly. 'You hae the land and a house - a home which any man wad be proud to live in now.' He gave a wry smile as he looked around the cosy room with its gleaming furniture and the firelight flickering on the white walls. Mattie's mother's blue bowl sat on the shining dresser. It was certainly different from the night they had arrived at Fairlyden. He looked up to find Daniel Munro's dark eyes fixed upon him.

'I will work at Fairlyden, but I need freedom to breed my horses and to sell them as I please; the extra cows will be needed to keep us all in food and clothes.'

To Sandy's relief, Daniel's dark face split into a wry grin.

'You would never make a "common labourer" -for Mistress Sharpe or anyone else, Alexander Logan. You have too much pride and too many ambitions. So be it. Welcome to Fairlyden - and its poverty.' He held out a gnarled and twisted hand and Sandy took it in both of his.

Mattie could scarcely believe that Sandy would soon be living and working at Fairlyden every day. She tried to control the pulses which sent the blood coursing around her body at twice its normal rate. Their separation during his time at Mains of Muir had made her even more aware of him, and not only as her dearest companion. It was an effort to turn her mind to more practical things. Her eyes glowed as though a lamp had been lit behind the delicate bones of her skull. Even her skin seemed to take on a rosy, translucent sheen, but it was her mouth, so soft and full, which held Sandy's gaze, her lower lip caught by two pearly white teeth. He could not look away.

Daniel watched with satisfaction.

Thirteen

Sandy and Mattie moved slowly over the field, no more than a yard or so of brown earth and sprouting plants between them. Their heads were bent, intent on the task of hoeing the turnips. The sky was a uniform bluish-grey. The distant peak of Criffel, their guide to the weather, remained clear of mist, but not clear enough to reassure them that the fine weather would last. Although they had hoed laboriously from dawn until dusk for a week, they were only halfway across the field.

One morning when the sun was almost overhead, Mattie looked up to see a child's figure alternately stumbling and trotting over the field towards them.

'Me name's Sean O'Leary, an' it's ten years I am, an' 'twas the Minister himself sent me,' he panted breathlessly, even before he reached them. Suddenly he remembered his mammy's training and swept off his huge cloth cap to reveal strands of straight black hair brushed roughly across his narrow scalp. His tentative grin revealed a gap where one of his front teeth had been knocked out a month ago when he had attempted to defend the reputation of his elder sister. His eyes looked east and west, or darted together towards the end of his nose - or at least Mattie thought it was in that direction. Since she could hear nothing of his explanations she studied him carefully while waiting for Sandy to explain the little urchin's presence; she wondered how he had arrived at Fairlyden alone. His coarse breeches were baggy, roughly improvised from a pair several sizes larger. His waistcoat was crudely patched and his shirt stained and torn. Behind the bright, birdlike eyes Mattie detected anxiety. The boy was painfully thin. Indeed his stomach was almost a hollow hidden by the ballooning trousers. The soles of his boots were worn through and parting company with the uppers.

The boy says the Reverend Mackenzie has sent him,' Sandy explained with a thoughtful frown. 'He wants work at the hoeing.'

Mattie turned her fine dark eyes on the boy in surprise. He gave her an expectant, almost pleading, smile. She sighed.

'We have no money to pay.' She doubted if such a small fellow would be capable of earning any either. He was desperately thin. She sighed again. 'Would you like to share our oatcakes and cheese?' she asked kindly. The boy nodded vigorously. Deafness was no barrier when a fellow was as hungry as Sean.

He wolfed the food down as Mattie had suspected he might and he accepted the bottle of buttermilk as if she had offered him the finest wine. Her heart went out to the half-starved waif and she looked inquiringly at Sandy.

'He says he came over from Ireland with his father. They walked from Stranraer, taking work along the way. His father is hoeing turnips at the Mains.' Sandy grimaced. 'He says the boss woman there thinks he is too small to earn his food.' Mattie looked at the boy and saw desperation in his one straight eye before he blinked and looked hastily away.

'Tell her, Mister, tell her that I came with Dada last year, to Liverpool. Tell her I worked for me food.' He turned to Mattie himself, jabbing his bony chest with a small finger. 'Sean - will - not - eat - much,' he shouted.

'Dinna shout, laddie!' Sandy exclaimed. 'Just speak slowly and clearly, and look at Mistress Munro.'

The boy nodded.

'The minister - he said you would be letting me sleep in the stable? I work hard.' Suddenly he fell to his hands and knees and started weeding and thinning the turnips, his small neat hands moving with surprising speed. Sandy and Mattie stared at him in amazement. He worked quickly, but he was careful, selecting the strongest plants with unerring accuracy. There was nothing wrong with his sight despite his squint.

'Where did you learn to single turnips like that, laddie?' Sandy asked him.

'From the Lancashire women - last year.' Sean did not halt.

Mattie and Sandy took up their hoes and proceeded with their own rows and the boy did not fall behind, or tire, as they had expected.

In return for a bed in the hay loft and food enough to satisfy a full grown man, Sean O'Leary stayed at Fairlyden until the hoeing was finished at Mains of Muir and his father was forced to move on to look for more work. Fortunately the hoeing at Fairlyden was already finished. A day and a half of gentle rain had provided a brief respite before the sky turned a brazen blue and Sandy started on the hay. He scythed the first field and moved on to the next, leaving Mattie to turn and re-turn the swathes as they dried. Sean was her constant shadow and willing helper.

She was almost as sad as Sean himself when his father called to take him away. She tactfully turned aside as he wiped away a tear. At least his clothes were clean and patched and his pockets filled with food. They had learned that he had two younger sisters back home in Ireland as well as an elder sister, Kate, who had been forced to stay at home to look after their mammy. It was clear that the boy loved his mother dearly, but he knew the coughing disease would have sent her to heaven by the time he and his father returned to Ireland at the end of the summer. Mattie wished passionately that they could have helped him more and bid him return if ever he passed that way again. It would have made her heart glad to hear the tales Sean told his sisters about Fairlyden and its kindly folk.

Although Sandy had bought two cows with the money he had earned at the Mains, they did little more than replace Constance and the minister's heifer. He knew more animals were needed for Fairlyden's acres if it was ever to regain its former prosperity. During his work at the mill he had heard there was a demand for good quality hay from the railway companies who needed it to feed cattle at the stations during long journeys to the English markets. Fairlyden had a plentiful supply of grass and he determined to make the most of it for as long as the fine weather lasted. He felt nothing was impossible when he had health and strength, land to work - and Mattie at his side.

Whenever Mattie was not attending to the needs of her husband, or milking, churning, feeding the pigs and hens, she helped Sandy in the fields. So they went on, day after day - scything, turning, shaking out and turning again, heaping and carting -until the sun gilded the distant hills with molten gold, and the evening sky became a vast tapestry of crimson and purple, light and shadow, before the day faded into night and the last streak of light clung lovingly to the far horizon.

Eventually Sandy took his scythe to the Hillanfit field - the most distant, and the most neglected, of the fields on Fairlyden. Even before they started Mattie realised this would be the hardest work of all. She thought how hard her father had toiled to improve Nethertannoch and she knew he would have approved of Sandy's plans to improve Fairlyden. Matthew had considered it a sin to neglect any gift from the Almighty - the soil, the sun, the sea were some of God's greatest gifts, second only to the gift of life.

So they worked on despite the energy-sapping heat and the dust. Each morning, almost before the dawn lit the sky and the birdsong heralded another new day, Sandy would set off for the fields. Before she joined him Mattie had to milk the cows, taking even greater care than usual. When the weather was hot and the air so heavy she knew it needed no more than a few flies, a straw, or a splash of dung in the pail, to turn the milk sour within a few hours. She did not know why this should be, she simply knew it was vital to keep her dairy clean and cool if she was to continue selling her butter to Mr Jardine's store. When evening came she was almost too tired to drag her weary limbs to bed. Both Sandy and Daniel expressed concern but Mattie knew the good weather could not last much longer and they must make the most of it.

'You should bathe in the pool in the high pasture,' Daniel said one evening, seeing the weary droop of her shoulders, and the dark smudges of fatigue beneath her wide brown eyes.

Mattie stared at him in surprise, wondering if she had understood correctly. She had read of gentlemen taking their wives and their servants for holidays at the seaside, but the ladies had their own special beach, and bathing waggons, and special bathing dresses. Daniel smiled indulgently at her shocked face but his dark eyes took on a dreamy, wistful look which held Mattie's attention and tugged curiously at her tender heart.

'I bathed there often in summertime where the burn flows into a deep pool, beneath the willow tree. It was so cool, like purest silk. It was a wonderful feeling, my dear. Surely Sandy bathes there?'

Mattie nodded, but she turned hastily aside to conceal the rush of blood which stained her pale skin, right down below the neck of her dress. Only yesterday evening she had seen Sandy's broad bare back sparkling with water as he stood in the pool. She had watched enviously, from a discreet distance of course, as he plunged his whole body beneath the clear water. She had seen him stand up and shake his cinnamon-coloured head like a shaggy dog; and plunge again in an ecstasy of delight. Oh, yes, she had wanted to plunge into the cool, clear water.

'Bathe your feet there, at least,' Daniel suggested. Mattie opened her mouth to voice her doubts but Daniel shook his head. 'Fairlyden is isolated from the world.'

The following day was hotter than ever. Mattie dragged her weary, sweating limbs back to the hay field after she had finished the evening milking. She worked doggedly, no more than a few yards behind Sandy, determined to finish raking the thick swaths of grass into rows of little haycocks. All that day the air had been still and heavy. Sandy listened as God raced his chariots with increasing frequency and the ceiling of the world seemed to get lower and lower with each ominous rumble of His mighty wheels. So far He had smiled on Fairlyden and its two lone labourers; the thunder showers had fallen all around the Solway Firth, but not on Fairlyden's high pasture. A thunderstorm now, however brief, would waste so much effort, especially if the hay was left lying flat upon the ground. So they worked on, pushing their bodies to the utmost limit of physical endurance.

Mattie could feel the sweat trickling through the dust in little rivulets, down her neck and between her breasts. Her head was hot despite the protection of her straw bonnet and the white muslin kerchief which protected the back of her neck. Even her thighs were sticky. One by one she had cast off her petticoats in desperation, but the thick calico of her long skirt and the wide harding apron still enveloped her in a bath of prickling, stabbing heat, dragging at her limbs, sapping her energy.

At last only the outer swath of the field remained. It had been shaded by the high, overgrown hedge, and the powerful rays of the sun had not penetrated the lower layers of grass. Mattie was sorely tempted to leave it overnight. The scent of newly mown hay mingled with the heady perfume of honeysuckle and wild roses winding through the thorn bushes. It hung on the evening air, and she lifted her head, breathing deeply, inhaling it into the depths of her soul. It had a soporific effect and when Sandy came and turned her face to his he saw that her dark eyes were soft and dreamy, her lips softly parted. He caught his breath sharply. He knew she was bone weary. He had seen it in her dragging footsteps and the slowing rhythm of her arms.

'Rest now. I will finish the last row.' His voice was sharp with sudden tension. Mattie was not aware of that, any more than she was aware of the effects of her wide, dreamy eyes, or her body, swaying with fatigue. Sandy clenched his jaw. The heat and sweat seemed to emphasise her womanly scents. They were not repulsive. Rather they aroused an animal desire which filled his own body with hot, coursing blood. He gripped her shoulders so fiercely that she winced.

'Rest. Sit by the burn. I will finish.' He spun her away from him abruptly and she moved obediently, like a sleepwalker.

The grass was soft and short and tinder dry. Mattie stretched her weary limbs gratefully and for ten whole minutes lay still, emptying her mind completely, allowing the waves of heat to wash over her. Gradually she realised that the storm was moving away; no more flashes lit the sky. The rain had not come after all. She sat up and scanned the field. Sandy had reached the far side; he was still working rhythmically. Mattie turned and gazed down into the burn. She remembered how she and Sandy had paddled at Nethertannoch when they were children. Her mouth curved upwards in a reminiscent smile.

'Bathe your feet,' Mr Munro had said. 'It is like silk '

Mattie glanced around almost guiltily. A little brown bird perched on a twig just above her head. He cocked his head at her and she imagined one bright eye winked conspiratorially.

'All right, Mr Sparrow,' she grinned, 'the temptation is too great to resist.'

It did not take Mattie long to unlace her boots and peel off her woollen stockings. Even that small freedom gave her a feeling of pleasure. She curled her toes in the grass. Then she was scrambling eagerly to her feet, clambering into the shallow burn, bunching her skirt in her hands. The clear running water was heavenly on her hot skin. Soon it was not enough and she bunched her skirts higher and rolled up the frilly bottoms of her drawers. Almost unconsciously she followed the burn downstream, gasping when unexpected hollows made her stumble and sent the water spraying up her legs, even damping her clothes. She did not care. She felt like a child again, free and unfettered by conventions, a little reckless even.

The water was so beautifully cool. She clutched her wide skirt in one hand so that she could scoop up the sparkling water with her other. She splashed it over her hot face, over her neck, patting her temples and the tendrils of hair which curled free of their thick coil. Her hat came loose and she lifted it from her head and tossed it carelessly on to the grassy bank. A few yards ahead the burn widened and it was here that the willow tree dipped its graceful branches low into the water, making a green tunnel, cool and inviting. Mattie moved towards it carefully, not consciously intending to do more than take a closer look. She was unprepared for the sudden slope of the polished pebbles beneath her feet. Her arms flew out instinctively in an effort to regain her balance and her skirt and apron escaped from her fingers and ballooned out over the water, then slowly sank, sodden and heavy around her legs. Mattie stared down at her clothes in dismay.

The sides of the burn were higher and steeper here and the weight of yards of wet material hampered her a little, but she scrambled up on to the bank. She reviewed her bedraggled garments ruefully, thankful there was no one around to witness her predicament as she tried to wring out the folds of material. Sandy was still at the bottom end of the field where the crop of hay was thickest.

Impulsively Mattie unfastened the sodden dress and apron and pulled them off, then she knelt on the grass and methodically squeezed the water from the dripping skirt a little at a time. When she had finished she shook it hard, glanced down the field to check on Sandy's progress, then hung it over a branch of the willow tree. She felt wonderfully free and cool, clad only in her drawers and chemise. Having no mother either to guide or upbraid her, Mattie had never worn the restricting, tightly laced corset favoured by the ladies of fashion, who rarely did anything more energetic than lift a needle of silk thread.

She looked longingly at the cool green tunnel beneath the willow tree and the water that no longer rushed and chattered over the pebbles. It was calm and clear and, oh, so tempting. Mattie slid gracefully over the bank into the water. She had known it would be cool and deep. She had not known it would feel so wonderful. Her weary, aching limbs felt weightless. The water lapped gently almost to her neck. She had only to bend a little and it would wash away the sweat and grime from the tips of her toes to the crown of her head. Swiftly she released the thick braids of her hair. She gasped with shock and delight the first time the water closed over her head. Her hair floated out behind her like a fan of brown silk.

Mattie lost track of time until Sandy's hand touched her shoulder. She was so startled she slipped and lost her balance. Sandy reached out to help her. He was unprepared for the gasping, laughing face which surfaced so close to his own. Mattie was beautiful! Truly beautiful. Her hair was like a dark cloud on the surface of the water and her creamy skin was soft and flawless. He felt his breath coming faster and faster as he stared down at her. The thin muslin of her chemise was almost transparent in the water, and the rosy peaks of her young breasts were clearly visible. Time seemed to stand still.

It was no more than the blink of an eyelid, yet it was enough to change their world. All the wisdom and the power of all the generations of women that had ever lived, became Mattie's in that fleeting moment when she looked into Sandy's eyes and saw his love for her shining there, naked and undisguised.

'Love me! Ah, love me, Sandy!' She had no idea whether she breathed the words aloud. She only knew they came from the depths of her soul - and Sandy understood.

'You dinna' ken what ye're asking!' he moaned softly, as her arms fastened around him with a strength which belied the delicate, bird-like structure of her bones. The thin layer of material which lay between them could not hide the heat of their trembling bodies.

'Love me!' Mattie's hands moved with an instinct as old as time - over his broad back, over his chest, his neck. She could feel the rapid beating of his heart against her cheek. The warmth and strength of his arms around her naked shoulders seemed to light a furnace within her, and its fire spread so swiftly and so fiercely that it left no room for thought. She had no recollection of the marriage vows she had made to Mr Munro, or the teachings on which her life thus far had been based. It swept her along like a rushing tide and Sandy had neither the will nor the desire to resist.

Between the broad trunk of the ancient willow and the burn there was a shelf of earth, held there despite the onslaughts of winter floods by the roots of the great tree. When the snows melted and the burn was in spate the shelf of land became no more than a mud-flat, but now it was covered in soft moss and grass. Above it the willow branches arched like the roof of a cathedral. It was on to this grassy bed that Sandy lifted Mattie with all the gentleness of a mother handling her newborn infant. It was here, beneath the green branches of the willow tree, with the music of the burn and the song of birds, with the air redolent of the scent of flowers, that Mattie and Sandy discovered heaven on earth.

Sandy had learned to respect Mattie long ago, as a child battling courageously to come to terms with her affliction. He had admired her loyalty and intelligence as his friend and companion. Now he loved her as a woman - a desirable woman to be cherished. He treated her gently, reverently; he would not take her ruthlessly as in his drunken dreams - and Mattie's response rewarded him a thousandfold. His heart swelled triumphantly as the truth dawned. Mattie was his - only his! His dream had come true. No wonder Reevil had continued his search for her. He had had no part of her; he had whipped her most cruelly - but he had not possessed her.

Slowly Sandy became aware of what he had done. He had taken another man's wife. He had committed adultery. He was swamped with guilt. But Mattie was not a real wife. Daniel Munro needed only her care, her comfort in his last painful months of life. They would care for him - and for Fairlyden - as long as he needed them. So Sandy soothed his troubled conscience, and loved Mattie again. They must be together always. He could never bear to part from her now that she was truly his.

Fourteen

On the twelfth of May, eighteen hundred and fifty-nine Mistress Munro of Fairlyden gave birth to a daughter.

Throughout the preceding months Mattie had remained remarkably healthy in every way; she had been carried along on a tide of undeniable joy, despite the niggling awareness that her baby had been conceived in sin. Her qualms of conscience had been overcome by an inexplicable buoyancy, but she still blushed with shame and shied away from the subject when Daniel tried to talk to her.

'Ah, Buff, your mistress does not realise the joy she has given me,' Daniel murmured whimsically. Mattie's little dog cocked her head on one side as though she understood every word. 'She would not believe what pleasure it brings, to see her body swelling with new life, to witness the brightness of her beautiful brown eyes.' Even when his pain was at its worst Daniel had resisted the temptation of Doctor Baird's laudanum. When the doctor himself made one of his infrequent visits he had been puzzled, disconcerted even, to find him in such lively spirits.

During the bleak winter weather Mattie had done her best to bring relief to his swollen joints with her herbal infusions and poultices, and had cooked nourishing soups with the vegetables she had grown in the garden. Buff had made her contribution as a rabbit catcher, or so Mattie fondly believed. Nothing was too much trouble. Daniel knew it did not occur to Mattie to leave him to suffer - and maybe to die - so that she could marry Sandy. He was grateful for her loyalty and affection, and humbled by it.

Barely six hours before the birth of her daughter, Mattie had been milking their four cows, stoically ignoring a nagging and most persistent backache. The birth was relatively swift and uncomplicated and when she gazed at the fuzz of dark hair which covered her baby's tiny, perfect head her heart swelled with pride.

She longed to show Sandy his daughter. Already Mattie fondly imagined that her wandering eyes held all the wisdom of the world as she thrust aside distracting fingers and eagerly sought succour from her mother's breast. The rose petal cheeks, so fair and delicately painted, reminded Mattie of Sandy's mother, and indeed of Sandy himself when she had first seen him, a thirteen-year-old boy with a skin still smooth and soft as fine silk, a sprinkling of freckles across his nose. Then, unaccountably, the bubbling fountain of joy and optimism which had sustained her throughout her pregnancy suddenly drained away with the birth of her infant daughter. In its place a pool of darkness began to grow and spread; a weight of despondency cast her down, filling her heart with dread. How could a baby, made in sin, be blessed with happiness, or with the health and strength to survive the terrible fevers, the sicknesses and coughing diseases which afflicted so many children? She had been selfish; she had indulged the physical yearnings of her body. She had broken the Lord's commandment; she had sinned grievously, not once but many times during the rapturous months when she and Sandy had discovered their great and wonderful love for each other. So Mattie's tormented spirit gave her no peace to rest. She felt an urgent need to see Mr Munro; to look into his deep dark eyes when they rested on her child - and Sandy's. She ignored the warnings of Mistress Clements, the dour, silent woman whom the Reverend Mackenzie had sent to help her during her confinement.

'Sandy! Come here! Quickly, man!' Daniel shouted in dismay. He was alarmed by the tension and anxiety on Mattie's pale face when she entered the kitchen carrying her baby in her arms only four days after the birth. Sandy rushed from the dairy where he was clumsily skimming the creaming pans. He drew to a halt, gazing in sudden awe at Mattie and the tightly swathed bundle clutched in her arms. She moved towards them uncertainly and gently eased the shawl from the baby's face.

Daniel had been disappointed when he learned that Mattie had given birth to a daughter. Now, as he looked upon the perfect oval face with its tiny rosebud mouth earnestly sucking a dimpled fist, his heart filled with emotion - and a strange pride. Tiny fans of thick, dark lashes lifted and he found himself staring into eyes which could so easily have been the reflection of his own. He sucked in his breath, almost ashamed of the delight and tenderness which filled his heart. He raised his brilliant dark eyes to Mattie's strained face.

'Sarah Munro - my daughter.' He smiled. 'Thank you, my dear, thank you.'

Mattie's heart surged with relief, but as she straightened up her eyes met Sandy's. She saw the shock, witnessed his pain, such pain that it smote her to the very depths of her soul. Here then was the price of sin.

Like Eve she had tempted Sandy with forbidden fruit. The child in her arms was made with his seed; given with all his heart, all his love - but Sandy would never call the child his own, or give her his name, or hear her call him Father.

'Her name will be Sarah Mary Munro,' Mattie amended more harshly than she knew.

Sandy's eyes flickered briefly. Mary had been his mother's name. His face remained stiff. Daniel Munro's words echoed with icy clarity in his brain. 'Any child born to my wife, within nine months of my death must bear my name.' How could he have for-gotten?

Mattie watched him with pain in her own heart. He swallowed convulsively, several times.

'You have a beautiful baby.' Only Daniel heard the bitterness in his voice but Mattie saw it in his eyes before he turned abruptly and strode from the kitchen. Her shoulders sagged.

During the weeks which followed nothing could dispel the depression which settled on Mattie. In the news sheet she had read about a Mr Darwin who had shocked the world with his belief that all men were descended from apes, and not made by God as it was written in the bible. Mattie almost wished she too could believe such theories, but she could not forget the teachings of the bible and the strict beliefs of her beloved father. She had broken her marriage vows, she had sinned against God and against man; she had brought unhappiness to Sandy. Would the Lord, in his vengeance, take away her child? Her beautiful child? Already Mattie loved Sarah with a fierce possessiveness. She was almost jealous of her husband who had so much time to watch over her, to rock the cradle at the slightest sound. In fact Sarah was a contented baby; it was Mattie who grew thin and pale and developed dark shadows beneath her eyes and a sharpness to her tongue.

Daniel was concerned. When Doctor Baird made another unexpected visit he temporarily set aside his suspicion of everyone connected with Strathtod - the glen of the fox, the home of his half-brother. He mentioned Mattie's unusually low spirits and his anxiety.

'Some women are beset with illness of the mind after the birth of a child. Nothing can be done,' Doctor Baird pronounced discouragingly. A moment later he remarked slyly, 'Perhaps there is something troubling

Mistress Munro? Something about the child? If I might look at your daughter ?' He bent to the cradle.

Doctor Baird had observed Daniel Munro's progress with surprise. The Earl had not been pleased by his reports, but the rumour that his half-brother had sired a child had almost driven him wild. Now the doctor peered suspiciously into the crib, only to stare into a pair of eyes as dark as Daniel Munro's own, eyes which he imagined bore a surprising resemblance to the youngest of the Earl's own sons, the eleven-year-old William Fairly. The infant sensed the doctor's scrutiny, and his hostility. She opened her mouth wide and exercised her lungs accordingly. Doctor Baird seized his bag.

'I have just the thing to quieten such noise!' He drew out a small bottle.

'The child requires nothing from you!' Daniel exclaimed in alarm. Laudanum appeared to be the physician's remedy for everything, he realised contemptuously. 'You disturbed her!'

'Then I shall make her sleep peacefully again -very peacefully.' Doctor Baird removed the glass stopper.

Sarah's first protesting yell had sent Buff shooting through the door to the scullery, and into the dairy beyond. Mattie had just finished churning the butter. When Buff's cold wet nose pushed urgently at her hand she knew something was wrong. Buff never entered the dairy. She hurried through to the kitchen.

'What are you doing?' She darted towards the whey -faced doctor, but he turned his back on her, still clutching the wailing infant.

'Give me my baby! You're hurting her!'

'Hysterics! A sure sign of an unhinged mind!' he declared triumphantly. 'The child should be removed from your wife's care without delay.'

'What does he say?' Mattie demanded in frustration. 'What is he doing with my baby?' Her eyes darted wildly, but Daniel was struggling to rise, to snatch the lethal bottle from the doctor's hand. His face was white with pain, and anger, and an awful fear. Mattie saw it. Her sharp eyes darted to the bottle. Instinctively she knocked it from the doctor's hand as he held it to Sarah's gaping mouth. Only then did she realise his intention. She knew well the effects of excess opium. Her father had welcomed the oblivion it brought, but only at the end. Taken by surprise

149

Doctor Baird turned on her furiously, but Mattie cared nothing for his anger. She snatched her struggling infant from his grasp.

'Do not touch my child with your medicine!' She spat the words with all the fury of a she-cat guarding her kitten. She saw the man's lips move in reply but Daniel had sunk back on to his chair and there was a look of intense relief on his damp, grey face. Mattie knew then that the doctor was no friend, either to them or to Sarah. She looked fearfully into her daughter's tiny crumpled face, still puce with angry indignation, then back at the stranger.

'Go! We do not want you here.' Again the man's lips moved, but Mattie did not even try to understand.

'If you do not go, I shall ask Sandy to whip you!' Whipping was the worst punishment she could think of since her ordeal with Jacob Reevil. Apparently the doctor did not relish the prospect either. He fastened his bag hastily and moved to the door.

'Do not return to Fairlyden again, Doctor!' Daniel Munro commanded coldly, relieved to feel his heart regaining a more normal rhythm. 'If anything happens to my daughter, you will hang!'

'Hang?' The doctor's face blanched.

'You were sent to spy. And I believe you were tempted to murder, Doctor!' Jeremiah Baird shuddered beneath Daniel's contempt. 'Now I understand the reason for your visits, and your uncommon generosity with the laudanum. Be gone!'

Daniel already loved the tiny, wise-eyed infant, and plans for her entertainment and her future absorbed his thoughts. The more attention he gave the child, the more desolate Sandy became. Mattie was increasingly conscious of his despair. She blamed herself entirely. There was a wretchedness in her dark eyes and in the droop of her hitherto smiling mouth. She began to avoid Sandy's company, hoping he might forget the joy of their illicit love - though she knew she could never forget.

When the Reverend Mackenzie called to discuss Sarah's baptism, Daniel voiced his anxiety for Mattie.

'It seems common for some mothers to be in dull spirits after the birth of a child,' the minister replied, but his brow creased in a thoughtful frown.

'Do not say that!' Daniel growled. He told his old friend of the doctor's visit.

'He may be right in his assumption that the baby is the cause of Mattie's low spirits, nevertheless,' Robert Mackenzie said slowly. He found himself in a quandary. He had no proof that the child had been conceived in sin. No one would guess, from looking upon the sleeping infant, that she was not the daughter of Daniel Munro. Yet he knew better than any one that Daniel's health, even during periods of comparative ease, rendered him almost incapable of siring a child. He was also aware of Daniel's over-riding desire to frustrate his brother's claim to Fairlyden. It was a desire which had become paramount since the onset of his own ill health and the knowledge that he was unlikely to outlive his half-brother. In acknowledging the child as his own, he was ensuring the succession of the Munro name through her, as well as through his wife.

As a minister of the church Robert Mackenzie could never condone the sin of adultery, and he understood the burden of guilt which must be crushing Mattie's sensitive spirit. She had been reared to accept the teachings of the bible implicitly, but isolated as she was in her silent world, it was possible that she had been ignorant of the ways of procreation. He knew she loved Sandy Logan with a deep and abiding love. And Daniel had been aware of that love when he gave her his name in holy matrimony. He had been equally aware that Sandy returned her love with all his heart and soul - yet he had been instrumental in bringing them together, in throwing temptation in their path. No doubt Mattie's tender conscience had been overcome by the natural instincts of a man and woman in love. Daniel was as guilty of sin as the devil himself; he had wanted Mattie to bear a child, to perpetuate another generation of Munros. Sandy Logan was not blameless either, if the child was his; but he was already paying for his sin. He must deny his own flesh and blood, deny the love which must fill his heart when he looked upon his child.

The Reverend Mackenzie prayed for guidance as he baptized Sarah Mary Munro in the name of the Father and of the Son and of the Holy Ghost. Mattie felt her spirits strangely uplifted by the solemn occasion although she could hear nothing of the minister's prayers. Before he left to return to the manse he asked her to walk with him in the garden. His eyes were grave and she trembled inwardly. In her heart she knew he had guessed her dreadful secret.

'Your husband is happy to have a daughter.' He formed the words clearly, and as usual she understood him without difficulty, but her eyes fell before his forthright gaze, and a painful flush coloured her pale cheeks. He lifted her chin with one finger.

'You must take care of your health, Mattie. Your husband needs you, and he will need you more in the months ahead. Your daughter also needs you too, to be happy in spirit, to take pleasure in her '

'I cannot! I have sinned. God knows I have sinned.'

'Then pray for forgiveness, for strength and for courage.'

'I have, oh, I have!'

'Mattie, do you not recall the scriptures? "Joy shall be in heaven over one sinner that repenteth, more than over ninety and nine just persons, which need no repentance".'

Mattie frowned, trying desperately to follow his lips, longing for comfort; yet already she felt relief. She had shared her burden, and the minister had not condemned her as she had feared.

'Surely you know God is merciful to a sinner who truly repents, Mattie?'

'Do you believe God can forgive all sins?' There was a plea in her wide brown eyes which even the hardest man would have found difficult to resist, and Robert Mackenzie was not a hard man. He too had loved, and known the heartache of parting. He bent and picked up a flat stone from the garden. With another he scratched upon it, 'Luke 15, v 6 to 10'. He handed it to Mattie.

'Read your bible. Take comfort from the story of the lost sheep, and the widow's mite '

The Reverend Mackenzie came face to face with human frailty every day of his life, and often the frailty was his own. He knew temptation would remain in Mattie's pathway every day, and every night, that she and Alexander Logan shared the same roof and worked in the same fields. Her dark-haired, dark-eyed daughter would be accepted as Sarah Munro, and therefore as heir to Fairlyden - but a second child, especially a child bearing any resemblance to Alexander Logan, would cast doubts upon the legitimacy of both children for Robert Mackenzie was all too familiar with the Earl of Strathtod's jealousy and his inherent spite.

'When the devil tempts you, think of your vows and the promises made before God. Think of Jesus in the wilderness! Avoid temptation. You must be strong!' he counselled urgently, and his face was sterner than Mattie had ever seen it.

'I will try.' She shivered. Even now she yearned to feel the strength of Sandy's arms around her again, the hardness of his body next to hers; she longed to banish the shadows from his blue eyes and see again the laughter - and love. But the sins of the fathers will be visited upon the children She shivered again, despite the warmth of the summer evening.

'Sandy needs my help.'

'I know there is much to do. Your cattle are increasing and Fairlyden has been long neglected.' Robert Mackenzie frowned thoughtfully. 'There is a boy in the village of Bentaira. He is thirteen years old; small for his age, but he would be a willing worker.'

'We have so little money.'

'His mother has nine younger children. She would be pleased to have one less to feed.'

'Certainly I could feed him for his labours,' Mattie agreed eagerly. 'And with more cows and more butter, maybe we could pay a few pounds by the November term.'

The Reverend Mackenzie smiled. His day's work had brought an unexpected reward. Louis Whitley's parents were desperately poor, and their two-roomed cottage was overcrowded. At Fairlyden the boy would be treated with kindliness and he would provide a youthful, if unwitting, chaperon. The minister sighed with satisfaction.

A few weeks after Sarah's baptism Mattie was cheered by the receipt of a letter. It was from Mistress Lowe and she felt a stab of compunction that she had not written to her dear friend and teacher herself. It was the Reverend Mackenzie who had informed her of Sarah's birth, and suggested she might visit Fairlyden. The prospect of such a visit delighted Mattie, but even as she read she realised she had been too absorbed in her own guilt and depression to consider the health of her old friend.

After the first few lines of greeting and warm congratulations, it became clear that Mistress Lowe was too ill to travel, or indeed to leave Caoranne Castle, where Lady Irving was presently caring for her.

'Does Mistress Lowe give news of the glen?' Sandy asked. 'Has Captain Irving returned from the army?' Mattie read on, unaware of Sandy's eager questions, and her face paled as it became clear that Mistress Lowe did not anticipate inhabiting God's earth much longer. She seemed to be obsessed by memories of Jacob Reevil and his treatment of Miss Emilia; she was tortured by suspicions that he had been responsible for Mr Lowe's death. Mattie read on:

'I have thanked God many times, for guiding you in an alien world, Mattie, and for delivering dear Sandy from the glen. There was cruel vengeance - indeed murder - in Reevil's black heart when he found Nethertannoch deserted. Perhaps he was insane. It is said he even accused Sir Douglas Irving of being Miss Emilia's father!'

There was more about Jacob Reevil and his sudden disappearance from the glen, but the letter did not reflect Mistress Lowe's usual clarity of thought and her clear script had a habit of deteriorating by the end of each paragraph - as though her hand had grown too weak to hold the quill. There was news of several other people from Glen Caoranne, but it was the postscript, written on a separate sheet, and in a feeble hand which made Mattie gasp in dismay.

'Captain Charles Irving is dead!' she exclaimed, looking up at Sandy. 'The young laird - he's dead!' Sandy hurried to her side and glanced at the paper in her hand, screwing up his blue eyes to decipher the writing.

'He died in Gibraltar - from fever and a sickness of the bowel!'

'It is an illness which has killed many of the Queen's soldiers serving in foreign lands,' Daniel commented sadly.

'Captain Irving did not choose to be a soldier! He did not want to join the army!' Sandy protested. He turned his attention back to the letter in Mattie's hand. 'The death of the young laird has caused great unhappiness between Sir Douglas and Lady Irving. The laird has returned to France again. Still he seeks proof that Miss Emilia and her child are dead. I fear for his sanity. He is overcome with remorse,' he read aloud. 'And so he should be,' he muttered darkly. 'He banished his only son from the glen. Now Miss Emilia is also dead, if Mistress Lowe's mind is clear on that matter.' Sandy felt a pang of grief for the young laird, and the girl he had adored. And the child? Was it possible that Charles Irving had given Emilia a child - or was Reevil himself responsible? Surely even he would not be base enough to rape his own daughter?

Slowly Sandy began to realise how fortunate he was in comparison to Charles Irving. He was alive. He was free. Every day he could see the woman he loved, and watch over her and their child. It was his duty to protect his daughter, to work for her, even though she did not bear his name. One day Fairlyden would be hers, as Daniel Munro had planned. Sandy would make it a place she would be proud to call her own.

Mistress Lowe's letter had a salutary effect on Mattie also. She was deeply saddened by the news of Emilia's death and she thanked God that she herself had escaped Reevil's evil lusting. God had indeed guided her; she had repaid Him with sin, yet He had shown mercy. He had made their child beautiful and blessed her with good health. Mr Munro had accepted her into his home, given her his name; he loved her as his own daughter. God willing, Sarah would grow in strength and grace - to be worthy of her name, and of Fairlyden.

Gradually the awful depression began to lift. Mattie's strength and cheerfulness returned but she made a firm resolve to be a good wife. She would not tempt Sandy with her body, however much she longed for his touch; she must obey the will of God as her father had done, and as he had taught her to do.

Fifteen

Sarah was a lively toddler and Mattie delighted in each new accomplishment.

'The p-wince has died!' she announced, imitating Daniel's stunned expression. 'P-wince Albert!'

Mattie regretted her own lack of hearing more than ever before. Sarah was quick to grasp the situation, and mischievously used it to her own advantage; her tiny hands sought forbidden tit-bits whenever her mother's eyes were averted. Chunks off the sugar frequently disappeared as well as the precious raisins, afforded only for special occasions. Yet Sarah, with Buff's help, always found a way of attracting her mother's attention when she needed comfort, and as time passed a remarkable rapport developed between them.

Daniel took great interest in every facet of Sarah's development. As soon as she was old enough to understand, he forced his twisted hands to hold the pencil and patiently drew pictures on her slate, and from there they moved to letters, numbers, and eventually to words. It was not long before she began to read simple sentences. She could count and write by the time she was five years old.

One of her greatest pleasures was to accompany Sandy to the pigs or horses and this brought him some consolation at last. Darkie, the mare, was her special favourite and when a colt foal was born the day before her own birthday Sandy allowed her to name him Prince. He was proud of her observant eyes; she recognised the animals as individuals, even within a litter of pigs, which to most children would have seemed identical. Even so he suffered many a pang when he heard Sarah address Daniel as 'Papa'.

His patience, and the sacrifices he had made to keep the horses, had been rewarded. He had reared two colts since the one bought by Abraham Sharpe. They were by a stallion which had been traveling the district and the first one had sold for twelve pounds ten shillings at the Lanark sale. The waggoner had been well satisfied with the strength of bone and the docile temperament inherited from Dark Lucy, and the following year he had paid seventeen pounds twelve shillings for the second colt. More recently Dark Lucy had produced the long desired filly foal.

'I intend to keep young Bess myself,' he informed Daniel. 'Darkie is getting older and I shall breed with Bess, when she is old enough.'

He had refused to use the Mains of Muir stallion after his year's work ended, and to Abraham Sharpe's chagrin, his opinion of the horse was being proved correct. Two older geldings sired by the Mains stallion were already suffering from poor eyesight, and they had never developed the size and strength which the waggoners demanded for carting heavy loads. As Matthew Cameron had forecast, the best stallions were in great demand; some had recently spent the whole season travelling in England and Scottish Clydesdales had been sent to Australia and New Zealand, such was their popularity and the demand for good, strong, Scottish-bred draught horses. Everywhere things were changing.

'I don't know where it will all end,' Daniel said to Sandy one day as he was reading his newspaper. 'Who could have foreseen that men would make enormous ships all driven by steam, or light whole towns by gas?

Every day it seems men build new railway lines to transport bigger and bigger loads.'

'Aye, nothing stays the same,' Sandy agreed.

'It says here that a new fuel called petroleum has been discovered in Pennsylvania.' Daniel studied the news sheets and political trends as carefully as Mattie studied the butter and egg markets. 'I think farmers in Britain will find it hard to make a living soon.'

'There'll aye be a need for food,' Sandy reminded him. 'Surely ye're feeling pessimistic today. The folks keep on flooding to the new towns, but they still demand bread, and more bread. The price o' wheat is still good in spite o' the laws for free trade. We have had two good crops at Fairlyden, especially considering our wet climate.'

'I still think you should be canny,' Daniel insisted stubbornly. 'It is only the civil war in America which has prevented large quantities of grain from being imported. I tell you, Britain has the ships to carry it now, and railways to move it from the ports all over the country. They say the American and Canadian prairies are vast.' Sandy smiled tolerantly at Daniel's gloomy predictions. He was young and strong and unafraid, but he did listen.

The Earl of Strathtod fumed at his brother's survival, especially when he saw Fairlyden's increasing prosperity and knew he would never be able to demand any rent. He continually repeated his threats to any of the Strathtod tenants who might be tempted to help with the Fairlyden harvests.

Daniel was aware of his brother's spite, and it troubled him that Sandy and Mattie toiled doubly hard to compensate for the lack of neighbourly help with the hay and harvest. Mattie was efficient and thrifty. The calves she had reared were now producing calves of their own and she had as much milk as she could handle alone.

'It is a pity we are so far from Muircumwell,' she said one day to Sandy. I could have sold fresh buttermilk and skimmed milk to the cottagers instead of making cheese. Mr Jardine only pays threepence halfpenny a pound.'

'Mmm, but the pigs thrive well on the whey,' Sandy reminded her, though he knew it entailed a lot of extra work and the household had increased to five since the minister had sent young Louis to Fairlyden. It meant a never-ending round of washing and cooking and cleaning, but it was her husband's deteriorating health which caused Mattie most concern. Daniel needed help for the most basic bodily functions now and his helplessness made him impatient and irritable, sometimes sending Sarah into floods of tears when his temper was short. The ageing Buff frequently sought sanctuary beneath the table. The summer weather had brought a temporary improvement but Daniel could no longer teach Sarah all the things she needed to learn.

As soon as she was old enough to cling to the cart, Sarah had accompanied Sandy or Mattie to Muircumwell. Beatrice Later was fourteen months older than Sarah and they had become instant friends, playing happily together at the mill while the bags of corn and meal were being loaded or unloaded. When Joseph Miller had realised that Sarah could already write and count, he insisted that Beatrice must attend the village school without delay.

'Can I go to school, Papa?' Sarah pleaded after one of her trips to the mill. She missed Beattie's company.

'You would have to walk four miles to Muircumwell every day,' Daniel reminded her with a frown, 'and back again, whatever the weather.' Mattie knew he would miss her lively company, as she would herself.

'I could do that!' Sarah cried eagerly.

Eventually Daniel agreed that she should attend Dominie Campbell's school. Sandy cut two large tree trunks and laid them across the burn, carefully embedding them into the banks to form a narrow bridge so that Sarah could cross in safety and keep her little boots dry.

The end of summer, the struggle to gather in the harvest, the coming of chilly autumn mists, brought other changes too. Daniel's pain intensified. Only Mattie's calm acceptance of his needs and the efficiency with which she performed even the most unpleasant chores, made his dependence bearable. He was increasingly aware of the shadows in Sandy's blue eyes as they followed her slender figure, and he could not fail to notice his wife's tension whenever Sandy was close.

Mattie felt guilty and distressed because she could not give her husband all her attention, or give him more relief from his pain. The end of autumn was a particularly busy time for her as she gathered and preserved the autumn fruits and vegetables, as well as helping in the fields with the constant stooking and re-stooking of the corn sheaves, in addition to her work in the dairy and in the house.

Edward Slater was well aware of her busy life.

'I ken a guid lassie who wad help ye at Fairlyden,' he suggested slyly. Mattie always had difficulty following the movements of his mumbling lips, and he was not adept at writing. After a good deal of repetition and a little laborious use of her slate, however, she felt she had grasped the gist of the conversation. He knew a young woman who had given up her work to care for her ailing grandmother. The old woman had died suddenly; now the poor girl had no home, no family and no job, and the hiring fairs were still some weeks away at the end of November.

'I cannot afford to pay her,' Mattie declared regretfully. She was harassed and Master Slater had delayed her, consequently she failed to give him her usual careful attention.

'Alice Simm wad be glad tae work for her food and a roof o'er her head. Just for a few weeks until the hiring fairs?' This time Slater spoke as clearly as he knew how and some of his urgency communicated itself to Mattie. If she had been on more familiar terms with Jeannie Slater she would have known that Edward's own wife was almost as much in need of assistance as herself. As it was, Mattie clearly recalled her own plight when her father died. Without Sandy she might have been forced to share the roof of the obnoxious Reevil. The help of a kindly young woman such as Master Slater described would be a great benefit to Mr Munro.

'Where can I find the girl?'

'I could ask Alice tae meet ye here, at the mill,' Edward suggested eagerly. 'It wad save ye the trouble o' finding her hame, for it's in an awfy quiet bit o' country.'

The following day Mattie was disappointed with her first impression of Alice Simm. The girl seemed incapable of meeting her eyes. Her gaze darted continually in the direction of Master Slater and three other men who were making deliveries of corn. Maybe the girl's desperate need made her nervous, Mattie thought, trying to put aside her doubts. Surely Alice Simm must be kind to have cared so deeply for her grandmother and she did look as though she would make a good dairy worker; her clothes were neat and clean. Indeed her gown was prettier than Mattie's own, and her white apron and cap were freshly starched and ironed. Yet even as Mattie agreed to give the girl a temporary home in return for her help, she was filled with misgiving.

It was quite by chance that Jeannie Slater was glancing disconsolately out of the window of her bed-room at that time of day. She stared in disbelief when she saw Alice Simm dressed in her own second best dress and clean white apron. Jeannie had been sick again that morning, but even the physical sickness which always seemed to drain away every vestige of her energy and spirit, was nothing to the sickness which filled her heart and soul.

Apart from six-year-old Beatrice, she had born three sons, all with Edward Slater's lanky brown hair and small eyes. None of them resembled her, Jeannie thought with some resentment, for she found them hard to love with their constant petty jealousies and squabbling. Now she was expecting another Slater brat and her hatred of Edward was growing beyond endurance. He never missed an opportunity to humiliate her. The demands he made on her body were those of an animal, utterly devoid of feeling, without any form of gentleness - indeed, Jeannie believed her husband deliberately sought new ways to degrade and punish her, both in body and mind. Since the initial shock and horror of those first weeks as Edward's wife, she had suffered his attentions in grim and absolute silence, refusing to grant him the satisfaction of hearing her cry out, either in pain or protest. How she hated his malevolent smile! Humiliation in their bedchamber was one thing. Giving her clothes to one of his sluts was quite another. Some of Jeannie's former spirit returned briefly. She resolved to tackle Mister Slater at the first opportunity.

It came after the mid-day meal. Her mother was not in good health. Ruth Miller was as sick at heart as her daughter and she had formed the habit of resting in her bedchamber each afternoon, as the doctor had advised. Today Joseph Miller was delivering meal to an outlying farm. Edward had considered the order too small to be worth bothering with. Jeannie knew her father was constantly worried by the number of customers they had lost on account of her husband's offensive and sullen manner. Whenever she remonstrated with him his reply was the same.

'Mind your ain business, unless ye want your father and the rest of the parish to ken about Logan's bastard.' Usually the threat was sufficient to ensure her silence. Today Jeannie was more determined. She set her husband's meal upon the table with a thump, then she moved to her own place. She did not sit down, neither did she bother to hide the loathing and contempt she felt at the sight of Edward's greasy brown hair and black, dirt-ringed finger nails, his slobbering lips as he wolfed at the food, wiping dribbles and snivels away with the back of his hand. Her stomach heaved, but she clutched at the table and breathed deeply, willing the spasm to pass. It did.

'Alice Simm was here again!' Her voice was sharp and cold. Edward looked up briefly and a sneer brought his pointed nose almost to his short upper lip.

'So?' He went on shovelling the mutton stew into his mouth.

'You said she wadna come here again!'

'She needs work.'

'Work? What decent woman would have Alice Simm in her home?' Jeannie felt the peculiar faintness again. Surely even Edward would not dare bring his slut to the mill to work?

'Mistress Munro would.'

'Ah!' Jeannie understood. Mistress Munro could not listen to village gossip, of course; indeed it was doubtful if anyone up at Fairlyden heard any. Sandy rarely came to the mill or the Crown and Thistle now. She felt a brief moment of relief for she had half feared that Edward intended to flaunt the Simm woman in front of her parents - and Beatrice. She slumped on to her seat. Then she sat up straight, alerted by the familiar, sly gleam in her husband's narrowed eyes.

'It's time Logan paid his debts.' A malicious smirk played around his thick lips. Jeannie's face whitened. Already she looked twice her twenty-four years.

'What d'ye mean?' Edward's eyes narrowed until they almost disappeared. Despite all his treatment of her, Jeannie still managed to look proud and contemptuous.

'I gie'd her some o' your clothes. I thoucht she wad please Mistress Munro - and your friend, Logan. Nae doot Alice will soon hae him buying everything she wants - including a wedding ring!'

'Ye're crazy! Sandy wadna look at Alice Simm!'

'Alice has a way wi' men.' Edward smiled malevolently. 'He wadna reject her. She's no' a cold, limp fish in a man's arms.' He knew Jeannie had only married him in desperation, and to save her own pride when she had failed to attract Sandy Logan. She had never wanted him and the knowledge angered him. 'Logan will hae to marry her, and soon! Ye'll see!'

Jeannie stared, her blue eyes widening, fully aware of the mockery in her husband's tone. His jealousy and malice towards Sandy had not abated. He never failed to remind her of the sixpence a week it cost to send Logan's bastard to school, yet Edward would have had nothing without her parents' generosity. She felt the bitterness of bile rise in her throat but she swallowed hard. She would not give the devil the satisfaction of knowing he had filled her with his damnable spawn again! Nor would she let him see her dismay.

'You mean that slut is with child? Your child?' She kept her voice calm, but it was an effort.

'If Alice Simm is a slut, then so are you!' He scowled angrily. He had expected hysterics, not contempt. 'I gave Logan's bastard a name, now I mean tae see he repays his debt wi' yin o' mine!' He pushed his chair away from the table, deliberately making a nerve-tearing screech on the flagged floor. When he had hauled himself to his feet he bent over, threateningly. 'And if ye've any plans for warning Logan, dinna! Remember your father and his precious mill. I can talk as well as you - whore!' He strode out of the door without a backward glance.

Long before the end of Alice Simm's first day at Fairlyden Mattie knew she had acted too hastily. She blamed herself for not making inquiries - perhaps from the Reverend Mackenzie. She knew Mr Munro and Sandy had been surprised when she brought Alice home and explained the arrangement.

Matters did not improve. Alice continually ignored Mattie's instructions. Greasy dishes were barely washed because the girl was too idle to ladle hot water from the boiler. Dirt, straws, and hairs appeared in the milk, and Alice would not bother to strain it through the scalded cloths, as Mattie had instructed. Instead she flounced out of the dairy with a pitying grimace, as though Mattie was a delinquent child instead of the Mistress of Fairlyden. Mattie was angered but loath to give in. She really did need help if she was to give her husband the care he needed. She decided to persevere in trying to train the girl.

Sandy had long since deemed it wise to sleep as far away from Mattie as possible, therefore he occupied the large room above the kitchen, originally intended for the maids. When the minister brought Louis Whiteley to work at Fairlyden Sandy had resolved to give the boy better treatment than he had received himself at Mains of Muir; he had devised a rough partition in the room, giving Louis a small cubicle of his own near the top of the stairs. The boy had been overwhelmed with gratitude after sharing a lumpy mattress with four young brothers. Mattie knew Louis followed Sandy's example and took pride in keeping his own small space neat and tidy, so she thought it strange when Alice spent so much time cleaning up there, especially since she neglected everything else. The room was accessible only by way of narrow stairs leading directly from the kitchen and Mattie was further astonished when the maid began invading Sandy's privacy in the evenings. He had always reserved a precious hour for reading, after the day's work was over and Louis had fallen into a sleep of youthful exhaustion. Alice Simm had been quick to recognise that Mistress Munro was Sandy Logan's Achilles Heel

'I wad like ye tae teach me tae read and write,' she pleaded. 'I want tae gie Mistress Munro a surprise, so we maun keep the lessons secret, eh?' she suggested slyly. Sandy soon despaired of teaching Alice Simm anything which required more concentration than batting her ridiculous eyelashes, but Mattie did need help and he knew that few maids would choose to live in isolation at Fairlyden. So for Mattie's sake Sandy tried to be tolerant.

Sixteen

'This butter is bad!' Mr Jardine shouted. Mattie stared at him. She guessed he was shouting but it did not help her to understand the words pouring from his lips in an incomprehensible stream. There were other people in the store and she felt her cheeks grow hot with embarrassment. Suddenly the colour drained away as under-standing dawned.

'Bad? All of it?' she gasped in dismay.

'All of it! I've had nae end o' complaints. Ye're loosing ma customers. I willna pay! Tak it awa', and I dinna want any mair!'

'N-no more? B-but'

Mr Jardine saw her white face and relented a little. Fairlyden butter had always been the finest quality until recently.

'I ken ye're awfy busy wi' Mr Munro being sae sickly, but the butter willna dae, Mistress. I'll take a wee bit next week, but only if it's better, mind!'

Mattie knew Alice was at fault but the responsibility was hers and they could not afford such a loss, especially when the milk was getting less every day. Any butter should stay fresh in cold weather. Alice Simm's filthy habits were to blame, she reflected gloomily, as yet another November day started with bone-chilling dampness and a sneaky, penetrating wind.

Sarah had set off for school happily. She was a strong, healthy child. Warmly dressed in the petticoats and skirt so lovingly sewn by her mother, she rarely felt the cold. She enjoyed all the lessons taught by the stern but kindly dominie, Mr Thomas Campbell. Beatrice had remained her best friend and the two little girls shared many childish secrets. Sarah had also made friends with the three Jamieson children who came from the Mains of Muir cottages. So Mattie did not worry unduly about her small daughter when the day darkened ominously. She did not hear the rising wind screaming around the buildings, crashing doors shut with alarming force. Sarah did not worry either. She was safe in the small schoolroom, engrossed in mastering multiplication tables.

Around the middle of the afternoon curtains of grey, lashing rain shut out the rest of the world. The smoke gusted down Fairlyden's wide chimney in a choking cloud. Daniel Munro frowned. His thoughts were not on the black pother of smoke and soot. He knew only too well the damage which could be done by the winds if they caught the spring or autumn tides. There was real danger for any man foolish enough to venture on the surging Solway, or near its tidal rivers. Strathtod burn did not flow directly into the Solway Firth so it was rarely affected except when the tides were exceptionally high in spring and autumn. Then they were driven on by the raging winds, forcing water back up the burns. Today the burn would be full from the heavy rains; it would be running fast and high, red with mud brought by a myriad swollen streams tumbling from the hills. Daniel had seen the burn in spate. He had been truly awed by the transformation of the gently flowing stream into a sudden fearsome power, sweeping away small bushes and boulders as well as sheep and lambs.

Sandy and Louis were gathering turnips in the field. They pulled, chopped and threw to the cart repeatedly, working doggedly; the rain trickled coldly down their necks, penetrating their thick jackets and coarse shirts, chilling their hands. Still it continued, lashing mercilessly, making little rivers between the ridges of soil. In the sheds cows and bullocks waited hungrily. The two horses stood perfectly still, heads down, dejected; their shining chestnut coats were black with rain and mud. They waited patiently, unmoving, bedraggled.

In the byre Mattie had started the milking earlier than usual on account of the rapidly fading light. She had been on the point of sending Alice to feed the pigs, but some instinct made her send the maid to meet Sarah instead. The child was fiercely independent but the path was dangerously close to the burn in places and it was a long walk, totally without protection from the vicious wind and rain. Mattie might have gone herself but she was determined not to allow Alice near the milk after Mr Jardine's threats to cancel the butter order. Buff lay with her head on her paws watching the milk streaming rhythmically into the pail as Mattie worked expertly, her fingers firm and gentle on the warm fat teats of the cows, a little slower on the smaller teats of two young heifers. She could not hear the rage of the ever rising wind and she was almost oblivious to the lash of the rain, except when she had to dash to the dairy to empty her pails of milk.

Alice had watched sullenly when Mattie went into the byre, then she had run to the house, spattering her skirt with mud. Why should she trail after the brat while the mistress stayed in the warm byre? It was not that Alice wanted to milk the cows, in fact she did not want to work at all, but at least with a man for company most things were bearable. She sauntered into the kitchen. Daniel Munro looked up in relief.

'The wind will be driving the tides far and fast today. You must hurry. Wait for Sarah at the burn as Mistress Munro bid, but if the water has risen tell her to seek shelter at the mill with her friend, Beatrice Slater.' He broke off incredulously as Alice threw him a defiant, mocking glance and sauntered deliberately towards the stairs. The bairn would be home before the milking was finished. Daniel shouted urgently. Alice gave a harsh laugh.

'Ye're only a shell of a man, except for those deep dark eyes,' she muttered, and pushed open the door of Mattie's bedchamber, knowing she would not be disturbed until the mistress finished outside. All her own clothes were either dirty or torn, including the ones Edward Slater had given her from his wife's closet. She had quite fancied the dark blue gown which she had seen Mattie sewing in the evenings.

*

In the little schoolroom the children worked on. The fire burned low in the grate for the day was almost ended and Dominie Campbell could not afford to waste fuel. An insidious chill numbed the small fingers which grasped the slates, but the dominie was a conscientious and honest man and he knew how hard most of the parents had to struggle to pay the few pence each week for their children's' education. But when the room darkened with encroaching shadows and the single window became a sheet of grey water, the good dominie's concern for his small charges overcame his qualms of conscience and he released them thirty minutes before the appointed hour. Boys pulled ragged jackets closer to their thin bodies, the girls wrapped themselves more tightly in their shawls, then they were out, some running before the wind, some against it, all heading eagerly for their homes, however humble.

Sarah and Beatrice ran together, then with a breathless farewell they parted and Sarah ran on alone, head down against the rain and wind, past the cottages which marked the end of the village, past the high wall at the bottom of the Manse ground, out into the open country towards the burn, the little bridge, the fields beyond, and home. There would be no time to linger to search for wee fishes today, nor to peep at the toad which lived under the big flat leaves.

There was no sign of the tree trunk bridge! Sarah's eyes grew round with surprise and awe. Brown water was spreading over the ground, eddying and frothing. Soon it touched the toes of her little boots. Then Sarah saw the tree trunks, or at least one of them. The broom bush had been washed away, and the curve in the bank where the primroses always grew was gone! She could see the grass of the field through the water at her feet. It was not deep. She could easily get to the trunk if she held her skirts up - and she did long to be home, beside the fire and Papa. She could almost smell Mama's broth on the swee, warming ready for her and Uncle Sandy and Louis. They would be wet and cold too. She tucked the little canvas satchel more firmly on her shoulder. Mama had made it for her to carry her slate and pencil and the bread and cheese she took for her dinner.

Sarah had no fear of the rushing, tumbling burn as she picked her way daintily towards the trunk, stepping carefully over the swaying, swirling grasses submerged by an ever widening stretch of water. Even so she frowned when she felt the water squelch over the tops of her leather boots and her small toes curled coldly. Before she reached the trunk the hems of her skirts were sodden and the water was up to her knees. She paused uncertainly. The single trunk looked much, much narrower than two trunks, and the water swirled above it instead of trickling gently down below. Sarah turned then and looked behind into the lashing curtain of rain. She was half blinded by the cold sting of the wind, and the water seemed to stretch behind her forever. She had to cross the trunk. It was the only way she could get home to Mama. She saw one end of the remaining trunk move, and then wash back again, lodging against the boulder which Uncle Sandy had placed there so that it would be secure. She hitched the canvas satchel again and clutched her skirts more firmly.

The moment Sarah put her feet upon the log it rolled precariously and she swayed and dropped her skirts, flinging out her arms to regain her balance. She was halfway across when another powerful surge and sucking rocked the tree trunk from its hold. Sarah screamed. The rolling movement of the log threw her off balance into the icy water. She clutched at the log instinctively and scrambled on to it, clinging, shivering, hampered by the dragging weight of her wet clothes. The little canvas satchel was carried away on the foaming water. Above her head the wind howled in triumph. The burn was angry now. It bucked and lifted and lowered just like the colt had done before Uncle Sandy had broken its temper and gentled it to the shafts. Sarah wished Uncle Sandy was with her now to gentle the burn. He was so big, so strong, and she loved the way he smiled at her. She didn't know what to do, except cling to the log. Her arms were cold, so cold, and aching. Tears rolled silently down her cold, wet cheeks, but she bit her lip and shook them away. She waited and waited.

Her eyelids were so heavy. She stretched them wide. Surely she had heard a voice? Suddenly the water heaved the trunk, and her with it, and sent it whirling down the burn. Sarah clung desperately. Her arms felt as though they were dropping off. They were not very strong arms yet. She wondered if Jesus would take her to be one of his angels, like the ones Mama had read about in the bible. One of the big boys at school said his sister had gone to be an angel. She thought she heard his voice, calling to her. Her eyelids drooped wearily.

*

When Mattie returned to the dairy to empty the bucket of milk for the third time, Buff followed anxiously; the little dog persisted in lifting her paw and Mattie regarded her intently. Buff moved to the door which led into the scullery. Mattie opened it and Buff pawed urgently at the second door. Mattie pulled it open impatiently for there was still much to be done and darkness was falling fast. She stopped in horror.

'Mr Munro!' Daniel had half crawled, half dragged his useless body across the floor. He lay still, almost fainting with the effort and the pain in his knees and back. He pointed to the flag floor.

'Bring Sandy. Sarah! Tides.' Mattie watched his lips carefully and her face paled, her dark eyes rounded in alarm.

'Surely Sarah is home?' She gazed wildly towards the hearth, expecting to see Sarah's small body crouched upon the rag rug, before the fire. She bent urgently to help her husband, but he shook his head.

'Alice? Where's Alice?'

Daniel pointed upwards to the bedrooms above. 'Bring...Sandy! Leave me!'

The urgency in his tormented dark eyes made Mattie obey instantly. She grabbed Agnes Lowe's old cloak from behind the door and ran out into the lashing rain. Long before she reached the field above the steading her sides ached and she panted desperately against the wind, but still she ran on.

'Sandy! Sand-eey!' she called, vainly. The wind blew her words back at her. She was almost upon them before she saw the horses looming out of the wet, grey gloom. Sandy saw her slithering over the watery ruts, stumbling desperately in her haste to reach them. He ran to meet her, his heart thumping. He grasped her shoulders as soon as they met.

'The burn!' she gasped, clutching her side. 'Floods! Sarah is not home! Oh, Sandy '

He squeezed her shoulders briefly, then turned back to the mare and loosened the rope from the harness, coiling it as he ran, shouting to Louis to take the carts back to the steading. Mattie bent double, catching her breath in gasping sobs.

'Please God, don't let the burn flood!' She could not imagine the little burn being a danger, but she knew Mr Munro would not have struggled so desperately to reach her without good reason. And Alice? What was she doing?

Daniel crawled painfully back to the fire, but he could not raise himself to the chair and the bands around his chest tightened with every breath. He lay still, forcing himself to relax. By the time Mattie returned the spasm had passed and she helped him into his chair, her face devoid of colour. She wanted to question him, but he looked drained of life. She wanted to follow Sandy, but it was almost dark now. If Sarah was in danger she could not hear her if she called. But Louis could hear. He would help! She ran to the box bed and seized a blanket, rolling it tightly.

She ran out into the storm again, oblivious now of the cold rain and tearing wind. Louis led the horses, with their carts tied one behind the other, into the yard. As soon as he had tipped out the loads of turnips, Mattie took the bridles.

'I will unharness them and rub them down. Take this blanket to Sandy. Sarah has not returned from school. She will be cold and wet. If-if Sandy finds her.'

She saw the boy's face whiten. He had lived all his life in the area. He knew how dangerous the autumn floods could be when the winds and high tides came together. Even small burns could become raging torrents. They could sweep away a child as easily as a dandelion seed upon the wind. Louis turned and disappeared into the shadowy, teeming, darkness.

A cold terror, more deadly than that of the fiercest weather, struck Sandy's heart when he saw the water-covered field stretching out to him. He waded towards the burn. There was no sign of the little bridge or of the tree trunks. The roaring of the water filled his ears and his head. He shook himself, making a determined effort to think clearly. Would Sarah see the floods in time and go back? Would she go to the mill? Would Slater bid her welcome?

'Sarah?' he heard himself calling out. 'Sar-aah!' There was no answer, and no sign of any living thing. Surely no child could have crossed the burn during the last two hours?

*

The wailing of the rising wind, the splatter of rain upon the tiny windows of his mother's cottage, had drawn Rory O'Connor like the wild spirit of his Irish ancestors. He had left the house early and walked many miles that day. Still the whining wind beckoned him on. He knew the wild geese had arrived; they were early this year but he had not seen a single one braving the leaden skies today. He had not intended to go near the Strathtod burn. Every instinct told him that it would rise above its banks today. The rushing power of it exhilarated him, the creeping waters reaching over the banks, spreading great clutching fingers across the fields, mesmerized him. Yet as the short day drew to its close the lure of the burn was irresistible. Once he thought he heard another sound above the whine of the wind. He listened intently, but it did not come again. His foot-steps carried him through the shallow waters, nearer, ever nearer, to that relentless force of churning, thrashing water. It made him think of a great giant holding the waters at bay, pushing them back from the Solway Firth, back even to the hills from where they had flowed so merrily. Now the tide would have turned and that same giant was sucking the pent up waters down again, relentlessly taking everything they had gathered, drawing the flotsam and jetsam from the flooded banks, taking it away to the surging Solway, to be lost forever in the ocean.

Seventeen

Rory O'Connor saw the tiny canvas satchel caught around the branch of a submerged sapling. He retraced his steps, peering into the foaming waters. The tree bridge had gone! The satchel belonged to the little one from Fairlyden - but where was she? He hurried downstream, straining his eyes in the deepening grey shadows of the dark November afternoon. He dodged the overhanging branches, oblivious now of soaking boots and cold, wet feet. He heard the voices in his brain: 'Do not go to Fairlyden. Do not help. Do not go ' The rain had plastered his hair to his head and he rubbed it in an unconscious gesture of agitation. He had to go on! The wind had beckoned him, and the burn had called to him with its thunderous roar.

Then he saw the small bundle attached to a log, floating and bouncing over the foaming water. He called, but his voice was carried away on the wind. The bundle did not stir. He ducked away from the burn where the water was too fierce and too deep for him to wade. The bushes hid the log from his view. Then the bushes cleared and he saw clearly a small girl, clinging desperately to a tree trunk. He grasped an overhanging branch and leaned over the water, calling again and again The child raised her head briefly. He reached out a hand.

'Jesus,' Sarah whispered, and closed her eyes. She would be all right now. Jesus had come to help her, just as Mama had promised he would if she said her prayers every night. Her small frozen arms slid away from the log. Sarah gasped as the icy water rushed over her head.

Rory yelled in dismay. He could not reach. He let go of the branch and grasped frantically at Sarah's soaking skirts as the water dashed over her head a second time, taking away the last of her breath. Rory clutched the sodden bundle more firmly but he could feel the current sweeping him away. He tried to catch the branch he had just relinquished but he was carried along by the water and it evaded his outstretched fingers by a hair's breadth. The burn curved naturally and Rory was swept off his feet by the sudden surge, but the current carried him and his bundle to the opposite bank, throwing him up hard against a protruding root. He clung to it grimly with one thin arm, gasping for breath, exhausted by the brief fight with death, for Rory was more aware than most of the danger of the burn in spate.

He tried to pull himself upwards into shallower water, but he almost lost Sarah in his efforts. He knew he could save himself if he let her float away down the stream. He smiled gently and looked down into her still face. It gleamed like marble in the faint light. He had no thought of releasing her slight body to the relentless waters. He put his wet face against her chest but he could not tell whether her heart still beat beneath her sodden clothes. Twice he almost lost his grip on the slippery root. Rory had often been cold, he had often been wet to the skin, but he had never had to remain in one place getting hungry. He could run like the deer and usually his young blood coursed through his veins and warmed him - until he reached home and submitted to his mother's clucking tongue and tender smile. He had not eaten since early morning. He thought of the pan of hot gruel his mother would have simmering for her ravenous brood, and his stomach kinked with longing. He could scarcely feel that part of his body beneath the water now. He had tried to hold

Sarah above the foaming swirls but her clothes added considerably to her weight and his arm ached

'Sarah! Sar-aah… ' Rory started at the sound.

'Haeloa-oa-oa,' he yelled in excitement. Someone had come at last to look for the little one. 'Haeloa-oa-oa-oa!' He stopped, breathless. An iron band seemed to be tightening around his chest.

'Where are you?' Sandy called back instantly. 'Call to me! Where are you?' His voice was harsh with worry.

'Haeloo-a ' Rory called weakly. Then suddenly the iron band slackened, his breathing eased, and he shouted strongly, again and again. He could hear Sandy crashing through the bushes on the opposite bank, following his voice. It was barely possible to see now. Still the pent up water rushed on. Then Sandy loomed out of the bushes, tall and strong. He had seen them, crouched against the bank, but how would the big man from Fairlyden get across? Rory wondered faintly. Almost as though he sensed Rory's unspoken question Sandy shouted.

'I have a rope. I will tie this end to a tree and try to wade across to you. Stay there!' Sandy's voice was clear and calm now, hiding the terror in his heart. Swiftly he tied one end of the rope to a stout bush and the other around his waist, for he guessed the force of the water might sweep him off his feet; it might even snap the rope. 'Guide me with your voice!' he called, but Rory could not reply coherently, the words jumbled in his throat and around his tongue as they always did. 'I have come to help you as well as the child. Do you understand?'

'Aya-a-a aya-a-a.'

Sandy grasped the rope and stepped into the water, moving backwards, using the rope to steady himself against the swirling current.

He grasped Sarah thankfully and felt tears mingle with the rain on his weathered cheeks. She was so cold. So still. His heart missed a beat and he clutched her tighter, willing her to be alive.

'Wait here. I'll come back for you,' he gasped. 'I can never thank you. Never!'

Rory smiled his wide sweet smile. 'Yours,' he nodded at Sarah.

Before Sandy had reached the safety of the far bank, Rory had scrambled up the slippery root and hauled himself on to the opposite bank, then he was away, stiff and cold but moving now, alone, into the darkness.

When Sandy turned he called urgently, thinking the boy had lost his grip and been born away by the water.

'Haeloa-oa-oa ' The voice echoing through the darkening shadows reassured Sandy that he was safe.

Long before Sandy returned, Mattie had the fire stoked high and the bathing tub ready to fill with hot water from the copper boiler. The wooden clothes' stand was draped with towels and a blanket to keep the draughts away. A new candle was standing ready to be lit. Mattie could not stand still. If Sarah died, she would never forgive Alice Simm, never! She clenched her teeth unconsciously, and snatching up a candle stub marched towards the staircase and the upper floor.

Mattie's anger almost exploded when she pushed open the door of Alice's bedchamber. The girl was sound asleep, sprawled on her back across the bed -and she was wearing Mattie's own gown! As she stared at the maid, Mattie's eyes widened further. Alice was taller and broader than herself. The dress was stretched tautly over her body and the distinctive swelling of her stomach was clearly outlined. Mattie frowned. The girl was with child! She was useless and unreliable but she was carrying an innocent child. Mattie turned away. How could she, a sinner, condemn?

Daniel saw her troubled face when she returned restlessly to the kitchen.

'Leave the girl to me,' he commanded, and his dark face was grim, but Mattie just shook her head helplessly. She was sick with worry. Please God, don't take Sarah from me because I am a sinner, she prayed silently.

When Sandy pushed open the door and carried Sarah into the lamplight, Mattie rushed to take her from him. Her heart filled with despair as she stared at her daughter's white, still face. She looked up into Sandy's wretched blue eyes. He was depending on her to bring the merry young life back into their child's inanimate figure.

'Oh, Sandy,' her voice shook, 'our own innocent bairn. The sin was ours! She must not be made to pay!' Her words shook Sandy out of his despair. He met Daniel's gaze, but Mattie was already laying Sarah on the thick rag rug before the fire, tearing at her sodden clothes, chafing the cold little limbs. Gently she put her mouth to Sarah's ice-cold lips.

'She breathes, Sandy! She breathes! Oh, thank God, thank you God!' She began to rub Sarah's chilled body with the warm towel. 'Bring hot water to the tub!' she commanded.

'Jesus,' Sarah sighed softly, but she did not open her eyes. She was barely conscious of being bathed and fed like a baby and cuddled in her mother's arms in the big bed warmed with a shelf from the oven.

The following morning Sarah awoke with nothing worse than aching limbs and a feverish chill. Even that did not prevent her from pattering barefoot down the stairs. She had inherited a strength and stamina for which she was to be truly thankful during her eventful life.

Her appearance, so lively and normal except for the unusually high colour on her rounded cheeks, and a livid bruise on her temple, made Mattie quite emotional. Sarah was surprised when her mother scooped her up in her arms and hugged and kissed her - especially so early in the morning. When Mattie turned and looked into Sandy's face, alight with relief and love, she hugged him too.

'Thank you for saving her, Sandy.'

Daniel's dark eyes were shadowed as he watched the tenderness in Sandy's face. He knew how much effort it took to keep the fires of their love from flaring out of control; he knew too that the strain and tension between them deserved the natural release of their shared love; yet neither one ever treated him unkindly or showed resentment as his useless life dragged on, an obstacle to their happiness. Today Mattie's imprudence stemmed from relief and gratitude, and he understood, indeed he shared it. He loved Sarah as much as if she had been the seed of his own flesh.

'It was a laddie who truly saved Sarah's life,' Sandy's voice interrupted Daniel's thoughts. 'I do not even know his name. How are we to repay him?' Daniel frowned thoughtfully.

'If the boy lives on the Strathtod Estate he will not want to be known as the saviour of a Munro. Already he may have put himself, and his family, in peril of eviction from my brother.'

'But we owe him a greater debt than...'

'Leave him in peace. He will know that he has saved the life of an innocent child, and be glad, I think. Some day you will find a way to repay him.'

There was almost an air of celebration in the air at Fairlyden that November morning. Mattie had risen early, as usual, to empty the ashes, clean the range and kindle up the fire before she milked the cows and fed the young calves. Sandy and Louis had attended to the horses and bullocks, and fed the pigs. The sheep were still foraging on the hill, and the hens, ducks and geese were safer in their houses until the sky grew light and the fox had returned to his own den. It was Sandy who helped Daniel to rise from the box-bed and dress with painful slowness while Mattie made porridge for breakfast.

When Alice Simm sauntered into the kitchen, still dressed in Mattie's gown, now crumpled from sleep, there was a tense silence. The sight of her, flaunting herself in Mattie's clothes, the provocative smile on her face as she gaped owlishly at Sandy, the sheer conceit of the girl, exploded Daniel's pent up anger. He remembered the contempt and mockery on her face the previous evening. She had left Sarah to drown, she had mocked him in his helplessness

'Take your things and leave this house!' he commanded through gritted teeth. 'Now!'

Everyone stared at him in surprise, even Sarah, her cup of warm milk poised in mid-air. Alice glared at her with venomous eyes. The brat had come to no harm, so why such a fuss?

'I'm no' ready tae gang yet!' she retorted insolently. Edward would never forgive her if she didn't get a father for his bairn - and not just any father. He wanted Sandy Logan; but he only had eyes for the mistress. She shrugged. It would have to be his word against hers if that old crab tried to get rid of her. She had nothing to lose. She pulled a chair from the table, but before she could sit on it Daniel bellowed furiously: 'Get out of this house, you murderer!' Alice Simm's face paled then flushed angrily. No man had ever spoken to her like that!

'If I hae tae gang, I shallna' gang alane, I'm warnin ye!'

'Don't you threaten me.' Daniel was almost beside himself with fury. 'Get out of my house!'

'An' dinna think you can threaten me. We all ken fine the braw Sandy fancies your ain wife. But he's no content jist tae fancy.' She glowered at Mattie who was straining to understand. 'Naw he wants mair. He's taen advantage o' me, a puir lassie biding i' the master's hoose '

'What!' Daniel almost exploded.

Sandy gave a single incredulous gasp. His face went white with shock.

Mattie frowned, her dark eyes darting from one furious face to another. 'What did she say?' she demanded impatiently.

'Tell her then!' Alice taunted. 'Tell her, her blue-eyed Sandy,' she mimicked Mattie's pronunciation, 'will hae tae marry me.'

'She's lying!' Sandy jumped to his feet.

'Is she?' Daniel asked flatly. Was that the reason Alice Simm had spent so much time in Sandy's chamber? Had his desire for Mattie been frustrated too long? Daniel groaned aloud. Had he deprived her of happiness while she nurtured his useless life?

Sandy was staring at him in disbelief.

'Naw, I'm no' lying!' Alice Simm insisted. 'His seed is in me! Why dae ye think he wanted me in his ain room every nicht? Ye all ken he did!' She looked triumphantly around the shocked faces.

'You lie! I wadna touch you if...'

'Time will prove ye did!'

Mattie stared anxiously at Sandy's clenched fists and angry face. He strove for control.

'Tell me what is wrong, Sandy?' Her heart raced.

'She!' He glared at Alice contemptuously. 'She accuses me...' Sandy looked bitterly at Daniel, then suddenly he grasped Mattie's shoulders and stared intently into her eyes. 'She says I've fathered a bairn.' Mattie paled. 'Her bairn,' he choked. 'It isna mine, I swear it!'

'Of course it is not yours.' Mattie's face cleared. Sandy and Daniel stared at her in amazement. 'The bairn was in her before she came to Fairlyden.'

She turned and laid a hand calmly over the girl's stomach. Alice jerked away angrily, but not quickly enough. 'The child grows already,' Mattie declared, but she felt a stab of compassion for the hapless maid. Had she herself not used Mr Munro as a father for her own child? But Mr Munro had wanted her child he loved Sarah. Sandy did not want Alice Simm or her child. His angry white face and the dismay in his blue eyes told her that plainly.

'You had better go now,' Mattie told Alice gently. 'You may keep the gown and the other garments you have taken from my chamber.'

Alice's face paled. The mistress was not stupid after all. You could get a nasty time in prison for stealing. The sooner she was clear of Fairlyden the better. She would return to the quarry huts. Edward Slater would have to feed her and the brat. It was his, and he knew it! She stalked out of the house muttering curses.

As the year eighteen hundred and sixty-six dawned, Daniel knew he was fortunate to have survived almost a decade since death first stared him in the face. He had learned to regard Mattie as an angel in disguise, far superior to her heroine, Miss Nightingale, whose book Notes on Nursing she had read so avidly. She had never allowed her own handicap to dim her smile and she withstood even his ill temper.

Mattie was aware of her own limitations, however, and it troubled her to see Mr Munro so subdued. Ever since the flood she had noticed the bluish lines around his mouth and the weariness in his dark eyes. She feared the effort to crawl across the kitchen floor, followed by his angry outburst towards Alice Simm, had had a lasting effect on his health. So when he asked her to prepare a special meal and invite the minister to dine with them on the first day of the New Year, Mattie did her utmost to please him.

Robert Mackenzie was not unduly surprised to receive a summons from his old friend. He and Daniel frequently discussed the news sheets and the changing world. He went eagerly to Fairlyden. He had other news with which to interest Daniel.

He enjoyed an excellent meal. Mattie had made carrot soup and, after much diligent cleaning of the flues in the big black range, had roasted a fine piece of mutton. There was a piquant caper sauce of her own concoction, and two kinds of potatoes as well as parsnips and Brussels sprouts; to please Daniel's sweet palate, she had devised a custard mould made with eggs and milk, and swimming in a golden caramel sauce.

'If you please, Sir, I will eat your pudding if you cannot,' Sarah piped earnestly when he paused to savour the delicate flavour. Daniel had not chastised her as he sometimes did when she spoke at meal times or out of turn. Instead he had given the little girl a sweet, strangely wistful smile.

Afterwards, when Sarah was safely tucked up in bed, Robert Mackenzie settled down to enjoy a pipe of tobacco with Sandy and Daniel. Mattie carried the dirty crockery into the scullery where she could scoop hot water from the copper boiler and there was a large stone slab table on which to stand the wooden bowl. Sandy had installed two shelves where she could store the clean plates and cups. She frequently offered a silent thank you to the old Earl for his thoughtful arrangement of the kitchen, scullery and dairy. She always had a plentiful supply of hot water now that she had fuel to light the copper fire each day; the kitchen was tidier too, and Mr Munro had warmth and peace beside the range.

When she had finished in the scullery she stoked up the kitchen fire to keep her husband warm during the night, but as she was about to retire Daniel touched her arm. She turned with her usual gentle smile. Surprisingly he reached out and clutched her hand.

'You made a fine meal for us, my dear, thank you.' Mattie blushed in confusion. Mr Munro was not a demonstrative man; he rarely expressed his gratitude openly, though she knew he appreciated all her efforts to bring him comfort. 'Thank you, Mattie, for everything. Good night, my dear.'

Sandy had made a last round of the animals in the stable and byre, as was his habit before going to bed, and it was only when he had mounted the stairs to his chamber that the Reverend Mackenzie broke his news to Daniel.

'The Earl of Strathtod has suffered an attack of apoplexy.'

'Gordon? He's ill?'

'He is confined to his bedchamber. I am told he can neither speak nor move, and the doctor fears for his life.'

'When?'

'In the last hours of the old year. Daniel, as a minister I must pray for his soul. But, God forgive me, I cannot forgive your brother. He destroyed the happiness of all those around him: Your father's with your mother - and with yourself; and he killed Elizabeth, his own sister, more surely than the Indians who wielded the axes in the massacre in which she died!'

'He certainly destroyed your happiness, my friend,' Daniel murmured pensively. 'And now he lies abed, dependent as I am dependent?'

'More so. He cannot speak and must wet his blanket like a babe. He cannot ask for water. May God forgive me!' Robert Mackenzie repeated passionately. 'I cannot feel compassion for him.'

'Perhaps it is God's punishment,' Daniel mused. Strangely he could feel no triumph in the knowledge that his half-brother had been stricken, the brother who had resented him before he was born, hated and envied him, taunted, threatened and hounded him. 'Is Reggie home?'

'They have sent for him, though it is young William who understands the estate. Aye, and loves it, as your father did. I met him out riding a few weeks ago. He is the image of Lord Jonathan, his grandfather.'

'Poor William - the youngest son by so many years, and the one my father would have welcomed into Gordon's family more than any other. How old is he now? Sixteen years?'

'Almost eighteen. I hear he and Reginald get along well together, but Stuart is said to be as filled with petty jealousies as his father, while James ... I fear James was spawned by the devil himself.'

'Then we may feel sorry for them,' Daniel sighed. The Reverend Mackenzie looked searchingly at his friend and smiled wryly.

'I could almost believe we have exchanged roles tonight. Have you put your bitterness aside? Have you developed a spirit of Christian charity, Daniel? Do I detect a sudden repentance of all your sins?'

Daniel did not reply. He stared broodingly into the fire and Robert Mackenzie was disturbed by this new quietness, the strange serenity which seemed to have settled upon his spirited friend. The news of Lord Gordon's illness seemed to Daniel to be an omen. The time had come to carry out his plan, the plan he had considered for so long. Had Robert Mackenzie not written to Mistress Lowe, had Mattie and Sandy Logan not come to Fairlyden, he would have had little option. They had given him those extra years of life; care, companionship, aye and joy, the joy of watching Sarah - Sarah Munro.

The Reverend Mackenzie was even more surprised when Daniel asked if he would read a passage from the bible before he left. He knew he ought to be gratified by such a request from a man who had long declared himself a doubtful believer, an earnest student of the new theories of the man Darwin. Yet Robert Mackenzie was troubled as he turned to Daniel's chosen passage from the book of Numbers and the story of God's guidance to Moses.

"The Lord bless thee, and keep thee:

The Lord make his face to shine upon thee, and be gracious unto thee:

The Lord lift up his countenance to shine upon thee, and give thee peace.

And they shall put my name upon the children of Israel; and I will bless them."

When he finished reading, a peaceful silence fell upon the cosy hearth. Daniel nodded.

'Thank you, Robert. You are a good shepherd, even to your most erring sheep.

"And God shall wipe away all tears from their eyes;

and there shall be no more death,

neither sorrow, nor crying, neither shall there be any more pain:

for the former things are passed away." ' He quoted the lines himself, almost inaudibly. Robert Mackenzie heard them in astonishment.

'You wish me to read another passage? From the New Testament?'

Daniel stirred and sighed softly.

'No. You have been a good friend, Robert.' He smiled. 'A very good friend.'

There was a tranquillity in the dark eyes which Robert Mackenzie had never seen there before, and he had known Daniel Munro since he was a boy.

'Perhaps you would help me into bed before you leave?'

'Of course. And tell me what kind of night it is out there for the journey.'

'Journey?'

'Your ride back to Muircumwell.'

Robert Mackenzie looked up at the stars shining crystal clear in the January sky. Already the ground was sparkling white with frost. He turned back into the firelit kitchen and looked at Daniel, lying in the bed beside the wall, close to the broad chimney breast.

'It is a fine night ... a beautiful night. The sky is filled with stars; they shine more brightly than any earthly diamond could ever shine.' He sighed. 'It will be a hard frost before morning.'

'Aye, but a peaceful night.'

'Yes, it is calm. Good night, Daniel. Sleep well, if you can.'

'I will; yes, indeed I will. Good night.' Daniel waited until the sneck of the outer door fell gently into place. 'God bless and keep you, my friend.' He raised his eyes to the ceiling and thought of Mattie sleeping in the big bed which had been his mother's, with Sarah curled up beside her. And Sandy, asleep in the room directly above his head. 'God bless you all.'

Long before he had succeeded in removing the loose stone which concealed the hidden cavity beside the fire, Daniel was exhausted. The bands around his chest tightened with the excruciating pain which had become so familiar. But it had always gone away before. He had waited in vain for death to claim him in the last few months. He had to reach the laudanum. This time he had to be sure. He lay still, gasping, his gnarled fingers a fraction away from the stone.

Eighteen

The morning air was bitterly cold when Sandy clattered down the wooden stairs into the kitchen. He saw Mattie standing motionless beside the box bed. He raised his candle high and moved swiftly across the stone-flagged floor to her side.

In death Daniel Munro's face was serene, devoid now of the lines of suffering and pain which had ravaged it in life. Gently Sandy bent and closed the dark, sightless eyes for the last time. He sensed that Daniel had welcomed the sweet release from pain, which only death could bring. Later he would miss the man's friendship, his learning, and their discussions; but now there was much to be done.

Sandy knew his happiness with Mattie was almost assured, but they had both learned to appreciate Daniel Munro's wisdom and courage and they missed his presence in the chair beside the fire. So, despite his impatience to make Mattie his bride, Sandy understood her wish to show proper respect for the man who had given her his name. Moreover, to marry hastily would have aroused suspicion and gossip, causing misery for Sarah. Nothing must be allowed to cast a shadow on their love. Soon they would be joyfully united at last and although the interval was one of mourning, an air of peace and contentment settled over Fairlyden.

Neither Mattie nor Sandy guessed that their own good fortune was viewed with envy, or that it might influence the lives of others, however indirectly. Edward Slater had resented Sandy since the day Joseph Miller employed him and his horse at the mill. Jeannie's open admiration of him had only intensified that jealousy. Slater had been temporarily placated by his marriage to Jeannie, especially since Sandy Logan's own aspirations had already been frustrated by Mattie's marriage to Daniel

Munro. Now things had changed. Logan's future seemed brighter than Edward's would ever be, for not only would he marry the woman he loved, but he would also be master of Fairlyden; even his horses were in demand. At the mill the trade grew less with every passing week; the millhouse was full of hungry mouths to feed - and one of them was Logan's bastard. He knew Jeannie despised him. He blamed Alexander Logan; he hated the man who had stolen her love. Every time he looked at Beatrice he thought of her mother in Logan's arms and his malice against Jeannie's only daughter grew.

Mattie had also experienced something of Slater's true character since Alice Simm's dismissal from Fairlyden. More than once he seized her by the waist with only the slightest pretence of helping her climb from the cart; his touch had become insultingly familiar; his increasingly bold stares made her uncomfortable. She began to avoid the mill whenever she could.

Sandy guessed the reason for Mattie's reluctance to buy her flour and oatmeal from the mill, but he remembered Joseph Miller's early kindnesses and he took the Fairlyden corn to the mill himself. He grew increasingly displeased with the quantity, and the quality, of the meal he received in return for the grain he supplied. After a particularly angry exchange with Edward Slater, he decided to try the Strathtod mill. The Earl still lingered on the fine edge between life and death; he barely recognised those who attended him and seemed to have lost all interest in the affairs of the estate.

John Benson, the Strathtod miller, greeted Sandy warily, but small country mills could no longer afford to turn away trade. He dealt fairly and Sandy was well satisfied. Sarah accompanied him on his second visit to Strathtod. While she was waiting patiently in the cart a young man rode into the mill yard. The Honourable William Fairly was mounted on a spirited black horse and Sandy found himself admiring the youth's calm manner and gentle hands. Sarah was a friendly child, ever eager for new acquaintances and experiences and she gave the young man a winning smile.

'Ah! You must be the queen of the fairies!' he declared gallantly. 'Have you journeyed from Fairyland, Your Majesty?' He doffed his hat with a grin.

'No-o, of course not!' Sarah giggled delightedly. 'I am not a queen! My name is Sarah. I live at Fairlyden up that long track.' She supplied the information with childish innocence. William Fairly's own smile wavered, but Sarah chattered on, unaware of any constraint and quite oblivious to the stares of the three men repairing the wall beside the mill-lade.

Sandy finished loading the cart. He touched his cap courteously and Sarah waved as they drove away. To his surprise the youth returned Sarah's gay salute, but Sandy fancied his smile was a little wistful as he watched them turn on to the track to Fairlyden. He thought the Honourable William Fairly bore an uncanny resemblance to Daniel Munro.

Slater used every excuse to keep Beatrice away from school so more than a week passed before Sarah could tell her friend of her meeting with the smiling, dark-eyed stranger. They shared all their childish secrets. As they waited for Dominie Campbell to open up the schoolroom, Beatrice listened to Sarah's account of her meeting with the young man on the black horse.

'Why did Mr Logan go to Strathtod Mill?' Beatrice asked miserably. Sarah's cheeks grew pink and she looked away. She had not intended to hurt her dearest friend. 'It's because my father cheats, isn't it?' Beatrice asked bitterly. 'Mama says he cheats. She says he does not like Mr Logan.' Still Sarah stared silently at the ground, scuffing the toe of her little boot. 'I hate my father!' Beatrice hissed vehemently.

'Oh, Beattie!' Sarah was shocked.

'I know 'tis wicked. It says in the bible, "Honour thy father, and thy mother" but I canna', Sarah! I hate him!' Her blue eyes were shadowed with exhaustion. She had spent half the night trying to soothe little Joe, but he was getting another tooth and he could not sleep. Her mama was sick again and Beattie knew there would soon be yet another baby at the Millhouse. Sarah was her best friend in all the world but she could not tell her how cruel her father was to dear Mama, or how he had begun to beat her until she could scarcely sit upon her stool at the table. She shuddered suddenly, remembering the way he had come striding into the kitchen while Mama was bathing her in front of the fire. He had pushed Mama aside and just stood there, staring at her with his small awful eyes - hard, horrible eyes.

Sarah gazed at Beattie in dismay, seeing her distress but unable to understand it. She wished she had never mentioned Strathtod mill, but she had liked the fine black horse and the young man. He had nice manners and such kind, laughing eyes.

Suddenly she turned and hugged Beatrice impulsively.

'I will not go back to that other mill. Maybe Uncle Sandy will not go back either, if I tell him you are my best friend, Beattie. I have no papa now and you do not love yours, so we will love each other and we shall be friends for ever and ever.'

'Do you promise?' Beatrice asked with pathetic eagerness. 'My father says - he says you are to have a new papa. Is it true that your mama is to marry Mr Logan soon?'

'Yes, it is true, but I shall always, always be your friend!' The two little girls smiled at each other.

'Grandfather Miller likes Mr Logan. I shall tell him about father cheating.'

Sarah nodded and they turned and walked side by side into the schoolroom as Dominie Campbell opened the door.

As it happened Sandy was making his third visit to Strathtod mill that very morning. He was in high spirits. It was almost fourteen months since Daniel Munro had died. In two more weeks Mattie would be his bride. He was only halfway along the narrow road when he saw two young men on horseback, galloping madly across an adjoining field. To his amazement they urged their horses straight at the hedge instead of heading for the gate. They landed clumsily on the narrow track, narrowly missing the back of the cart. Fortunately the placid Darkie remained unaffected by their wild yells and halloos.

Even before he reached the mill Sandy guessed they were two of the Fairly brothers from their over-loud voices and arrogant manners. They were clearly looking for trouble. The miller obviously had the same impression. Except for a fearful flicker in his eyes, he gave no sign that he had ever met Sandy before.

'You are from Fairlyden! You have no business here!' James Fairly announced haughtily. 'You were blocking my path, causing a nuisance upon a public highway. I have a mind to summon the constable and have you arrested!'

Sandy looked at the pale-faced young man and could not hide his contempt. He judged him to be in his twenties, totally lacking in any form of grace, either in manner or in looks. Even his eyes seemed colourless and his mean mouth was pursed so tightly that his lips were scarcely visible. It was clear the brothers wanted excitement. Trouble with the occupants of Fairlyden would probably give them extra satisfaction. He remembered the wide gap which had mysteriously appeared in the low meadow where the in-lamb ewes were grazing. It had not been there two days ago; now he understood. The Fairly brothers were intent on provocation. They had been summoned to their father's bedside, cutting short their travels in Europe. The old Earl had rallied again, and while he lingered, his sons kicked their heels and looked for mischief. No doubt they assumed Daniel Munro's deaf widow would be easy prey.

Sandy was taller and stronger than either of them. Despite his being thirty years old; he knew he could punish them both severely in a straight fight. Whatever happened he would not get his corn ground at Strathtod mill today, or any other day, while these two arrogant pups were around. His mouth tightened. He could see the huge wooden mill wheel already turning; he had no wish to go back to Muircumwell and Edward Slater.

Suddenly Sandy remembered another provocation, another fight. He remembered Jacob Reevil at Nethertannoch. That day's evil work had cost him his happiness with Mattie. Now he had been given another chance. In two weeks Mattie would be his. No amount of provocation was going to interfere this time. Nothing must stand in the way of their marriage.

He caught the gleam of anxiety in the miller's eyes. The man would probably lose his job, and his home, if these two knew they had done business together. Calmly Sandy flicked the reins, hiding his frustration with a careless shrug.

'Since you do not care to increase the trade of the Strathtod mill,' he looked pointedly at the empty mill yard, 'I will bid you good morning - gentlemen.'

Neither his surprisingly precise speech, nor the irony in his tone, were lost on the two men. The estate had deteriorated during the past year, but James did not care to hear the truth. Their father was no more than an empty shell, but Reggie had no real authority while he lived, and in any case their elder brother spent most of his energy coughing his heart out in his bedchamber.

Sandy gave the miller a brief salute as he drove his cart out of the mill yard with all the dignity of a gentleman. He was rewarded by the shine of gratitude in the man's eyes. James and Stuart Fairly sat upon their horses and stared after him, open-mouthed. They had wanted a quarrel! The fish had refused the bait!

James Fairly narrowed his eyes angrily. Without further thought he dug his heels viciously into his horse's flanks, sending the startled beast forward at an alarming speed. The miller jumped for his life. Stuart followed his elder brother instantly, blindly, as he had done all his life. His horse sprang forward. It was nearer the mill-lade. Stuart's reactions were slow. He pulled frantically on the bridle, but the wide gap in the tumble-down wall rushed to meet him. The frightened horse tried desperately to respond. He whirled around on his hind legs like a pierrot upon a coin. The miller was momentarily frozen to the spot as horse and rider plunged through the air to crash against the great, ponderously turning mill-wheel.

Sandy had barely driven the cart on to the road when the horse's terrified squeal mingled with Stuart Fairly's inhuman scream. He vaulted from the cart almost before he had pulled Darkie to a halt. Then he was running back across the mill yard, down the slope leading to the back of the mill, the pond, the lade. The miller was there before him, white-faced, staring helplessly at the swirling water.

'Stop the wheel, man!' Sandy cried. 'And bring a rope!'

James Fairly still sat astride his horse, staring in horror at the thrashing limbs of his brother's horse and the peculiar angle of the gleaming neck.

'You are to blame!' he yelled wildly at Sandy. His face was chalky with fear. The miller ran back to them carrying a coil of rope.

'Are you going to rescue your brother?' Sandy demanded curtly.

'In there? The wheel I-I cannot see Stuart.'

'He is trapped below the horse there, see! Against the wheel.' There was no time to argue. Sandy knew the Honourable James Fairly lacked the courage to help his own brother. 'Hold the rope then! Quickly now! Fasten it to your saddle and be prepared to pull back. You direct him!' he added to John Benson, the miller. Sandy could feel the cold sweat breaking out on his forehead. Oh Mattie! Why had he turned back - and for a Fairly? He had so much to lose.

'God help me!' he muttered as he scrambled into the cold, churning water.

Stuart Fairly survived. His horse did not. No one knew whether the Earl understood the full extent of his son's accident or not. He could give no sign, but the flame of life which had flickered so feebly, for so many months, expired three weeks after the accident.

Mattie had been sewing secretly for several weeks in preparation for her wedding to Sandy. Although the ceremony was to be a quiet affair in Fairlyden's front parlour she wanted to look her best. She had re-fashioned a dress which had been carefully stored in the chest belonging to Daniel's mother. The material was dark blue satin with paler blue stripes and Mattie knew she could never have found such beautiful stuff in Mr Jardine's store, even if she could have afforded to buy it. The bodice was covered in tiny sewn pleats and the skirt was very full. She had no hoops to make a fashionable crinoline but she wore all the petticoats she possessed and the tight, pointed waist emphasised her small neat figure. The sleeves were ruched and below the elbow she had stitched bands of blue velvet which exactly matched the little cap she had made and adorned with ribbons and tiny silk flowers.

It was the last week of March, eighteen hundred and sixty-seven.

'Mama!' Sarah almost squealed in excitement. 'The Reverend Mackenzie is coming! He has Mistress Turner, the clogger's wife, in the trap too!'

Mattie was grateful for Mistress Turner's assistance and support. Sarah was already dressed in a gown of lemon-coloured silk embroidered with tiny rosebuds which Mattie had made for her. Her excitement was infectious and it was almost impossible for her to keep still as she hopped from one foot to another in a fever of impatience.

'My, but ye're a real bonny bride!' Mistress Turner exclaimed softly as she gave the ribbons on Mattie's hat a final tweak. She had no daughters of her own and was touched that Mattie had asked for her help. 'I've heard tell Master Logan has waited a long time for this day, but I ken he'll think it has been worth every minute when he catches sight o' ye!' Mattie could scarcely understand her words but she blushed like a young girl at the expression in her eyes.

In the front parlour at Fairlyden the square of carpet had been lifted and beaten, Mattie had polished the mahogany cabinet and two small tables with beeswax and gathered a huge bunch of daffodils from the garden. Their golden yellow trumpets seemed to play a silent fanfare as Mistress Turner held open the door and bid her enter. Sarah followed as sedately as she could manage while Buff padded beside them, tail wagging joyfully. Mattie's eyes flew instantly to Sandy. He was standing stiffly in front of the black horsehair sofa with Joseph Miller at his side. She was rewarded by the light of admiration which shone in his blue eyes, the tender smile which curved his lips as they formed one word.

'Mattie!' He held out his hands and she moved towards him in a dream of happiness. She was unaware of the old miller's nostalgic sigh, or the Reverend Mackenzie's affectionate regard. Louis was standing very straight in his best Sunday suit and his mouth seemed set in a permanent 'O' as he watched Mattie in her fine new gown.

They made their vows with deep reverence before the Reverend Robert Mackenzie, and there was no doubting their enduring love for each other.

Afterwards they ate their meal in the freshly whitened kitchen. Mattie had been saving every farthing she could for this special feast. She wanted Sandy to be proud of her skills as a cook and to repay their guests with suitable hospitality.

She had prepared a light creamy soup with leeks and potatoes; there was a roast chicken with thyme and lemon stuffing and a creamy sauce, slices of succulent pink ham from their own pig, Brussels sprouts fresh from the garden, and glazed parsnips and carrots as well as golden roast potatoes. The dessert was Sandy's favourite trifle topped with cream from the dairy; Mattie had also made a fluffy yellow sponge streaming with golden sugar syrup which Louis and Sarah adored. Sandy was indeed proud of his wife as he basked in the praise heaped upon her by their appreciative guests.

Sarah was unaffected by the marriage, except that she moved from her mother's bedroom to a small chamber of her own. Sandy had delighted her by making a shelf on which she could arrange her small treasures, and he had given her a new book entitled Alice in Wonderland.

Mattie, on the other hand, felt like a shy young girl again, on the very threshold of life, instead of a widow of twenty-five.

Sandy felt his life was complete at last. He had always known there was no other woman who could fulfil his desires and share his dreams as Mattie did. They were more than lovers, they were companions and friends. Together they had faced death, and poverty, even despair; now happiness was theirs. The exchange of a smile or a glance conveyed a whole conversation - between them alone. Mattie's radiance seemed to bathe everyone around her in perpetual sunshine.

It was a week after their marriage before Sandy found time to move his small oak chest to the chamber they now shared. They had retired early that evening, for they cherished the privacy afforded by their bedchamber. Sandy was sorting out his few personal possessions which had lain untouched in the false bottom of the chest since they fled from Nethertannoch. His eye fell upon Matthew Cameron's parting gift, still wrapped in the grey linen. He untied the parcel with a reminiscent smile. Mattie's father had been right after all - he did have many reasons to thank God now. His fingers stilled as he remembered the fine man who had given him a home at Nethertannoch, and treated him as a son.

Sandy glanced up and saw Mattie watching him, her soft dark eyes luminous in the candlelight. Her lips curved in a smile. A faint blush still lingered charmingly in her cheeks as she sat up in the large feather bed, demurely fastening the buttons of her frilled white nightgown for the second time that evening. Sandy's eyes gleamed with love and gentle laughter and her blush deepened. Then her husband's gaze became tender, and serious once more.

'Shall we read a passage from the bible? This was your father's last gift to me.'

Mattie nodded, pleased. She always read a passage from the bible each evening, as her father had done, but she knew Sandy's mind held many doubts - most of which had been planted there by the men of Caoranne: Sir Douglas Irving, the Reverend Lowe, Dominie Butler. Sandy unfolded the linen. He recognised the bible immediately. It was bound in red leather with a brass clasp which kept the flimsy pages intact. It was not large, like the family bible from which Matthew Cameron had read each day and which had been left behind in their hasty flight. This had been Matthew Cameron's own bible, given to him by his father when he was fourteen years old. Sandy opened the worn leather covers reverently. It was almost like meeting his old friend and mentor face to face again. He wished with all his heart that he had opened the package sooner.

Suddenly his hand shook and the colour left his ruddy face. Mattie watched in surprise as he stared at the two cards which had fallen on to the bed, along with a thin sheet of paper. She guessed they had been tucked inside the cover of the bible - perhaps for Sandy to find when he opened the packet?

Sandy passed one of the thin folded cards to her. It bore the name of the Savings Bank near Glen Caoranne. It also bore her own name. There were many entries, sums of money deposited regularly, twice in every year since eighteen hundred and forty-nine. That would be soon after Sandy and his mother had come to live at Nethertannoch. Some of the entries were small, shillings only, some as large as two pounds, ten shillings. As Mattie gazed at them her eyes misted. Her father had saved these precious sums of money since the fever had deprived her of her mother and infant brothers, and left her in her world of silence. She guessed that the smaller sums had been carefully, even painfully, hoarded in years when crops had failed or the cows had not given much milk, or perhaps when disease had killed off the young pigs. She looked up and saw Sandy smoothing the thin sheet of paper. If anything his face was whiter than ever; he finished reading and sat staring sightlessly at the floor.

Gently Mattie took the sheet from his nerveless fingers and Sandy buried his head in his hands, filled with remorse. Matthew Cameron had trusted him implicitly. Why, oh why, had he not shared the older man's faith in God as he had urged him to do? Within the pages of Matthew Cameron's bible lay all the proof Sir Douglas Irving had required. They need not have left the glen or Nethertannoch. He had wasted so much time - so much happiness with Mattie.

She was puzzled by Sandy's reaction. The letter had been written before her father lost the power of his right hand. Perhaps he had had a premonition. Yet why should Sandy be so upset? Her father had trusted him completely; it said so in his letter. He had asked Sandy to take care of her until she reached her sixteenth birthday. After that she was to have the money he had put in the bank for her and she would make her own decisions for the future. Mattie smiled. Her father had known that she possessed the Cameron pride - too much pride to want to be a burden, even to Sandy.

She touched his shoulder gently. 'What troubles you so? You have done all that my father asked - and more.' She shuddered. 'You left the glen for me; you saved me from Jacob Reevil.'

He looked up into her eyes. 'I failed you! I failed your father. "Oh ye of little faith",' he groaned bitterly. 'I should have unwrapped the bible, Mattie! I should have read it, as your father intended.'

'But you have opened it now. The money is safe in the Savings Bank. The minister, Doctor Henry Duncan, made certain of that when he started the first Savings Bank for the poor people in his parish.'

'Ah,' Sandy groaned, 'there's the money too! In every way he treated me as his son.' He handed her the other card. It was the same as her own, except that it bore his name.

Mattie watched him, bewildered. If it was not the safety of her father's savings which bothered him, what was it? Suddenly he grasped her shoulders - as he had always done since she was a child, when he wanted her to understand something important to him.

'It is my fault you had to flee from Nethertannoch! Leave the cattle and pigs - all your possessions! We could have married, Mattie. Sir Douglas Irving demanded proof of your father's wishes. It is there. If only I had listened! "You will find help and guidance in the bible" - those were his words to me! If only... ' He groaned again. Mattie did not understood all his words but she saw the distress in his blue eyes.

'Sandy,' she spoke his name urgently, 'The laird might have accepted my father's letter after his death - but Jacob Reevil would never have heeded anyone's wishes, even if my father had been alive, I think.' She shuddered, 'He wanted more than Nethertannoch! More than a wife for his son. You know he did! He came all the way to Fairlyden to find me!' She trembled at the memory. 'No one could have protected me from that - that beast!' Her soft mouth firmed. 'It was God's will that we should come to Fairlyden, and I am so happy now, with you.' She patted the soft feather bed and blushed shyly. Sandy began to smile, his regrets forgotten - at least for a time.

'You are a witch!' he mouthed silently, but Mattie only smiled and snuggled beneath the woollen blankets, offering an extra little prayer to the Almighty for such a wealth of happiness.

Nineteen

Joseph Miller looked down at Beatrice's small pinched face, framed by the matted golden curls which had once shone so brightly. He saw the bruise on her cheek bone and the purple shadows beneath her eyes, yet he was powerless to interfere between a father and his child, or a man and his wife, even when that wife was his own beloved daughter.

'So Sarah said Mr Logan took her to Strathtod mill.' This time Beatrice knew she had gained her grandfather's full attention. Joseph looked intently at the rosebud mouth which rarely had cause to smile these days. Little Beattie was the only one of his six living grandchildren who looked like Jeannie. She bore no resemblance to that spawn of the devil who had claimed to be her father. He thought of his wife. Every night after Jeannie's marriage to Slater, until the day she died, his Ruthie had grieved in his arms.

'I will deliver the meal to Fairlyden myself,' he decided impulsively. 'I'm getting old, little Beattie, but not so old I want to lose my friends; and the mill canna afford to lose any more customers.' He knew Alexander Logan was not a man to desert a friend without good reason, just as he knew Edward Slater would aggravate, aye, and cheat, the Almighty Himself.

Again Joseph stared into space and his faded blue eyes were troubled. Beattie tugged at his sleeve.

'May I come with you to Fairlyden, Grandfather?'

'Aye, that ye can, my lassie. Sandy has made a fine bridge o'er the burn since the flood, wide enough for the horse an' cart. We'll go on Saturdays when Miss Sarah is home frae the school. I reckon Mistress Logan will make me a cup o' tea while you twae bairns have a wee chat.' He frowned and a line from the scriptures sprang to his mind. "Love is as strong as death; jealousy is as cruel as the grave." Edward Slater had no conception of love, but he had always been consumed with jealousy ever since Sandy Logan first came to the mill and gained Jeannie's admiration. She was rarely outside the mill house door these days, and she had borne him eight children, even though two of them had died at birth - yet still Slater treated her cruelly; recently he had extended his cruelty to Beatrice; he had stopped her going to school because he resented her intelligence and her friendship with little Miss Sarah. 'We'll keep oor visits to Fairlyden a secret, eh, Beattie?' he remarked softly. 'I'll speak tae your mama mysel'.'

Beatrice nodded eagerly, and the old smile shone briefly. She loved her grandfather dearly, but he hardly ever stayed in the mill house now. During the day he was always down with the pigs or milking the cow or attending to his mare. In the evenings he went to the Crown and Thistle. Her father went out in the evenings, too, but she knew he did not go to the Inn as he had told Mama. She had seen him going across the fields to the shacks on the edge of the old quarry. She often wished he would never come back. Then she had to say a hasty prayer and beg Jesus to forgive her.

*

It was a very wet afternoon at the end of September. The previous evening Buff had laid herself wearily at Mattie's feet for the last time; the faithful little dog had earned her final sleep. Mattie thought of Jem Wright, the carrier at Nethertannoch, who had brought her the furry golden bundle eleven years ago. How quickly the little dog had learned to accept her deafness, how eagerly she had tried to help. Buff had been more than a well-loved pet; she had become Mattie's ears, her guardian, her most loyal companion. Now she felt as though one of her own limbs had been severed and her heart ached with sadness. But she was a married woman of twenty-six and must hide her grief from the world. Only Sandy had been allowed to witness her tears in the privacy of their chamber. He understood how much Buff had meant to her - how much his wife had grown to rely on the dog's presence and her intelligence. Sandy had been so tender ... so loving last night.

Today Sandy had work to do and the wet autumn day made Mattie keenly aware of Buff's absence beside the fire. She looked forward to the visit from Joseph Miller and Beatrice each Saturday afternoon. Today their company was doubly welcome. Beattie was such a kind thoughtful little girl, despite the heavy load she had to bear at the mill house. Now she was sitting in front of the fire on the rag rug and Mattie guessed Sarah was telling her about the daffodils she had planted on Buff's grave under the beech tree at the corner of the garden. Sarah fully expected the bulbs would bloom immediately, in honour of the little dog.

Mattie watched the miller's kindly face intently and realised he was promising to get her another puppy. She accepted gracefully. A puppy would comfort Sarah, but Mattie knew no other dog would ever fill the special place Buff had held in her own heart.

Joseph sensed Mattie's need for company and knew how much Beatrice enjoyed her visits to Fairlyden. Also he had hoped to see Sandy, so he lingered longer than usual. The rain had not slackened by the time Mattie and Sarah had to bring in the cows for milking, and the daylight was already dimmed by the curtain of lowering cloud. Joseph shivered at the prospect of the dismal ride back to Muircumwell. His old bones were protesting already. Beattie put her hand in his and they hurried together to the stable where they had left old Daisy, the mare. Sandy had just returned and was rubbing down his horses. Joseph always enjoyed a chat and today he had wanted to tell Sandy about a farm sale which was to be held some miles north of the town of Lockerbie. The farmer had died and his widow was selling everything, including a yearling colt which had all the qualities of a fine Clydesdale stallion. Sandy was just as interested as Joseph had supposed and they discussed the colt's breeding at length. Before they parted they had arranged to travel on the train together to the sale. They had talked longer than they realised and the day was fading fast when they trooped out of the warm stable. Sandy scooped up Beatrice's slight figure and deposited her safely in the cart.

Her skirt and shawl were soaked long before they reached the mill yard and she looked anxiously at her grandfather's hunched shoulders. She knew better than anyone how he hated the wet weather. Her father was never around to help him lift the heavy sacks, she thought bitterly. Wet though she was, she insisted on helping him remove Daisy's harness and brought her some chopped hay and corn while he rubbed her down and brought her a bucket of water.

They both knew the evening meal would be over in the noisy, overcrowded mill house, but they knew there would be a pot of broth waiting by the fire. They looked forward eagerly to its comforting warmth. Unfortunately they had reckoned without Edward Slater's presence. It was long past the hour when he usually set out on his nightly excursions, but Edward always avoided discomfort and trouble. After such incessant rain he guessed Alice Simm would be waiting to nag him again about the safety of the hut which she occupied, along with the two children she had borne him. The last heavy rain had washed away much of the ground and left the dilapidated shacks precariously near the edge of the quarry. So Edward had chosen to stay warm and dry in the mill house, but was finding the querulous demands of his sons intensely irritating.

'Where's that lazy slut?' he demanded for the sixth time. He grabbed Jeannie's arm roughly. 'Answer me! Where is she? And dinna gie me any more lies! She's not in the wash house!'

Jeannie often needed to protect Beatrice from his petty grievances. She knew he enjoyed beating her because she was Sandy's child. He was a brute and a bully - and he was getting worse. She tried to hide her loathing, but she felt deadly tired tonight. She was with child again - her ninth. She was still trying to think of another excuse for Beattie's absence when the door opened. Joseph and Beatrice dashed thankfully into the warm kitchen. They looked like two drowned rats. Edward Slater released his wife at once, but he flew at her daughter, slapping Beatrice's small cold face with the full force of his dirty hand. He grabbed her long wet hair, dragging her into the lamplight. Her teeth were chattering but it was as much from fear as from cold.

'Where have ye bin, you lazy, good-for-naething trollop!' His eyes narrowed suspiciously. 'Have ye been tae Fairlyden?' Beatrice glanced fearfully at her grandfather. Joseph shook his head imperceptibly, but Edward Slater did not need an answer. 'What dae ye think I keep ye for? Do ye think I work like a navvy jist tae mak ye a lady?' He caught the contempt in Joseph Miller's eyes. They both knew that he had never done a decent day's work since the day he arrived at the mill, a snivelling, whining urchin, without kith or kin. Joseph's presence did nothing to calm his filthy temper, though. Indeed it seemed only to goad him further.

'Mama! I'm cold an' 'tis dark up here,' one of the boys cried fretfully from the top of the narrow wooden stairs.

'You get up there and see tae Wullie!' Edward Slater snarled, giving Beatrice a hefty push towards the stairs. She would have fallen on her face had she not crashed into the old dresser first.

'The bairn's soaked to the skin! See how she's shiverin',' Jeannie protested wearily. 'You get some soup, lassie, an gie yer grandfather some, then ye'd better rub yoursel' dry and get intae bed.' She flashed Beatrice a warning glance. They both knew what happened when Edward Slater was in one of his venomous moods and Beatrice shuddered fearfully. 'I'll go and settle that wee demon,' Jeannie added quickly as Wullie shouted again. Joe began to cry somewhere above their heads, wakened by his older brother's noise.

'I said she was to gang tae the lads!' Edward Slater bellowed furiously. 'It's time that madam knew that I'm the master.'

Beatrice fled as she saw him stride towards the wall where he kept a stout leather belt.

'Leave her be!' Jeannie cried despairingly. 'She'll see tae the boys - not that they need anything.' She looked after Beatrice's slight figure, disappearing hurriedly into the darkness above, and without even a towel to dry herself, let alone the hot soup and crust of bread her mother had kept ready.

Edward glowered and paced angrily about the untidy, crowded kitchen. He moved to the window and listened at the wooden shutter. The rain was falling as heavily as ever. There would be no sport with Alice tonight. His glance turned speculatively towards his wife. It was time she gave him some wifely attention, he decided malevolently. He'd left her alone for nearly a week.

Jeannie saw his look and interpreted it correctly. Her heart sank. She hated Edward Slater more with every passing week. There would be no chance to smuggle a warm towel and a wee drop of soup up to Beatrice this night. But there was nothing to stop her looking after her own father. Even Edward only dared go so far with Joseph Miller. While he lived, her husband could only claim half of the mill; he could not turn them out of the house.

She turned and lifted two towels off the wooden frame before the fire, surreptitiously folding them together. She had known Beattie would be soaked and chilled and had warmed the towels specially, and saved some hot water, intending to let her bath in front of the fire when the boys were in bed. She reached for a large enamel mug and filled it with soup from the pot hanging near the fire. She handed it to her father, and as she did so glanced from it towards the stairs, raising her eyebrows.

'Maybe ye'd like tae drink this while ye're getting oot o' yer wet clothes, Faither. There's more i' the pot, if ye've a mind tae come doon for it when ye're dry.'

'Aye, aye, lassie, I'm michty hungry tonight after sic a drookin. I'll sup some more later.' Father and daughter exchanged glances and Jeannie smiled wanly in relief. Perhaps it was fortunate that Edward was so dull-witted.

Joseph shared the upper floor of the mill house with his grandchildren. The boys were together in the biggest room; he had the room which had once been Jeannie's; Beatrice's room was little more than a large cupboard beneath the eaves, with a tiny square of glass in the roof. Joseph found her in the boys' room, kneeling beside Wullie's bed, trying vainly to soothe him into sleep and to still her chattering teeth. He had placed the mug of soup carefully on the clothes chest in his own room, along with his lighted candle. Wullie was the image of his father, in looks and in nature, and Joseph knew he carried tales to Edward, especially if it meant trouble for Beatrice.

'Do ye intend to be a baby all yer life?' he demanded sternly. 'Leave the laddies tae sleep, Beatrice, and get ye oot o' them wet clothes before ye earn yer death.' Beatrice gladly obeyed. Once they were on the small landing, Joseph's expression softened and he beckoned her into his own room and bade her drink the soup.

She accepted gratefully, cupping her hands around the mug in an effort to warm them as she drank. Then as she set the mug down he passed her a towel and instructed her to strip off her wet garments and rub herself dry while he fetched her nightshift. When he returned she was standing with her back to him, trying to rub some warmth into her thin shoulders, while modestly concealing her slight child's body as her mother had taught her always to do, not that she ever felt shame or embarrassment in her grandfather's kindly presence. Joseph Miller was dismayed to see the red weals across her skinny buttocks and shoulders. He handed her the flannel shift and she slipped it over her head gratefully. The bairn must have been severely beaten to have so many marks. He wondered what she could have done to deserve such a thrashing for Beatrice was a kindly little maid, without sullenness or defiance. He turned her shivering body towards him, and while she buttoned her shift up to her neck he took the towel and vigorously rubbed her blonde curls. His own clothes were wet but he was not as affected as Beatrice. Still her teeth chattered and she shivered uncontrollably.

'What ails ye, lassie?' he demanded with gruff concern. He wanted to hug her slight, shaking body and give it warmth but to hold her against his own wet clothes would do no good. 'Come, I'll tuck ye intae yer ain wee bed, like Granny Miller used tae dae when ye were but a babe. Do ye mind o' yer grandmother, Beattie?'

'Oh, yes! I w-wish she was here st-still. Th-then F-father wouldna' flay me wi' his belt, would he?' She turned and her blue eyes were round with fear. She trembled. He knew then what ailed her. It was more than cold or wet. She was shivering with fear - fear of her own father. Well, the bairn had done no wrong this day. If she had come home late, and with sodden clothes, then it was his fault for lingering too long at Fairlyden. Not for the first time he wished passionately that Sandy Logan had been his son-in-law instead of the loathsome Slater.

'Jump into my bed, lassie. Say your prayers there tonight. I'll warm ye in a minute.'

Beatrice obeyed instantly and he saw the relief in her eyes before he blew out the candle. He fumbled to rid himself of his own wet clothes and rub himself dry and warm. He pulled on his thick nightshirt, then as an afterthought groped in the chest and pulled on his clean woollen drawers. He climbed into the big bed and hugged Beatrice's thin little body close to his chest, instilling her with some of his own warmth, gradually dispelling her fears. In a little while he heard the sound of her gentle breathing and knew that she was asleep. He turned on his back and lay staring into the darkness.

'Aye, Ruthie, I wish ye were still here tae!' he muttered softly, thinking of his dead wife with a familiar stab of longing.

A little while later he heard the creak of the stairs and recognised the heavy tread of his son-in-law. His heartbeat quickened. Jeannie and her husband slept downstairs. He heard Edward lift the stiff latch of Beatrice's door. Swiftly Joseph pulled the blankets over her head so that she was shielded from view if her father peered in. He was glad he had kept Beattie with him, but he would prefer her father not to find her hiding in his bed. As it happened Edward Slater assumed Beatrice had curled up beside the boys to quieten them, as she often had to do. He had no wish for their whines and tales. The punishment could wait. He had other things in mind for this night's entertainment.

Jeannie had long since learned to suffer her husband's attentions in silence, longing only for him to be done with her, waiting for him to roll on to his own side of the straw mattress and begin his usual loud snoring. That night, however, Edward was even more brutal than usual. She could not stifle the cry of pain which escaped from her. He had left the candle burning. She saw the smirk on his thick lips and the gleam of malignant satisfaction in his eyes. She knew then that he had planned the night's mischief. Her torment would not be brief. But even Jeannie had not envisaged the cruel degradation Edward Slater devised for her that night, or the length he could sustain such animal lusting.

She could barely crawl from her bed the following morning, much less contend with the squabbles and complaints of her boisterous sons. It was unfortunate that Wullie, unable to command his mother's attention, chose to inform his father of Joseph Miller's sharp words of the previous evening. Edward was tired after the night's orgy.

'She slept wi' ye, didn't she?' He glared balefully at Beattie.

'Naw she didna! An' it was dark!' Wullie complained, ever in search of sympathy.

Edward's small vindictive eyes followed Beattie speculatively. He would give her a real beating tonight then. Beatrice was too concerned by the sight of her mother's white, pained face to pay attention to Wullie or his father.

Long before evening Doctor Kerr had been called. The child which had barely begun to form was emitted from Jeannie's torn and bruised body with riving and bloody force. Beatrice was banned from the chamber but she saw the basins of blood red water which were brought out, and the serious expression upon the doctor's usually reassuring countenance. Her grandfather's lined face was anxious; he refused to leave the house all that day. Beatrice was very frightened. Even the boys were unnaturally subdued and spoke in hushed whispers when they returned from school. They fed the hens and pigs and milked the cow without protest. Only Edward seemed unmoved, until a weary Doctor Kerr, his sleeves still rolled above the elbow, took him aside and spoke to him long and sternly.

'What did the doctor say?' Joseph demanded anxiously, as soon as the door closed behind him.

'She's tae have nae mair bairns!' Edward snorted. 'She's never been much of a wife! Now she'll be nane at a'.'

'Jeannie has been a good wife to you, you scoundrel!' Joseph rose angrily to his feet, his old face tense in his anxiety for his only daughter. 'Will she live?'

Beatrice gasped, but soundlessly. They had for-gotten her presence as she sat in the corner by the fire, struggling to mend the great hole in her brother Bert's stocking.

'Aye, she'll live, if she disna get the fever - more's the pity!' Slater added callously.

'Pity, is't?' Joseph grabbed his son-in-law's jacket and pulled him around. 'An' who would look after your sons then? An 'who wad...?'

'There's ither women wad be glad tae live here wi' me!' Edward sneered. 'Women who ken how tae pleasure a man!'

'Why you - you!' Joseph was too shocked and dismayed to find words - but only for a few seconds. He was an old man, but he was not dead yet. Suddenly he realised he still held one weapon to make Edward Slater see no more harm came to Jeannie at least for as long as he was alive himself.

'Aye then, and who would be feeding and clothing ye, and your sons, and your women, if Jeannie wasna' here?' he asked softly.

Edward stared at him stupidly. Beatrice held her breath. What did Grandfather mean?

'It's law. What belongs to her belongs tae me ' Edward blustered.

'Aah, but this hoose belongs tae me! And the pigs, an' cow! Aye, and the mare! Even the twae fields are rented in my name, remember? We should all be starving if we depended on you. Ruth was right, God rest her! She knew I should never hae given ye a share o' the mill when ye married Jeannie. It wadna keep ye now - never mind yer women!' Joseph rarely lost his temper, and for Jeannie's sake he had held his tongue, but tonight he was too distraught. 'Every man in the parish kens ye wad cheat your ain soul. If Jeannie dies this night, I'll see ye beg for bread on the street before I let ye have anither crust!'

Edward's slack mouth gaped with shock. His pasty face went white with rage. He began to threaten but Joseph cut him short. The floodgates of his own anger and contempt had opened at last.

'We took ye in and treated ye as our ain son. What did ye do, you lazy, guid-for-naething son of a witch? Ye've lied an' cheated! Ye even took an innocent lassie under the roof that sheltered ye! Aye, 'twas a sorry day, the day you married Jeannie. You broke her mother's heart aye, you killed my Ruth.'

'Aagh!' Edward gave such a bellow of rage that Beatrice almost jumped out of her skin, and even her grandfather released his grasp on her father's jacket and stepped back.

'I didna' take an innocent lassie! Your precious Jeannie married me tae save her ain character,' he sneered. 'An' her mother's holy pride. An' the Miller name!'

Beatrice's eyes grew round and anxious. Grandfather looked so white. He had gone so quiet. Joseph sensed that Edward was on the point of telling him something important.

'Then who?' he croaked. Suddenly he remembered Beatrice and spun round, catching her wide-eyed stare. She plied the darning needle with agitated speed. It pricked her finger and she gasped aloud, drawing her father's attention. He fixed her with a hard speculative gaze, his slow wits pondering his dilemma.

If he told the old man that Logan was her father, he might take her to Fairlyden, especially if Jeannie died. She was welcomed there already; she had always been too friendly with the deaf woman's brat. Aye, Mistress Logan an' her bible preaching ways, she would take her in - even if she was Logan's bastard. Supposing Logan ever found out that he had beaten her? Edward's face whitened as his thoughts progressed. If Jeannie had not been so proud she would have guessed he didn't want Logan to find out the truth, any more than she did herself. As usual he resorted to bullying.

'It'll be the worse for her,' he glared at Beatrice, 'if ye dae the wrong thing by me - whether your ain precious daughter dies or no'!' His voice was low and filled with menace. Joseph turned away from him in disgust. Edward lifted his hat from the peg and slammed out of the door.

At last Joseph understood some of the things which had puzzled him - why Edward treated Jeannie so cruelly, why he hated Beatrice. Ruth had been convinced that their beloved granddaughter had none of Slater's blood in her. Joseph was glad his wife had been right about that. If only he had listened to her advice. He sighed. It was too late for regrets. Maybe Jeannie would confide in him when she recovered. He prayed fervently that God might allow him a few extra years to help her and Beattie.

Jeannie survived, but her mind could not accept the shock and pain, the ordeal and torment she had suffered at the hands of the man who called himself her husband. She sought refuge in solitude and silence. Her life had become a long shadow where unspeakable horrors lurked around each and every corner.

At Fairlyden they heard little of Mistress Slater. News of her illness was overshadowed by accounts of the landslide at the old quarry. Two of the shacks had collapsed into the bottom of the quarry. The bodies of a woman, known as Alice Simms, and two young children had been found amidst the debris. The story which circulated in the village claimed that the tragedy had been discovered by Edward Slater, who had been walking alone. He had supposedly been seeking solace after learning that his wife's mind had been deranged by a severe loss of blood.

Beatrice was not yet ten years old but she had long since learned to wash and scrub and cook. Now she looked after her mother and did her best to feed her hungry brood. There was rarely time for visits to Fairlyden. Mattie regretted the little girl's heavy burden but there was little she or Sarah could do to help in the face of Edward Slater's hostility.

Twenty

Christmas came and went and Mattie awaited the dawn of the New Year with growing anticipation. She left the candle burning so that she could see Sandy's lips and watch his face. The grandfather clock in the hall of Fairlyden had once belonged to Lord Jonathan Fairly. Sandy listened to its sonorous tick, waiting for it to strike the midnight hour, infected by Mattie's unusual excitement. At last he heard it. The year of eighteen hundred and sixty-eight had begun. He leaned over and kissed his wife gently, his blue eyes glowing.

'A happy New Year to you, Mistress Mattie Logan!'

Mattie had waited for this moment to share her news with Sandy, news which she was sure had been born out of her husband's tender loving during those autumn nights after Buff's death, when she had missed the little dog's company so dreadfully. Her face was alight with joy in the dim light of the flickering candle. She was unable to keep the secret a moment longer.

'You will be the father of another bairn before this year is half over, Sandy.' She watched the incredulous joy, tenderness and love which chased each other over his face, and her heart seemed to overflow with happiness. Long after she slept, Sandy lay awake contemplating Mattie's news.

Son or daughter, this child will be truly mine! It will bear my name! It will call me Father. He laughed exultantly to himself. He loved Sarah dearly, and knew she loved him, but she must always think of Daniel Munro as her true parent. The deceit surrounding her birth would always irk him; he had too much integrity to accept the situation easily. It was true that Strathtod was a wealthy estate and Fairlyden's one hundred and twenty-five acres were relatively insignificant against it, but it was the principle which troubled him and especially the denial of his love for his own daughter.

He reached out and felt Mattie's soft warm body at his side. A fountain of happiness rose in him as his thoughts turned once more to the child she carried. Secretly he hoped she would bear him a son - maybe several sons. They would all be good farmers and stockmen for they would be Mattie's sons too, possessed of the Cameron blood. His heart soared within him.

The year ahead promised real happiness for Mattie and himself. Even the horses were beginning to bring in a little money at last. One of the Fairlyden colts had earned the stallion premium from the district Agricultural Society for his new owner. His own dream of keeping a fine stallion was getting nearer; one day breeders would send their mares to Fairlyden and be pleased to pay for the privilege,. So Sandy's thoughts wandered as he listened to Mattie's gentle breathing, loving her with every fibre of his being as he drifted into sleep.

*

As the weeks passed and the snowdrops heralded another spring, other changes were taking place at Fairlyden. Louis Whiteley had left his boyhood behind and manhood brought both joy and responsibilities.

'I-I want tae get married,' he told Sandy shyly one morning as they were working together, spreading the little heaps of dung scattered over the field.

'Is that so?' Sandy exclaimed, feigning surprise. He had noticed Louis walking down to Muircumwell whenever he had an hour to spare in the evenings last summer, and he had taken to going to church regularly without any persuasion on Mattie's part. 'I wonder if the lucky lady is the maid at the manse?'

'Aye, her name's Janet,' Louis informed him eagerly, then his face fell. 'The thing is, Mr Sandy, I dinna want tae leave Fairlyden. I hae bin here since I left school but I'll need tae look for a place wi' a cottage.'

'We shall be sorry to lose ye, Louis,' Sandy said slowly. 'Very sorry. Fairlyden willna be the same without ye.'

When they were alone together, Sandy told Mattie of Louis's plans.

'Oh dear, we shall miss him!' she said with a note of consternation. 'Especially at this time.' She looked down at her swelling body. 'We shall need to hire another boy unless...'

'Unless what, my love?' Sandy asked tenderly.

Mattie knew Louis would never possess the inborn instinct of the true stockman, but he was a loyal, hard-working young man and with Sandy's guidance had become one of the best ploughmen in the area. He had even won some of the big ploughing matches. She remembered how glad they had been of his puny labours when the Reverend Mackenzie had brought him to Fairlyden nine years earlier!

'Do you think could we afford to build a cottage at Fairlyden?' she asked diffidently. 'Maybe Janet would be willing to help me with the milking and the dairy? I shall be glad of help when the babe comes.'

'Why, Mattie, that is an excellent idea!' Sandy exclaimed.

The young couple were delighted at the prospect of having their very own home, as well as a garden where they could grow vegetables and build a sty for a pig.

'Janet is a good, clean girl,' the Reverend Mackenzie assured Mattie. 'She has no experience of dairy work but she is eager to learn, especially from someone who has a reputation for making the best butter in the parish,' he added with a smile.

Mattie was almost as delighted as Louis at the prospect of having Janet at Fairlyden. There would be extra work with the baby and she had no wish to make Sarah a young drudge like her friend, Beatrice. Sandy had promised that Sarah could stay at school until she was thirteen so that she would learn everything the good dominie could teach her.

Gradually a track had formed directly from the house, across the fields, to the new bridge. Although it was very muddy in winter, it was almost a mile shorter than the meandering path round by the burnside. Sandy and Louis had planted young hawthorn bushes and several beech trees along either side. Already they were growing into thick hedges, providing shelter for the animals in the fields, as well as keeping them from wandering over the track. The hedge also sheltered Sarah's small figure from the full blast of the winter's icy winds as she trudged to and from school, and recently Sandy had bought a light trap and a pony so that Mattie could continue taking her eggs and butter into Muircumwell. The track had gradually become the main access to Fairlyden and they all agreed that Louis and Janet's cottage should be built beside it.

The new track also had the advantage of being as far as possible from the boundary with Strathtod. The young Earl was suffering from the wasting disease and his brother, the Honourable James Fairly, had taken advantage of his sickness to flaunt his own authority. He had inherited his father's vindictive nature, and to make matters worse he lacked Lord Gordon's knowledge and his desire to preserve and improve the estate. Sandy avoided James Fairly and his petty provocations whenever possible. It was one more reason for building the cottage as far as possible from the Strathtod boundary.

Spring was almost over. The ploughing had long since been completed, the hedges neatly laid. Young lambs were frisking in the fields. Sandy had finished sowing the corn - twelve acres in all. Only the turnip drilling remained. This year they were to be grown in the fields furthest from the steading, according to the rotation which Sandy had devised to restore the fertility to each of the fields in turn. Louis had carted all the manure from the cattle sheds during the winter.

'If we could just have a shower o' rain, conditions would be right for drilling now,' Sandy declared one fine May morning. He had learned from experience that if the corky covered clusters of turnip seeds lay dormant too long they would be picked out by the birds, or smothered by weeds before they had had time to grow; it was vital to get the right time and conditions. 'We must have the drilling finished before the wedding in two weeks' time!' he grinned at Louis. Janet was leaving the manse at the May term and the wedding had been planned for then. She would just have time to settle into her new life at Fairlyden before the birth of the baby around the middle of June.

Already Sandy insisted on carrying the water from the burn, and Sarah had learned to help with the milking. She had her own small three-legged stool and dealt competently with two of the older cows each morning before she went to school, and again in the evening. Sarah was quick and eager to learn any new skill and Mattie was justifiably proud of her nine-year-old daughter. Even so she secretly looked forward to having Janet to help with the churning, and the hens and pigs, as well as some of the heavier work in the house. She had been troubled with backache for some months and had begun to think that Sandy's son - and she was convinced the babe must be a boy - had feet like the largest mare in the stable, and twice as many of them! If he was not punching her stomach to make her sickly, then he punched at her bladder and had her running to the privy or searching beneath the bed for the chamber pot in the middle of the night. Two months ago her ankles had begun to swell and she now found it impossible to tie up her boots. She had taken to wearing her clogs all the time, but even then she had had to ask Mr Turner, the clogger, to make a bigger pair than usual.

So Mattie watched the progress of Louis's cottage with as much satisfaction as his bride to be. The Muircumwell mason had finished building the walls, and the roof had been thatched. All that remained was for Dick Anderson, the carpenter, to finish the windows and the stout oak door.

It was the last week in May. A gentle shower during the night had made the ground ideal for sowing the turnip seeds. There was no time to lose. A good crop of roots was essential to keep the cows milking well, and the bullocks in good condition through the winter. Sandy found himself murmuring an involuntary prayer of thanksgiving for so much contentment. He and Louis planned to work until evening and make the most of the long, perfect day. As the field was some distance from the steading Mattie packed bread and cheese and a bottle of cold tea for their lunch, and Louis had a bag of chopped hay and oats for the horses. She waved them off with a smile. She intended spending the morning weeding her vegetables, for she was proud of her productive garden.

She had been weeding for about half an hour when she stood up to stretch her aching back. Over the garden wall she saw one of the ducks waddling away on her own.

'Ah!' she muttered gleefully. She had been sure one of the khaki-coloured ducks had a nest hidden somewhere; so far she had not been able to find it. She had no intention of leaving the silly bird to sit there hatching ducklings for the fox to eat. She must be brought back to safety, and her eggs along with her. Sarah usually kept her sharp young eyes on the broody hens, watching over their chicks when they hatched, but the ducks wandered further away and were not so easy to find. Today Sarah was at school and Mattie was determined to follow the roving duck to her hiding place.

She skirted the garden wall and caught sight of the duck waddling through the long grass at an oblique angle, towards the burn. She followed carefully, keeping her distance in case the duck should become alarmed. Mattie was surprised how far and how fast the duck could waddle on her short legs. At last she paused, cocking her head first to one side and then to the other. Mattie stood perfectly still, knowing those bright eyes would be peering around to make sure no one had seen her; all nesting birds were surprisingly wily, and exceedingly clever at camouflaging their nests from human eyes. Suddenly the duck darted through the grass, heading straight towards the burn. Mattie followed. She lost sight of the little dun-coloured bird amongst the long dried grasses and reeds which grew along the banks of the burn at this particular point. It was low, barely more than a trickle in places, and there was no sign of the duck enjoying a morning swim. Mattie frowned and stared around with fierce concentration. The duck must have reached her destination. Even now she was probably crouching upon her nest, laying another egg, before she decided to hatch them. Mattie bent as low as her considerable bulk would allow, and peered through the gently waving grasses. Slowly she moved nearer the edge of the burn, reluctant to give up the chase now that she had followed the duck so far.

Over the years the burn had washed right into the bank in places, forming miniature caves which were ideal hiding places when the water was so low. Mattie scanned several of these overhanging ledges, but there was no sign of the duck. She sighed in exasperation. She had wasted almost an hour and now she was hot and tired. She turned round to retrace her steps but the toe of her clog caught in a knot of twisted grasses and she gasped at the pain which shot through her ankle as she fell, groping helplessly for something to save herself. The sandy bank had been undermined by years of minor floods. It trembled beneath the sudden weight of her fall. Suddenly it crumbled completely, catapulting her ungainly bulk heavily on to the washed pebbles beside the burn.

Normally Mattie would have scrambled lightly to her feet with little more than a grimace at her rapidly swelling ankle, but it was not advisable for a heavily pregnant woman to go hurling herself on to the hard bed of a dried up burn. She lay for a moment, too dazed by the fall to consider her predicament. The old Mattie might have bathed her ankle in the clear, cold water and eventually hopped back to the house. There was no question of hopping anywhere in her present condition and she soon realised that. Tears of angry frustration sprang to her eyes, but she blinked them swiftly away. It would be hours before anyone missed her. Sandy and Louis would not be back until dusk Sarah was at school.

Her ankle was throbbing. She sat up and began to edge her way towards the burn intending to bathe it in the cold water, to soothe it. Suddenly her whole body seemed to convulse with pain, a pain far worse than that in her ankle - and far more alarming. She lay still, panting softly. Gradually the spasm passed. She sat up again, breathing a prayer of thankfulness as she eased off her clog and stretched her foot towards the shallow water. She tried to wriggle her toes but the pain shot up her leg and she contented herself with resting her throbbing ankle in the cool, soothing flow of the stream.

Mattie was unprepared for the next onslaught of pain which grabbed her body like the clenched fist of some bestial giant. She felt the perspiration break out on her brow. Again the pain eased and she lay back thankfully on the smooth pebbles. She passed the tip of her tongue over her upper lip and tasted the salt from her own sweat. She clenched her jaw and tried to swallow the fear which threatened to overwhelm her. She must keep calm. She guessed her fall had precipitated the birth of the baby. The pains came again, and passed; but they returned with increasing regularity and force. She felt the warm thrust of fluids spilling out of her. She did not know whether she cried out or not; she only knew she had to keep calm, she had to take care of her unborn child - Sandy's child, Sandy's son.

Each time the pains subsided Mattie forced herself to rest, to relax her tense muscles with a conscious effort. She was powerless to halt the force within her. She knew she must go with it; she must help her child, and Sandy's, to live. Mattie had never lacked courage and although the pains were fearsome the labour was relatively short. Her son lay there, bawling angrily, still bound to her by the life-giving membranes. Mattie pulled the hem of her cotton petticoat up to her mouth and with her teeth tore a strip of clean white cotton to tie the cord which joined them together. Then she fell back exhausted, collecting her strength, knowing she must lift the child to her and give him the warmth of her own body.

Eventually she managed to wrap the baby in her shawl and cradle him against her breast. He stopped crying and closed his eyes and she gazed at the small perfect body with pride and joy. His tiny face was waxy and unwashed as yet but she could see how fair his skin was and the fine covering of hair on his tiny head was the colour of ripening corn. He would be just like Sandy had been when he first came to Nethertannoch when he was thirteen, Mattie decided proudly; before his hair darkened and only red-gold lights remained to glint in the sun. Before he attained the weathered skin of manhood. She felt a glow of satisfaction as she visualised his surprise and delight. When he returned to the house and found her absent he would search for her. She grimaced at the pain in her ankle as she edged herself back to a more comfortable place close against the bank of the burn, sheltered from the breeze by the overhanging miniature cliff. Exhaustion claimed her and she slept, the baby snuggled warmly against her breast.

She wakened suddenly, with a feeling of alarm, wondering where she was. Then she felt the pain and knew that was what had wakened her. It was as though a violent storm was going on inside her. She had a terrible desire to push it out of her. She was being turned inside out, and yet the pain went on and on. There was no respite - none! Suddenly Mattie understood. There was another child! Twins! Her mother had born twin sons, how could she have forgotten? Yet she scarcely remembered the young brothers who had died along with her mother all those years ago. She knew now why the last months had been so physically unpleasant. Carefully, gasping a little, she wrapped the shawl more tightly around the baby and put him aside on the dried grasses.

She was filled with a new burst of strength; the desire to push this second small demon into the world was intense. She felt the sweat on her body. She tried, and tried, but the child would not be born! The pain was unbearable. Mattie thought perhaps she screamed in her agony but she did not care. She panted, gasping for breath, praying for strength to deliver her child. She felt herself sinking into darkness and summoned all her will power. But still the child refused to enter the world.

'Please God, help me!' she screamed aloud. Ten yards away the duck she had followed earlier rose from its comfortable nest in alarm and waddled away with a series of anxious quacks. Mattie neither saw nor remembered it. She lay with clenched fists, struggling to combat the dreadful beast within her. It sought to tear her apart with a thousand sharp fangs and she was powerless to help herself.

Twenty-One

Sarah hummed softly as she wandered up the track on her way home from school. It had been ages since she had last seen Beatrice. They had had a lovely time catching up on each other's secrets. Beatrice said her grandfather had got a black puppy named Jet and would be bringing it to Fairlyden soon; if only Mr Slater had not forbidden Beatrice to come too, Sarah thought with a frown. Why was he always so horrid to Beattie?

A blackbird darted out of the hedge. Sarah stood still and watched. She knew it had a nest. She had seen it; it had four greeny-blue eggs with red-brown speckles. As she waited, the bird returned with a worm in its mouth and Sarah grinned. The eggs must have hatched into little birds. She would have liked to look at them but Uncle Sandy said it was cruel to frighten them. She walked on again.

At the cottage she stopped to watch Mr Anderson, the carpenter, making curls of paper-thin wood as he painstakingly fitted the window frames to the cottage where Louis and Janet were going to live. A few weeks ago there had been nothing but a patch of field. Soon there would be a real house with smoke coming out of the chimney. Mr Anderson smiled at her and stopped for a minute, just long enough to reach for his piece-bag and take out a biscuit. He always saved a biscuit for her.

'I must go now,' she said when she had demolished the last crumb. 'I have two cows of my own to milk,' she told him proudly.

'Aye,' Mr Anderson nodded solemnly but there was a twinkle in his crinkly blue eyes, 'ye're a real pretty milk-maid, Miss Sarah.'

She was surprised to find the cows still grazing in the meadow when she passed. She was even more surprised to find the door of the house firmly closed when she reached home. She stretched up to the sneck to lift the latch. No smell of cooking reached her. She had heard Mama promising to make Uncle Sandy's favourite stew with lots of meat and onions and potatoes, for when he came home from the turnip field. Sarah loved her mama's stew and so did Louis. Mama had promised to teach Janet how to make it when she came to work at Fairlyden. There wasn't even a fire nothing but dull grey ash.

'Mama!' Sarah called instinctively, although she knew her mother could not hear. Mattie usually had a glass of buttermilk waiting when Sarah arrived home from school. There was none today. She ran outside eager to impart the news of the newly hatched eggs, and the new windows in Louis's cottage. The byre was empty and clean; no warm smell of cows, no soothing strum of milk flowing into the piggin.

'Mama!' Sarah called again. She ran back to the house, through the dairy this time. There was no one there. She clattered up the stairs to her mother's bedchamber. It was empty, the patchwork cover neatly smoothed. There was no sign of Mattie anywhere!

Perhaps Mama had needed more water? Perhaps Uncle Sandy had forgotten to bring any because he had been in a hurry to get to the turnip field? Yes, that would be it, Sarah decided and ran to the burn.

A few hundred yards away Mattie lay, fighting the rolling waves of pain-filled darkness which kept enveloping her. Her face was grey and damp with fatigue. Her world was a solitary, silent place. Beside her the baby lay wrapped tightly in his mother's shawl, missing the comforting beat of her heart beneath his tiny cheek.

Sarah did not hear his faint mew as she turned back to the house. She had walked four miles to school that morning, and home again; she had run hither and thither and her legs felt weary, but she began to run. She was a sensible child but a strange panic gripped her now and she called out - again and again, her child's voice shrill with a fear she did not understand, for there was nothing about the familiar surroundings to frighten her.

She went to the meadow. The cows looked up with interest. Some of them ambled towards the gate. They always knew when it was time for milking, and Sarah knew her mama never kept them waiting but she was nowhere in sight. Sarah bit her lip to stop it trembling.

'Mama-a-a, where are you?' she called loudly now. In her distress she forgot Buff was no longer there to alert her mother to her calls. Again Sarah searched in the byre and in all of the little wooden hens' houses; she peered over the doors of the pig sties; she even looked in the deserted stable. She could see the cows beginning to gather at the gate now, wanting to come in for milking. She had to find Mama! There was nowhere else to look except the far field where Uncle Sandy and Louis would be drilling the turnips. It was such a long way and Sarah's legs ached, but she set off determinedly, panting, even sobbing a little beneath her breath as she stumbled across first one field and then another.

*

Rory O'Connor had never fully recovered from the effects of the chill he had suffered the night he rescued Sarah from the flood. It had taken many months before the terrible wheezing in his lungs had lessened and he had been fit to venture out. Ever since, the slightest chill had brought on a recurrence, making his thin chest pump painfully. He had been recovering from another of these attacks during the past few weeks, but when he wakened and saw the fresh May morning, the whole world of sky and fields and woods so newly washed, he felt the pull of his old haunts. He remained indoors reluctantly, but only on account of his mother's earnest pleading. After a meagre midday meal she took her basket and set out for the village store and Rory could no longer resist the voices which seemed to beckon him forth.

He walked slowly, savouring each blade of grass, each bird and flower. He moved aimlessly, breathing deeply in the pure air. After a while he sat on a fallen tree trunk and surveyed the scene around him. Already many things had changed since the death of the old Earl. He had never been popular with his tenants, but he had kept the estate in good order, the houses and buildings in repair. He had dismissed tenants who could not, or would not, maintain his property - all that is, except Mr Munro. Now Fairlyden was the best farm of them all, Rory mused. It was a pity the young Lord Reginald was too ill to see it. He would have appreciated the green grass and the corn and cattle. A raging thirst brought Rory to his feet.

He considered returning home for a drink of his mother's rosehip cordial but somehow he found his footsteps heading in the direction of the Strathtod burn. He was some distance downstream when he heard the shrill cry of 'Mama'. He paused in the act of drinking the water from his cupped hands, but the cry did not come again. Sarah had already turned disconsolately away to make another search of the farmyard.

The sun was moving towards the western skyline and Rory knew he ought to retrace his steps, if only for his mother's peace of mind. Yet he wandered along, up the burnside, as though drawn by some invisible thread. His hearing was acute and he paused; a faint cry reached his ears, like that of a kitten in distress. He looked about him in surprise, moving forward cautiously, following the tiny, persistent sound.

Rory had seen many wonders of nature, and he had seen many of her cruelties, but he had never seen a woman in childbirth, nor considered the agony - and despondency - of such a natural phenomenon. Both were evident in Mattie's dark, pain-filled eyes. He moved closer, disturbed by the blood-stained pebbles and grass. The mewing began again and he saw the shawl. He bent and pushed the folds gently aside and gazed upon the unbathed infant. His eyes darted in alarm. Here was the babe, tightly swathed and protected by the mother's own shawl - yet still her body writhed and strained and without result. He knew instinctively that the needs of both mother and child were urgent. He picked up the crying infant, cradling the bundle in his arm, then he bent over Mattie.

'I bring help!'

She stared up at him without comprehension. Then her vacant stare fixed upon the child and her brown eyes dilated with fear. She struggled to raise herself. Rory pushed her back gently. He began to gabble, bending closer, trying to offer reassurance. As usual, in his agitation, the words tumbled over each other and Mattie saw only his fumbling lips.

'Tam Reevil!' she screamed. 'Go! Leave my baby! Oh, please leave me!' Her wide, wild eyes glazed with the onslaught of renewed pain and she sank back, swallowed by a suffocating darkness.

Rory ran all the way home, carrying the newborn child against his heart, ignoring the searing pain in his chest. Maisie O'Connor's relief swiftly turned to dismay when she saw his ashen face. He passed the bundle to her and the infant cried in protest. She stared down incredulously, then she looked up at Rory and her eyes filled with fear.

'Where did ye get this? Take it back! Take it back before ye get hung.' She thrust the bundle towards him.

'Need help!' he gasped. 'Come, Mother, come!'

He turned back towards the door, but his mother stilled him with a hand on his arm. She gathered her senses. Rory would never harm anything, least of all a child. Something was amiss.

'Tell me, laddie. Slowly now.' Rory relaxed a little and his breathing eased.

'By the burn. Fairlyden.'

'Fairlyden? Oh, no!' Maisie's face blanched.

'The mother ' Rory glanced desperately at the bundle in her arms 'lying by burn. She ' He frowned, then simulated Mattie's straining. He pointed to the floor. 'Blood! Much.'

'We cannot leave the babe here,' she muttered. 'It might die.' But Rory was already outside. Swiftly she grabbed her shawl, a clean white apron and a towel. She had little idea what lay in front of her.

Maisie O'Connor arrived at the burnside, panting breathlessly for she was no longer a young woman, but when she saw Mattie her heart filled with pity. The girl was barely conscious. Maisie wasted no time as she gently made herself familiar with Mattie's situation. Her lined face looked suddenly old.

'We must get her tae the hoose. Bring her man, Rory!' She forgot her son's recent illness in the urgency of the moment.

He stared from his mother to Mattie and back again.

'Help her? Now?'

Maisie O'Connor rose up stiffly and put her face close to her son's.

'Listen well, son.' Her voice was soft, but Rory recognised the desperation in it, and in his mother's overbright eyes. 'I canna help her. She needs a doctor - a doctor, Rory.' She watched her son's eyes widen.

No one in the O'Connor house had a doctor unless it was a choice between life and death.

'Aye, aye!' he gabbled and turned to run. He knew exactly which field Mr Logan had prepared for this year's turnip crop and he knew he would find him there on such a day.

'Take care, son, take care!' Maisie muttered under her breath.

*

Sandy heard Sarah's call as he reached the edge of the field. He smiled to himself but did not halt; the bairn often came to meet him and ride home on the horses. Sarah almost sobbed in frustration.

'I canna find Mama!' she screamed. 'Mama's lost!' Only one word registered in Sandy's mind: 'Mama'. He pulled the horses to a halt and gave Sarah's stumbling little figure all his attention now. He realised she was upset - sobbing - and Sarah was not a child given to hysterics.

He ran towards her over the straight brown rows, gathering her in his arms, brushing away her tears with a gentle, dusty finger.

'Tell me, Sarah, what is it?'

'I couldna' find Mama,' she muttered, feeling suddenly foolish, staring down at the little lumps of soil. Sandy screwed up his eyes at the westering sun.

'Surely she will be at the milking?' He tried to hide the anxiety which suddenly filled his heart. The baby was not to be born for at least three weeks, Mattie had said, and she had been smiling and bright this morning.

'The cows are still in the field.'

'I will come home with you. You can ride home on Prince's back, eh?'

Sarah nodded eagerly. Her legs felt very tired and she loved a ride on the horses, so long as Uncle Sandy or Louis walked close by. Sandy swiftly unhooked the chains, but as he straightened he saw Rory O'Connor's thin figure in the distance. He beckoned wildly, then he bent almost double, shaken by a spasm of coughing which left him gasping for breath. Sandy led the horse as quickly as he could towards the lad. As he got closer he saw that his face and lips were alarmingly blue.

'Surely you are the laddie who saved Sarah's life?' He exclaimed in surprise. Rory nodded.

'Go!' he gasped. 'Quick. Babe '

'Mistress Logan? She's all right?' Sandy knew his voice was sharp with fear.

'You go. Get doctor,' Rory gasped for breath, but at least it stopped his words pouring forth unintelligibly.

'Get on the horse with Sarah. Save yourself now,' Sandy said kindly, but Rory shook his head. Sandy's mouth was tight. 'I must run ahead.'

'By the burn! Bring him ' Rory pointed to Louis. 'Get doctor soon. I…' His thin body shook with another spasm of coughing and afterwards his breath whistled painfully from his congested lungs. 'You go.' he groaned, and glanced at Sandy in despair.

'You have done well.' Sandy's face was white as he cupped his hands to his mouth and shouted for Louis. 'Sarah!' He lifted her from the horse's back and stared into her frightened eyes. 'Mama needs me. Be brave now. Wait here for Louis. Ask him to tie the horses together. Tell him to follow as quickly as he can. Do you understand?' he demanded urgently. 'You must lead the mare, and Prince will walk beside her.' He looked into Sarah's anxious face. 'Bring them home to the stable. Take care now, there's my brave girl!' He did not wait for an answer.

Maisie O'Connor was a practical woman and she had seen many troubles while rearing her own large brood. Twice she had believed her own time had come, but each time the good Lord had spared her. She greeted Sandy calmly, but she was relieved to see Louis not far behind him running down the slope, with Rory some distance behind; her beloved Rory who had once been as fleet as a young stag, and never tired. She pushed her own anxiety aside.

'You have a son,' she nodded at the bundle in her arms.

'But…' Sandy brushed her aside, ignoring the child he had longed for as he sank to his knees beside Mattie and tried to cradle her in his arms. He spoke her name desperately, willing her to open her eyes so that she would see and understand him. Maisie O'Connor watched him with compassion for a moment or two, but as soon as Louis panted up to them she became brisk.

'Send him for the doctor. We must get her to the house. There's no time to waste.'

Sandy stared up into Maisie O'Connor's grave grey eyes and his heart thudded sickeningly. She was a stranger to him but her eyes spoke a thousand words in that single steady glance. He obeyed instantly.

'Take the pony and trap to Muircumwell. Bring Doctor Kerr. Hurry, Louis!' Maisie O'Connor hesitated then spoke quietly, her grey eyes holding Louis's intently.

'And the minister. Tell them both to hurry, laddie.'

Doctor Kerr arrived with his pony in a great lather. Louis followed with the minister. Robert Mackenzie had brought Janet too. He understood every aspect of his peoples' needs; he knew that no matter what happened at Fairlyden on this beautiful May evening, the cows would still have to be milked and the animals fed. He dispatched Louis to take charge of the two ponies, and the horses which the white-faced Sarah was nervously leading into the yard.

Maisie O'Connor had kindled up the fire and boiled water. When an almost inhuman cry echoed from the bed chamber, she decided this was not the place for an innocent, wide-eyed lassie on the very threshold of womanhood herself. She dispatched Janet to gather in the cows and instructed her not to return until she and Louis had finished the outdoor work. She had already sent Rory home, smothering her anxiety at the sight of his blue lips, and sallow skin, and the labouring of every precious breath.

Sarah was a different matter. The child's feet dragged with exhaustion and she slumped on to the rag rug before the fire. Maisie lifted the muslin cover from a jug of buttermilk she had found in the dairy and filled a cup. Sarah drank it gratefully. It seemed to revive her and she looked at Maisie curiously.

'Who are you? Where's Mama?'

'I'm Mistress O'Connor. And what wad your own name be, m'dear?'

'Sarah. Sarah Munro.'

'Ah, Sarah Munro.' Maisie's face clouded as she remembered she was at Fairlyden - helping its mistress too! She hoped that fiend, the Honourable James Fairly, never had cause to hear of this day's work. Already he had dismissed the factor who had mediated between the tenants and the young Earl.

'Wad ye like an oatcake spread wi' honey?' she asked Sarah hastily, trying to forestall the child's questions as hurried footsteps sounded on the stairs and the doctor called for her to bring more hot water. She passed Sarah two oatcakes and told her to wipe her sticky fingers when she had finished.

'Then ye can rock this wee mite if he cries.' She led Sarah to the shadowy corner beside the wide range, where Mattie usually stacked her kindling wood to dry. Maisie had bathed the baby while she had waited for the doctor to arrive and Sandy had silently brought her the little chest of flannel gowns which Mattie had sewn all winter long. Now he lay, sleeping peacefully, at least for a little while, and looking like an angel. Sarah gazed down at the tiny infant in wonder and delight, her tiredness forgotten.

'Can I keep it?' she asked excitedly.

'Aye.' Maisie sighed heavily. 'He is your ain wee brother. Ye'll hae tae look after him well now, eh?'

'Oh I will! I will!' Sarah cried ecstatically. 'He will be even better than a puppy! What's his name? Do you know?'

Maisie O'Connor shook her head as she listened to Sandy's heavy footsteps pacing relentlessly back and forth outside his wife's chamber. Every now and then she heard the voice of the minister talking to him calmly. He had a nice voice, the minister, even if he did belong to the Free Kirk. She sighed again and lifted the kettle of boiling water and carried it upstairs.

Presently she returned. She lifted the baby in her arms and beckoned Sarah to follow her upstairs. Her kindly eyes were shadowed.

'Come, ma bairn. We'll show your mama the babe.' Sarah followed eagerly.

'Can I hold him?'

'Aye, if ye're careful, when we're safely up the stairs.' Maisie opened the door and carefully transferred the tightly swathed bundle to Sarah's eager arms. Sarah was surprised to see so many people upstairs. She faltered uncertainly. There was a man standing at the little window with his back to them all. He was in his shirt sleeves, just standing staring out at the fields, muttering.

'There was nothing more I could do - nothing!' Doctor Kerr was a good and conscientious physician. It distressed him to lose a patient, especially a mother in childbirth. Chloroform had been used to assist Her Majesty, the Queen, during the birth of Prince Leopold, but he knew so little of its use. In his heart he knew he had been powerless to help from the moment he arrived, but the plea and the courage in the girl's wide dark eyes would haunt him for the rest of his life.

Sarah stood beside her mother's bed with her precious bundle. It puzzled her when her beloved Uncle Sandy turned his head away. He was holding Mama's hand in both of his.

'See, Mama. Look at our baby ' She held the white woollen bundle forward but Mattie did not open her eyes. Sarah looked uncertainly at Sandy.

'Why are your eyes wet, Uncle Sandy?' she asked in concern, but he dashed a hand across his face with a muffled groan. Sarah bent and touched her soft lips to Mattie's pale, cold cheek. Her touch was as gentle as the wing of a butterfly, but Mattie felt it and her eyes opened and focused on her daughter's eager young face.

'See, Mama! A baby!' She held out the bundle carefully but Mattie had no strength left to raise her head. 'We can keep it! It's a boy.' Sarah pronounced the words with her usual exaggerated care. Mattie's mouth lifted in a faint smile.

'Care for him, Sarah.' Her voice was no more than a silken thread of sound, but Sandy's head jerked towards her, his blue eyes ablaze with hope, heedless now who witnessed the weakness of his unmanly tears.

Robert Mackenzie also heard. He moved closer, towering above Sandy's kneeling figure. His voice was calm and quiet but his words, like Sarah's, were also formed with the greatest clarity he could muster.

'You have a son, Mattie. Shall I baptize him?' He took the baby gently from Sarah's arms and made the sign of a cross over the tiny forehead and raised his eyebrows questioningly. 'What is his name?'

Mattie's eyes moved until they rested on Sandy; they were full of love and tenderness. She smiled, the sweetest of all smiles. His clasp tightened on her fingers and he felt her faint response.

'It grows so dark ' Her eyes lifted to the Reverend Mackenzie, still waiting for a name.

'Alexander,' she breathed softly, then gently she released her fingers from Sandy's clasp and her eyes lifted upward and beyond him, beyond the minister. Her hand fluttered as though in the greeting of a well-loved friend.

'Dani—' The last syllable was lost on a final fleeting breath.

Robert Mackenzie laid a hand on Sarah's shoulder and squeezed it gently before he returned her, and the sleeping infant, to Maisie O'Connor, waiting gravely at the door of the bedchamber.

'Come, ma wee lassie,' Maisie instructed kindly. 'This wee manny will be needing to be fed, and there's a real problem, for sure!' she muttered under her breath.

'Danny. Mama said his name is Alexander Danny, not "manny",' Sarah murmured as she followed Mistress O'Connor to the kitchen. 'So I shall call him Danny.' There was no one to contradict her.

Maisie O'Connor scalded a piece of white butter muslin and was patiently dipping it into a small bowl of honey and water and squeezing it into the baby's mouth when Doctor Kerr and the minister came down the stairs. Suddenly the full enormity of the day's troubles hit Robert Mackenzie like a physical blow. How was Mattie's son to survive without a mother to succour him?

Sandy came slowly down the stairs like an old man in a trance. His face was ravaged by grief. He did not even pause to look upon his son. He would have walked past them all in silence had the minister not stepped in front of him.

'Let me pass!' he commanded harshly.

'You have a son, Sandy,' the minister reminded him quietly. 'He needs a mother's milk, if he is to survive.'

'His mother is dead!' Sandy cried bitterly. 'Dead, I tell you! I should have died, not Mattie. Let me pass!'

'It is God's will. You cannot hide from grief, Sandy.' The Reverend Mackenzie acknowledged softly, 'I know you have a terrible burden to bear, but Sarah needs you. Remember, she has lost her mother too; you have a duty to your children. Mattie's children. Your son needs a wet nurse.'

'It will be necessary to send the babe to a woman in the town,' Doctor Kerr began.

'No, you cannot send Danny away!' Sarah cried out involuntarily, forgetting the good manners Mattie had taught her.

'There is not a woman in the whole of Muircumwell who can help.' Doctor Kerr said stiffly, quelling Sarah with a frown.

Maisie O'Connor looked at the girl's trembling lips, the huge, pleading dark eyes which almost swamped her oval face. The bairn had lost enough already.

'There's a woman in Strathtod,' she said reluctantly, continuing with the task of dribbling liquid into the baby's eager little mouth.

'But would a woman from there dare to help? And could she nurse another child?' The Reverend Mackenzie asked anxiously when Sandy remained silent, staring at some hidden spectre within the dark recesses of his own tormented soul.

'She is a traveller. An Irish woman.' Maisie O'Connor was proud of her own Irish ancestry but there were rumours about this woman which she would not repeat to anyone, and certainly not to a man of God. She wished she could have named a good, decent woman to succour the innocent, motherless babe. 'Her own babe died at birth yesterday.'

'Is she alone? Could she come to Fairlyden?'

'She was following her man. She reckons he moved on - looking for work.' Maisie had seen the woman in the store at Strathtod. She had ogled every man who chanced to pass, even old Jocky Mathieson and he with one foot in the grave already. Widow Taylor, who had let her a room in her own house until after the birth, believed she had smothered the babe while she was out of the house.

Danny choked, recalling Maisie's full attention. She lifted him to her shoulder, and looked across at Sandy's bowed head and inward-looking eyes. She shrugged. The baby needed milk and by the looks o' things his father wadna' be looking at another woman for a while even one as free with herself as the Irish Maureen.

'She's biding wi' Mistress Taylor. I think her name is O'Leary. At least she talks of a laddie who once worked at the turnip hoeing in these parts. Sean O'Leary I believe was his name.'

'Thank you, Mistress O'Connor, for everything you have done this day,' the Reverend Mackenzie said warmly. He turned to Sandy. 'You must call on the Irish woman without delay.' Sandy made no reply. He didn't seem to hear. The minister sighed.

'I will call on her myself then, if you will lend me the pony and trap? Shall I bring her here to Fairlyden if she is willing? Sandy!' His tone sharpened and Sandy started out of his reverie.

'Ach, do as you please.' Subconsciously Sandy held his innocent son responsible for Mattie's death, but deep down he blamed himself. He looked vacantly at the minister, then he stepped past him like a sleepwalker, outside, moving instinctively towards the burn, to the place where Mattie had lain. Had she prayed for help? Where was the mercy of the Heavenly Father now? he wondered bitterly.

All night he paced, and even when his body was exhausted to the point of collapse his mind would not allow him peace. Mattie was dead. His wife. His beloved.

Twenty-Two

Sarah knew it was important that Maureen O'Leary should stay at Fairlyden if the doctor was not to take Danny away, but she disliked her instinctively from the moment she arrived with the Reverend Mackenzie. Child though she was, she sensed a brazenness in the green-eyed woman with her wild tangle of red hair and her voluptuous body. She did not even wait for the minister to leave the room before she lifted Danny carelessly from the crib, draped her bulk over a chair, and blatantly displayed her full, white breasts. Then, with an arch glance, she guided the baby's tiny mouth to her oozing nipple and settled herself comfortably. The moment the minister had left the house, she gave Sarah a hard assessing stare.

'Now, you young varlet, just you be a passing a cup o' the buttermilk tae Maureen O'Leary!' she ordered 'An' a bite to eat.'

Maureen O'Leary was quick to sense Sarah's feelings of unease and insecurity and she took full advantage. 'To be sure it's an orphan ye are now, an' don't ye be forgettin' it.' Sarah looked back at her with wide, anxious, brown eyes. The Irish woman put Danny into his crib and covered him roughly. Then she turned back to Sarah and grabbed her shoulders, glaring down into her frightened face.

'You know what an orphan is, eh?' Her green eyes lit with cruel malice. 'It means yer mammy an' yer daddy have gone to the devil.'

'No!'

'You be listening to Maureen O'Leary now.' She shook Sarah viciously. 'And don't you be thinking o' telling tales to Master Logan or I'll be having ye sent to an institution.'

'Wh-what's an institution?' Sarah asked fearfully.

'It's a place where they send wicked children like you. A long way from Fairlyden, I will be making sure!'

Sarah shivered. She had heard the Reverend Mackenzie saying she was a burden to Uncle Sandy. Supposing he listened to the horrid Irish woman and sent her away from Fairlyden? Away from Danny? She could not bear it!

In the days between Mattie's death and the funeral, Sandy rarely entered the house, even to sleep, for sleep eluded him, so Sarah was left alone with her fears. For three days she clung to the conviction that her beloved mama would waken up; she would come from her bedchamber and send the horrid O'Leary away; she would make Uncle Sandy happy again. In her heart Sarah knew it was impossible. She had encountered death before. Her papa had never wakened up, and Buff had been buried under the tree in the garden. She had never seen the little dog again.

Maureen O'Leary derived a peculiar satisfaction from watching Sarah's fear whenever she used her vicious tongue. Like her mother, Sarah quickly realised she must hide her fear, but at nine years old she could not conceal her fierce, protective love for her new brother; Mama had entrusted Danny into her care. Maureen O'Leary played upon her weakness, making Sarah fetch and carry for her. The awful thing was that Danny seemed to like the Irish woman. When he cried it did not matter how gently Sarah rocked him, or how tenderly she sang, he would not be silenced until Maureen O'Leary plucked him from his crib and thrust him impatiently to her ample bosom. Danny needed the O'Leary woman and this had a far greater influence on Sarah than any threats.

When Mr Anderson, the carpenter, arrived at Fairlyden, dressed in his best black Sunday overcoat and tall hat, leading his black horse with its harness all freshly polished, and his waggon, newly washed, Sarah knew in her heart she could not pretend any longer. All the things which Maureen O'Leary had said must be true. He had made a wooden box; he had come to take Mama away in it. O'Leary had said he would screw down the lid and Mama could never get out! The Irish woman had laughed, the harsh, jeering laugh which made her green eyes sparkle like those of the little spitting cat in the stable. Sarah felt icy shivers run down her spine.

'Go to your room and take the bairns with you until 'tis over,' Sandy instructed Maureen O'Leary bleakly.

Sarah looked at him pleadingly, but Sandy was too frozen with grief to see her. She turned and stared out of the window with hot, dry eyes at the men gathering in the little yard, all of them dressed in their sombre Sunday black. Maureen O'Leary lifted the sleeping Danny and tucked him roughly under her arm, then she flounced sulkily up the stairs, ignoring Sarah's dark, apprehensive eyes.

I can't bear to be closeted up there with Maureen O'Leary's smelly body, Sarah cried silently, wringing her small hands in desperation. Her tongue is so sharp, so cruel. Oh, Mama! She glanced wildly around the kitchen and then darted frantically through the door into the scullery, and from there through the dairy and out into the yard.

There were people everywhere! She sought refuge in the fork of the old apple tree in the garden. She could just see over the wall into the yard in front of the house. Sarah was surprised to see so many men, all so grim and unsmiling. She recognised Mr Jardine from the store, and his son; there was the clogger, and the blacksmith, and a group of men she did not know. They had weathered faces like Uncle Sandy. There was the mason, and the thatcher, and of course Mr Miller, Beattie's grandfather had arrived, but he went into the front parlour with Uncle Sandy and the minister and Doctor Kerr and three strangers. Sarah shivered and wished passionately that Beatrice could have been with her in the apple tree. She felt shivery and afraid - and very, very lonely. Even Uncle Sandy had scarcely spoken to her, and he had always comforted her before.

Sarah did not notice the young man who had ridden up the track from Strathtod on a jet black horse. He had tethered it to the fence and quietly joined the crowd of mourners. It was quite by chance that he looked up, over their heads, and glimpsed the edges of Sarah's petticoats amongst the green leaves, and the pale gleam of her small strained face peering through the branches. Then with the other men he moved closer to the door of the house. A hushed silence fell.

At last the prayers were said and heads were raised. Slowly the bearers carried the coffin out of the house. Sarah watched tensely as they placed it carefully on the carpenter's waggon. She stuffed a small fist in her mouth and bit hard on her knuckles. The tears she had held in check for three whole days rained silently down her pale cheeks as she watched the waggon draw further and further away - down the track, taking away her own, dear, beloved Mama forever.

Sarah watched until the last of the mourners moved over the crest of the slope and were lost to sight. A hard, dry sob escaped from her aching throat and she flung herself out of the apple tree and rushed headlong across the garden, across the yard, over the fields - heedless of direction.

'I must get away from here! I must! I must!' she cried, imagining Maureen O'Leary's mocking face. 'Mama! Oh, Mama!' She began to sob openly, with only the birds to witness her distress.

The Honourable William Fairly, youngest son of the late Earl of Strathtod, did not follow the funeral cortege to Muircumwell. He scarcely knew what had urged him to attend the funeral service of Mistress Logan of Fairlyden, except that he felt a peculiar gratitude to the young woman who had given care and comfort to Daniel Munro, his grandfather's bastard son, the unknown relative whom he was said to resemble. Young Miss Sarah would inherit Fairlyden now, but James and Stuart would never call her 'cousin' or welcome her at Strathtod Tower. Indeed, James was so short of funds he would probably stoop to some mean trick or other towards the Logans while Reggie was too ill to know what he was doing.

William turned his horse's head towards the fields, reluctant to return home. His face was sombre, his thoughts on his eldest brother. Reggie would have welcomed their orphaned cousin with warmth and compassion. He bore the Munros no grudge but time was running out for Reggie too. It grieved William to contemplate his brother's approaching death. Despite the difference in their ages, Reggie had been his friend and confidant since he was old enough to walk and talk. He had protected him from James's petty spite and resentment. Reggie had understood his reluctance to become a Minister of the Church too, but it was their father's wish that William should do so, and his small inheritance depended on it. As the Earl, Reggie had a duty to carry out their father's wishes, but he had asked William to remain with him for the little time that was left to them. He would leave for St Andrew's in the autumn.

William cared nothing for his other brothers. Since his return from Europe for their father's funeral, James's only interests had been gambling, horses and women; when he could not get enough excitement from them, he made his own amusement by stirring up trouble on the estate. Already he had distressed Reggie by his presumptuous dismissal of the factor. Mr Soames had known the estate and its tenants all his life, he had been loyal and trustworthy; Reggie, in his sickness, had depended upon him to act as a mediator and adviser.

If James had any softness in his heart at all it was for Stuart, for there was less than a year between them and Stuart had followed wherever James had chosen to lead - until the accident which had paralysed him from his waist to his toes. Now he whined constantly, while James blustered and blamed Alexander Logan for his brother's helpless state. It was the sight of Sarah's small figure running in the direction of the burn which distracted William from melancholy thoughts of his family. He remembered her clearly from their meeting at Strathtod mill. She had the most enchanting smile he had ever seen.

Sarah, believing she was alone and unobserved, flung herself face down on the turf beside the burn. Harsh sobs shook her small body, rendering her deaf to the faint jingle of harness. William dismounted while he was still some yards away, and tethered his horse to the branch of a tree. He moved closer and looked down at Sarah's slight, shaking figure with compassion. She had lost her cap and a wild profusion of curls reached almost to her waist. Her hair was not as dark as he remembered. Indeed, when the sun's rays fell upon it, it reminded him of a polished chestnut. He stepped on a twig and Sarah's head jerked up. When she saw him she jumped to her feet and turned her back. Like Sandy she felt ashamed that anyone should witness her grief, but still her shoulders shook with the sobs which would not be stifled.

'Leave me alone!' she cried angrily, fearing the young man from Strathtod would mock her, as Maureen O'Leary mocked.

'I came only to share your grief,' William murmured gently.

'How c-can you sh-share? You d-did not know m-my mama. G-go away!' Sarah felt humiliated because her sobs would not be controlled. 'G-go away!' William simply stood there, helpless. At length her sobbing ceased, except for an occasional hiccup. She thought he had gone, but when she turned he was still there, his dark eyes filled with sympathy and understanding and Sarah almost began to cry again. This time she bit her lip instead and scrubbed furiously at her eyes and cheeks with a grubby, moss-stained fist.

'Now you look almost like a chimney-sweep!' William chided softly, but his expressive dark eyes were kind and gentle. Sarah turned away;

she heard him move to the edge of the burn and glanced over her shoulder, watching as he dipped his white linen handkerchief in the water. When he returned he crouched in front of her and cupped her chin firmly in one hand, turning her face up to his. Sarah was so surprised she did not even struggle as he proceeded to wipe away the grass and tear stains. He reminded her a little of her dear papa, except that he had no lines on his face. She closed her eyes obediently so that he could complete the treatment. When he had finished, he dropped a feather-light kiss on each of her eyelids.

'Wake now, my princess, thy beauty is restored.' Sarah's dark eyes flew open and stared into his. He took her hands, one at a time, and cleaned them too. She felt suddenly shy.

'I'm not a princess - and you'll get into trouble with your Mama when she sees your dirty handkerchief.'

'Then we shall pretend you are my princess. Now don't refuse me, that would be cruel, because you see I have no mama either.'

'Oh.' Sarah looked at him doubtfully. 'Does it make you very sad too?'

'Not anymore.'

'Do you have a papa?' Sarah asked wistfully, and watched William shake his dark head. His eyes did not mock her. 'I havena' got a papa either but I have got Uncle Sandy, only he's very sad too. I hope he never dies!' she added sharply, her dark eyes wide with apprehension.

'I am sure he will live for a very long time, Miss Sarah,' William assured her comfortingly, 'but you must come to me, if ever you need a friend. Promise?'

Despite her grief, Sarah was a practical child. She frowned. 'But where could I find you?'

William thought for a moment. His offer was sincere, but he had spoken hastily. Neither James nor Stuart would welcome her at the Tower. She was a Munro, a continuing reminder of their grandfather's indiscretion - not that James cared about the family honour, but the child was now the legal occupant of Fairlyden; land meant rents and James would always be greedy for more money. Already he could scarcely wait for Reggie to die; he boasted to Stuart of his gambling, and his debts.

'Can you write, Sarah?' he asked.

'Oh, yes. Dominie Campbell never raps my fingers with his cane,' she informed him proudly.' Papa taught me to write and to read. I write

227

messages for...' She stopped, remembering. She gulped down a knot of tears.' I wrote messages for Mama. She could not hear.'

'Then you must write a message for me, if you need me. Leave it under a stone at the foot of the tree, the one nearest to the new bridge which Mr Logan built.' William had an extraordinary desire to befriend this young girl - perhaps because she was almost his cousin, he thought.

'But how will you know if I leave a message?' she inquired forlornly.

William understood how desperately lonely and in need of friends she must feel - as he would feel when Reggie was gone. 'If I do not ride that way, I shall send someone to look. Someone I can trust!' he declared firmly. 'Do you know Rory O'Connor?'

'Oh, yes. He saved me from drowning when the burn flooded. And he ...' Her mouth trembled but she bit her lip. 'He brought Mistress O'Connor to help Mama and Danny.'

'Mistress O'Connor? She went to Fairlyden?' William exclaimed in surprise and his face grew grave. 'We must never tell anyone that Mistress O'Connor was at Fairlyden, Sarah.'

'But I like Mistress O'Connor! I wish she could have stayed instead of the O'Leary woman. I hate her!' Sarah declared with a vehemence which surprised him.

'O'Leary?' He frowned. He knew no one of that name. 'Does she feed your brother?'

'Yes.'

'We-ell then, you would not want him to die of hunger, would you, Sarah?'

'Oh, no!'

'She will leave as soon as Danny can do without her,' William said comfortingly. 'Can you endure her until then, for his sake?' Sarah looked at him, crouching before her.

'I could do anything for Danny! Mama gave him to me.' Suddenly she smiled, right into his eyes. The transformation was like sunlight on a winter's day. William caught his breath. She was a pretty child. In a few years she would be a beautiful woman. 'I like you, William Fairly,' Sarah declared firmly, as though she had reached an important decision.

Sandy had watched the first soil fall on Mattie's coffin. He had listened to the minister's words: 'Ashes to ashes dust to dust.' Without Mattie, his dreams were dust!

*

The days passed slowly. He could not bear to stay inside the house which reminded him so painfully of Mattie. He was blind to the Irish woman's blatant efforts to attract him. Indeed, he had scarcely spoken to her except for a single sharp reprimand when she had caused Sarah to be late for school.

It never occurred to him that the Irish woman was the cause of Sarah's misery when he found her beside Buff's tiny grave, beneath the beech tree. His heart went out to her then. Her dark eyes reminded him painfully of Mattie. He longed to gather her in his arms and tell her she was his daughter; she was all he had left of Mattie. Then he remembered that her future at Fairlyden depended on his silence. He must control his impulses or keep away from her. He had promised Daniel Munro he would never tell her the truth.

As he stood looking down at her, Sandy did not realise how badly Sarah needed the reassurance of belonging. She was too young, and too innocent of evil, to realise that Maureen O'Leary had no power to banish her to the dreadful place she called an 'institution'. Sarah was determined never to tell any tales which might incur the woman's awful wrath. Yet when Uncle Sandy stroked her head with his big, gentle hand she almost blurted out her fear that O'Leary would carry out her latest threat and take Danny away. Instead she brushed away her tears and told him she was crying for Mama. Sandy accepted her explanation without question for his own heart was weeping too.

As Danny grew the sight of his dimpled hands and cherubic smiles made Sarah's misery and confusion bearable. Yet her pleasure was frequently over-shadowed by Maureen O'Leary's quick temper.

'Don't ye be drooling over that spoiled brat all day!' she yelled. 'To be sure an' I think it's across the sea I'll be a taking him! Get the work done! Do ye hear me, now? You'll never see the boy again if I take him to dear old Ireland!'

Sarah hated the increasing dirt and squalor of her home. She tried hard to keep herself clean and tidy, but the Irish woman jeered at her efforts and delighted in ordering her to empty the chamber pots, clean the privy, empty the ashes and scrub the scullery. Indeed, O'Leary seldom moved from her chair to do anything, except on the rare occasions when Sandy was in the house, then she swayed her plump hips and simpered foolishly. Sandy remained oblivious to her crude overtures, and Sarah bore the brunt of her temper and frustration.

'I shall be late for school again!' Sarah protested one morning when Maureen O'Leary's demands seemed to go on forever.

'Aah, and will the good dominie be a giving ye the belt then?' The green eyes gleamed spitefully. 'And is it afeared ye are?'

'No, I am not afraid!' Sarah declared proudly. She would not tell the horrid O'Leary she was ashamed -ashamed of her unwashed clothes, her dirty matted hair, despite her efforts to brush it as Mama had done. But she hated the humiliation of public chastisement most of all. Dominie Campbell had overlooked her unusual lapses at first, but he firmly believed that punctuality was an essential part of self-discipline. He was a fair man and Sarah knew she deserved to be punished when she was late so often. She wished Beatrice could have shared her troubles, but the two friends rarely met now. Mistress Slater was half crazed and the Slater boys were rough and continually hungry; there was always washing and cleaning and mending to be done at the mill house. Sarah was beginning to understand Beatrice's misery in a way she had never done before the death of her beloved mama.

The summer weather was suddenly interrupted by one of those freak days properly belonging to the month of February. About midday the rain began to batter the windows, making dusty rivulets. The wind rose in playful gusts, but as the sun left the sky, whining squalls penetrated every crack and crevice. Joey Slater panted up the track to Fairlyden with an urgent plea.

'Grandfaither Miller says can ye come, Mr Logan? It's the mare. She's three weeks past her time. He said tae tell ye "the foal is big an' it willna come". Will ye help?'

'I'll come back with ye at once!' Sandy declared with concern.

Maureen O'Leary flew into one of her rages as soon as the door had shut behind him. Sarah's heart sank. She sought refuge in the byre. Even after she had milked her own cows, she stayed to help Janet with the rest. Louis's new wife was not used to milking and she liked Sarah's company; things had not turned out quite so well as she had expected, with Mistress Logan gone and that red-haired she-cat screaming obscenities and banning her from the house. Janet knew better than anyone how much of the work Sarah had to do and how she had to suffer the lash of O'Leary's cruel tongue whenever Mr Logan was away.

Sarah was almost sorry when the milking was finished. They turned the cows back into the field as usual on summer evenings, but they moved slowly, heads down, reluctant to leave the shelter of the buildings. Sarah watched them huddle together, backs up against the hedge. It was horribly wet but she had no wish to spend the rest of the evening alone with O'Leary. She ran across to the dairy, and quietly opened the door into the scullery where she had left the basket of eggs she had collected earlier. She put six of the biggest eggs into a small basket. In the dairy she filled a stone bottle with milk, then pulling her shawl tightly around her head and shoulders, she set off across the small field towards the glen which separated Fairlyden from the rest of Strathtod.

She had not seen Rory O'Connor since he tried to help her mama, and she had never forgotten it was he who had saved her from drowning on the night of the flood. The burn was narrower near the head of the glen. Although Sarah got her boots wet, she managed to leap across in safety with the help of a large stone in the middle. Her shawl and skirt were very wet by the time she eventually reached the O'Connor farm. It was further than she had anticipated for it looked no distance at all from Fairlyden's high meadow.

'Mercy me!' Maisie O'Connor exclaimed in amazement when she opened the door. 'Ach, come awa' in do, my bairn! What brings ye out on such a night?' she asked with a motherly concern that warmed Sarah's young heart instantly. Maisie drew her close to the cheery fire and took her shawl to dry, bidding her put her boots on the hearth to warm a while.

'I-I brought ye some milk an' some eggs,' Sarah said diffidently, 'for helping M-Mama.'

Maisie was deeply touched by Sarah's gifts; she missed the rabbits and other spoils which Rory had supplied. Sarah responded to Maisie's welcome like a flower to the sun. She chattered happily while Maisie pushed the pot of broth further over the fire.

'Ye must tak a bite o' supper wi' us, afore ye gang home tae Fairlyden,' she insisted. 'Look, Rory, see who has come to visit ye!' Rory was delighted to see Sarah.

It was the first day he been out of bed since Mattie's death. He smiled but remained silent. All his energy was concentrated on breathing.

*

In the town of Dumfries the rain was falling relentlessly. James Fairly was bored. He had ridden into town early that morning and by late afternoon had lost a considerable sum of money at cards and drunk a vast quantity of whisky. The weather did not help his mood. He almost decided to stay the night in the tavern; he had shared a bed several times with Bessie, the comely maid, but his pockets were light and the evening stretched ahead. He decided to leave his own horse in the inn stables and travel to Strathtod by train. He could hire a horse at the station and be back at the Tower in time for a hot soak and a good dinner, along with the French brandy his father had secretly hoarded.

The train was ready to leave as James hauled himself drunkenly into a carriage, his brain too befuddled to notice whether it was first, second or third class, or even whether there was an empty seat. As it happened there were only two other occupants. One, a ruddy-faced farmer, stared gloomily out of the window. He was travelling to Annan and he had a five-mile drive in the trap from the station. His business had gone badly and he was disinclined to talk.

'Whither are you bound, fellow?' James boomed drunkenly to the shrinking youth in the far corner.

'I-I'm bound for St-Strathtod station, Sir!' Normally he would have walked and saved the train fare, but the night was wild and likely to get worse. He had been amazed when Lord Fairly's brother entered the same compartment as himself. James peered at him. The jolting of the carriage and the amount of liquor he had consumed caused the young man's features to form themselves into extraordinary patterns.

'I don't remember seeing you before?'

'I'm the n-new apprentice at the Sm-smiddy. I'm lodging with ma grandmither er Mistress Taylor, S-Sir.' The young man supplied the information nervously, awed that anyone from Strathtod Tower should bother to speak to him even if the words were slurred and jumbled.

'Taylor, eh?' James frowned. His brain churned slowly. 'Ah, yes, I remember. She has a green-eyed Irish wench lodging with her!' James had seen Maureen O'Leary in the village. Despite her cumbersome burden there had been an invitation in her flashing eyes and James had recognised the latent promise of her swaying hips. Soon she would move on, but first there was sport to be had. 'Surely the babe has arrived by now?'

'Aye. It was d-dead, S-sir. It wasna' ma Grand-mither's fault!' he added hastily.

'No, no, of course not.' James Fairly smirked. He had judged the Irish woman correctly. 'So!' His pale eyes gleamed. 'Is she about yet, eh?'

'Oh, aye! She went to Fairlyden the verra next day.'

'To Fairlyden!' James echoed incredulously. His cold eyes narrowed suspiciously. 'Why did your grandmother send her to Fairlyden?' he demanded sharply.

'The M-minister came for her, S-Sir!'

'Minister?' James scoffed loudly. 'You're lying, boy! What would a minister want with such a woman? Tell me that!'

'He took her to f-feed the b-babe at Fairlyden, S-sir!' The boy stuttered in alarm. His grandmother had been worried because the Irish woman's own babe had died after it was born.

'Babe! At Fairlyden? Mistress Logan is dead, and her child! You lie, boy!'

'No. There is a l-live b-babe at Fairlyden! It w-was the Minister frae the Free Kirk, ower at Muircumwell. He came and took the Irish woman awa' in his t-trap, S-Sir! Mistress O'Connor sent him.' His voice faltered and trailed to a halt at the sight of the man's apoplectic expression.

'Mistress O'Connor! Mistress O'Connor sent the minister for a wet nurse?' James bellowed so loudly that the farmer grunted in protest. 'Are you telling the truth, boy?'

'Aye, I am, S-Sir. Grandmither d-did naething wrong, S-Sir!'

The youth fidgeted uneasily. The Irish woman had threatened to put a curse on his grandmother if she gossiped to the women in the village but she had already told Mistress O'Connor the babe had been born alive.

'So Mistress O'Connor went to Fairlyden!' James Fairly muttered viciously. 'She went to help!'

The lad shivered before the drunken man's malevolent gaze. As the train jolted to a halt, he jumped down on to the platform and darted away, glad of the curtain of cold grey rain and the darkening sky which quickly hid him from view.

The station master was reluctant to lend his own horse to James Fairly; he was known to have a vicious hand on the bridle, even when sober, and tonight he seemed possessed of the devil. But rumour had it that he would soon be the next Earl.

The wind and rain were more ferocious than James had realised once he left the shelter of the little station. Although it was almost midsummer the early evening sky was already darkened by the lowering clouds. The wildness of the elements, added to the effects of the alcohol, stirred a primitive exhilaration in his blood.

Twenty Three

In Maisie O'Connor's firelit kitchen, boots and coats steamed gently on the hearth after the day's labours. The young O'Connors who were still living with their parents were surprised and delighted to have Sarah as their youthful guest. Only Rory had little appetite for food as they gathered round the table.

They had barely started to eat their meal when they were startled by a loud kicking at the door as James Fairly came crashing into the room. His lip curled when he saw Maisie's face blanch. Rory's breathing became even more laboured than before. His eyes popped in agitation. Sarah sensed the tension. She stared wide-eyed at the stranger.

James Fairly looked around the circle of upturned faces - Maisie and her husband; Bruce and Bobby, their eldest sons, who worked the farm with them; Vicky and Dick, the twins, both employed on the estate. His eyes rested on Sarah, taking in her dark eyes, the small proud chin. Maisie held her breath. James frowned. His head was far from clear, and he had never met Sarah Munro. He had seen apprehension in all their faces and he savoured his power as his gaze moved back to Maisie. His grey eyes glittered.

'You! You helped the woman from Fairlyden!' he thundered accusingly. 'You told the Minister about the Irish woman! Well we shall see how the Minister will repay your help now! Get out, all of you - get off my land!' He rocked on his feet, almost over-balancing. It was not only the liquor which intoxicated him now but the feeling of power as he heard the gasps of dismay.

Sarah stared. This man was turning the O'Connors from their home because Mistress O'Connor had tried to help her mama and Danny. She

234

bit back a sob of distress, but as she opened her mouth to protest, Vicky O'Connor pinched her hard beneath the table. Vicky's anxious eyes and the imperceptible shake of her head held a warning which Sarah was intelligent enough to heed. She shrank in her seat, wishing she was invisible. Maybe her own presence might make things worse! James revelled in the fear and alarm he had aroused. Rory rose with an effort, holding on to the back of his chair. His lips were blue, his breathing painful to hear, but he spoke with a slow clarity which amazed his family.

'Mistress Logan was dying.' He gasped for breath.

'Sit doon, Son, sit ye doon!' Maisie cried in distress. 'Yes, I helped the puir lassie!' She faced the intruder defiantly now. 'Naebody wi' any mercy in his heart could hae left a woman in childbirth to die alane.' James Fairly's face went purple with rage.

'She was Munro's widow! She deserved to die! Her and her whelp!' Maisie glanced nervously at Sarah's white face and Vicky squeezed her hand urgently beneath the table. 'Get out, I say! You and your brood! Take your filthy rubbish with you! Now!' James lifted a hand and swiped two small figurines and a photograph from the high mantle above the fire. The O'Connor men rose to their feet as one. Vicky gasped indignantly, but Maisie swiftly shook her head at them. They all knew how much she had cherished the little figures. Now they were smashed into a thousand pieces. Vicky's blue eyes flashed and twin flags of angry colour stained her cheeks. James's eyes narrowed insolently as they fixed on her heaving breasts. Maisie saw. She recognised a new danger. Swiftly she pressed a restraining hand on her daughter's shoulder, but it was only the anxiety in her mother's eyes which made Vicky hold her tongue, and her temper. Her father had seen it too.

'We will move out as soon as we can get another farm,' he began placatingly.

'Another farm!' James jeered. 'You will move now! Tonight!' They stared at him incredulously. No amount of pleading could move him, even on such a night. James stood over them, watching. They began to carry the pieces of simple, solid furniture out into the rain-drenched yard.

'We must make room in the barn for tonight,' Walter O'Connor muttered to his eldest son. James overheard.

'You will not go near the barn, O'Connor! See that everything belonging to you is cleared away from here by noon tomorrow!' Walter saw the frenzied light in his eyes. He guessed he had been drinking heavily and his old heart sank. There would be no reasoning with him tonight. They would have to wait until he had gone before they could take shelter.

James waited relentlessly until the kitchen was empty, then the attic, and the single bedroom. Blankets were bundled beneath the temporary shelter of the kitchen table and Rory lay amongst them, wheezing and shivering helplessly while Sarah crouched beside him in an effort to keep him warm.

It was the plight of her son which brought Maisie to her knees in the mud, in a final futile plea. James wheeled his horse deliberately, sending a shower of mud and grit over her. It was too much for Vicky to see her mother and brother treated so callously. She sprang forward and grabbed the horse's bridle. Standing on her toes, she spat right into James Fairly's face. He uttered a vile oath and kicked out viciously, but Vicky had already jumped out of reach.

'I shall not forget that, you slut!' James shouted angrily. 'If you so much as enter this house or the buildings, I shall burn them to the ground, and you with them!' Vicky merely turned her back contemptuously. He jerked furiously at the reins and hurled his horse towards her.

'Vicky!' Sarah shrieked in horror as she realised his intention. She sprang from under the table and grabbed Vicky's skirts with all her strength. Vicky almost fell on top of her, but the horse's hooves missed her by a hair's breadth.

'Stop it! Stop it!' Sarah screamed wildly. 'Rory is sick!' Tears of anger and frustration and sheer disbelief mingled with the rain. James Fairly pulled his horse to a surprised halt and stared down at the small figure with the long black hair streaming out behind her; he peered down into a white face, almost swamped by a pair of wild dark eyes - eyes which condemned him utterly. Just for a moment James Fairly though he was staring at a ghost. Then his senses cleared. She was no more than a child! His fury boiled anew. A child!

'A Munro?' he bellowed. 'You dare to harbour a Munro! I shall see you starve for this!' he almost screamed in his drunken rage.

'You are wicked!' Sarah sobbed in frustration, heedless of his anger. She had tried to help, but her presence in the O'Connors' house had made every-thing worse. 'God will - will kill you!'

James Fairly stared at her flashing dark eyes. Was the child cursing him? Uncertainty flickered in his pale eyes. He shrugged uneasily; he had had his sport for one night.

The O'Connors watched in amazement as he kicked his heels into the horse and sprang away into the gloomy deluge. Sarah tugged Maisie O'Connor's shawl. Her young face was pale but determined.

'You must come to Fairlyden with me. Uncle Sandy will give you shelter, I know he will!' she insisted earnestly. Then, in a choked whisper, 'I know you are in trouble because you helped Mama.'

'Naw, lassie,' Maisie murmured brokenly. 'There'll aye be trouble wherever there's James Fairly. I've heard tell his grandmother was the same, and bad blood aye comes oot.'

'Rory saved my life. You must bring him to Fairlyden. He is so cold.'

Maisie looked at her youngest son, shivering amidst the sodden blankets. She turned a stricken face to her husband.

'If the bairnie can help us, jist for tonight? For Rory's sake.' Walter O'Connor nodded and asked Bruce to harness the horse and bring the cart. They lifted Rory gently and covered his shivering body with the blankets. Vicky obeyed her father's instructions and climbed in beside him, trying desperately to warm him with the heat of her own body, for it was several miles round by the road. Tired though she was, Sarah refused to ride in the cart. She preferred to cut through the glen with Mistress O'Connor and her husband so that she could warn Uncle Sandy and help prepare warm blankets and gruel for Rory and his brothers. She thought of Maureen O'Leary and her sharp tongue and prayed that Uncle Sandy would have returned.

Sandy had not returned. Maureen O'Leary had been snoring before a roaring fire and she glared angrily when Sarah entered the kitchen with the drookit figure of Walter O'Connor close behind her. Walter swayed slightly and blinked the rain from his eyelashes, but Maureen O'Leary chose to ignore his exhaustion. He was past sixty and no use to her. Walter had done a long day's work. He was cold, and hungry, and very tired after his battle against the elements, but most of all he was desperately worried. Maisie had fallen behind. O'Connor looked at

Maureen O'Leary's angry face as she berated Sarah. The woman was a disgrace to his own Irish blood, Walter thought contemptuously.

Sarah felt strangely calm. Suddenly, just for a little while, she was unafraid of Maureen O'Leary's wicked tongue. It was almost as though Mama was standing beside her, telling her to befriend the O'Connors, as they had befriended her.

'Please come to the fire, Mr O'Connor, and warm yourself.' Then, to Maureen O'Leary, 'Mama would not be pleased if we did not...'

'She's dead!' Maureen screeched furiously. She did not want any disturbance.

'Uncle Sandy will be angry if you turn them away. Rory O'Connor saved my life and now he is sick. We must help him.' She spoke with a quaint dignity which left Maureen O'Leary gaping, but not for long. She soon realised there would be work to be done when she saw Maisie O'Connor coming in from the yard. Like her husband, the shock of the evening's events had exhausted her. Maureen O'Leary flounced out of the kitchen and up to her bedchamber, leaving Sarah, a child of nine, to cope.

She led Maisie O'Connor into the kitchen and her sharp young eyes noted the anxiety and the many new lines which creased her friend's kindly face. Again it was as though Mama stood at her side, guiding her hands and putting words of comfort on her lips.

Rory was chilled to the bone and barely conscious when his brothers carried him into the kitchen. They undressed him and rolled him in the blankets which Sarah had taken from the box bed. Then they laid him to rest there, gratefully obeying the child's bidding; Sarah helped Vicky O'Connor fill the iron kettle and together they made gruel.

Sandy did not return that night. Joseph Miller's mare had had a long, difficult time. The foal was already dead and it seemed doubtful whether the mare would survive. Joseph was getting too old for such a night of labour and Sandy knew Edward Slater would give him no help. Unaware of the crisis in his own household, he offered to wait with the exhausted beast until morning.

A pale grey light was creeping over the edge of the horizon before Sarah fell asleep. Her child's mind could not accept that anyone could be as heartless as the man who had turned the O'Connors out of their home. When she crawled sleepily downstairs to the kitchen, barely an hour later, Sandy had not returned. She went through to the dairy but it was Louis who was collecting the piggin and stool to start the morning milking. She told him and Janet of the night's events as she milked her own cows. Janet had no liking for Maureen O'Leary and expressed her anger at the woman's callousness. Louis was quiet. He could offer no comfort. He knew about the feud between Fairlyden and Strathtod. If the Honourable James Fairly used his influence against the O'Connors, they would never get another farm. They would be lucky even to get work.

Sarah ate the porridge which Maisie had made for them all but when she looked at Rory, lying in the box bed, so still except for the shallow, laboured breathing, she felt desperately afraid. She remembered William's promise to help; he was Rory O'Connor's friend too. She ran to the drawer in the dresser where Mattie had kept her account book. She opened it and saw the rows of neat figures. She was surprised that Uncle Sandy had not made any entries; Mama had always been so particular. She resolved to pay more attention to the figures which Dominie Campbell taught at school. Soon she would keep the lists which Mama had said were important. If she worked hard and learned to do Mama's work, perhaps Uncle Sandy would not be quite so sad, she thought innocently. Meanwhile she turned to the back of the big blue ledger and carefully tore out half a page. Then, taking Mattie's quill, she pushed aside the brass lid and dipped it in the ink. Carefully she wrote a message to William Fairly.

'Rory O'Connor is very sick.

Your Friend,

Sarah Munro. P.S. He is in our kitchen bed.

She folded the paper and tucked it carefully into the pocket of her grubby pinafore.

I must go to school now,' she told Maisie O'Connor. 'Please do not go away. I know Uncle Sandy will want you to stay.'

'Bless ye, bairn!' Maisie O'Connor smiled tiredly, but she was grateful for Sarah's cheering words, child though she was.

William Fairly had awakened early. He knew Reggie was fighting a losing battle with the dreaded disease of the lungs. It would be some hours before he was ready to be disturbed. William decided to go for his morning ride. The clouds of the previous day were dispersing and he rejoiced in the sight of the newly washed world, just as Rory O'Connor had so often done. He sat easily upon his spirited black horse, and Diablo moved into a canter, then into a full gallop. William revelled in the sensation of wind rushing past his cheeks and lifting the dark hair from the nape of his neck. He jumped the hedge which marked the boundary between the Home Farm and the O'Connors. He noted absently that the O'Connors' cow was still in the field, apparently unmilked.

He was at the top of the rise, overlooking Fairlyden, when he caught a glimpse of Sarah's small figure running down the track towards Muircumwell. He smiled, and turning Diablo's head, galloped downhill towards the burn. He had almost reached it when he saw Sarah stoop to put something under the stone beside the bridge. His eyes widened. He stood up in the stirrups and waved his hat, calling her name. She heard him. She waved back, but dared not linger. She would be late for school again.

William put Diablo to the boundary hedge and the burn in one big leap, and galloped on. He paused just long enough to retrieve Sarah's brief note, then with a lithe jump he sprang into the saddle again and rode after Sarah, swinging her up beside him with barely a pause. She cried aloud as his strong arm held her securely against him, but as she screwed round her head to look at him she saw his nose wrinkle and a look of distaste pass fleetingly over his expressive face. Sarah knew immediately that it was the smell of her own unbathed body, her dirty clothes and matted hair, which offended him. Her cheeks blazed with humiliation.

'Put me down! Put me down!' She wriggled frantically.

'Keep still, Princess, or you'll unseat both of us.'

'Let me down!' Sarah yelled angrily.

'Be still! You need a ride if you are not to be late for school; and I need to know about Rory, if I am to help.'

'I am not a princess!' Sarah's bottom lip trembled but she caught it firmly between her small white teeth. 'Princesses are not dirty - and they don't smell, so don't pretend, if you please Sir!' she commanded grittily.

William threw back his head and laughed at her autocratic tone. He saw her dark eyes widen in surprise which rapidly turned to fury. She twisted in the circle of his arm, trying to beat at his chest with her small fists, yet half afraid she might fall from Diablo's back and end up beneath his feet.

They were almost at the school before William pulled the horse to a halt. All the other children were there and they stood staring at the new arrivals. Even Dominie Campbell paused in the act of summoning them into school. William lifted his hat and gave him a polite smile, but it faded as he looked into Sarah's mutinous face.

'I would not have asked for help for myself,' she hissed proudly, 'but Rory O'Connor is very sick, and your brother is wicked. He put Rory and all his family out of their house last night.' Her voice sank and her dark eyes stared at him anxiously. 'I think Rory is going to die, like Mama.'

It was William's turn to stare. He forgot about the smell, the tangled mass of Sarah's matted hair. He jumped to the ground and lifted her down. She saw his face had lost some of its healthy glow and he hooked the reins over his arm and walked towards Dominie Campbell.

'With your permission, I would like to detain your pupil a little while, Sir? She has brought a message for me from a friend.' The dominie inclined his head stiffly in acknowledgement and called the rest of the children to their lessons.

Sarah had to repeat her story of the O'Connors' plight three times, and William asked her many questions, before he could take it in. Then his dark eyes grew cold and his young face hardened. He bade her a brief good-bye, and before she could reply had jumped on Diablo's back and was galloping up the track to Fairlyden to see the O'Connors for himself.

Lord Reginald Fairly was as incensed and shamed by James's actions as William. He felt sick with dismay. If only he had more time more strength. His mouth tightened. Whatever time he had he would put to good use, he vowed silently. He dispatched William to Fairlyden with instructions to reinstate Walter O'Connor and his family in their own home immediately; he ordered food, blankets and fresh straw mattresses to be taken from Strathtod. But he was powerless to restore Rory O'Connor's health.

James showed no remorse when his elder brother confronted him with news of Rory O'Connor's death a few days later. In his anger and frustration Reginald accused James of murdering the boy. Already he could visualise Strathtod's decline but he was powerless to prevent James inheriting the estate.

As he lay on his couch, hour after weary hour, he wished passionately that he could do something to comfort Maisie O'Connor in her loss. Other aspects of the affair also troubled him. Vicky O'Connor had already left her work in the Tower kitchen; her brother, Dick, had been one of the best young horse-men at the Home Farm, but he had not returned to his work either. James's irrational desire to turn the O'Connors from their home had been thwarted, but only for the time being. Even as a small boy, he had always wreaked revenge when he did not get his own way.

Reginald suddenly sat up straighter. Just because he was confined to his room by his body's weakness did not mean he was incapable of thinking - or of acting! He rang the little bell on the side table with a touch of impatience. One of the maids came scurrying in, her face expressing concern. Reginald smiled reassuringly.

'Ask my brother to come to me, as soon as he can be found.' The maid bobbed hastily and departed.

'Are you feeling worse, Reggie?' William inquired anxiously, the moment he entered the room.

'No. Better, if anything. I have thought of a plan to protect Walter O'Connor and his sons from James's revenge. I want you to ride to Dumfries and bring back Mr MacDonald. Have the maid prepare a room for him. I wish him to stay here until he has drawn up a document to my exact instructions. There must be no delay. It must be witnessed and made legal before he leaves.' He began to cough, vainly trying to hide the large scarlet spots on his white handkerchief. 'Go today, William,' he gasped, 'I fear there is not much time.' William nodded, his young face shadowed with sadness. He loved Reggie more dearly than anyone on earth.

Sarah was sorry when she found the O'Connors had left Fairlyden by the time she returned from school. She knew instinctively that she must not visit them again, but she longed for news of Rory. As the days passed she decided that William Fairly was too shamed and disgusted by her appearance to come near her, even to bring her news.

Janet heard her muffled sobs as she was passing one of the little hen huts. No doubt O'Leary's bin up tae her tricks again! she thought bitterly, and clamped her lips tightly together. She and Louis had had their first quarrel two days ago, and it was all because she had dared to criticise Mr Logan.

'Surely he must ken Maureen O'Leary aye leaves the greasy cooking pans and dishes for Miss Sarah tae wash when she comes frae school, and maist o' the dirty clothes?' she had declared irritably.

'It's nane o' oor business, Janet!' Louis had been angry. 'Mr Logan is the finest man I ever kenned. He taught me everything! He's too sair at heart the noo tae see ordinary things!'

'Well, he must ken O'Leary only stirs hersel' tae rinse a few mugs if he's aroon'. I've seen her when I gang intae the scullery for the hot water for the dairy, up tae her tricks, simperin' at him!'

'It's not oor business!' Louis had declared angrily.

Janet felt another wave of irritation towards Mr Logan as she heard Sarah sniffing in an effort to stem her tears. Sandy would have been dismayed to know he was the cause of the first real quarrel between the young couple. He would have been even more dismayed had he realised his own heartache had made him so blind to Sarah's insecurity. He sincerely believed she derived a comfort from Danny which in his own bleakness he could not. It did not occur to him that Maureen O'Leary would use Sarah's love for Danny to ensure her silence. He shunned the house and the slovenly Irish woman who had taken over Mattie's little kingdom. When he asked Sarah how she fared, he accepted her mumbled reassurances with relief and without question.

This time it was not Maureen O'Leary who had caused Sarah's distress, however, but the thought of William Fairly's revulsion. She knew she would never forget the sight of him wrinkling his nose in disgust! She was sure he must be keeping away from Fairlyden because he did not like her any more, with her matted curls and dirty clothes. She had no way of knowing of Rory's death, or that William was busy carrying out his brother's urgent instructions to protect the O'Connors.

At the sound of Janet's footsteps she brushed away her tears, leaving another dirty streak across her cheek. I will bathe myself every night from head to toe, even if the water in the ewer is freezing cold, she resolved silently, even if the horrid O'Leary does laugh and jeer at me. Yet her tears fell faster as she remembered her beloved mama and the luxury of bathing before the fire, screened from draughts by the wooden horse draped with an old bedsheet.

'What ails ye, lassie?' Janet called softly from the door of the hen house. Janet was young and brisk and Sarah blinked hastily, ashamed of her tears. She was too young to realise that Janet might have problems of her own, or that she might be lonely when Louis was out at work from dawn till dusk, except on the Sabbath. Janet had, in fact, experienced a number of doubts since she came to live in the cottage at Fairlyden. She had looked forward to having a little house of her very own and to being a good wife - for she loved Louis very much; she had wanted to work for Mistress Logan and learn how to make the best butter in Muircumwell. Instead she had had to learn to make the butter as best she could - and sometimes she was not very proud of her efforts when Mr Jardine refused to buy it. Then again, the cottage was so quiet compared with her life at the manse. There had always been somebody knocking at the door wanting the minister; and Mistress Simmons was always bobbing in and out of the kitchen; and Miss Prisset had come twice a week to do the washing and the ironing; there had been Billy White as well, coming in for his dinner every day. He looked after the stables and helped with the garden and the glebe.

'What are ye greetin' for?' Janet persisted now, but her voice was gentler than usual as she looked at Sarah's small hunched figure, bending over a nest, pretending to look for eggs so that she could hide her tear-stained face. Her answer was a muffled, but determined sniff.

'It's that O'Leary woman bin at ye again, I suppose,' Janet declared flatly, but she bobbed into the little wooden hut and put her arm around Sarah's thin shoulders, drawing her against her. The unexpected gesture and the sympathy in Janet's tone penetrated Sarah's defences and with a few gulps and sniffs she confided some of her troubles.

'Ah, but ye hae real bonny hair!' Janet soothed. 'I tell ye what, Miss Sarah,' she said with a note of excitement, 'how wad ye like to come to my wee hoose? I'll boil a kettle o' water and then I'll wash your hair in my new wooden bowl.'

'Will you really?' Sarah asked with pathetic gratitude.

'Aye, I will!'

Sarah's wealth of long, thick curls made it difficult to wash her hair herself and she welcomed Janet's help. It was wonderful to feel clean again and she gave Janet two newly laid eggs for her trouble.

The arrangement became a weekly ritual which they both enjoyed. Unfortunately it did not endear either of them to Maureen O'Leary. Her temper became a thing to be feared, especially when it was exacerbated by her other increasing weakness.

Twenty-Four

Danny had grown into a lovable if mischievous toddler in the year since Mattie's death, but Maureen O'Leary had no intention of weaning him. She had used all her wiles to consolidate her position at Fairlyden, but Sandy remained oblivious to her efforts to inveigle him into her bed. All her life she had revelled in her power over men. Her frustration grew.

When she was only ten years old she had brought shame and despair to her proud Irish mammy. Later she had listened to her neighbours' young brother, Sean O'Leary, telling his tales of Scotland and the welcome he had received at Fairlyden, and him no more than a ragged urchin, desperate to help with the turnip hoeing. At last she had crossed the Irish Sea herself and headed in the direction of the place young Sean had once described. She had adopted the lad's name of O'Leary, believing it might bring her better fortune. She had already conceived four babies but had reared none until she took Danny Logan to her bosom. She would have refused him succour too, had the Minister not mentioned the name of Fairlyden which reminded her of Sean's talk of the fine man called Logan. It seemed as though fate had played into her lap, striking down Logan's wife and leaving his son. Maureen had had an instant picture of a life of ease. She was confident she could make any man forget his wife, alive or dead. So far her confidence had been misplaced, despite her more recent efforts to stir herself into action on the rare occasions when Sandy was in the house.

A life of ease was not without boredom, for the likes of Maureen O'Leary without a man to pleasure. Increasingly she turned to gin for solace. Sandy was too immersed in work, or with his own brooding thoughts, to notice her habits. During the summer he worked until he fell exhausted into bed. On winter evenings he sought the company of Joseph Miller and several other Muircumwell men at the Crown and Thistle. He bought himself a light cob. When his memories were particularly poignant, he sought to drown them with liquor, and his trusty steed carried him safely home.

So as Danny grew, Maureen O'Leary began to fear for her position at Fairlyden. Even when he reached his second birthday she still put him to her breast before he went to bed, insisting that he needed the comfort only she could give him before he would sleep. Danny himself brought this ritual to an abrupt end when he playfully sank his teeth into her soft flesh. She pushed him from her with a screech of pain and fury. Hurt and bewildered, Danny rushed into Sarah's arms for protection.

'I'll wash ye and put ye to bed,' she whispered eagerly after that painful incident. It was the beginning of one of the happiest periods in Sarah's young life, despite the misery of the never ending tasks which Maureen O'Leary set her. Each morning after she had milked her two cows and fed the hens, she helped Danny to dress before she went to school. Slowly, with infinite patience, she taught him to speak and to say his prayers as their mama had taught her.

'Can I come, Sari?' he would carol merrily whenever he saw her leaving the house. He followed her everywhere when she was not at school. For Sarah his merry chuckles and childish adoration made up for O'Leary's jealous rages and increasing demands.

Everyone loved Danny's sunny smiles and placid, happy nature. When Sarah washed him and put him into bed she was sure he must resemble one of God's own angels, with his cheeks as delicately flushed as the petals of a wild rose and his halo of shining curls. His baby hair had already deepened to a beautiful reddish gold which reminded Sarah of her dear friend, Beatrice Slater. It was the thought of Beatrice, looking after her brothers at the mill, which prompted Sarah's idea. As time passed she had lost most of her fear of the Irish woman's threats to herself - at least regarding the 'institution'. She had confided some of her anxiety to Janet.

'She willna send ye awa', Miss Sarah,' Janet scoffed. 'Mr Logan wadna let her do such a thing! Anyway, who would do the cleaning and cooking then? Not herself to be sure!' Janet mimicked wickedly. 'She wadna help with the milking or look after the hens either!'

Sarah had enough sense to realise this was true, but her fears for Danny remained; no one would be able to find him if the Irish woman took him away across the sea. If I could stay at home all the time with Danny, like Beatrice does, she reasoned, then Maureen O'Leary could never take him away.

It had not been easy to speak to Uncle Sandy alone since Maureen O'Leary came to Fairlyden. When Sarah saw him entering the stable one morning, she ran after him.

'Uncle Sandy!' she called eagerly. He turned and crouched down beside her and took her hands in his.

'What is it, Sarah?' His smile was kind, as it had always been, but there was an awful sadness in his eyes. Sarah knew it was because he missed her beloved mama, as she did herself. How could she trouble him with tales of Maureen O'Leary's dreadful rages and her trips to Mr Jardine's store in the pony and trap, while he and Louis were working in the fields or away from home?

'Can I - can I stop going to Dominie Campbell's school?' she asked hesitantly instead. 'I want to look after Danny.' She thought her beloved uncle looked sadder than ever, but her heart sank when he shook his head slowly.

'I promised your mama. It was her wish that you should learn everything Dominie Campbell could teach you, Sarah. You are not yet twelve years old, and the Reverend Mackenzie tells me Dominie Campbell regards you as one of his brightest pupils. One day he will award you a certificate to say how much you have learned. You will be very proud of that, and I shall be very proud of you - as your mama would have been,' he added huskily.

He saw Sarah's disappointment, but she was still a child, too young surely to be burdened with a house and a toddler though he was beginning to suspect that she did a large part of Maureen O'Leary's work already. He frowned. He had no liking for the woman and avoided her company whenever possible, but he was reluctant to put her on to the road after she had given succour to Mattie's son, and especially when she was kin to Sean O'Leary, the lovable urchin who had been their first helper and who had claimed a corner of Mattie's heart; he would permit her to stay until she was ready to move on.

Despite his angelic appearance Danny was a sturdy, independent little boy. Like Sandy as a child, he was rarely afflicted by the common ailments of childhood and never whined or complained. The sight of his dimpled fists and limpid blue eyes filled Janet's breast with yearning. She would have helped Sarah to care for him willingly now that he no longer needed a mother's milk. So far she had failed to conceive herself and the situation was beginning to cause her some anxiety. Maureen O'Leary was cruelly perceptive in such matters and Janet suffered her jealous taunts whenever Danny displayed his affection for her.

Even Sandy was drawn out of his melancholia at the sound of the lilting voice eagerly chirruping 'Papa, Papa!' whenever his small son caught sight of him, but a glimpse of Sarah following behind him with her basket of eggs or a handful of vegetables would bring the bitter-sweet memories flooding back. Sarah was so like Mattie the way her hair sprang from her temples in soft abundance, the sparkle of her brown eyes when she was happy, her tenderness when she was with Danny. He loved his children, but the sight of them, without Mattie, wrenched his heart.

So he continued to find consolation in work, especially with the horses. In the spring of Danny's third year he found himself busier than ever. Dark Lucy, the mare he had brought from Nethertannoch and on whom so many of his early dreams had rested, had produced a fine young stallion - her final foal. Sandy named him Logan's Lucifer.

He put the horse through his paces before the group of men who were to select the best stallion for use in the district during the coming season. Despite his weight and size, Lucifer demonstrated exceptionally good movement, lifting his feet cleanly from the ground, displaying well-formed, perfectly set limbs. His ribs were sprung like the hoops of a barrel, his back was short, strength and quality showed in every line.

'Ye know exactly what they're looking for, don't ye, Lucifer?' Sandy murmured proudly when the massive stallion arched his long neck and pricked his ears, gazing at them with clear intelligent eyes. Sandy imagined there was even an element of his own disdain in the inclination of his noble head as he looked down upon the Earl of Strathtod; his was the only dissenting voice amongst the men who had the power of selection. The Earl was outnumbered. Lucifer was awarded the coveted premium of fifty pounds. Sandy was elated; his patience had been rewarded at last.

The award of the premium, and the selection of Lucifer as the district's stallion, meant that Sandy was obliged to travel through the surrounding parishes calling on those breeders who requested his services. Even Abraham Sharpe at Mains of Muir swallowed his pride and put forward three of his best mares. Sandy found it ironic that Mistress Sharpe now considered him worthy of entrance to her house. He smiled at the prospect of sharing this trivial triumph with Mattie, until he remembered. Again and again memories reared up out of his subconscious mind, stabbing his heart with renewed grief when he least expected it.

Sandy welcomed the prospect of journeying with the stallion, of getting away from everything that was so poignantly familiar.

'Ye'll have tae put the past behind ye,' Joseph Miller repeated again and again. 'Ye must be strong, laddie, for the sake o' the bairns. They're Mattie's tae, remember.'

As though he could ever forget, Sandy thought bitterly, but he was determined Fairlyden should not be neglected during his absence with the stallion. He knew Louis could not manage the spring work alone, especially with the increased number of ewes and lambs. When he heard that Dick O'Connor was intending to put himself up for hire at the next May Fair, Sandy lost no time in offering him work at Fairlyden. The O'Connors were known to be canny men with animals and Sandy felt he would have no qualms about leaving them in Dick's care.

'Och, Mr Logan, there's naething I could want better!' Dick declared with delight. 'I wad be near enough hame tae return every nicht. Ma mither an' faither will be fair pleased tae. They think the hoose is empty noo.'

'Aye, I'm sure they do, Dick,' Sandy agreed with compassion.

Before his death Lord Reginald Fairly had drawn up a lease to protect Walter and Maisie O'Connor which even his malevolent brother James would be hard put to break. But the dead Earl had been unable to protect the jobs of the young O'Connors and they had been forced to move away from the Strathtod Estate.

Sandy had met Lord Reginald Fairly only once but the young Earl had earned his immediate respect; he had shown courage in the face of death; he had also shown wisdom and compassion when Sandy sorely needed it, for his conscience had been greatly troubled. He knew that Sarah had no real claim to Fairlyden since Mattie's death, and in his grief-stricken state he had half believed her death was his punishment for the sin of adultery.

He had received a most cordial welcome at Strathtod and Lord Reginald had even expressed an urgent desire to meet Sarah whom he regarded as his cousin. Such amiable sincerity had only served to heighten Sandy's guilt and he had almost broken his promise to Daniel

Munro and blurted out the truth. Looking into the young man's dark eyes, he had been aware of a wisdom and understanding far beyond Reginald's twenty-eight years - as well as an uncanny resemblance to Daniel himself. Sandy knew he would never forget Reginald Fairly's steady, penetrating gaze as he stumbled over his request for a similar lease to the one the O'Connors had been granted, a lease which would entail the payment of a fair rent but which would ensure Sarah's security whatever questions might be raised by a suspicious or evil laird. He had been disconcerted by the young Earl's reply.

'Surely you do not wish to usurp her right to Fairlyden?'

'No! Of course not. I love Sarah as though ... as though '

'As though she were your own daughter,' Lord Reginald had supplied quietly. The thin, sickly face had softened. 'It was my grandfather's intention that his son, Daniel Munro, should reap great benefit from Fairlyden. He could not have foreseen the illness which would beset him, and he would have been grateful - as I am - to all who helped him in his adversity. Clearly it was Daniel Munro's wish that Sarah should bear his name, therefore Fairlyden is hers - and yours, as her legal guardian. I have no wish to interfere. The farm is a credit to you. All I ask is that you should continue to act in Miss Sarah's best interests, at all times.'

The familiar words sent a shiver down Sandy's spine. For a moment he was back at Nethertannoch, at the side of another dying man. 'Ye'll aye dae what's best for ma bairn.' Matthew Cameron's words echoed as clearly in Sandy's mind as when Mattie's father had first uttered them. How terribly he had failed!

Lord Reginald Fairly saw the torment in Sandy's blue eyes and his heart was filled with sympathy. Then Sandy lifted his head and his square jaw clenched. He had failed Mattie but he would not fail her daughter, his own flesh and blood.

'I think you know I shall always do what is best for Sarah,' he had replied quietly, meeting Lord Reginald Fairly's steady scrutiny unflinchingly.

It still saddened Sandy that there had been no opportunity to take Sarah to Strathtod before the young Earl's death, but his own conscience had been easier after their meeting. In his heart he knew Lord Reginald suspected that Sarah was his own daughter.

Dick O'Connor had proved honest and utterly trust-worthy.

'Will ye be hiring at Fairlyden for another year then, Dick?' Sandy asked when the hiring fairs came round a year later.

'Ye ken fine I'll hire wi' ye, Mr Sandy,' Dick grinned happily. 'While ever ye have a place for me at Fairlyden, I'll be mair than content tae bide!'

'Mmm, well, I'm pleased that's settled then, Dick,' Sandy admitted with relief. 'Now that another Fairlyden stallion has been awarded the hiring premium for the district, I'll need tae be awa' a good many days. Aye, an' a few nights too nae doubt.'

Success with his horses kindled new hope in Sandy's heart. Danny was almost four years old now. His and Mattie's son must have a future. There was talk of higher premiums now that the best horses were in demand all over the country. There would be greater honours to be won. The Glasgow Agricultural Society had begun the new decade of eighteen hundred and seventy by selecting the best Clydesdale stallion in the whole of Scotland and the north of England. It was Sandy's ambition to breed a horse worthy of that accolade. Mattie had died giving him a son. Now he resolved to make Danny proud of the Logan name, proud of the Logan horses too.

Sarah was too intelligent a child not to realise that her beloved uncle's attention was now divided between the farm and his obsession with breeding the best horses in the country.

'If only Maureen O'Leary didna go to Muircumwell so often whenever he is away,' she said anxiously to Janet as they finished the milking. Even Janet kept out of the way when O'Leary had made one of her trips to the village.

'I ken how ye worry about Danny, Miss Sarah,' Janet sympathised. 'I dinna ken where she gets the money tae buy so much gin! Of course she wadna admit it was gin but her temper is something terrible after it. One o' these days Mr Logan will be catching her!'

'I wish he would!' Sarah agreed fervently. 'But whenever he's there she's...' She wrinkled her nose thoughtfully.

'I ken!' Janet muttered grimly. 'She puts on her Irish charm!'

Sarah had not wasted her time, or the money Sandy paid each week for her lessons at Dominie Campbell's school. She had made up her mind to earn her certificate of competence and to learn to keep accounts, as her Mama had done. The dominie sensed her new determination. He could not overlook any pupil being late for lessons, but Sarah knew he did not apply the cane with his earlier vigour. Indeed, her small work-roughened hands had become quite hardened to its mild sting. Dominie Campbell's wife was less sanguine when she came into the schoolroom to teach the girls to sew.

'Sarah Munro, your hands, girl!' she would screech in her high-pitched voice if torn finger nails snagged the finer threads, or soiled the linen. Mistress Campbell complained loudly, even though Sarah was already proficient in everyday needlework as well as spinning and knitting. Dominie Campbell came to her rescue by suggesting extra arithmetical problems. When Sarah eagerly agreed, his wife eyed her incredulously and not without suspicion.

'The child wishes to learn in order to keep account of the Fairlyden household as her Mama used to do. It is surely a worthy ambition - to know the price of candles and cotton, of mutton and meal; to know how much butter or cheese, and how many eggs, she must sell in order to buy the things she needs?' Dominie explained patiently, but Sarah thought she saw a wry gleam in his eye. Mistress Campbell was an expert with her needle, but she was not an intelligent woman.

'Her mama!' she exclaimed. 'Surely Mistress Munro ' she sniffed disapprovingly as she corrected herself, 'Mistress Logan was deaf? Totally deaf. She could not possibly have understood such things!'

'But she did, Ma'am!' Sarah declared indignantly. 'It is all written in her own hand, in a big book, in the dresser at Fairlyden.'

'1 believe that is correct, Madam,' Dominie Campbell assured his wife gravely. 'I have heard Mr Jardine say how quickly the child's mother could add a list of figures, and that she always knew exactly how much money her eggs and butter would bring. She never spent in excess of her income.' His wife glared at his bland expression suspiciously. She had little idea about budgeting and Mr Campbell was always adding up lists and telling her to economise.

'Surely you will agree it is a worthy example for the child to follow, my dear,' he said, 'especially as things are so greatly changed at Fairlyden?' Sarah looked at him sharply and saw a slight flush stain his thin cheeks as he caught her glance. 'Er that is, according to Mr Jardine,' he added hastily, but Sarah was uneasy. What had the dominie heard, and why should Mr Jardine mention their private business?

At Easter, a few weeks before her thirteenth birthday, Dominie Campbell presented Sarah with a scroll which proclaimed her to be proficient in Reading, Writing and Arithmetic, to have sufficient knowledge of the Latin to assist her in general life, as well as a sufficiency in French. She was also 'moderately skilled in needlework'. Sarah was delighted with the scroll, though she gave an inward grimace at the grudging comment Mistress Campbell had allowed. She knew herself to be at least as skilled as any of the other girls under Mistress Campbell's instruction. Now she could be with Danny every day! She would be able to help Janet in the dairy and make the very best butter in Muircumwell, as her mama had done. Already several of the hens were clucking broodily since the spring weather had arrived. She must set more eggs to increase the chickens, and perhaps Mr Miller would let her have some young goslings to rear?

As soon as this thought occurred to Sarah, she found herself running, taking the fork away from the village, towards the mill house, to share her good news with Beatrice and to ask her friend's grandfather about the geese. Beatrice was delighted to see her for it was a rare occasion now when the two girls had time to chatter. Sarah was immediately aware of an improvement in the mill house, and felt a spasm of shame at the thought of Fairlyden's filthy kitchen, festooned with cobwebs, the hearth continually littered with ashes, and the windows so grimy the sun could scarcely shine through them.

Beatrice was making scones on the girdle over the fire. Her mother sat in a corner, silent, bent forward, her arms clasped around her thin body as she rocked continually backwards and forwards. Sarah greeted her politely but she doubted if Mistress Slater was even aware of her presence; she stared vaguely ahead, unblinking. There was a faint bruise on her neck and her hair hung in untidy wisps. Sarah turned to her friend and thought how well, and how pretty and clean, she looked. Beatrice had grown taller since they last met, and she had put her hair up too. They smiled at each other and Beatrice pushed a newly buttered scone towards Sarah and poured her a cup of buttermilk.

'Eat it now before he comes in,' she instructed in a low voice. She pursed her lips in a grimace and turned back to the griddle to lift the last of her scones on to a cloth.

'Where are the boys?' Sarah asked.

'In the mill, likely - or meddling in some kind o' trouble!' Beatrice muttered gruffly. 'Tell me your news, Sarah, while we're on our own. My, 'tis grand to see ye!'

Sarah looked towards the dim corner. Beatrice caught her glance. 'Mother willna' hear us. She lives in a world o' her own these days; scarcely eats as much as yon wee robin out there.' She smiled, almost merrily. 'Cheeky wee fellow, he is! Comes every day for crumbs. What brings you to the mill, Sarah?'

Sarah started at the sudden change of topic. She had been thinking how pretty her friend looked when she smiled.

'You're almost a woman, Beattie, and pretty too.'

'Aye.'

Sarah was puzzled by the brooding shadows which darkened her friend's bright blue eyes, then the shadows lifted and she smiled again.

'What goes on at Fairlyden these days? I hear the O'Leary woman is often i' the village running up debts for your poor uncle.'

Sarah frowned. 'I wish she would go away!' She brightened. 'I have finished at the school, Beattie!' She held out her scroll proudly for her friend to inspect and admire, and Beatrice did so, generously, without envy. 'I am going to make Fairlyden clean and shining again. I shall persuade Uncle Sandy to buy four more cows at the market - as many as Mama had. I shall help Janet with the dairy now, and we shall have more eggs because I shall set eggs under the broody hens. I thought er that is, I wanted to ask your grandfather if he would tell me about keeping geese?'

'He will.' Beatrice smiled wryly. 'Ye ken how much he loves to talk to you or to your Uncle Sandy. He's doon at the stable just now. We have a new foal - a beautiful wee filly.' Her eyes sparkled. 'She is by your uncle's stallion. Grandfather says it will be the best foal he has ever had.'

'How do you know who its father is? I-I mean ' Sarah frowned, then she muttered in a sudden rush, 'Beattie, do you know how real babies are made? I mean babies like Danny. Maureen O'Leary keeps saying - well, things! Horrid things - to Janet.'

Beatrice blinked and stared hard at her friend. 'My, what an innocent you are still, Sarah,' she murmured softly, affectionately. Sarah flushed.

'I have a secret,' she muttered shyly. She bent forward and whispered in her friend's ear. Beatrice was not shocked; neither did she mock her as

Maureen O'Leary would have done. Sarah was greatly relieved when Beatrice nodded sagely, understanding, but her young face grave.

' 'Tis a sign ye're almost a woman then, Sarah. Sometimes I wish I had been born a boy. They don't have that bother. They don't have trouble with men -or babies, either!' she added darkly, and Sarah gazed at her wonderingly. Beatrice suddenly seemed so very, very much older. 'Ye must be careful now, Sarah. Ye're pretty, wi' your lovely hair and dark eyes and your pink cheeks. Don't ye be letting any man have his way wi' ye!'

'What do you mean?' Sarah asked with a puzzled frown.

Beatrice grimaced. 'Och,' just dinna let any men near ye - touch ye, ye ken!'

'Trying tae make her as prim as yoursel' and that bitch over there, are ye?' Edward Slater snarled from the doorway. Neither of the girls had heard him enter and they spun round, startled by his harsh voice. Sarah sprang to her feet.

'I-I must be going home now.'

She was alarmed at the way the colour had drained from her friend's face and when she turned Sarah saw the faint blue shadow of a bruise at her temple. Beatrice's eyes were dark now, their sparkle gone. Sarah had never liked Mister Slater much, and she hated the way he was staring at her now. She moved towards the door but he reached out and caught her arm in a vice-like grip, holding her still while his gaze roved all over her. He frowned as his eyes rested on her face, noting the small straight nose with its smattering of freckles, the full, soft mouth, the chin, still rounded but with that same determined tilt. His gaze moved to Beatrice. The eyes were different and the colour of the hair. Edward's eyes narrowed speculatively, but he released Sarah abruptly. With a hasty good-bye to Beatrice she sped down the path. She did not pause at the stable to speak to Joseph Miller about the geese, after all.

Sarah was still running when she passed the wall which encircled the glebe land. She almost ran into the Reverend Mackenzie as he came through the gate, leading his horse.

'Why, Sarah, what a hurry you are in today!' He smiled his usual kind, friendly smile while she stood there, panting breathlessly, wondering why she had imagined there were so many demons chasing her when all the world was so normal. 'How are you getting on at school?' Robert

Mackenzie inquired. 'I have not seen you for some time - not even at church.'

Sarah flushed guiltily and looked up at him. No wonder she imagined Master Slater had sent a thousand devils after her, when she didn't go to church! Perhaps they had only stopped chasing her because they had seen the Minister? She could not resist a quick look behind, but of course there was nothing there.

'I will come to church, I promise. I don't have to go to school anymore. The dominie gave me a scroll.'

'Ah, so you know everything now, eh?' Robert Mackenzie smiled down at her flushed face as he reached for her scroll and read it.

'No, I don't know everything!' Sarah declared earnestly. 'But Dominie Campbell says I can learn more if I read the news sheets. He read about a railway which goes for miles and miles and miles, right across the continent of America. He says it will "open up a whole new world", and Dominie Campbell says no one will be short of food any more. The wheat is grown in big fields and it will be transported on the new railway and brought across the ocean in the new steamships,' she ended breathlessly.

'Yes,' the Reverend Mackenzie agreed gravely, 'but I fear there will always be men and women, somewhere in the world, who will starve. Daniel, your father, studied the news sheets too. He believed the farmers in our own country would be unable to sell their food when the people of America settled down to farming, instead of fighting wars amongst themselves.'

Sarah chuckled. 'Well, they might send wheat to make flour,' she declared practically, 'but they can't send butter and cheese and eggs across the ocean! They would go bad! Sometimes Janet's butter goes bad before she gets it to Mr Jardine's shop. I am going to make the best butter in Muircumwell, like Mama did. I shall be able to help Janet milk and churn and Danny will be with me all day long.'

Robert Mackenzie looked down into her radiant face, so full of youthful optimism, and his heart ached with regret for the things that were past, the fine people he had known - Sarah's own mother among them. How proud Mattie would have been of her daughter and her small, smiling son!

'I hope you will learn to cook better than Mistress O'Leary,' he smiled mischievously, 'then I shall visit Fairlyden often.'

Sarah sighed. 'Mama cooked many things. There is so much to learn.'

'You will learn everything, Sarah, in time. Your mama learned many things from her books, and I think you have deserved a reward since you have worked so hard in Dominie Campbell's school. I shall buy you a very special book. It was first written in many parts for the Englishwoman's Domestic Magazine by a lady named Isabella Beeton. The articles were so popular that Mr Beeton had them bound together in one large volume. He has called it Mrs Beeton's Book of Household Management. When next I visit Dumfries I shall purchase a copy for you, Miss Sarah Munro! Then perhaps you will make gingerbread when I call at Fairlyden, as your mama used to do?'

Sarah smiled up at the Minister and thanked him happily. She had known him all her life and she was not in the least afraid of him, as some of the children at school had been. He was her friend. Her friend! Why had she not thought of it before? The Reverend Mackenzie would have known what to do about the O'Leary woman and her threats. She stared at him intently, thinking.

'What is it Sarah? You seem troubled?'

'It is nothing now, because I shall be there to look after Danny all the time, and O'Leary will not be able to take him away across the sea.'

'The Irish woman threatened to take Danny?' The Reverend Mackenzie gave a wry smile and shook his head. 'And you believed her, no doubt. Poor Sarah! I suppose that is what she said every time she wanted you to do the things she should have been doing herself! I wondered why she had stayed at Fairlyden so long. Well, you had no need to worry, child. One day you will learn that women such as Maureen O'Leary rarely care for their own children. Certainly she would not have taken Danny!'

'But she said,' Sarah stared back at him incredulously. 'Anyway, I hope Uncle Sandy will send her away now.' She could not suppress a shudder. 'She flies into awful rages, especially when she gets the gin.'

'Gin!' This time the Reverend Mackenzie did not smile. 'You mean the Irish woman drinks gin? And she threatens Danny?'

'Why, yes.'

'Surely you have told your uncle this, Sarah?'

'No! I was afraid she might take Danny when I was at school. Anyway, I didna want to tell tales to make Uncle Sandy more sad, 'specially after you said I was a burden to him.'

'I said you were a burden, Sarah? Never!'

'When Mama died you said he had a burden because I needed him.'

'My dear child!' The Reverend Mackenzie was aghast that Sarah had remembered his words so clearly after all this time. How she must have worried! 'Dear Sarah, you have been under a misapprehension. His burden was his own terrible grief. But you and Danny - you are his salvation. You must tell him about Maureen O'Leary! He would be even more hurt and sad if anything happened to you, or to Danny.'

Sarah eyed him carefully, then she nodded. Her eyes lightened and she began to smile. Everything was going to be wonderful!

Twenty-Five

'Janet, wait for me!' Janet turned at the sound of Sarah's voice.

'My, ye're late today, Miss Sarah!'

'Yes. I have good news!' she declared happily. 'Are ye going to bring in the cows? I will walk with ye across the field.'

Danny had been waiting for Sarah's return from school, as he did every day. As soon as he saw her cutting across the field with Janet, he scrambled manfully over the gate, half falling as his short legs became entangled in his skirts. He picked himself up and ran to Sarah as though she had been away for several days instead of hours. She caught him and swung him in the air, laughing aloud at his chuckles of delight.

Danny was with her; the sun was shining; she need never run all the way to school again. Spring was in the air; there were primroses down by the burn and new green leaves on the hedges. It was enough to make anyone sing and dance, and Sarah did just that, scooping Danny into her strong young arms. Laughing a little self-consciously, Janet joined her in a pirouette as the cows ambled in front of them towards the byre. Neither of them was aware of Maureen O'Leary sullenly watching. The Irish woman rarely stirred from her chair in the afternoons, but Sandy had returned unexpectedly and his searching questions had sent her stamping into the garden, seething with vengeful anger.

'Let's dance some more, Sari,' Daniel coaxed happily as Sarah came to a breathless halt.

'My ye're in fine spirits today, Miss Sarah,' Janet smiled. 'What good news have ye then, to be putting that big smile on yer face?'

'Oh, Janet, Dominie Campbell gave me my certificate today. I shall never need to go to school again. Just think of it! Now I can help ye milk the cows and churn the butter. I'm going to have more chickens, and I shall make the cleanest house ye ever did see! Oh, yes, and another surprise. The Reverend Mackenzie is going to bring me a book so that I can learn to do all the things Mama used to do.' Her smile faded at the thought of her beloved mama. To Janet, watching, it was as though the candle of joy inside her had been blown out; then the fleeting sadness was gone as Daniel tugged at her skirt, laughing up at her, willing her to be happy again.

'Maybe "she" will go away now, Miss Sarah?' Janet suggested hopefully. Janet detested Maureen O'Leary, and feared her rages almost as much as Sarah.

'Yes!' Sarah grinned jubilantly. Her conversation with the Minister had banished most of her fears and given her a new confidence. 'Mama looked after Uncle Sandy and grandfather when she was thirteen.'

'Aye,' Janet murmured slowly, 'but she didna have a bairn to mind.' She looked at Danny, now skipping happily ahead of them. 'Not that he's any trouble,' she added fondly, and a new note of optimism crept into her voice. 'I wad help ye wi' the scrubbing and the washing, Miss Sarah - if that O'Leary wad only gang awa'! I saw her driving doon tae the village again this morn - an' it wasna' meal she was bringin' hame i' the cart!' she added darkly. 'Best watch out for her temper tonight.'

Sarah bit her lip. O'Leary's drunken rages were fearsome. She had always assured Uncle Sandy that everything was fine when he asked how she was, but after her talk with the Reverend Mackenzie she knew she must tell him the truth. She raised her chin and Janet brightened at the determined glint in her eye.

'There's Uncle Sandy, standing by the gate. I must show him my scroll. Then I will ask him to send O'Leary away forever!' She clutched Danny's small hand and led him eagerly towards Sandy's silent, brooding figure.

'Papa! Papa!' Danny carolled eagerly, even before they reached the gate. Sandy turned and his expression lightened at the sight of his small son and Sarah, her pretty face alight with some inner happiness. 'Papa, will you give me a ride on the horse's back?'

Sandy smiled down at his son. 'The horses are all working in the field with Louis and Dick.' He frowned. It was the first time he had noticed how Danny's small legs were hampered by his skirts. 'If ye're tae ride a horse, then it's time ye had some breeches and became a man!' He bent and lifted his son in his arms and turned to Sarah. 'When I return, I will take him to Muircumwell, to the tailor. No doubt Mr Nimmo will make a small pair of breeches, or perhaps we should ask Miss Totty.' There was a note of doubt in his voice. Mattie would have sewn her son his first pair of breeches.

'You're going away again?' Sarah could not hide her disappointment.

'Only for a few days, with Lucifer.' He grimaced and his expression hardened. 'If that woman can find me a shirt to wear, and clean collars to take!' Sandy had learned to overlook the untidy kitchen for he was rarely indoors, except to sleep; he had even learned to accept the haphazard cooking; but Mattie had always been particular about washing and changing their clothes. She had never bothered him with money matters either. As soon as she had her hens and a couple of cows she had seen they did not lack for food or clothes, and she had never run into debt. He knew now that he had neglected too many things concerning his household.

'Mr Jardine sent his quarterly account,' he told Sarah with a frown. 'It is even bigger than the last one! Maureen O'Leary says he has charged for two hams, but ye ken we kill our ain pigs. Then there were bolts of cloth Do ye ken anything of that, Sarah?'

She shook her head.

'I shall pay young Master Jardine a visit before I leave. In fact, I will go tonight.' Sandy's voice held a note of exasperation.

'Uncle Sandy,' Sarah exclaimed excitedly, 'see my scroll! Dominie Campbell says I do not need to go to school anymore. I-I can keep accounts now - of the meal and flour and candles and all the things from Mr Jardine's store, and the butter and eggs we sell, as Mama did?' she finished uncertainly, watching Sandy's face cloud with sadness, but he put out a hand and patted her head with tender affection.

'Why, Sarah, ye're almost a young lady! Ye've done well with your lessons.' He sighed. 'In truth, I shall be glad o' your help. So many things need the attention o' a good woman.'

'Will you tell Maureen O'Leary to leave Fairlyden now?' She persisted eagerly. 'Danny does not like it when she rages. Janet does not like her either.'

Sandy stared down into Sarah's anxious dark eyes. His own narrowed suddenly. 'And you, Sarah?' he asked urgently. 'Have you been afraid? Too afraid to tell me?'

'She - she threatened to take Danny away if I - if I grumbled or told ye tales. And Mama said I was tae take care o' him. I can look after him now!'

'Ah, Sarah, my poor lamb!' Sandy groaned aloud. 'How blind I have been. How unforgivably blind!'

Sarah was astonished when he hugged her fiercely against him with his free arm. She did not see the moisture in his eyes; she was too young to understand how his heart ached for the woman he had loved, or the terrible remorse he felt for leaving her children so long in the care of a vagrant woman. He had shut his eyes, and his mind. He had not wanted to remember how things had been when Mattie was alive. In his heart he had known the O'Leary woman was a lazy slut but he had accepted the assurances of a child - a frightened child. He looked into Sarah's innocent, upturned face and set his wriggling son on his own sturdy feet.

'Dear God, how terribly I have failed,' he muttered brokenly.

'Uncle Sandy?' Sarah's dark eyes were wide with concern. She had seen that haunted look on his face before - when they had taken Mama away.

'Forgive me, Sarah. I have neglected you shamefully - you and Danny - Mattie's children. My ain bairns.' He whispered the last words under his breath.

Sarah's heart lifted, despite the sorrow on her beloved uncle's face. The Minister was right. He didn't consider her a burden! He had called her his own bairn. 'When will O'Leary leave?' she asked eagerly.

'Tomorrow.' His face was grim. 'In the morning I shall tell her to leave Fairlyden and never return! First I shall call upon Mr Jardine at the Muircumwell store.'

Sarah's eyes glowed up at him, so dark, so like her mother's.

'Will ye stay at home when O'Leary's gone, Uncle Sandy? We shall all be happy again then.'

He hugged her. 'Aye. We shall all be happy,' he repeated softly against the top of her head.

Sarah gave a joyful whoop, and rescued Danny from the mud where he had begun to play, a few feet away.

'Come on, Danny.' She clutched his small hand in hers. 'We must tell Janet the good news.'

Sandy watched them go. 'Forgive me, Mattie,' he groaned silently. 'I'm no use without ye.'

As soon as Sarah reached the house, towing a reluctant Danny, Maureen O'Leary began to bawl at her.

'I have to change into my milking pinafore and my clogs,' Sarah interrupted the tirade hastily, hoping to avoid further argument. 'Janet has already started the milking and, '

'That trouble-causing, idle besom! You will be letting the bitch get on with it. Leave her, wad ye be hearing now?' The screeching voice went on and on but Sarah didn't care now. Soon Maureen would be gone. She grabbed the coarse apron hanging behind the kitchen door.

'There's work in here for you, you lazy good-for-nothing, dawdling, why are ye late anyway? Ye needna be thinking Maureen O'Leary will be adoing of the washing and slaving after yourself and the brat, and that uncle o' yours! Him thinkin' he's a swell gentleman indeed! Comin' in here demanding his clothes to be washed and ironed. And him just going a travellin' wit' an old horse, and me wit' not a minute to meself. Humph! Let him be daring to tell me how to wash dishes again! Tells me not to hang 'em on the nails above the boiler, he did. Says I, they'll dry clean i' the steam - an' I've hung 'em there again!' she screeched defiantly.

Sarah threw her boots swiftly into a corner and grabbed her wooden clogs in one hand and Danny in the other but the harsh voice followed her across the yard. 'I'll smash the pots ower his head or me name's not Maureen Mary Kelly! An' dinna think Ye'll be gitting out o' the washing. I've left that ol' boiler full. Aye, an' boilin' fit tae be bursting, it'll be!'

Sarah guessed the Irish woman must have been drinking already; she couldn't even remember her own name. She sighed as she found Danny a comfortable place to squat while he watched the milking.

'When can I learn tae milk a cow like you, Sari?' he asked, his blue eyes sparkling.

'Och, it'll no' be long, wee man.' It was Janet who answered. The byre seems so peaceful. A happy place after the noisy kitchen, Sarah thought happily.

She was relieved to see that Uncle Sandy intended to eat the evening meal with them when she and Danny returned to the house, for she had learned to recognise the ugly mood simmering behind O'Leary's glittering green eyes. The Irish woman set down the plates of ham-bone soup with a thump which set the grey, unappetising liquid sloshing on to the table. Sandy wondered if it had ever seen anything more of a ham bone than the salt. He picked up a piece of the dry bread and noticed the blue mould on the back. His eye caught Sarah's. Her lips lifted slightly, a mere flicker of a conspiratorial smile, but it cheered him immensely.

Danny never dared to refuse his food if O'Leary had made it, but after the first few spoonfuls of the salty brew he stirred and stirred, and none of it found its way to his mouth.

'Eat it!' Maureen O'Leary bellowed and he immediately gulped down several spoonfuls in quick succession.

'A mug of buttermilk and an oatcake would be better for the boy,' Sandy said grimly without even lifting his eyes to inspect his son's plate.

Maureen O'Leary glared furiously at the unfortunate Danny. He recognised the threat in her green eyes. Sarah always got into trouble when she tried to defend him. It did not occur to him that his father would fare rather better in a confrontation with the formidable Irish woman. He swallowed the vile liquid with a speed which made him feel sick.

Sandy pushed away his own unfinished meal and rose from the table. The sooner he had spoken with the Jardines, the sooner he would be home. Then he would deal with Maureen O'Leary! He searched the mantle shelf high above the fire. He had propped the account there earlier.

'Have you seen the letter from the Muircumwell store?' he demanded.

'Must've blowed into the fire,' she muttered defiantly, but he saw the flicker of resentment - or was it fear - in her eyes? He was not in the habit of receiving letters which suggested, however politely, that he owed a large debt, especially for household goods. He had retained Mattie's arrangement with the store; the account was to be settled each quarter, either way. He had stuck to his side of the bargain, paying promptly when the sales of butter and eggs were low, and receiving money from the Jardines when they were high. He had trusted them, father and son. Tonight he would settle the affair, but he was sure now that Maureen O'Leary was the culprit.

He took Mattie's ledger from the dresser drawer where she had always kept it. His concentration was plagued by a raging thirst but it did not take him long to realise that the winter quarter was always the most expensive - candles, and extra oatmeal, and oil for the house lamp, and with fewer eggs and less butter to sell. Even so the amount he owed was more than three times as much as any in Mattie's accounts. He shut the book with a snap. The salty soup had given him a craving for a drink of fresh cold water straight from the spring. That would help set his thirst right. A talk with the Jardines would put his other problems in order.

Maureen O'Leary's harsh, whining voice started immediately Sandy had closed the door behind him, but tonight Sarah was cheered by her knowledge that this would be the last time.

'Hurry you up wit' the mending o' them socks, ye lazy varmint! Don't ye be tinking Maureen O'Leary'll be a doing o' his washing! Him demanding his shirt an' clean collars, if ye please,' she muttered, and drew the cork from the bottle which she had hidden earlier beside her chair. 'It's not slaving after him that I will be a doing!'

Sarah sighed heavily. She was very tired after her day at school, the long walk there and back, helping Janet with the milking and feeding the hens.

'The clothes must have boiled for hours. I'll take them frae the boiler now. Did ye bring the water to the tub for the rinsing?'

'Indeed and I have not! To be sure you will have to be getting it at the burn yoursel'. It's idle ye are!'

Sarah laid down the sock she was darning, determined not to argue tonight. She suspected the Irish woman must have consumed a considerable amount of gin already, and the evening was only just beginning. She hoped Uncle Sandy would not be too long with the Jardines.

'Finish the mending, do ye be hearing me?' Maureen O'Leary suddenly screeched perversely.

'But it's almost dark!' Sarah protested, wide-eyed. She had never heard of anyone washing clothes at night. 'Uncle Sandy's shirts will not be dry.' Maureen O'Leary never usually stirred herself to light the boiler fire, even in the mornings. Sarah guessed she had only done it tonight to be contrary because Uncle Sandy had criticised her slovenly ways.

'Can I have a drink of water, please, Sari?' Danny asked wearily, watching O'Leary gulping at the bottle she kept pulling out of her large pocket. Sarah put aside the sock with a tender smile.

'Yes, I'll get'

'Get on wit that mending! It's a needing of the stockings he is. Leave that spoiled brat be.'

'I'm thirsty, Lealy,' Danny pleaded, using the name he had always used for the Irish woman; few hearts could have resisted the appeal in his sleepy blue eyes.

'I'll just get him a wee drink o' water frae the ewer in the scullery,' Sarah began.

'Stay where ye are!' O'Leary thundered menacingly.

'But he's thirsty. I'm thirsty too,' Sarah pleaded, though she was always a little frightened of Maureen O'Leary when she flew into her rages. 'It was the soup,' she faltered, then clapped a hand over her mouth.

The moment the criticism was uttered she knew she had said the wrong thing. Apart from the several large swigs of gin she had taken, the Irish woman had been acting strangely ever since Uncle Sandy had announced his intention of going to Mr Jardine's store. A spate of abuse poured into their innocent ears. The absent Janet was blamed, Uncle Sandy, the gods, the little green men - everyone was to blame except O'Leary herself!

Sarah lowered her head with a yawn and tried to concentrate on the darning, deriving a little comfort from the knowledge that the horrible woman would leave Fairlyden tomorrow. She had learned from experience that protesting only inflamed O'Leary's awful temper and she was quite likely to throw the first object which came to hand. Yet the more she thought of a drink of water, the greater her own craving and her sympathy with Danny became. She did not see him creep quietly towards the scullery and push the door ajar.

The scullery was in darkness except for a faint glow from the small fire beneath the boiler in the corner. Danny knew Sarah always filled a big jug of clean water and left it on the stone slab ready for morning. He needed to pour some into a mug. He licked his lips in anticipation and looked up at the row of mugs which Maureen O'Leary had hung to dry above the steaming copper. They were beyond his reach. He peered around for the little stool Sarah had to stand on when she needed to ladle hot water from the boiler. He was a little bit frightened of the shadowy corners, but thirst urged him on. He found the stool and climbed up, but he was much too small. In a trice he had hoisted up his trailing skirts and climbed nimbly on to the stone slab, next to the boiler. He could just see the row of pottery mugs gleaming palely on the nails above it. He could feel the warmth of the steam escaping from the peculiar-shaped tin cover on top of the bubbling clothes. He stretched his short arm as far as it would go but he couldn't quite reach the end mug. He looked down at his feet. If he stood on the corner of the boiler - the thought had no sooner entered his curly head than he had stepped up. Now he could reach any of the mugs and he had always liked the yellow one best. He stretched forward. One small foot rested lightly on the wobbly edge of the tin cover which Maureen O'Leary had slammed in place earlier. She had left it slightly askew. Danny was light but there was nothing - nothing at all - to stop the cover tipping.

As long as she lived, Sarah would never forget Danny's screams. Never!

The scullery was full of billowing steam. She couldn't see Danny. Maureen O'Leary just stood there. She was frightened out of her drunken wits, gabbling: 'O, Mary, Mother of God,' over and over.

It was Sarah who grabbed the candle. It was she who tugged the slobbering creature frantically to the boiler; pleading, nay, commanding her to help. Maureen O'Leary was at least a foot taller than Sarah and she plucked Danny from the steaming clothes by his curly hair, but it was Sarah's arms which lowered him to the floor, heedless of his scalding skirts.

Danny's screams grew silent. In the dim shadows cast by the light of the candle Sarah saw his blue eyes, clouded with pain and shock.

'I'se hurted, Sari,' he whispered. His eyes closed.

'Get the doctor! Send Louis. Oh, you look after Danny!' she sobbed at the stupidly staring woman.

Both Louis and Janet stood up in alarm when Sarah burst into their tiny cottage. Her breath came in gasping sobs.

'Bring the doctor!' she cried frantically. 'It's Danny!'

Louis acted instantly, pushing away his half eaten meal. Sarah turned and ran back. She would not leave Danny with Maureen O'Leary a moment longer than she had to. She was barely aware of her own stinging flesh, the breath tearing at her lungs.

At the sight of Sarah's wild, tormented eyes and white face, Janet had grabbed her shawl. They arrived at the house almost together - in time to see Maureen O'Leary's bulky figure shuffling away into the shadows of the April evening.

They found Danny where she had left him, alone on the scullery floor, his small, painfully scalded body wrapped in a scrap of filthy blanket.

Twenty-Six

Sarah found it impossible to forget Danny's painfully cruel death. Her love for her little bright-eyed brother had been deep and sincere. He had been the sunshine in her young life.

As the weeks grew into months the scars on her arms and hands faded, but Sarah felt the scar on her heart could never heal. She viewed the world as through a sheet of ice - cold, clear, at a distance. It was a barrier no one could penetrate, not even her beloved uncle. She believed she had no right to his love, despite Sandy's new gentleness and unfailing patience. Sarah thought he was doing his duty towards her, keeping his promise to the woman he had loved beyond all others, her own dear mama.

'I loved ye, Danny,' she sobbed into her pillow during the dark hours of endless nights. 'I shall never love anyone else like I loved you. Please, please, forgive me!' She blamed herself and she could not forget.

Sarah could not know how near Sandy came to telling her that she was his daughter when she was inconsolable in her grief and remorse. The shock of his son's death, and the depths of Sarah's grief, had catapulted him out of his own trough of despondency.

'Sarah is all I have left of ye, Mattie,' he would murmur aloud in his anguish in the darkest hours of the night. 'I mustna fail again. I have been selfish in my ain grief. I neglected my bairns when they needed me. Dear God, forgive me.' Sandy prayed more fervently than he had ever done in the months when Sarah's spirits were at their lowest ebb. It seemed nothing could comfort her, not even a visit from William Fairly. She refused to see anyone.

As time passed Sarah learned to accept that life must go on, however much she missed Danny, but she was haunted by an insidious loneliness and the belief that she had no one of her own to love, or to love her. Sandy's kindness and gentleness only added to her guilt; she had allowed his son, his only child, to die. She began to regret her stubborn refusal to see anyone; she longed for the friends of her childhood - the laughing dark eyes and kindliness of William Fairly, the affectionate loyalty of Beatrice Slater.

Beatrice had grown into a young woman now and had problems of her own, problems she seemed unable or unwilling to share, even with her childhood friend. As for William Fairly, no one knew where he had gone.

William had not learned of Danny's death until three weeks after the tiny coffin had been laid beside his mother's in the kirk yard. He had left the university at St Andrews immediately and ridden through the night to Strathtod Tower. He knew how deeply Sarah had loved her young brother. He longed to see her, to offer what comfort he could. He was dismayed when Sarah refused to see him. He had believed she was the one person in his barren life who would always welcome his presence; yet he had been absent, he had failed her in her hour of greatest need.

How can 1 ever become a minister? he asked himself bitterly. When I cannot help the one young person whom I promised to befriend at all times? I shall never be a worthy man of God. He refused to return to St Andrews and he abandoned his studies.

'You have forfeited your right to an allowance from the estate!' Lord James Fairly announced triumphantly. 'It was our father's command.'

The new Earl cast aside the burden of his youngest brother with unwarranted speed. William was left with no option but to support himself. He sold his beloved horse Diablo and journeyed to Liverpool. There he persuaded a ship's captain to take him on board.

As the years passed, time helped to assuage Sarah's grief, and common sense eased her guilt. She still saw Beatrice but it saddened her to know that her dearest friend could not confide in her since they had left the innocence of childhood behind. She sensed that Edward Slater resented her presence whenever she visited the mill house, and his baleful scrutiny made her uncomfortable.

At twenty, Sarah was taller than Mattie had been, with firm, graceful limbs and a lithe, enviably curved young body; her skin was clear and soft, emphasised by dark, finely curving eyebrows above wide brown eyes; but her youthful chin had a determined tilt, and a careful observer might have said it bore a remarkable resemblance to Alexander Logan's, as did the copper lights which glinted in her hair. Recent years had brought an unyielding firmness to a mouth that had been shaped for laughter - and loving. To the casual observer it gave the appearance of a young woman who was entirely self-sufficient; to Edward Slater it spoke of aloofness and disdain. It reminded him of Alexander Logan.

The prosperity of British agriculture seemed to have passed with the years, just as Daniel Munro had forecast. Rumours concerning the future of Strathtod estate abounded, but no one seriously believed the ancient traditions and wealth could crumble, even though the stories surrounding the present Earl were legendary.

'The Earl might survive, but some o' his tenants have already given up their farms,' Sandy declared grimly one evening when he and Sarah were discussing the latest victims with the Reverend Mackenzie. 'More will follow if he insists on raising their rents at such a time as this.'

'Mmm, there is much anxiety amongst my parishioners,' the Minister agreed with some concern. 'The British government seems convinced that cheap food is essential to keeping wages down and the industrialists demand cheap labour because they think it is the way to ensure their monopoly of the world's industrial markets.'

'I dinna ken whether cheap food will ensure anything except richer owners and poorer labourers. Aye, and fewer farmers!' Sandy remarked with rare cynicism. 'They want food imports so that they can export their iron and steel goods in exchange, but they dinna care about the country folks struggling to survive when the other governments dump their ain excesses in the British ports.'

'I am disappointed that Prime Minister Disraeli has taken no steps to help, after his protestations that the Free Trade policy was too inelastic,' Sarah remarked. She had continued to follow Daniel Munro's example of studying the news sheets. 'He declared that a strong agricultural industry would always be Britain's greatest asset.'

'Aye,' Sandy agreed, puffing at his pipe with a worried frown, 'but politicians canna be relied on. As for the new industrialists, they would murder Mother Earth and every living creature for the sake o' selling their ain products.'

'Well, at least we must be thankful that the Earl of Strathtod has no power over Fairlyden,' Sarah said fervently.

This was a fact which had never ceased to anger Lord James Fairly, especially when he heard of the growing demand for Fairlyden horses. He forgot that it took a whole year to breed a single foal and often another three years before it could bring in money, and like every other animal, horses could die when one least expected it.

Sarah studied all the trends and reports and gradually Sandy grew to accept that she was now a young woman with a mind of her own. She had inherited much of her mother's shrewd judgement. He listened to her views and Sarah began to enjoy their discussions. She had read about farmers in the country of Denmark who were increasing their numbers of pigs and hens and buying cheap American grain to feed them on instead of growing their own. More stock meant more work but Sarah had never been afraid of hard work. She expressed her ideas with an eloquence which would have made Mattie proud of her.

Louis Whiteley and Dick O'Connor were secretly doubtful about a woman making plans which affected anything beyond the house and dairy, but they knew their own livelihoods depended on Fairlyden's survival. Sandy agreed to increase the number of cows, pigs and hens. In future Fairlyden would grow only grass for grazing and for hay, enough turnips to last through the winter and a few acres of oats. All the other food for the animals, the linseed cake or bean meal, must be purchased from the merchants. Trade at the Muircumwell mill had dwindled drastically and Sandy only continued to trade there out of loyalty to Joseph Miller and for the sake of Sarah's friendship with Beatrice.

Sarah regarded sheep as weak and stupid creatures, although she loved to see the lambs in springtime.

'Ach, we must keep the sheep!' Sandy insisted. 'They manure the higher fields. Anyway, the woollen mills are increasing. Maybe there will be more demand for wool soon.' Neither he nor Sarah could have guessed that Fairlyden's relative prosperity would attract the attention of one of these new mill owners.

Meanwhile Lord James Fairly noted the changes at Fairlyden and his resentment grew. So too did his debts. He insisted on increasing the rents of his overstretched tenants yet again and the decline of Strathtod estate continued on its downward spiral.

Janet and Louis Whiteley now had three children and a fourth was expected before Christmas.

'I have hired Agnes Jamieson to help milk the extra cows, and to work in the house,' Sarah announced one Friday when she had been to the market with her butter.

'Agnes Jamieson? Frae Mains of Muir?' Sandy asked.

'Yes. She was telling me she has had enough of Mistress Sharpe. She is leaving at the term.'

'Mmm, she'll be a fine lassie, I think. Her father was Nicky Jamieson. He was killed at Mains of Muir.'

'Yes, I remembered you telling me that, and how good her mother is with the dairy. She is only five years older than me and she always seems so calm and neat. I'm looking forward to having her in the house.'

Dick O'Connor had proved a valuable asset at Fairlyden. Amongst other things he had taken over the job of collecting the meal from the Muircumwell mill. Sarah was surprised that he seemed to look forward to this particular task when Master Slater was such an obnoxious creature. Dick could always be relied on to take care of the young animals when she had to go to the market at Annan with her butter and eggs. She had long since given up hope of selling all her produce at the Jardines' store, and even the town markets were becoming fiercely competitive.

'Who would have believed they would ever bring cheese all the way across the Atlantic Ocean from Canada?' she muttered one evening. 'It is selling at twopence a pound, cheaper than I can produce it myself. It was bad enough when they brought whole cargoes of frozen beef from Argentina a year ago.'

There were rumours that many of the farmers on the Strathtod estate were now poorer than the Fairlyden workers, whom they had once regarded as common labourers. Sarah knew their position at Fairlyden would have been untenable had it not been for the protection afforded by Lord Jonathan Fairly, and she could never understand Uncle Sandy's shuttered expression whenever she mentioned her grandfather.

The O'Connors were also grateful for the protection which Lord Reginald had given them before his death. Dick would never have dared to work at Fairlyden if his parents and eldest brother had not been secure from the present Earl's greed and spite. Lord James Fairly was only too aware of the privileges enjoyed by the O'Connors and bitterly resented his brother's action. Reggie would have been horrified by the chain of events the Earl's vindictiveness would set in motion.

Rumours that Strathtod was actually to be sold to pay the Earl's gambling debts had been rife for weeks. Creditors were said to be both angry and anxious. They were all silenced when the Earl suddenly made a most unexpected announcement: he was going to marry a French heiress.

The lady in question was neither young nor pretty, but she did have a certain charm and dignity. Every-one hoped Lord Fairly would mellow in her presence. This appeared to be the case for a while. Then stories began to circulate amongst the maids at Strathtod Tower once more.

'His Lordship has fallen intae his auld habits again.'

'Her Ladyship has banned him frae her chamber until the birth!'

'But the bairn's no due for several months.'

The Earl submitted to his wife's ruling with bad grace. He frequented the Dumfries taverns in search of excitement; but after trips to London and Paris, he found the small town tame. His frustration and ill temper increased, along with an absurd obsession to wring the last shilling out of every single tenant.

On a misty autumn morning the Earl was riding home after a long night of excesses. It was later than he had intended so he was hurrying to reach Strathtod Tower before his wife noted his absence. It was the Sabbath day and she always insisted that he must accompany her to church, to set an example to his workers. He had still several miles to go when he came upon the neat figure of a woman walking briskly along the path in front of him. She walked gracefully, and the thick coil of auburn hair beneath her white cap glinted in the first rays of the early morning sun. As he passed, she stepped aside and he slowed his horse, curious to note whether her face matched her figure. He was not disappointed. The exercise had given her fair skin the hue of a delicate pink rose, and even from his exalted position in the saddle he could see the light of contentment in her blue eyes; her lips were parted as though she had been humming a tune.

James's head was aching and he needed a wash. He thought no one should look so fresh and happy. He frowned down at her, even turning in the saddle to stare back at her. He saw her raise her eyes, saw them dilate at the sight of him. Her slim figure stiffened with disapproval - or was it fear? He looked again, through bleary eyes.

'By Gad!' he exclaimed. 'If it isn't the O'Connor wench.' His eyes narrowed as memory came flooding back. A dull colour suffused his pasty cheeks beneath his bristling whiskers. It was the spirited filly who had spat at him! He jerked at his horse's reins and turned it around in the narrow path.

Vicky O'Connor stared up at his glaring, bloodshot eyes defiantly, but her heart was thudding with fear beneath the neat bodice of her best muslin dress. Just for a moment she thought the Earl intended to dismount, but instead he felt beneath his riding cape and pulled out his gold pocket watch. He snapped it open and peered closely, blinking his gritty eyes several times before he could decipher the hour. His head ached abominably and he knew he could not cope with his wife's hysterical raging, if she were to discover he had been out all night again.

He sighed irritably and put his watch away. Vicky stood tensely, for he and his horse were blocking her path. There was a cruel twist to his mouth and she sensed that any move on her part might be sufficient to trigger some insane reaction. She held her breath as his gaze travelled over her, inch by inch, as though measuring each individual limb for a new garment. Then he gave a little nod, wheeled his horse in the direction of the village and cantered away.

A huge sigh of relief escaped Vicky's lips. Davy Peterson, the coachman at the big house where she worked, had wanted to come with her this morning, and she was beginning to wish she had agreed. She blushed like a young girl at the thought. Vicky had almost given up any idea of marriage until she met Davy. They had not rushed into anything, but they knew in their hearts that they would be happy together. Now Davy wanted to speak to her father. Her heart soared. Her parents were sure to like him. Lord McAndrew had already promised them a cottage of their own when they were married. He valued Davy's integrity and his absolute reliability. He occupied all Vicky's thoughts as she stepped out jauntily, pushing the memory of her encounter with the obnoxious Earl from her mind.

Nevertheless when her brother, Dick, offered to walk part of the way back with her that evening, she did not refuse as she often did. Instead she chattered happily to him about Davy and their plans to marry next spring, if her parents approved. Dick smiled affectionately. He and Vicky were very close.

'Wad ye like me tae meet you an' Davy, on your next visit?'

'Och, that wad be fine, Dick, if ye wad give him your support. He - he's a mite shy, for all he's a guid man. We'll wait for ye where the paths fork, in the wood. You know the place, a few hundred yards south of the old boundary cottage?'

Dick nodded, 'I'll be there, never fear.'

The next ten days were depressingly misty and wet; coughs and sneezes abounded everywhere, but to Vicky's delight the weather changed again before her free Sunday arrived. It was the middle of October, one of those beautiful golden days which come as a rare gift before the winter's bleak unsmiling weather. The rosehips and rowans glowed like scarlet fairy lanterns in the hedgerows. Overhead the leaves still clung, clothing the trees in a vibrant glory of gold and brown and richest red. The early morning air had held a hint of frost but as the sun rose overhead the grass became crisp and dry underfoot and the air was still and calm, better than it had been at any time during the dreadful summer which had just passed. Vicky was almost ready to leave when Davy entered the kitchen, his face clouded with disappointment.

'Morrison has a cold. Sneezing all over he is,' he announced flatly. 'Her Ladyship willna have him drive tae the kirk wi' her.'

'Oh, Davy!' Vicky's face echoed his own disappointment. 'Then I'll bide here as weel. We could go walking after the kirk.' Davy smiled and shook his head. He was a kind, understanding man.

'Your mither wad be disappointed, I'm thinkin? Anyway, I expect I'll need tae drive His Lordship to the evening service. Ye'd best go hame, lass.'

Vicky nodded. It was true, her parents did look forward to her visits, and Dick would be waiting for her. She nodded, and smiled mischievously at Davy. 'I'll prepare the way for ye!'

At Fairlyden Sarah had also been affected by the cold. She rarely ailed anything and never shirked her work. This time not even her mama's recipe of honey and butter and vinegar had soothed her aching throat. Dick O'Connor could see she was wretched despite her denials. On Sunday mornings he always went straight home as soon as the milking was over and the cows and pigs had been fed and watered.

'I think I'll stay a while longer today, Miss Sarah,' he said in the slow, considering way he had. 'One of the sows is farrowing.'

'Oh no, Dick. Sunday is your day off,' Sarah mumbled croakily. 'You must go home. Anyway, I thought you were meeting Vicky?'

'Och,' Dick grinned. 'Davy Peterson will be wi' Vicky. I'd rather stay, 'specially when Master Logan's no' back frae Ayr. Auld Betsy is real heavy this time. I reckon it'll be a big litter, an' ye ken she has a way o' lyin' on her youngsters if we dinna watch '

Sarah frowned. She often wondered how they would manage without Dick. He had an uncanny instinct for trouble with any of the animals. 'We-ell,' she agreed slowly, 'Uncle Sandy only went to see a filly foal he wants to buy. He must have missed the train back to Dumfries last night.'

'Aye.' Dick smiled. 'That's it then, Miss Sarah. I'll just ask Agnes if she has a mug o' tea and a bite for me, then I'll settle down nice an' quiet tae keep an eye on that old rascal.'

'Well, I don't feel much like sneezing through the Reverend Mackenzie's sermon,' Sarah grinned feebly, 'so perhaps I could do a good deed instead. I will ride Duke over to the Strathtod woods and tell Vicky and Davy Peterson not to wait for you, shall I?'

'That wad be fine, Miss Sarah,' Dick answered gratefully.

Vicky's eyes sparkled and she sang softly as she walked. She had almost reached the fork in the track where she was to meet Dick when she heard the snap of twigs underfoot.

'That you, Dick?' she called cheerfully. There was no reply. Vicky shrugged. Probably a young deer, she thought with a smile.

275

The Earl had made his inquiries thoroughly. He knew exactly where Vicky O'Connor worked and when she visited her parents. He had risen early that morning, and having spent the last few days closeted with his moaning brother and the demands of his expectant wife, was now ready for a little excitement. He had tethered his horse in a small clearing and walked some distance along the woodland track to await Vicky's coming.

When the figure suddenly stepped on to the path right in front of her, Vicky was startled but unafraid, until she recognised the Earl of Strathtod. She turned instantly and began to run back the way she had come.

James uttered an oath. He had not expected immediate capitulation, he had known the O'Connors had too much spirit for that, but her reaction had been swift and she was fleet of foot. He was a tall man, however, and the prize was worth the winning.

In her heart Vicky knew she could never outpace him - and there was no place to hide.

'Oh, Dick!' she sobbed breathlessly. 'Dick!' Then she uttered a stifled scream as the laird grabbed her, bringing her down heavily on the path, his bulky weight on top of her, pinning her beneath his panting body. Vicky struggled wildly, but she was like a fly caught in the web of a giant spider.

James Fairly enjoyed watching her struggle as he regained his breath. Then suddenly, without warning, he grasped the neck of her neat dress and ripped it ruthlessly to her waist.

Vicky was as angry as she was humiliated. The mistress provided three calico dresses and aprons for working in and she was expected to keep them clean and mended. The muslin she had made herself with painstaking effort. She had saved hard to buy the soft blue material and thread, and a length of precious ribbon from the packman who called once a quarter. Her blue eyes narrowed and twin flags of furious colour stained her cheeks. She struggled violently to free her arms, pinioned at her sides by the pressure of the laird's knees. Lord James Fairly was unprepared when she succeeded in reaching his leering, florid face, dragging short, strong nails down his flabby cheek. Vicky knew she would pay the penalty, but she was not sorry; he would make her pay anyway, but not without a struggle!

Vicky was totally ignorant of the price a man like the infuriated Earl could, and would, demand. He bent his head and sank his teeth into the tender white flesh revealed by her torn bodice. Vicky screamed in pain. He gave a gloating laugh and nipped viciously at her other breast. She almost fainted - but not quite, unfortunately. She was made of sterner stuff, and pride made her fight like a vixen, unwittingly increasing the pleasure of the sadistic Earl.

There was no one at the fork of the two paths when Sarah arrived. She waited, wondering whether she had missed Vicky or whether she and Davy Peterson had lingered along the way. Once she thought she heard voices but no one answered when she called. After a while she turned Duke's head towards the woodland path, ambling slowly, wondering whether Vicky had been detained by her mistress.

Vicky felt as though her body had been torn asunder. Her back and shoulders had been ground into every stone and pebble on the hard-packed earth by the Earl's considerable bulk.

'That will teach you a lesson, you bitch!' Lord James Fairly declared venomously. Never for a moment had he forgotten her defiance.

Vicky lay still, her eyes tightly closed against the stinging tears she would not allow to fall. She heard him get to his feet but she remained there, her little world shattered, the sparkle of happiness dimmed forever. No man would want her now!

The Earl of Strathtod stared down at her. Even bruised and dusty as she was, her hair and clothes in disarray, she was still far more beautiful than the woman he had married - but then, he had not married Maria for her beauty but for her wealth. The left side of his mouth lifted in a silent snarl. A wife's wealth belonged to her husband - but Maria's father still insisted on protecting his daughter's interests. He gave her only a yearly allowance, retaining the bulk of her fortune in France, under his own vigilant management. To make matters worse, Maria seemed well satisfied with the arrangement. James squirmed inwardly as he recalled the faint mockery in her shrewd grey eyes, the way she had of rocking back on her heels and coolly surveying him. He knew she had only married him for his title, and to escape from her spinster's mould. He knew she suspected he had married her for her fortune, despite his gentlemanly play acting. He believed she enjoyed tormenting him, releasing enough of her allowance to bind him to her, and no more.

Perhaps things would be different once they had a son. Meanwhile James knew there were some things the Countess would not accept. He looked down at Vicky's prone figure. He thought he heard someone call. It would not do for anyone to find her, he thought with a stab of alarm.

'Get up! Get up, you lazy bitch!' he grunted, and kicked Vicky viciously in the ribs so that she groaned involuntarily and opened her eyes.

Behind his head she saw her own best white cap caught on a twig, fluttering like a huge snowy butter-fly. Her face creased in sudden anguish. How could she ever tell Davy Peterson of this day's evil work? She could never tell him - or anyone else. Never!

'Get up, I say! Get up!'

Vicky struggled to her knees, wincing at the pain; it brought a resentful glare to her eyes. James watched her, fascinated; even now she still had spirit.

Suddenly he grabbed her arm and yanked her to her feet, dragging her after him through the trees, feeling the heat rising in him again at the touch of her smooth flesh. They were well clear of the path when he pushed her down amongst the dried leaves.

'No! Not again!' Vicky cried aloud as she realised what he was about. But she would not plead.

When he had done with her there were no tears in her - just a wild, burning hatred. She forced herself upright and all the gentle laughter and loving kindness inherited from her Irish ancestors were submerged beneath a tide of bitter fury. She cursed him aloud, calling on spirits she had never even heard of, wishing him every evil form of retribution she could think of. So strong was her voice, so vivid her words, that the arrogant Earl shrank beneath the onslaught. Vicky O'Connor's curses would remain with him to his dying day.

This time Sarah was certain she had heard voices and she urged the old cob to quicken his pace. Further into the wood her attention was drawn by an urgent rustling and she saw the receding figure of a man hurrying towards a tethered horse. She thought it was Lord James Fairly but of course he would not be abroad in the woods so early on a Sabbath morning. She called but the man did not answer. A few yards in front a white cap fluttered on the end of a thin branch. Sarah's heart began to thump. She urged Duke nearer and bent to retrieve it. It was then she saw the quivering figure some distance from the path.

As soon as she was alone Vicky had thrown herself on to her stomach and sobbed into the dry leaves and damp earth beneath - deep, shuddering, heartrending sobs. She wished she could die - but death did not come so easily, except to the weak. Sarah tethered her horse and scrambled beneath the branches towards the prone figure.

'Vicky! Oh dear God in heaven '

Vicky started violently. She stared up at Sarah's horrified face, her eyes wild. She wanted to run. She wanted to hide. Sarah fell to her knees beside her, cradling her in her arms as though she were a child.

'Who did this to ye, Vicky? Who?'

Vicky shook her head mutely, but slowly she gathered her senses and released herself from Sarah's arms. She pulled her torn dress together and wrapped her arms tightly around her quivering body.

'It was the Earl!' Sarah exclaimed. 'I saw him! Scurrying away - like the rat he is!' she hissed furiously. 'He did this to you, Vicky, didn't he? Tell me! He must be made to pay.'

'No!' The single word broke from Vicky's white, bruised lips. She shuddered violently. 'No one must know! Ever! Promise me, Miss Sarah! Oh, promise me,' she sobbed brokenly.

'But, Vicky, surely Dick?'

'No! Please promise ye willna tell him?' Vicky pleaded brokenly. 'He - he would - God only knows what Dick wad do.' She shuddered.

'He should have been here, with you, instead of caring for the sow at Fairlyden. It's my fault. You must let me help you, Vicky.' Sarah took off her shawl and wrapped it around Vicky's trembling shoulders. 'The horse is tethered. I'll help you up, if you can hold on to his mane. I'll take you back to Fairlyden and help you bathe '

'No!' Vicky drew back sharply. 'Dick?'

'He will have gone home by the time we get back. Agnes Jamieson always visits her mother after the Kirk on Sundays, and Uncle Sandy hasna returned frae Ayr. The house will be quiet today. I will give ye hot water to bathe. Then you must rest a while.' Sarah could scarcely imagine the full horror of Vicky's ordeal, but she knew the older girl was in a state of shock.

Vicky felt quite unable to face her parents or Dick. Neither could she return to Davy Peterson. She was sure she would never be able to look into the faces of those she loved - and who had loved her. She longed to wash away the filth of the animal who had mauled her. Sarah saw the thoughts chasing each other over Vicky's ravaged face. Gently she helped her to her feet and led her towards the waiting horse.

Twenty-Seven

Sarah had been glad to use the excuse of her cold to avoid any questions, and Dick assumed his sister and Davy Peterson had been detained by their employers. Two weeks later when Vicky visited her parents alone, they attributed her white face and unhappy eyes to a lovers' quarrel, but as the weeks passed Vicky grew more thin and pale, her lovely face haggard. She refused to mention Davy's name, even to Dick.

Sarah could not get Vicky's stricken face out of her mind. On a Sunday morning just before Christmas Vicky waylaid her at the bridge on her way to Church. She looked frozen, as though she had been waiting some time. Fortunately Sandy had ridden on ahead to inquire after Joseph Miller's health and Sarah was alone in the trap. She drew the pony to a gentle halt; subconsciously she had been hoping for such a meeting. She longed to know if Vicky had recovered from the shock of her terrible ordeal, but her heart sank at the change in the once bright, brisk young woman.

'I dinna ken what tae do,' Vicky confessed dully. 'He has left his evil spawn in me. The mistress is a guid woman, but she'll put me oot when she kens.'

'What of Davy Peterson?' Sarah asked tentatively.

'I couldna tell Davy, I couldna! He must never know! Promise me, Miss Sarah?'

'But surely he?'

'Please promise? I had tae talk tae somebody.' Vicky's head drooped. 'I shouldna burden ye, Miss Sarah, but I darena tell anybody else. What am I tae do?' She wrung her hands. 'Mother has had trouble enough o' her ain, an' money's scarce for everybody.'

Sarah was shocked by this further ruination of Vicky's life. The girl's plight was even worse than she had imagined. The sacrifice, the shame and punishment these should have been the Earl's. But it would be Vicky who would be shunned and condemned as a sinner.

'Ah, Vicky!' Sarah scarcely knew how to comfort the young woman whose happiness had been so wilfully destroyed. She offered the only help she could give. 'When your time gets a little nearer, you must leave your position and come to Fairlyden. There will always be a roof for you, and enough to eat, with us.'

'Oh no, Miss Sarah, I couldna dae that!' Vicky looked shocked. 'I shouldna hae troubled ye. There'll be the bairn tae. I shall hate it!' she hissed vehemently. Then, 'God forgive me,' she sobbed softly.

Sarah took her cold blue hands and chafed them gently. She felt as though she was the woman and Vicky the girl. Her tone was firm. 'Courage, Vicky,' she urged. 'The O'Connors never lack courage. Uncle Sandy will agree that you must come to Fairlyden. We owe your family greater debts than we can ever repay. There will be a place for you with us when you need it.'

Vicky nodded silently, unable to express her gratitude. Tears streamed down her pale cheeks as she turned wearily in the direction of her parents' little farm. Sarah watched sadly. Vicky must have made a three-mile detour already to meet her at the bridge. Now her shoulders drooped and all the spring had gone from her step.

Sarah went on her way to church, but her heart was heavy. There seemed no justice in the world. 'Vengeance is mine: I will repay, saith the Lord.' Would He, and would He help Vicky? Sarah's thoughts were distracted all through The Reverend Mackenzie's service.

Suddenly it occurred to her what she must do. Her own Grandfather Fairly had sired a child out of wed-lock, but he had made sure his child had a home. It was true he had loved his mistress, but surely Lord James Fairly had a duty to provide for Vicky and his own child? She would not stoop to plead with him, and Sarah admired her pride, but the Earl was almost her own cousin. Sarah shuddered at the thought. She was not proud to have him as her kin. Nevertheless, she would make him aware of what he had done. She would see that he paid, somehow.

Sarah told no one when she set out for Strathtod Tower that same afternoon. The footman was surprised to see a young lady visitor on the Sabbath, especially alone. Sarah gave her name and there was no doubting her determination to wait on the doorstep if the Earl refused to see her immediately. She was shown into a large room where Lord James Fairly sprawled in a chair beside a huge log fire. His brother Stuart was gazing morosely out of the large window, but he turned at Sarah's entrance, eyeing her with interest. The cold December air had given her cheeks a healthy colour and her brown eyes glinted with the light of battle.

'So this is our cousin from Fairlyden?' Stuart remarked before Sarah could speak.

Her lip curled involuntarily and words fell from her lips before she had time to think.

'It is a relationship I prefer to disown,' she announced coldly. Then, to Lord James, 'I wish to speak with you alone, My Lord.'

James insolently eyed her slim, erect figure. Perversely, he refused to grant her wish.

'Very well, My Lord, if you prefer your brother to learn of your indiscretions, I will come straight to the point. I have no wish to linger here.' Sarah saw James's eyes narrow and a dull flush mount in his face. She hurried on before he could have her thrown out. 'The young woman you assaulted in the wood near the Strathtod boundary, Miss Vicky O'Connor '

'Get out, do you hear? Get out of here, you lying wench!'

'Oh no, My Lord, it is no lie. I saw you with my own eyes. Miss O'Connor is now expecting a child - your child.'

'You lie!' James's voice was louder than he had intended and he jumped to his feet, standing over Sarah menacingly. She did not flinch; neither did she hide her scorn.

'Methinks our young cousin has the Fairly spirit!' Stuart chortled, enjoying his brother's discomfiture.

'Shut up! She lies, I say. I remember now. She was ever friendly with the damned O'Connors.'

'I do not lie, My Lord, and you know it.' Sarah's own anger was rising now. 'You assaulted Vicky most brutally. It is your duty to provide your child and its mother with a cottage and money to keep them. Vicky will be forced to leave her employment on account of your...'

'Why, you insolent wench! I'll teach you to come here telling me what to do!' He grabbed her by the shoulders and was about to propel her to the door, but Sarah resisted and twisted to face him again.

'Remember the book of Hosea, My Lord! "They have sown the wind, and they shall reap the whirl-wind." You will pay for your wickedness!' James Fairly saw the twin flags of angry colour in her cheeks and the glint of her dark eyes. He smelled her lavender-scented clothes and hair. His grip tightened on her arm.

'Maybe you have come looking for sport yourself, eh?' he leered. 'Is that why you came unaccompanied? Just like your grandmother, lusting for a lord!'

'Take your hands off me!' Sarah snapped furiously, but James grabbed her face in his sweating fingers and squeezed her cheeks brutally so that she could scarcely speak. She knew he intended to kiss her and the thought was nauseating.

'Let me go!' she tried to protest, and James Fairly jeered at the peculiar sound which issued from her lips.

'What did you say, my dear?' he taunted.

'You heard what she said, My Lord.' The woman's voice was quiet, but there was no disguising the steel in it.

James Fairly released Sarah as though she was a red hot coal. She turned to see his Countess standing in the open doorway. None of them knew how long she had been there.

'So!' She looked at her husband. 'We have a guest? Surely you should have sent for me, My Lord, to entertain a young lady. Yes?' Even Sarah could hear the mockery in the soft voice.

'You were supposed to be resting, Madam,' the Earl growled angrily.

'Mais non. I shall welcome a little feminine company. Come, my dear.' The Countess beckoned, and Sarah knew she must follow. But she had not yet achieved her purpose. She turned at the door and looked back at the Earl.

'I learned a text from the Reverend Mackenzie today.' Her voice was quiet, but there was no disguising the thread of steel in it. 'It is from Isaiah. "Set thine house in order: for thou shalt die." You will remember, My Lord, to set your house in order?'

The colour drained from James Fairly's face. The text reminded him of Vicky O'Connor's curses; they had echoed too often in his mind. He gritted his teeth. He was aware of his wife watching from the hall with that enigmatic smile on her face. How much had she heard? he wondered.

'Damn you, I will remember nothing from that Free Church hypocrite!'

Sarah's dark brows rose. In that instant she knew he was afraid and would not be able to put the text out of his mind. Her eyes held his steadily, her contempt plain to see, then she turned and followed the Countess.

Lady Maria Fairly had watched Sarah approaching from the window of her chamber. She had noted her graceful walk, the proud set of her head, her neat, though unfashionable dress. Maria was curious. The sound of her husband's raised voice had made her more so and she had glided silently down the stairs, only to freeze on the threshold as she caught the gist of the conversation.

She smiled as she faced Sarah across the small ornate table in her private sitting room. It was a very pretty room, furnished with pale damask-covered delicate gilt chairs and a chaise longue which Maria had brought with her from France. Sarah was enchanted, and temporarily distracted from her original purpose in visiting Strathtod Tower. The Countess was charming. Sarah was taken off guard when she suddenly set down her dainty cup and asked: 'So who is this Veecky for whom you seek help from my husband, Miss Munro?'

Sarah's face flushed and then whitened, but her lips set in a firm line and she held the Countess's gaze steadily. Maria sighed.

'In France, many noblemen seek pleasure, when their wives are - how do you say -enceinte. This must be accepted, yes?'

Sarah gasped and stared wide-eyed at the French woman. She would hate to have a husband who sought his pleasures with others while she bore his children.

'So,' Maria went on calmly, `I do not like it, but it is not so bad if the women are unknown to me. Far away - in the town, perhaps?' Still Sarah stared at her in silence. 'This silly Veeky has got herself into trouble, yes?'

'Vicky is not "silly", Your Ladyship!' Sarah denied indignantly, as Maria had intended. 'And it was the Earl who got her into trouble.' Sarah bit her lip hastily.

The Countess nodded calmly, but inwardly she was furious. She had no intention of having her husband's bastards on her own doorstep.

'Where does she live, this girl? Does she wish money to go away? To London, perhaps?'

'Oh, no! The O'Connors have a farm on the estate.'

'Ah!' The Countess's eyes narrowed. She knew about the O'Connors. She had already gathered that Lord Reginald Fairly had done his best to give the family protection from her husband's hounding. They were poor but respected. Her anger against her husband increased. He was a fool.

'So Veeky would not wish to leave her family, her Scotland - with its rain and wind. Then I shall try to help her in another way.'

'You will, Your Ladyship?' Sarah was astonished, but she was far too innocent to understand the Countess's meaning.

Maria Estelle Fabliau had spent frequent spells in Paris and Rome. Even in the most respectable circles there were women who had found ways to dispose of their 'troubles'. She herself had chosen to marry Lord James Fairly. She had never had any thought of denying life to the child of an artist whom she had dearly loved. It would have a name - a title, too, if it was a boy, as she hoped - and neither the Earl of Strathtod nor her own father would suspect. Yet already she had cause to regret her hasty marriage to Lord James Fairly. She would help Vicky O'Connor, both for the girl's sake and for her own. First she would make discreet inquiries. 'I must give this matter many thoughts,' she informed Sarah. 'Then I will write Miss Veeky a letter.' Sarah frowned. She did not understand.

'Vicky's parents do not know.'

'Then I shall address the letter to Miss O'Connor and send it to Fairlyden, yes?' Sarah nodded. She had done all she could to help Vicky for the present.

Dick O'Connor was crossing the yard after stabling his horses when the groom from Strathtod rode up the track. It was already dark and beginning to rain.

'Will ye deliver this to Miss Munro?' the man asked and handed Dick a bulky letter. The groom did not linger and Dick glanced down curiously at the package. His eyes widened when he saw it was clearly addressed to 'Miss Vicky O'Connor'. The groom must have made a mistake when he mentioned Miss Sarah's name.

He decided to deliver it to Vicky in person. She might confide in him if they were alone. He knew she would have some time to herself the day after Christmas. The family for whom she worked always joined a shooting party during the festive season; they usually stayed away for several days. Dick asked Sandy's permission to leave Fairlyden for an hour or two.

As soon as Vicky saw Dick she flung herself into his arms and burst into tears. He was her own twin. She thought he must have guessed what had befallen her. Dick held her tightly until she had regained some of her composure. Then he gave her the pack-age. He realised she was as bewildered as he had been.

'It was delivered by the groom frae Strathtod '

Dick faltered when he saw Vicky sway. Her face had drained of colour. He began to read the letter over her shoulder and his own face whitened with shock. Gradually he began to understand Vicky's secret -the burden she had been carrying alone.

'What does Davy Peterson say?' he asked at length.

Vicky choked back another sob. 'Oh, Dick, I-I couldna' tell him.' She knew her silence had hurt Davy badly, but she could not bear to see rejection in his eyes.

'But you are without blame, Vicky! Surely Davy wad understand?' Dick's voice tailed away uncertainly at the look on his sister's face.

'No!' She shuddered. ' He - he was like - an animal! I couldna - I couldna be a wife tae Davy! Tae any man ever!'

Dick looked into her pale desolate face. He took the letter from her and read it again. Vicky began to tremble, but Dick's eyes narrowed.

'Perhaps it is the way '

'It is a sin!' Vicky gasped.

'It is a sin when the devil forces himself on an innocent maid!' Dick spat with contempt. 'Her Ladyship has enclosed money to pay. Perhaps it is the way - with gentry?'

'Twenty pounds!' Vicky whispered hoarsely. 'That is a year's wages, Dick!'

'Aye.' He frowned. 'But the - the place is some distance away - in Carlisle.'

'I canna go there!' Vicky protested fearfully.

Dick was silent for a while, then he spoke, his mind made up. 'Do ye want the babe, Vicky? Ye ken I'll help all I can if 'tis your wish.'

'I hate it! Tis his!'

'Then we must take the train to Carlisle today,' he said resolutely.

'Today? We? But, Dick,'

'We must go while your mistress is away. Today I am free to go with you. I wadna' have ye go alone, Vicky - and no one must hear tell o' this.'

Her face puckered uncertainly and her blue eyes were wide with fear, but then she bit her lip and nodded. 'It is what Her Ladyship wishes.'

Dick summoned an encouraging smile, trying hard to hide his own doubts and fears. Surely Her Lady-ship would not have suggested such a course if there was danger - or if there had been any other way?

'Can ye find a crust to eat, Vicky? I've been up since before four this morn and 'tis a fair walk tae the station; we'll need a wee bite tae be taking along for the journey.'

They tramped the streets for an hour before they eventually found the muddy lane and the narrow, grimy little close whose address the Countess had written on the piece of paper she had enclosed in her letter. Even before the slovenly old woman peeped round the edge of her door in answer to their knock, Dick's heart was filled with misgiving. He saw the fear in Vicky's eyes, but almost before they knew it the old crone had hauled them swiftly into her dim, dingy little room. She seemed to know why they were there and wasted no time in naming her price. She appeared momentarily surprised when they agreed to it woodenly, scarcely knowing what to expect or what to do. Before they could ask any questions, she pulled Vicky into an alcove screened by a filthy, tattered curtain. Dick turned his back and stared out of the single pane of glass which sufficed for a window. It was thick with grime but he did not notice. His eyes were closed in fervent prayer. He felt cold and sick. He heard Vicky give a fearful whimper of protest. He half turned. Suddenly his nerves were shredded by a high, involuntary scream. He flung himself across the room, whipping the curtain aside.

'Leave her be!' he commanded urgently. 'We hae changed our minds!'

Tha's t'late, lad!' the old crone snapped. 'Get 'er out uv me 'ouse!'

Vicky was lying on a dirty pallet, panting in shallow little gasps, her eyes fixed unseeingly on the low, smoke-grimed rafters; her face looked suddenly old and deathly white. The old woman clawed at her arm, jerking her upright as though she were a rag doll.

' 'Ere y'are! Take 'er away frum 'ere!'

It was then Dick saw the fear in her eyes. 'What have ye done tae her?' His voice was raised in alarm.

It galvanised the old crone into action and she half jerked, half dragged Vicky to the door, and shoved them both out, barring it firmly behind them.

Dick almost carried Vicky back to the station. There was a train coming in, bound for Dumfries. It would stop at Strathtod. He bought tickets and helped Vicky into an empty carriage.

' 'Tis the wrong train,' she whispered faintly. 'I must... get back to work '

Dick frowned and bit his lip. He had acted impulsively. It was already getting dark and a chill wind had sprung up. At least Vicky had a seat and shelter in the train.

'I'll take ye hame for tonight, lass,' he muttered gruffly, but Vicky was too busy fighting the waves of pain and nausea to pay much attention.

He had to lift her from the train when it drew into Strathtod station, and he knew she could never walk the three miles to their home. She slumped limply against the station wall, her eyes closed. He went to ask McAllister, the station master, if he could hire his pony and trap. People like the O'Connors did not waste money hiring traps when they had two good legs to walk. Dick knew he would need to offer an explanation.

' Tis ma sister, Vicky. She's come o'er sickly; maybe eaten bad fish,' he muttered. Dick was not used to lying. The station master nodded and did not question him further. The O'Connors were only small farmers, but they were well respected in the glen, especially since Lord Reginald had drawn up a special lease for them.

'But Ye'll hae tae have it back here before the last train comes in. His Lordship's no' hame frae Dumfries yet. He'll no' be fit tae sit his ain horse. Often hires my trap, he does. Peggy kens the way tae the Tower noo.' He nodded towards his pony.

By the time Dick had the pony saddled and yoked to the trap, Vicky had sunk to her knees against the station wall. Dick was thankful to see the glimmer of lights as they drove into the farmyard. His mother could not hide her dismay at the sight of Vicky's condition but soon had her into a clean shift and tucked up in bed, just as Dick had known she would. He sank on to a low stool before the fire and dropped his head into his hands. Almost immediately his mother returned to him. Her face was white and strained. There was a fear in her eyes which would not be denied.

'Ye'll hae to bring the doctor right away, Dick! She - she's in a bad way.' He thought he heard reproach in her voice, but it might only have been his own guilt and remorse. Vicky had trusted him.

It was the new doctor. He held out little hope of saving Vicky. Even if he could stop the bleeding, he was afraid she would develop a fever. Dick remembered the dim, filthy room, the slovenly old crone. How could he have let her touch Vicky? Why had he allowed himself to be influenced by the advice of the gentry? He paced restlessly round and round his mother's kitchen. He almost forgot his promise to return the pony and trap, unwilling to drag himself from the house - and Vicky.

He arrived at the station as the train was drawing in. He heard the raucous voice and drunken laughter of the Earl of Strathtod, saw him pushing aside the other passengers, swaggering up to Mr McAllister, demanding the trap. Dick thought of Vicky lying so still, her pretty face deathly white, her merry laughter silenced, her joy quenched. Usually Dick was one ol the calmest and most tolerant of men but now anger boiled in him. He slipped silently into the shadows.

He heard the trap behind him on the track and stepped aside. As it drew level he grabbed the slouching figure of the Earl and jerked him bodily from his seat. He fell heavily and before he had gathered his drunken wits Dick clenched his fist and hit him squarely in the face. The laird reeled with the pain and shock. He spat out a bloody, yellowed tooth, then began to bellow drunkenly, shouting his blustering threats. Dick waited while he struggled to his feet. He made no effort to hide his face from the dim light thrown by the flickering lantern on the corner of the station trap; the pony waited patiently. As soon as the laird was on his feet Dick struck again, feeling his knuckles sting with the impact. Pain and fury dispelled the fumes of intoxication a little and the Earl threw himself at Dick, knocking him to the ground by sheer weight. Dick was light but he was wiry; he rolled aside and jumped to his feet. Vicky's white face floated into his mind. He aimed with deadly accuracy at the florid leering face of the man who had harmed her so grievously.

'If my sister dies, you are her murderer!' he panted, lashing out again with his fist.

'What sister? By Gad, I'll have you hung for this, you scoundrel!'

Dick no longer cared what his own fate might be. He was filled with guilt and fear and anger, and all his emotions were finding release in pulverising the arrogant, bloated face in front of him.

James Fairly was afraid! He sensed an implacable will behind Dick's blows. He began to shout for help, with little hope of anyone hearing him. In that he was wrong. Two of the passengers who had alighted from the train were walking in the direction of Strathtod village. They ran back to the station master, believing that a band of ruffians must be lying in wait. Mr McAllister considered such a thing unlikely, but he sent a man to bring the constable and went himself to discover the cause of the disturbance. He arrived in time to see Dick O'Connor knock the Earl to the ground for the fourth time. His lordship lay there groaning and clutching his throbbing jaw, but when he saw the station master he stumbled unsteadily to his feet.

'Hold this man! He - ' Dick would have silenced him with another punch but Mr McAllister grabbed his arms.

'Laddie, 'tis Lord Fairly ye're attacking!' he gasped in shocked tones.

'Aye, an' I will be killing him if Vicky dies!' Dick gasped.

'Whisht!' McAllister hissed. 'What's got in tae ye, Dick O'Connor?'

'Lord Fairly!' Dick snorted with bitter contempt. 'He forced himself upon my sister - and if she dies this night he's no better than a murderer!'

'He lies! He lies, I tell you! Have him arrested! By Gad, I'll have him '

'Here comes the constable now, M'Lord,' McAllister muttered unhappily. He had no mind to see Dick O'Connor thrown into a stinking gaol for defending his sister's honour. He believed the lad when he said Lord Fairly had forced himself upon her, yet he knew there was nothing he could do except try to calm Dick, to prevent him making matters worse for himself.

But Dick would not be calmed. He felt a contempt and hatred for the flabby-jowled, foul-tongued Earl such as he had never felt in his life before. He was beside himself with anguish and remorse for the part he had played in Vicky's terrible trouble. In his heart he knew she was dying. He no longer cared what happened to himself. He deserved to die too but so did this beast. He struggled against McAllister's restraining arms.

The constable knew the O'Connor family well. He could scarcely believe the Earl's accusations, but his battered and bloody face bore its own evidence and Dick made no effort to defend himself. He had an insane desire to tell the world what Lord James Fairly had done to Vicky. He knew what his own fate would be for striking a so-called gentleman. Tomorrow he would regret his outburst, for Dick valued his freedom, the song of the birds, the clear, pure air. The dark, damp confines of a prison cell would be death to him - but he could feel no regret for what he had done.

'Arrest him! The man is mad,' the Earl insisted furiously, and the constable could do nothing but obey.

The Countess had risen from her bed and was sipping a glass of hot raspberry cordial in her small boudoir when she heard her husband stumble into the hall and bellow for his valet. It was very late. She frowned. He was the most loutish and inconsiderate man she had ever met. She heard Simpson gasp in dismay.

'Oh, M'Lord, your face!'

As soon as she saw her husband she knew he had been beaten. She did not feel in the least sorry for him. Had she been a man, she would willingly have delivered such punishment herself. She tied her silk wrap more securely, and clutched her thick woollen shawl around her. The night was growing colder and the rising wind was sending flurries of cold air through the draughty passages. She shivered, but could not resist the temptation to gloat a little

Lord Fairly was not pleased to see his wife. He commanded her to return to her room, but his mouth was swelling badly and his words were no more than a mumble. He had lost some teeth and several livid bruises were already darkening his jaw and cheek bones. He saw his wife raise one eyebrow in that infuriating way she had - mocking him. He cursed beneath his breath and bellowed at his hapless servants.

'Mon dieu, M'Lord!' the Countess murmured sweetly. 'The poor face! But how er uglee it will be in the morning! Oui?'

'No! Damn you, Madam, get back to your chamber!'

'M'Lord! The servants!' Maria pretended to be shocked. She was enjoying her husband's discomfiture, but she waited until his valet had gone to fetch a glass of brandy, and the other servant had left the room with the bowl of bloody water, before she hissed, in almost perfect English and with an unholy gleam in her eyes: 'And what is it you have done to deserve such a beating, M'Lord?'

'Nothing!' He grunted and cleared his throat. 'Some drunken lout attacked me on the way from the station.'

'Were you not the one who was drunk?'

Again he saw her eyebrow raised in mockery, and his irritation increased. His jaw was throbbing, one eye had closed already. He was going to be a laughing stock.

'I'll see O'Connor pays for this!' he muttered furiously. He did not notice his wife stiffen.

'He is the man who? The drunken lout?' she asked carefully.

'Insolent, hot-headed, young devil!'

'But why did he beat you, M'Lord?' Lady Fairly asked in cool, soft tones which demanded an answer.

'Some cock and bull story about getting the doctor to his sister because she's supposed to be dying.'

'Dying! Did you say dying?' Maria asked sharply, sitting suddenly erect on the edge of her chair. Her husband rubbed his brow.

'How should I know? Where's that dratted Simpson with my brandy?'

'There is time enough for that. Tell me! Is Veecky O'Connor dying?' Lord Fairly's senses cleared briefly; he peered at his wife through one half-shut, bleary eye.

'You know the O'Connor wench? Answer me, Madam!' Maria's mouth curved in contempt but she did not reply. She felt slightly sick. Surely the girl could not die!

'You! You sent O'Connor - that bitch's brother! You told him to wait for me! To beat me! Why, you '

'Calm yourself!' Maria hissed contemptuously. 'Remember the servants. They keep from their beds for you. I told to the brother nothing! Mais, oui, 1 know everything. You deserved to be beaten! Oui, My Lord Fairly!'

There was so much contempt in her eyes that even James winced. She turned on her satin-slippered heel and left him - but her thoughts were with Vicky O'Connor. It was dawn before she fell into an uneasy sleep.

Twenty-Eight

It was late when the Countess awoke. Her husband remained in his own chamber and had given orders that he was not to be disturbed. Maria spent the short dark day in a fever of anxiety, wondering about Vicky

O'Connor and the fate of her brother. The following morning her maid brought a message with her breakfast tray. The Earl would not be accompanying her to Church. He had already gone to the railway station. He was bound for the Highland shooting lodge belonging to his friend, the Honourable Wyndham Pilkington; he intended to spend Hogmanay there, celebrating the advent of the year of eighteen hundred and eighty.

The Countess guessed her husband was running away from the gossip and the speculation which his battered face would certainly arouse. She did not care what he did any more. She hated the cold, draughty rooms of Strathtod Tower; she abhorred the sight of the dilapidated farms and buildings belonging to the estate. The laird had bled his tenants dry to finance his own pleasures. There would be nothing left here for her child - only the title, and scandal. How many more bastards had he sired? In that moment she made up her mind. She would return to France, to her father's chateau, to the sun.

A more immediate concern was to obtain news of Vicky O'Connor. As the day wore on the wind rose and rain lashed at the windows in grey sheets. Maria paced restlessly before the wide stone hearth, sighing at the gusts of black smoke when the wind whistled down the wide chimney. There was only her crippled brother-in-law for company and Stuart had more complaints than ever when dismal weather prevented him getting into the gardens. Usually Maria was patient and compassionate towards him but today her tension had been mounting since she awoke. Her irritation exploded. She poured out her frustration on Stuart's defenceless head. She told him of his brother's shameful conduct, of her own part in the affairs of Vicky O'Connor, of the Earl's cowardly escape. She could not hide her anxiety for the girl, or for the brother; no doubt he was languishing in a grim prison cell, awaiting her husband's return to give evidence against him.

'I shall leave this dreadful Tow-air. I shall return at once to mon pere,' she finished in a fine fury.

Typically it was the last piece of information which riveted Stuart's attention. Strathtod Estate could not survive without the Fabliau fortune; James had been furious, and alarmed, when he discovered he was not to have complete control of his wife's money.

'But what is to happen to me?' Stuart whined pathetically. 'If you go away?'

Maria halted her pacing in surprise. She frequently felt sorry for James's brother but he did so little to help himself. She looked at him now.

'You must come to visit at the chateau. Ah, it is so warm, so sunny there!' She closed her eyes, dreaming for a moment. 'Maybe you will sit in the sun in your chair. Maybe even learn to swim.'

'I cannot walk!' Stuart growled.

'I have heard of people who cannot walk and yet they swim. Mon pere, he may get a teacher.'

'I am not a child!' Stuart exclaimed angrily.

'Non! But you behave like the spoiled leetle boy! Forget your own troubles. Tell me, how can I find out how is Miss Vicky O'Connor today?'

'Take the carriage and ask her!' Stuart snapped waspishly.

The Countess looked at the streaming window panes - then at the petulant face of her brother-in-law. She sighed.

'I will go. I cannot rest if I do not.'

The news which the Countess received at the O'Connors' home had filled her with horror. She could not sleep that night while her restless mind considered ways of helping them. Her plans were rudely shattered when the maid entered her chamber with the announcement that a messenger wished to speak to her most urgently.

The man stammered nervously. The terrible storms of the previous day, Sunday the twenty-eighth of December, eighteen hundred and seventy-nine, had caused a fearful tragedy: the Tay Railway Bridge had been swept away. The Countess stared at the man. Why had a special messenger been sent to Strathtod Tower with such news? It did not concern her. The man twisted his cap between his hands. The massive ironwork structure of the bridge had crashed a hundred feet into the boiling river below, he reported haltingly. It had taken the train with it, just as it had been about to emerge from the high girders at the north end.

'How very sad,' Maria offered, bewildered.

'All the passengers and crew were rushed to instant death, Your Ladyship,' the man faltered unhappily.

It was some moments before the Countess of Strathtod grasped the full implications of the news. 'The Earl of Strathtod?' she gasped. 'He - he was on that train?'

294

It was perhaps ironical that the minister of Strathtod parish should, on the same day, conduct the funerals of Vicky O'Connor and the man she had cursed so vehemently. News of the Earl's death had been greeted with a variety of emotions, but not one of his tenants expressed sorrow.

At Fairlyden it was Vicky's death, and Dick O'Connor's arrest, which caused distress and dismay. Dick had become a vital part of life at Fairlyden. Sarah refused to believe he had intended to kill the Earl of Strathtod. She had seen him saddened too often by the death of a young animal to believe he could kill anyone - and yet she would not condemn him if he had. Lord James Fairly had been a vile creature, unworthy of his name and title. She shared Dick's grief, and his anger over Vicky's death, but he had been her twin and his sorrow must be infinitely greater.

Dick was finally given what the judge considered 'an extremely lenient' sentence, due to the Countess's intervention and goodwill. To Dick, and to those who knew and loved him, even a sentence of two years seemed interminable.

Beatrice Slater was secretly devastated by Dick's imprisonment, but her grief was a private thing and must remain so. No one suspected her blossoming feelings for the man who treated her with such tenderness, who had made her feel as a woman should. She knew her father would have found some way to debase their innocent relationship, as he had tried to debase everything Beatrice had ever cherished.

The Countess owed no allegiance to the dilapidated Strathtod Estate. Within weeks of her husband's death, she announced her intention of returning to France. She decided that her crippled brother-in-law should accompany her. She had grown fond of him, in a sisterly fashion, and if her child should be a girl, Stuart would inherit the title, albeit an empty one now. She knew nothing of the youngest Fairly, save that William had not acknowledged her letter or returned for his brother's funeral. According to the terms of his father's Will, he had forfeited his inheritance when he refused to become a minister of the church, and in any case the whole estate was heavily in debt on account of the late Earl's gambling debts.

It was not a propitious time to be selling land, especially when nearly every farm on Strathtod was in a state approaching dereliction. There was only one prospective purchaser of any consequence and as soon as his lawyers advised him of the conditions attached to Fairlyden, he refused to conclude the transaction. Cuthbert Bradshaw had pulled himself out of the poverty of the gutter by his own bootlaces, or lack of them. He thrived on challenge. He had come to Scotland intending to buy a woollen mill. He knew little about farming, but he recognised neglect when he saw it. Only a fool could fail to improve an estate as badly run down as Strathtod - or at least that was his conclusion when he saw the one jewel in Strathtod's crown: Fairlyden.

The Yorkshireman was far from pleased to discover the peculiar conditions attached to this prosperous little corner of his proposed new investment.

'Are yer telling me t' best little farm ont' estate isn't for sale, Ma'am Countess - or whativer fancy title yer 'usband left yer?'

'Oh, oui, oui. Yes, Fairlyden is for sale!' the Countess assured him hurriedly. 'It is part of the estate. But it is not - that is, you cannot have the control, yes? The conditions are a little strange.' The Countess gave Bert Bradshaw her most beguiling, most feminine, smile but the Yorkshireman was not taken in so easily.

'No control! No rent! An' yer expectin' me t' buy it!' He shook his head. 'It'll not do. I don't want no pig in a poke! It's all or nowt wi' Bert Bradshaw!'

'A peeg in the poke? I am not selling you the peeg.' The Countess frowned; she was having great difficulty understanding the broad Yorkshire accent. Normally she would not have given the square, ruddy-faced man a second glance.

'Never mind t' pig! You tell the folks at Fairlyden they'll 'ave to pay t' rent same as every other tenant, if I buy t'estate!'

'Mais non, the conditions! The late Earl - the land was for his mistress. Even my husband could not demand the rent for Fairlyden. He was very angry.'

'I'll bet 'e was!' Bert Bradshaw laughed mirthlessly. He had heard all about the late Earl. 'It's t' best little farm ont' estate. Yon feller must know what 'e's doin'. I'd like to meet 'im sometime. I'd expect t'other farms to improve if I buy t' estate, mind you. If one man can manage, so can t' rest! I'd niver 'ave looked at Strathtod but for Fairlyden. It'll not do, y' know, Countess. You tell yer lawyers t' sort it out! T' old Earl's mistress'll be dead now anyway, ain't she?'

'Oui. Mais...'

'Well then, you tell them folks in Fairlyden to buy it from t' estate or pay me a rent. Let me know what's t' do, an' don't take so long! Good day t' yer, Ma'am.'

The Countess was desperately anxious to return to France before the birth of her child. Indeed, she longed to sever her ties with Strathtod as soon as possible. Strathtod's creditors were impatient. Mr Bradshaw's was the only respectable offer so far received and the solicitors had no wish to lose it. One bright young man delved deeply into the conditions attached to Fairlyden.

Neither Sandy nor Sarah suspected that the Countess's decision to sell Strathtod would affect their own lives until the arrival of the official-looking letter. Daniel Munro's father, the late Lord Jonathan Fairly, had never envisaged a time when his beloved Strathtod might be sold. His intentions towards his mistress, the first Sarah Munro, and her descendants might have been clear at the time, but the legal documentation was decidedly ambiguous, especially in such changed circumstances. There were anomalies which presented several problems.

Despite Daniel Munro's careful plans, and Lord Reginald Fairly's subsequent reassurance, Sandy had never been entirely happy about Sarah's tenuous right to Fairlyden, and in the new circumstances even Daniel's own claim could have been in dispute.

Sandy passed the letter to Sarah with some anxiety. The solicitors apparently regarded her as a child, or an imbecile, instead of an intelligent young woman with a mind of her own. Incredulity warred with anger as she read the letter for the third time. She had no reason to believe that Fairlyden was not her rightful inheritance - without need for negotiation or compromise.

'They call this a generous proposal!' she exclaimed indignantly. 'One more year without any dues. Time to negotiate a rent with the new owner - or to look for another farm. Or - this!' She tapped the letter furiously. 'We could offer to buy Fairlyden and exclude it from the rest of the estate. Ordinary farmers don't buy land! Don't they understand how hard we work just to have food and clothes, and maybe a little spare money to improve the land when we have a good year? My grandfather made it clear that the Munros should inherit Fairlyden - for as long as there were Munros! Papa instilled it into my head, over and over almost before I could read or write!'

'But Lord Jonathan Fairly could never have envisaged a change of owner,' Sandy reminded her unhappily. Her anger and distress troubled him.

'And this!' Sarah went on as though he had not spoken. 'The final irony! "Fairlyden would be expected to realise a higher rent than other farms on the estate, owing to the greater fertility of the land and the fine state of the buildings." How can they contemplate such a thing when you and Mama worked so hard to restore Fairlyden?' she demanded wrathfully. 'We must fight to keep it! It is our home - our right!'

'Hush, hush, lassie,' Sandy soothed. 'The Reverend Mackenzie is also your guardian. Nae doubt he will hae received a similar letter. We must consider. It takes money to fight the law.'

'But we must fight for justice.'

'The law is not always just,' Sandy said bitterly. His thoughts winged back to Nethertannoch and his flight with Mattie. Sarah must never be placed in such a vulnerable position. 'Lawyers always get their money, whatever happens in the end. We could be left with nothing.' If anyone suspected that Sarah was his own daughter instead of Daniel Munro's, that would certainly be the case, he thought uneasily. He looked at her bent head. There was more than a hint of his own copper colour in the shining coil of her hair, and he had long been aware of the mannerisms she had inherited from him. The Reverend Mackenzie was also Sarah's guardian. What if he was asked for evidence? Maybe even forced to swear on the bible!

Sarah was bewildered by her beloved uncle's reluctance to fight for Fairlyden when he had worked so hard to restore it. He knew how much she loved this house and the neat stone steading; she knew every inch of the fields and hedges - just as Mama had once done at the farm where she was born, the place called Nethertannoch. Uncle Sandy had always been bitterly opposed to the power of landlords! Why was he suddenly prepared to consider the decisions of men in neat suits who knew nothing of Fairlyden?

Sandy pondered Sarah's angry frustration as he walked to the Muircumwell Manse. He knew she would never understand his reluctance to confront the lawyers unless she knew of the deceit which had surrounded her birth. Would it be so wrong to break his promise now that Daniel was dead? What of Mattie? Sarah remembered her mother with love and respect. At twenty she was still untouched by the passions which could drive a man and woman to madness. How could she understand the love which had carried them to the very pinnacles of heaven, or the grief which had cast him into the depths of hell? Would she turn against him? Would she feel contempt for the mother who had borne her with such joy?

The Reverend Mackenzie shared Sandy's disquiet. Lawyers had a habit of delving deeply. Daniel Munro had given Sarah his name; it would be difficult to prove that she was not his daughter but all too easy to cast doubts, to fill Sarah's mind with distrust, to cast a slur on Mattie's character.

Sandy was relieved to find the minister was equally opposed to a confrontation with the lawyers. He had no heart for a fight based on deceit, especially one which compelled him to deny his own daughter.

'I - I've bin thinking. I could maybe use the money Matthew Cameron saved for Mattie an' me. I hae saved a wee bit frae the horses as weel. It wad buy the hoose and buildings, I think,' he said haltingly. 'Maybe even the two wee fields beside the burn. At least Sarah would have a home, a wee bit o' security. She wad still need to rent more land tae make a living though. I wonder if the new owner will be a fair man? Will he agree to a lease and a fair rent?' he mused anxiously.

'I do not like to see you cast out of Fairlyden either, Sandy,' the Reverend Mackenzie declared resolutely. 'You have given the best part of your life to improving it. It is only right that you and yours should reap the benefits.'

'We have little option,' Sandy sighed. 'I couldna buy more.'

'I have influence with one of the directors of the Savings Bank at Annan. If I can arrange a loan, perhaps you could buy the fields between the burn and the new track? If the Countess agrees, then you will have the best access to the fields to the north and east. I am sure the new owner would agree to a reasonable rent for them. You would be bargaining from a position of strength.'

'A loan?' Sandy stared at the Minister in astonishment. 'Borrow money from a bank?' Yet the idea was shrewd. 'I wouldna like to leave Sarah with the burden of a debt,' he said uneasily. 'That wad be worse than paying a rent.'

'Surely you are in good health, Sandy?' the Minister asked with swift concern.

'Aye, but the future is in God's hands,' Sandy remarked with a wry smile. 'You've preached that often enough, Mr Mackenzie!'

The minister acknowledged his reminder with a smile of his own. 'That's true. You will be missing Dick O'Connor, I suppose?'

'We are indeed!' Sandy agreed with feeling. 'The truth is, no other body could replace Dick but we must have help o' some kind, especially if I'm to be away with the stallion. The money frae the horses is valuable now that prices are so poor for everything else. Dick had begun to take the stallion out for me, on local visits.'

'And no man worthy of his hire will move until the term, I suppose?' the minister murmured, understanding Sandy's problem only too well. Sometimes it seemed the harder a man tried, the more problems God sent him to contend with. All his parishioners had been affected by the last two years of catastrophic weather and some of the farmers had sold their cattle and left for the towns, even in his own parish. He had heard things were worse over in Strathtod.

'This foot and mouth disease is another worry, I suppose? I hear the government has closed the markets to prevent infected cattle spreading the disease.'

'Aye, it's raging o'er the country. Many o' the town dairies have been wiped out since they made the law to slaughter. I heard o' some farmers carting milk to the railway stations in sealed tin churns, and sending it by train to the towns!'

The Reverend Mackenzie sighed. He was getting too old to cope with such problems.

'Well, Sandy, I have faith in you, or I would never suggest you might borrow a sum of money. I know you will do what you consider best for Sarah, but I shall be sorry if someone else benefits from all your hard toil. You and Mattie made many sacrifices for Fairlyden. Let me know if you need my help, after you have visited the Countess. 1 hear she is eager to settle her affairs and leave the country.'

Later that evening Sandy took out the two bank books which Matthew Cameron had left to him and Mattie all those years ago. Between them the accounts amounted to ninety pounds twelve shillings and sixpence. He had managed to save a little money from the premiums which had been awarded for the hire of two of his Clydesdale stallions, and he was fairly confident there would always be a demand for his horses. Dark Lucy, the mare he had brought from Nethertannoch, had established his reputation as a breeder. He was always on the lookout for new blood to keep up his reputation for strong, healthy animals, and Dark Lucy had passed on her docile temperament through her sons. It was a quality appreciated by those carters who worked in busy towns and he had already sold two draught horses at forty-six guineas each.

It was from the stallions that Sandy really hoped to make his reputation. Last year a well-known breeder from Fife had written to offer him four hundred and eighty guineas for Logan's Lucifer, the last and most prized of all Dark Lucy's offspring. The offer had been tempting, but Sandy had great hopes for his stallion's future and he had no other horse to replace him. Lucifer had already proved himself a good sire. Since then his latest crop of foals had performed well at the Highland Show at Perth. One of the biggest traders in Southern Scotland had requested Lucifer's services as a result. The man, named McKean, had even offered to pay the train fare for the stallion and his groom to travel the twenty miles to his farm.

When he thought of the horses, Sandy's earlier apprehension began to disappear. He passed the bank cards to Sarah as she settled beside the fire with her sewing basket.

'I'm going tae Strathtod tomorrow,' he told her. 'The Reverend Mackenzie agrees that I should use that money to buy the house rather than risk losing everything to the lawyers. If the Countess is agreeable, we may be able to buy the two wee fields adjoining the'

'No! Oh, no, Uncle Sandy!' Sarah was staring at the bank cards in horror. 'This money was given to you and Mama. I will not let you use it!' She jumped up in agitation.

'Ach Sarah, that money was saved by your Grandfather Cameron. I promised your Mama -that is, we agreed you might need the money one day. I know she would want you to feel secure at Fairlyden.'

'No.' Sarah's voice was no more than a hoarse whisper and her eyes were bright with tears. Sandy stared at her white face in consternation.

'Why, Sarah, lassie! Whatever...?'

'I canna let you do that for me. You have kept your promise to Mama. You have done your duty.' In her agitation Sarah did not see Sandy wince. 'You have worked so hard - now, without Fairlyden, you will never have repayment.' Her voice trembled and she shuddered. 'Maureen O'Leary was right! I am a burden to you, Uncle Sandy. Uncle!' She choked. 'You are not even my real uncle. I am nothing to you really. I...'

'You are everything, everything to me, Sarah!' Sandy jumped to his feet, his face whiter than her own.

Sarah saw the muscle pulsing in his clenched jaw. She shook her head helplessly, but Maureen O'Leary's harsh voice still echoed down the years: 'To be sure an' 'tis a burden ye are to the puir man, an' him needin' a woman of his own and nae bairn like you tae be taggin' along.'

Sandy took her hands in his large, work-roughened palms. Sarah bowed her head, but he lifted her chin with his forefinger. 'You must understand, Sarah.' His voice was gruff, yet almost urgent. 'You were never a duty to me. I loved your mother. We loved each other. Always! She was a good woman, believe me.'

'I-I know that,' Sarah whispered, but her dark eyes were puzzled by his intensity. So often when she was a child she had longed for Uncle Sandy to hold her close, as he was doing now, yet always he had drawn back at the last moment, and she had felt alone again, bereft.

'Did - did you always love Mama?' she asked a little wistfully. Her own heart had never quickened its beat for any man - only for a dark-eyed youth so long ago, and William had not returned for his own brother's funeral. 'Did you love her even when you were both young - before she married Papa?'

'Aye, we loved each other, even when we were bairns. Sarah ' he caught his breath. 'I am your father.'

The words dropped into the silence. It was Sandy who bowed his head now. Sarah stared at his coppery brown hair with its streaks of grey.

'My - father?' Her voice, when it came, was barely a whisper. She tried to draw away but his clasp tightened, almost as though he were a child clinging to her for support, Sarah thought fleetingly. She felt bewildered. Uncertain. Yet even as she stood there in the circle of his arms, even as she listened to the clock ticking away the seconds, memories of her childhood came winging back - happy memories now. Memories of laughter - and of love.

'I-I don't understand,' she faltered. 'Was Papa...?'

Slowly Sandy began to talk. He made no excuses, blamed no one, but his love for her mother, and for herself, shone through each simple sentence.

When he had finished Sarah began to understand, for the first time, the true depths of his feeling for her mother, the sacrifices he must have made, the pain when he let her marry Daniel Munro. Then to have her snatched away by death so soon!

At last Sandy lifted his head and looked at her steadily, unflinchingly, his blue eyes searching her face. Sarah's own eyes were filled with tears - tears of sadness for her parents' lost love, tears of happiness for the father she had found. She was no longer alone in this alien world.

Impulsively she threw her arms around Sandy's neck and hugged him fiercely.

'Father,' she whispered. 'My own father. My very own!' He felt the softness of her skin against his weathered cheek, he tasted her tears - and his heart swelled with love and a new happiness. Suddenly he was filled with a desire to buy the whole world for her, his own beloved daughter.

Sandy shaved and trimmed his sideburns with unusual care. Sarah had starched and ironed his shirt. He donned his best black coat and top hat and set out for Strathtod Tower. He had lain awake for several hours the previous night, mentally preparing for his meeting with the Countess. The February morning was crisp and bright and his spirits rose, despite the ache of regret when he thought of all he had done to improve Fairlyden, the money he had ploughed back in lime; he had even bought clay tiles and drained Low Meadow. He had believed it was all for Sarah's benefit, yet in his heart Sandy knew he would always want to see the farm at its best. He hated neglect.

It was some years since he had visited the Tower, shortly before Reginald Fairly's death. He was appalled by the dilapidation; even the grounds and the interior of Strathtod Tower itself had deteriorated.

The Countess greeted him warily. Stuart had convinced her that Miss Munro and her guardian would certainly fight to keep Fairlyden. Maria did not want her departure to be delayed by prolonged litigation; she only wanted to complete the sale, pay off her late husband's creditors and escape from Strathtod.

As she faced Alexander Logan across the heavy, ornate desk her spirits brightened. He had not come to demand or to badger; he had come to make a proposition! The Countess was impressed by Sandy's steady gaze and earnest expression. None of his apprehension showed as she looked into his clear-skinned, handsome face. He was erect and broad-shouldered; she admired the honesty in his blue eyes, the firmness of his mouth, and the quiet confidence in his voice. This was no ordinary country yokel, with greed his only motive.

'I willna pay more for Fairlyden than the value of the rest of Strathtod. If it is better, it is because we have put everything we had into making it better.'

'Mais oui, Monsieur Logan, I understand. Mon pere - my father, he makes many things better than his neighbours.' She was intelligent enough to realise that it was only the sight of Fairlyden which had attracted Mr Bradshaw's interest in the estate. She had already argued with the lawyers over that very question. Money was not her prime motive - freedom was.

So Sandy found himself smiling back at the Countess's eager face. It was all so much easier than he had expected. Suddenly he found himself mentally replanning his strategy. Perhaps he ought to take up the Minister's offer to arrange a bank loan - just a temporary one, of course. He could sell Lucifer to repay it after he had kept his promise to McKean. He ought to bargain for the extra fields now, while the Countess was so amenable. He wished passionately that he could buy all of Fairlyden, but even fifty acres would strain his resources to the limit. He selected the fields with care, indicating the ones he wanted to buy on the linen map which the Countess had unrolled.

Sandy was astonished when she offered no argument at all.

'Mais oui,' she smiled. 'You bargain well, yes? I am grateful you do not fight with the lawyers, Mr Logan. I am in agreement but I must discuss with Mr Bradshaw. There remains the rest of Fairlyden land - and only you will have the way to the - how do you say it? The burn.'

'If you agree to sell the fields I have marked, you may tell the new owner I will offer eleven shillings and sixpence an acre to rent the rest of the Fairlyden land - in one year's time, and if a fair lease can be agreed,' Sandy suggested swiftly.

The Countess clapped her hands in delight. 'I shall tell him. Already I think he knows you are a good farmer, too good to lose such a tenant! Mr Bradshaw is not a bad man, you understand. Just, he fights a long time to make his money. So! He does not give it away like...' She fluttered her fingers.

Sandy smiled wryly, but he was satisfied. Things had gone far better than he had dared to hope. Maybe one day they would be able to buy the rest of Fairlyden land, if he could breed more Clydesdale stallions from Lucifer's line. Meanwhile he would not tell Sarah the full extent of his purchase, not until the deal was completed and he had repaid the loan.

Twenty Nine

Cuthbert Bradshaw took up temporary residence at Strathtod Tower as soon as the Countess and her brother-in-law had departed. For a month the new owner rode around the estate, scratching his head, listening to complaints, gazing over fences. Eventually he called at Fairlyden.

Sarah was pleasantly surprised to find there was nothing condescending about Mr Bradshaw, except that he clearly did not expect a mere woman to be able to answer his questions.

'My business is manufacturing woollen cloth, Miss Munro,' he boomed in his broad Yorkshire voice. 'There's nowt a man can tell me about that. But I've plenty t'learn about farming an' no mistake! I mean to make this damned - begging yer pardon, Miss -this land pay, now that I've got it, see? I keep looking ower t'fences at Fairlyden, and says I to meself, "Why is that place better than't rest?" So now I've come to talk to your step-father, lass.'

Sarah smiled when he stopped talking at last. 'I'm afraid my - my father will not be back until it is dark. He is ploughing in Birchy Pasture today. He wants to get the ploughing finished because he is planning to set out early with the stallion this year.'

'Aye, I did 'ear he 'as t'best 'osses in these parts.'

' 'Osses? Oh, er, horses. Yes,' Sarah agreed proudly. 'He was one of the first members of the Clydesdale Horse Society when it began, three years ago. Last year Logan's Lucifer earned a premium of a hundred pounds from the Glasgow Agricultural Society.' She broke off with a little frown. The money had gone to buy new harness and a new farm cart. They would need all the stallion fees to pay rent to Mr Bradshaw next year.

Bert Bradshaw, as he was known to friend and foe alike, watched her expressive face with interest. He liked her high smooth brow and the finely marked dark eyebrows, like question marks. Intelligent, he decided, especially for a woman. The women in Bert's life were either haggard, harassed creatures who worked in his factories, or preening, pretty misses like Fanny and Freda, his two surviving daughters.

'You must come to t'Tower 'ouse when my girls come, Miss Munro. They'll need a bit cump'ny. It's a mite quiet for 'em round 'ere.'

'Oh!' Sarah looked at him keenly. 'We - er - we're not usually invited to places like Strathtod Tower.'

'Just "The Tower 'ouse", now, if you please!' Mr Bradshaw corrected firmly. 'And if I want me neighbours to visit, I asks 'em! And you and yer stepfather are me neighbours, lass.' He drained his cup of tea and stood up, a broad, middle-aged man with a round shiny poll and greying sideburns. 'An' a mighty pretty an' 'ospitable neighbour, if I might say so. That was t' best bit of bread an' butter I've tasted in a long time. And that cake!' He smacked his lips with relish. 'It reminds me o' me grandmother.' His eyes took on a reminiscent look. 'She lived in't country when I were a lad, 'ad a little bit uv land an' a cow. Aye.' He sighed heavily. 'It's covered in piles uv red bricks now - rows an' rows of mucky little 'ouses. Some things don't change for't better, lass - even if I've done well enough out of it all. Worked 'ard, mind you, iver since I was a nipper.' He bobbed his head beneath the door lintel and stepped into the chill air of the grey spring afternoon. 'Now I've enjoyed me little chat an' me tea, lass, an' I'll send you an' Mister Logan word to come t'Tower 'ouse next time I come up.'

Sarah watched with a little smile lifting the corners of her firm, too serious mouth, as he mounted his sturdy horse and cantered off down the road back to Strathtod. In all the years she had lived at Fairlyden, few people had used that track until now. Yes, she decided, she liked Mr Bradshaw - even if he was their new landlord. Not a man to suffer fools, nor to be taken for one, but he had evidently earned respect the hard way - and he was not afraid to admit his ignorance of farming.

As she hurried to join Janet and Agnes at the byre for the afternoon milking, Sarah's thoughts turned unbidden to William Fairly. She wondered what he would have thought of the changes taking place at his old home. Where was he now? Not for the first time she wished she had not been so stubborn in her refusal to see him all those years ago, when Danny died. Her heart ached, as it always did when she thought of

Danny, but today she pushed her melancholy thoughts aside. Her father had told her he had loved her mother since she was a child; surely it could not be love she felt for William Fairly? Yet she had never forgotten his warm smile and the gentleness in his dark eyes.

Sarah still knew nothing of the extra land Sandy had purchased from the Countess. She would have been horrified to know her father had borrowed money to buy it for her. Consequently she had not the slightest suspicion that he planned to sell Logan's Lucifer, his pride and joy, to pay off the debt.

Sandy had experienced several qualms himself when the transaction had finally been concluded. He had bought fifty-two acres in all, at twelve pounds an acre. Even after paying out Matthew Cameron's savings and his own, he still owed four hundred and forty pounds to the bank. He had no intention of burdening Sarah with such knowledge, but he did look forward to giving her a pleasant surprise once Lucifer had been sold and the loan repaid.

He had written to the Fife horse breeder informing him that Logan's Lucifer would be put up for sale as soon as he had kept his promise to service two of the mares belonging to the local breeder, McKean. The Fife breeder was a dour man named John Proudfoot, but to Sandy's relief he had replied immediately expressing his intention of visiting Fairlyden and offering four hundred and eighty guineas, provided the stallion was still up to his former condition. It was forty guineas more than his offer the previous year. It exceeded Sandy's expectations, though the thought of parting with Lucifer saddened him more than he cared to admit. His only consolation was that the money for the stallion would ensure Sarah's future at Fairlyden.

He realised why Proudfoot had replied so promptly, and with a definite offer, when he received an inquiry from a Clydesdale breeder in Lanarkshire. The two men were keen rivals. They had admired the stallion at the 1878 Highland Agricultural Society Show which had been held in Dumfries. Both men had exported Clydesdale horses to Canada and they wanted, and could afford, the best. Sandy was proud that Lucifer was in such demand and it was comforting to know that the bank loan would certainly be paid long before the summer was over.

Sandy was reluctant to leave Sarah and Louis with so much extra work, but while Dick O'Connor remained in prison he had no option but to travel with the stallion himself if he was to keep his promise to Jim McKean. Also he had high expectations of a young unproven stallion, a grandson of Dark Lucy's, and he was hoping to persuade McKean to try the young horse on his other mares. Other local breeders would be sure to follow McKean's example. He had a particularly good mare, although her temperament was too flighty for breeding good dray horses. Her progeny would benefit from Lucifer's placid temperament and Sandy was interested in offering for the resulting foal himself, especially now that he had to sell Lucifer.

So with Sarah's reassurances ringing in his ears he set off to the railway station in good spirits, walking briskly to keep up with Lucifer's prancing gait. The stallion's coat shone like darkly burnished copper. He was in fine fettle, his silky white feathers flapping around his massive hooves; his head was high, his ears pricked, eyes bright with anticipation. He scented spring in the air, and sensed the pleasurable mission ahead.

It was the last day of Sandy's visit to the McKeans. The young mare was definitely in season and Sandy agreed to give her a final trial before he left for the station. When a dealer arrived unexpectedly, to buy three draught horses, McKean instructed one of his men to lead out the mare. He knew Sandy would have little time to dally if he was to complete the three-mile walk to the station in time to catch the train back to Muircumwell.

The capricious mare sensed the stablehand's nervousness immediately; she showed the whites of her eyes and pranced and squealed. Nevertheless she behaved impeccably in response to Lucifer's attentions until the great stallion slid away from her. His forelegs had barely touched the ground when the mare kicked out in fury. There was a sharp crack. The mare wheeled wildly.

'Get her away!' Sandy shouted urgently. 'Take her away, man!' His face was a sickly white. He tried to soothe Lucifer. He bent to examine the stallion's foreleg. The stablehand strove valiantly to control the mare. She reared on her hind legs, lifting him bodily. Despite his long experience of horses Sandy's terrible anxiety for Lucifer had made him careless of his own safety. The mare kicked out again, sending Sandy's bent figure sprawling under the stallion's belly. Lucifer shifted uneasily. Shock and pain made him clumsy. Before Sandy could move, he felt the weight of the stallion's massive hoof crushing his knee.

A brief but merciful blackness descended on him. McKean and the dealer ran to drag him clear. McKean summoned his own doctor. He was a gruff countryman, but he had studied all the new medicines. Before setting Sandy's leg in splints he bathed the grazed areas with iodine, all the while indulging in gruesome mutterings.

'I have seen a man stiffen until he was rigid as a corpse after he was injured by a horse. Only his eyes could move. Man, but the pain afore he died was terrible!' Neither the pain nor even the doctor's graphic description of a horrible death could distract Sandy from his anxiety for his stallion.

'Ach, man, a horse wi' a broken leg is nae use tae anybody!' The doctor rasped impatiently. 'Noo keep ye still an' dinna fret. We'll shoot the horse an' he'll be oot o' his misery! But you, you'll be miserable for many a long day - but Ye'll live, if I've anything to dae with it!'

Sandy closed his eyes and gritted his teeth but it was not the pain which troubled him, intense though it was. Seconds later the sound of a gunshot echoed in his brain. The death of his proud, magnificent stallion was terrible to contemplate. This was not a dreadful nightmare. It was real. Lucifer was dead!

The following day Sandy insisted on being transported back to Fairlyden despite the slow, painful journey in McKean's flat cart, the only vehicle which allowed room for his leg. He felt sick to the heart. A wire must be sent to Proudfoot in Fife, instructing him to cancel his journey to Fairlyden. There was no stallion for him to see now, no stallion to sell; there was nothing to repay the bank loan.

Sarah and Louis found it impossible to keep up with all the work without both Dick and Sandy. Fairlyden could ill afford to lose the fees which the young stallion, Logan's Bobby, might have earned, but there was no one to handle him. Sandy fretted helplessly. The doctor had warned him that it would be many months before he could walk again. Still he was determined that Sarah must know nothing of the bank loan. Louis was fully occupied in the fields, sowing the turnips with the new two-row horse drill. After sowing there would be hoeing, with an abundance of weeds on account of the wet seasons. Fairlyden needed at least one more pair of hands, yet there would be no money to hire another man now.

The cattle had been turned out to the fields after their long winter confinement, but they seemed intent on making holes in hedges and straying on to the young corn crops. The sheds had to be emptied of manure and cleaned and limewashed. Sarah was almost heartbroken when one of the sows lay on four of her piglets.

Sandy had dealt with many problems and setbacks in his lifetime, but he had never been ill or felt so useless before. Small things irritated him.

'I should have died instead o' Lucifer!' he muttered bitterly.

'Please, please don't say that!' Sarah pleaded in horror.

Sandy stared at her morosely. How could he tell her that Lucifer would at least have paid off the loan and given her Fairlyden, while he ... he was just a burden!

Sometimes Sarah was almost relieved to escape from the house and dairy to help with the field work. Then she would feel guilty because her father was alone with his ill temper. She knew his leg gave him great pain, but had an uneasy feeling that it was more than physical pain which was troubling him.

She longed for Dick O'Connor to help with the animals, especially the sheep. She had often thought they must be the stupidest of all God's creatures, yet Dick, with only the aid of his dog, had taken them to the burn for their pre-shearing wash without any trouble. Now the collie was pining and would work for no one but his master.

So the weeks passed in unrelenting work. The oats were turning from green to gold before the doctor would consider taking the splints from Sandy's leg. Sarah could not hide her dismay when she saw the crooked shape of his wasted limb. He could barely hobble a few steps, even with the help of a stick.

'I shall never be able to walk again! How am I to work with such a useless leg?' Sandy fumed.

Sarah also realised that he would be permanently lame and her heart ached for him.

'It will improve in time. You must rest, Father,' she soothed gently.

'Rest! How can a man rest with hay to gather? The rain will ruin it!'

'Louis and I will manage and Agnes will help when she can.'

'You canna manage! It is impossible without help,' he raged impotently. As the days passed he grew increasingly depressed by his lack of mobility, especially as the corn was ready to harvest. Sandy could not forget the debt he owed. Everything was going wrong. He could not hide his increasing anxiety, and yet he would not confide in Sarah.

It was at this time that Mr Bradshaw made his second visit to Fairlyden. He had been away for most of the summer, supervising an extension to one of his factories and making agreements for the supply of wool, both British and Australian. He wanted only the best to make his famous worsted cloth and he always dealt personally with the merchants. At last he had returned to sort out the problems of his latest acquisition, Strathtod Estate.

He was almost ashamed of his purchase now that he saw the full extent of the neglect. He had granted every tenant a year without rent, but in return he demanded improvements. He wanted these put in hand before his son, Crispin, arrived to inspect his new investment. Sarah gained the impression that Mr Bradshaw was boyishly eager for his son's approval of his Scottish estate, and that such approval was not easily won.

Her assumption was correct but she had much to learn about Crispin Bradshaw. His early character had been shaped in a hard mould. Meanwhile Sarah welcomed any cheerful visitor who might bring a smile to her father's drawn face.

'We 'ave a young feller visiting t' Tower 'ouse,' Bert Bradshaw announced casually as he accepted his second slice of her gingerbread one afternoon. ' 'E was asking about a certain luvely lass.' His eyes twinkled in his round, chubby face. 'If I'd bin twenty years younger, I wouldn't 'ave stayed away from you all this while, Sarah lass.'

Her heart began to thump. A becoming blush crept into her cheeks.

'And which young man wad that be, Mr Bradshaw?' Sandy asked curiously. 'Surely young Jardine hasna started visiting the Tower House?' He knew that the storekeeper's youngest son had long been an admirer of Sarah but she had never shown the slightest interest in any young man. He had assumed it was because she did not want to leave Fairlyden.

'Why, 'tis William Fairly. He didn't know t'estate 'ad been sold until he arrived, poor young gent. Only got a letter a few weeks ago, 'e did - about t' Earl's death an' all. He came soon as 'e could. 'E had cholera or summat bad like that. Nearly died '

Sarah's face lost its colour.

'Oh, he's fine now, lass - or soon will be when Mrs Bunnerby 'as fed 'im up for a few weeks. Real good cook is Mrs Bunnerby. Better 'n them American women that were looking after 'im where 'e was. Nuns they was. Fed t' lad nowt but boiled corn!'

'Wh-where will he go? Now that the estate is sold?' Sarah tried to sound calm, but she felt as breathless as if she had run a mile.

'We-ell, he says the Countess owed 'im nowt. I told 'im 'e can stay a while, but I reckon he'll go back to America. He'll be ower 'ere soon as 'e recovers 'imself though, or my name's not Bert Bradshaw!' He beamed at Sarah. 'My, one look an' 'is eyes will not rove no more - you mark my words! You was t' only one 'e asked for - after he knew what'd 'appened to t' estate.'

Sarah did not see the frown on Sandy's face, nor was she aware of the colour ebbing and flowing in her own cheeks. She simply knew that the world seemed brighter, despite the terrible weather, the corn waiting to be gathered in, and her father's unusually low spirits. Her heartbeat refused to slow to its usual steady rhythm - even when she sternly reminded herself that she had not seen William Fairly since she was a child. Perhaps he had a wife and children. Also she must remember that he was a Fairly. The late Earl had been despicable, and he had made many enemies - especially the O'Connors.

Bert Bradshaw guessed that William wanted an excuse to stay in the area. He was too shrewd a Yorkshireman to let such a golden opportunity slip away. He soon devised a plan which would benefit them both. He was impatient to restore his new property, but business demanded his return to Halifax. William remembered Strathtod as it had been when he was a boy, and he had known many of the tradesmen and their families. It did not take long for Bert to persuade him to make his home at the Tower House for the next few months; in return William would oversee the work, deal with any minor problems and send regular reports to Yorkshire.

The continuing handicap of his twisted leg worried Sandy far more than the pain. Every pair of hands was needed to snatch in the harvest, especially when the weather was so unsettled. Consequently William Fairly received a more friendly reception than he had dared to hope when he rode over to Fairlyden and offered his assistance. Although Sandy eyed him warily, he knew he could not refuse such an offer.

Gradually Sandy began to welcome William's visits. The young man's conversation was interesting and it took Sandy's mind off his own troubles, if only for a little while. He could see no way of repaying the loan with Lucifer dead and himself no better than an invalid. Even finding next year's rent might prove a burden, unless his leg recovered enough for him to travel with Logan's Bobby to earn service fees in the spring.

Few men possessed Dick O'Connor's uncanny instinct with cattle and pigs and William admitted he would never have Louis's skill with the plough either, but he soon proved himself no stranger to harvesting corn despite the lingering effects of the cholera. He worked hard, scything with Louis, tying sheaves with Sarah and Agnes, stooking, and restooking after the rain showers delayed the gathering of the sheaves.

Sarah had been secretly dismayed at the sight of his gaunt face and the sprinkling of silver in his hair the first day he called at Fairlyden, but it was wonderful to see that his eyes still reflected the same kindness and compassion she remembered.

William fell into the habit of appearing at Fairlyden in time for breakfast each morning and Sarah soon began to feel that her childhood friendship with him had never been interrupted; indeed, as the weeks passed the threads of friendship strengthened, binding them together as they worked in harmony or relaxed in the evenings in Fairlyden's cosy kitchen. The teasing laughter in William's eyes often brought shy blushes to Sarah's cheeks, a fact which Sandy noted with some misgiving, though he was relieved to see William possessed none of the cruel spite which had been such a mark of his brother's character.

Since Dick O'Connor's arrest, Sarah had returned to the task of collecting the meal from the mill herself, so she often saw Beatrice. Recently she had detected a certain coolness in their relationship, and it puzzled her.

'What is troubling you, Beattie?' she asked one day while she waited for Edward Slater to lower the sacks of meal into the cart. Beatrice's soft mouth pursed stubbornly at first, then:

'You have always liked William Fairly! Ever since the first time you met him at Strathtod mill, when we were still at school!' she declared accusingly.

Sarah felt her cheeks flush. 'Of course I like him. We are grateful for his help '

'I suppose poor Dick means nothing to you now!' Beatrice could not hide her distress. Sarah gazed at her in astonishment.

'You must know how much we miss Dick, Beattie. There will always be a place for him at Fairlyden, but we need every pair of hands we can get.'

'Even a Fairly's!' Beatrice snorted with contempt. 'Have you forgotten it was his brother who caused Vicky O'Connor's death? Now Dick is in prison, and he does not even know of his own mother's death; he will never see her again.' Beatrice was almost sobbing and Sarah stared at her dearest friend in dismay.

'William had nothing to do with Lord James's vile conduct! He would disown his relationship to the Earl if he could. You know William was always a friend to the O'Connors, Beattie. He tried to help Rory, he took them back to the farm. It was he who helped Lord Reginald to fix their rent and protect their lease.'

'Then where was he when Dick needed a friend?' Beattie demanded coldly.

'He was fighting for his own life,' Sarah answered quietly, 'with the aid of some good nuns in America.'

'Oh.' Beatrice's shoulders slumped and the fire seemed to die out of her.

'What is it, Beattie?' Sarah asked softly. They had never quarrelled in all the years they had been friends. Sarah gazed at Beatrice's bowed head with widening eyes, remembering how eagerly Dick used to set out for the mill. 'You love Dick?' she murmured.

Beatrice shrugged and turned away, neither acknowledging nor denying her feelings. Sarah was glad Beatrice's father was nowhere in sight. She detested Edward Slater's sly looks and increasingly brazen stares, and knew he would have mocked Beattie's tender feelings most cruelly, especially now that Dick would be branded a criminal.

Thirty

Sandy listened avidly to William's accounts of life in America and the young man was only too willing to share the evening meal at Fairlyden and to linger afterwards. He told Sandy of the vast prairies and the man

McCormick, who had invented a machine that could cut the corn and bind it into sheaves before it even touched the ground. They had lengthy discussions on the breeding of horses and Sarah listened to their conversation as she sewed and darned and knitted beside the fire.

William refused to accept payment for his help with the harvest.

'I know you miss Dick O'Connor,' he said, when Sandy tried to insist, 'and I feel responsible in part.'

'Ye canna be held responsible for your brother's actions,' Sandy said gruffly, but did not press the matter of payment.

William had begun to suspect that Alexander Logan had some secret anxiety; certainly he had more integrity than money. William smiled wryly to himself as he contrasted the independence of his fellow countrymen with the men he had met on his travels. He had done most of the work towards building up an exporting business during his sojourn in America, but he had owned it in conjunction with a Frenchman and a Dutchman. His partners had barely stopped to consider him when he had been taken ill. Confounded by the intricacies of business, they had cut their losses, divided the available cash between them, dumped him in a convent with barely enough to pay for his funeral, and made their departure.

It had taken some time for the news of James's death to catch up with him, and indeed it was a wonder the Countess's letter had found him at all. He was penniless by the time he had recovered sufficiently to contemplate the journey across the Atlantic. Fortunately closer examination of his affairs had revealed that he was in sole possession of a lease for two empty warehouses and a third, still half full of grain. This had proved to be more valuable than money. Two years of deplorable weather in Europe, and the subsequent poor harvests, had increased demand and he had sold the grain at a substantial profit. Storage space near the docks was a valuable asset. The leases had another five years to run and he had sold them to other traders. He was not wealthy, but even after paying his return passage, he still had a few hundred pounds.

He had been filled with profound regret when he learned that the whole of his family's estate had already been sold, and was appalled by the deterioration of it. He realised he had little option but to return to America where he could make his fortune buying and selling grain - but this time he did not intend to travel alone.

Once, during his slow recovery at the convent, one of the younger nuns had smiled her serene smile and asked what he dreamed of in the long hours he spent alone.

'A young girl with thick brown hair and flashing dark eyes,' he had replied promptly. 'A child with a courageous spirit and a smile like an angel.' Yet even his daydreams had not prepared him for the reality of the slender young woman with the fair, flawless skin and lustrous dark eyes; he had an almost insane desire to bury his face in Sarah's shining tresses. He felt his pulses quicken at the very thought of her in a demure white nightgown, with her dark hair streaming down her back

He was no monk, but no woman had disturbed his thoughts as Sarah did now. He knew she was aware of him. He had seen her bright eyes watching him covertly beneath their thick crescents of curling lashes. Only yesterday he had come upon her unexpectedly in the dairy.

'You startled me!' she protested, pressing a hand to her heart, but he had seen the swift colour rush in her cheeks and knew she was aware of him as a man. At the table his hand had touched hers as she passed the dish of meat; it had amused and pleased him to see her small white teeth catch her lower lip in confusion. He found it more and more difficult to draw his eyes from her parted lips, or from the agitated rise and fall of her firm young breasts beneath the neat bodice of her dress.

Yet there was a barrier between them. William sensed it was not merely the shyness of an innocent, untouched girl. Sarah had an aura of reserve. It puzzled, intrigued, and even angered him. He knew he must have patience. She was eleven years younger than himself and his health might never be as robust as it had been before the cholera. He had no great fortune to tempt her away from Fairlyden either, and he knew how much she loved her home and her step-father. Yet William had a firm conviction that a man should provide his own house and be the master of it, and he could no longer do that at Strathtod. Time was passing quickly; the harvest would soon be over.

Ever since Mattie's death Sandy had insisted that the Sabbath day must be observed. Cows had to be milked and cattle fed, but there was no work done in the fields, and Agnes Jamieson usually returned to Mains of Muir to visit her mother and sister after attending the Reverend Mackenzie's church. William Fairly had no reason to call at Fairlyden, and for the first time in her life Sarah found the peaceful hours of the Sabbath dragging slowly.

She was not alone in this. William fretted restlessly as he prowled around his boyhood haunts on the Strathtod Estate and carefully checked the progress of the alterations and repairs for Mr Bradshaw.

It was a fine autumn morning and Sandy was feeling more cheerful as he drove Sarah home from church in the pony and trap. The weather seemed settled and he knew the last of the harvest would be safely gathered in before the dawn of the next Sabbath. He resolved to put aside his anxiety over his debt to the bank, at least for this one day. He was surprised when he looked up to see William riding towards them on his chestnut mare. He glanced at Sarah and saw she was blushing.

How pretty she looks in her lemon muslin dress, with the matching ribbons on her bonnet, he thought with a sigh. William Fairly echoed the thought, judging by the look in his eye, Sandy decided. He made a determined effort to put aside his own troubles.

'Would ye like to join us, William?' he asked cheerfully.

'It is a very simple meal today,' Sarah said hastily. 'Agnes is visiting her family and...'

'And you will brighten up the simplest of fare!' William smiled, enjoying her confusion and the lovely colour in her cheeks.

An hour later he found himself watching her slender figure as she removed the dishes from the table to the scullery. Almost without conscious thought he pushed back his chair and followed her, closing the kitchen door behind him.

'Walk with me a little way, Sarah,' he said softly. She spun round from the stone bench where she washed the dishes, just as Mattie had once done.

'Oh! I did not hear you follow me,' she said breathlessly.

'Will you walk with me as far as the burn?'

'I canna. I have the dishes to wash.'

'Surely they will wait a while, Sarah?' She stared into his dark eyes and found she could barely breathe. His gaze would not release her.

'But you have your horse. Surely you will be riding home?'

'Are you so eager to see me gone then, or is it that you wish to ride with me?' William's dark eyes sparkled. 'Remember you rode with me once? I will hold you tightly '

'William Fairly!' Sarah gasped, but her indignation was mostly pretence; her eyes were very bright.

'Do you remember riding with me, Sarah?' he asked curiously.

'Yes, I do. And you wrinkled your nose in disgust!' Even now her voice shook at the remembered humiliation.

'But I'm sure you smell delightful today - of lavender and rose petals, perhaps?'

'Maybe, maybe not.'

'Perhaps I should come a little closer so that I might know for certain what pretty young ladies use to make themselves so enchanting.'

'No!' Sarah put out a hand, but William had already taken one step towards her. He was in a delightfully flirtatious mood. It pleased her, and yet she was afraid. She could feel her heart bumping erratically.

'Please walk a little way with me, Sarah.' William's dark eyes had changed, the laughter had gone. 'There are things I would like to tell you, many things I would like to ask but we are never alone.'

'No, I cannot. It is not seemly.' Sarah's face was pale now. What did William want to say? Well-brought-up young ladies did not walk alone with gentlemen unless they were betrothed. Perhaps Master Fairly had forgotten that? So many of the old traditions seemed to have been cast aside in the places where he had travelled. William waited, but Sarah could not give him the answer he wanted. She could not, dare not, walk alone with him in the quiet of the Sabbath afternoon.

'Then I must bid you good-day,' William said quietly.

He did not return to the kitchen. Instead he went through the dairy and down to the stables to collect his horse. Sarah watched him go. She felt curiously deflated. Surely he might have been a little more persistent? She had a feeling she had disappointed him - yet he could not really have expected her to go with him?

Sandy had watched William leave the kitchen and his blue eyes were troubled. He was aware of the increasing tension between Sarah and William and it worried him. How will he react if he discovers Sarah is not Daniel Munro's daughter? he pondered anxiously. Only the Reverend Mackenzie knew the truth. Other people assumed Sarah addressed him as 'Father' because he was her step-father, and also her guardian since childhood. Would William consider they had continued the pretence to cheat his half-brother out of the rent? Would his admiration for Sarah turn to contempt? He knew how closely Sarah had guarded her heart since Danny's death, but the love between a man and a woman could overrule even the strongest will. Had Sarah already given her heart to William Fairly? Sandy prayed she would not be hurt again. On the heels of that thought came another. Supposing William took Sarah to America? She loved Fairlyden, it was the only home she had known, but it could never be hers - he knew that now.

The problem of the loan loomed even larger in Sandy's mind when he received a letter from the bank two days later. The farming year was almost over. It was more than six months since the Reverend Mackenzie had arranged the loan on his behalf. The directors of the bank were concerned, in view of his promise to repay the money within three months, especially considering the uncertain future of British agriculture.

It was painfully clear to Sandy that he must tell Sarah the truth, but first he would try to persuade Mr Bradshaw to buy the land from him. If the Yorkshireman would not, or perhaps could not, offer the sum he had paid to the Countess, then they were completely ruined. Sandy dared not think of it.

'We must have a kirn to celebrate the end of the harvest!' William declared a few days later as the last sheaf was tossed from the cart, high up on to the cornstack.

'Aye!' Janet agreed enthusiastically. 'We could clean the barn and have a dance!'

'It would be an opportunity for the Muircumwell and Strathtod folks to get together too,' William agreed.

Sarah was excited by the idea. There had been little cause for celebration in her young life and the look in William's dark eyes made her blood tingle.

'Agnes and I will bake pies and plum cakes,' she said eagerly. And I will make myself a new dress, she thought with excitement. Sandy could not bring himself to cast a cloud on Sarah's anticipation.

As she worked with Agnes Jamieson and Janet, cleaning the house and baking and boiling ham, her thoughts were with William. He seemed happier than he had been since the afternoon she refused to walk with him to the burn; in fact, he was happier than he had been since he returned to Scotland. She wondered if the change had anything to do with the arrival of the Bradshaw girls at the Tower House; perhaps his idea of holding the kirn was really for them. The thought did not please her.

William had arranged for Sam Black, the Muircumwell blacksmith, and John Benson, the miller from Strathtod, to bring their fiddles for the dancing. Sarah felt guilty about the purchase of a length of sprigged muslin for a new dress, but as the preparations proceeded her excitement grew. She could never hope to compete with the fine silk gowns of the Misses Bradshaw, but without vanity she knew she was taller and more graceful than either of them, and she had no need to pinch her cheeks and lips to make them red. Just for a moment her hand hovered over the pastry she was rolling as she wondered whether William preferred girls who simpered as Freda Bradshaw did, or if he liked eyes as blue as cornflowers like Miss Fanny's. She thought of the parties the Bradshaw sisters enjoyed in Yorkshire or in London. Did William yearn for such gaiety?

The celebration was in full swing and the laughter and singing of the menfolk grew louder as the ale flowed freely. The skill of the fiddlers had every foot tapping to the music. Anxieties had been thrust aside, if only briefly. It was the first time that people from Muircumwell and Strathtod had celebrated together and there was a warmth and merriment in the air which was infectious. The Strathtod folk were beginning to get the measure of their new landlord. Bert Bradshaw respected those who worked hard, despite the difficult times; he was kind and considerate to those who were sick and could not help themselves; to those who whined and made little effort, he had delivered a stern warning. Beneath the jovial expression they glimpsed the steel which had made the ragged urchin into the urchins' master. He had brought strength and stability to Strathtod, and most of his tenants were learning to respect him.

Sarah was proud and happy that this unique occasion should be held at Fairlyden. Just for a moment she was alone. The food had been served, eaten, and generously praised; she was free from further responsibilities for the rest of the evening. The minister and Mr Bradshaw had retired to the house with her father, to share a pipe and a quiet chat.

William had insisted on opening the dancing with her. When it ended she had been breathless and the look in William's dark eyes had turned her legs to water. She had no idea of the effect on him of her own flushed cheeks and rosy lips; someone had interrupted them as he bent to whisper in her ear. Now her heart began to pound as she saw him striding towards her.

'It was a splendid idea to have a kirn, William!' she rushed nervously into speech. He did not answer. There was a look of determination on his face as he took her elbow and led her out of the barn into the shadow of the stable wall. The first silvering of the full moon was rising above a distant hill. The music and laughter blended into muted, pleasurable melody. Before Sarah could speak again, William turned her to face him.

'Will you marry me, Miss Sarah Munro?' He heard her startled gasp.

'Oh, William!' She murmured his name breathlessly, hardly able to believe she had heard the words her heart had dreamed of in the lonely darkness of her little chamber. He saw the gleam of her small white teeth as her lips parted in a smile. Suddenly she tensed. 'Sarah Munro' he had called her. He still did not know. Suddenly she was afraid - so afraid that she would lose him. She would be hurt again. She should never have allowed her heart its freedom. She trembled.

'Say you will marry me, Sarah, so that I may speak to your stepfather and to The Reverend Mackenzie tonight,' William urged huskily.

'Alexander Logan is…He is my real father.' Her voice was no more than a whisper, but William Fairly heard it.

He stared down into her upturned face, so strained, so pale - and yet so lovely in the light of the moon.

Thirty-One

Sarah lifted her head defiantly and looked William in the eye. 'I am proud that Alexander Logan is my father,' she declared fiercely. 'He loved my mother even when she was a child.'

'And I have loved you since you were a child, my fiery Sarah, and I cannot stop loving you now!' William drew her into his arms. His lips touched hers in a fleeting kiss.

Sarah knew then; all through the years she had been waiting for him, ever since he had comforted her beside the burn. Her heart sang.

'Will you be my wife, Sarah?' William repeated softly.

'Yes. Oh, yes!' she whispered fervently, without thought of his plans for their future together. Her eyes fell shyly before the dark intensity of his gaze.

'Come, let us go and ask your father's blessing.' William clasped her arm and guided her towards the house.

Sandy and the Reverend Robert Mackenzie were standing at the door, savouring the beauty of the moonlit night, while Bert Bradshaw prepared to take his leave.

'Will you be comin' back in t' coach, lad, wi' Fanny and Freda?' Bert asked when he saw William.

'No thanks, Mr Bradshaw. I, er, have some business with Mr Logan. In fact, now that the alterations to the Tower House are almost finished, I think I must be making plans to return to America.' He did not hear Sarah's stifled gasp.

'Don't you be worryin' yer 'ead about that, lad. It's t' farms that need attention now. I'm tryin' to persuade Mr Logan 'ere to be me steward. He knows what's needed.'

'I tell you it is a factor you need,' Sandy repeated for the third time. He had been astounded by the proposal. He regarded himself as no more than an ordinary farmer, and a crippled one at that! Still, he couldn't help being flattered by the shrewd Yorkshireman's proposition; neither could he deny that the challenge of restoring Strathtod Estate to its former prosperity would have appealed to him immensely. If he could earn some money, he might even be able to pay off his debt to the bank but it would take a long, long time, and he would have to find extra help for Sarah at Fairlyden. Sandy was lost in a dream world of his own.

Bert Bradshaw had been quick to see his interest and did not give up easily. Now he squinted through bleary eyes at William standing close to Sarah, eyeing her with that look a man gives the woman he loves. And she looking all shy and a bit pale. His attention returned to Sandy.

'Sandy Logan! I tell 't thee already - I've gotten meself a clerk to see to t' figures. He knows about costs an' prices. But as I said afore, 'e knows nowt about farmin'! I want a man who 'as learned every bloody thing for 'imself - from cleanin' t' shit from t' sheds to breedin' t' best 'osses in t' district! Er, beggin' yer pardon, Reverend!'

Robert Mackenzie inclined his head, and hid a smile behind his pipe. Bert Bradshaw had enjoyed several glasses of whisky and his Yorkshire accent and blunt manner had increased accordingly, but Robert Mackenzie liked him. His proposal was a good one too. Sandy's leg would never again allow him to walk long distances with the stallions or behind the plough, but he could still use his eyes and his head, and ride a horse.

'I tell't thee, Sandy Logan, I've made me inquiries. Any road, I've seen that tha's done more for Fairlyden than any fancy gentleman could 'ave. What do you reckon, Reveren'?'

Robert Mackenzie nodded slowly. 'I think it is a good idea. The farms and the tenants on the estate would benefit from Sandy's experience. Those who earn their living from the land will find hard times ahead, I fear.'

'There! Come on, man!' Bert Bradshaw coaxed. 'Tha'll not be needed at Fairlyden much longer if tha takes a look at these two luv birds! They'll be sailing off to America afore tha' knows!' He grinned knowingly at William, his accent thickening by the second. 'I allus knew that's the way the wind blew, lad. Ther's nowt makes a man as 'appy as t' luv of a good woman! Aye, by gum! Miss Sarah's a fine 'un. I tried to tell that lad of mine he ought to cum an' court her but Crispin wouldn't listen.' He shook his head sadly for a second while Sandy stared at William and Sarah in dismay. 'I wish thee 'appiness,' Bert Bradshaw boomed at William. 'So, 'ow about my little proposition then, Sandy Logan? Shake me 'and on 't afore I go 'ome. I've t' catch t'early train in t' mornin'. Cum on, lad, make tha mind up!' He extended his broad, stubby hand determinedly.

Sandy stared at it, then at the moon sailing overhead like a silver galleon. There would be nothing for him at Fairlyden without Sarah. What did it matter where he lived or what he did? She would be thousands of miles away across the sea - even if she did look up and see the same moon. Sandy felt his heart was breaking all over again. Slowly, as though in a dream, he reached out his hand.

Bert Bradshaw shook it eagerly. A man usually got what he wanted, if he persevered; he kept telling Crispin that.

When Bert had gone Sandy moved back into the house, his shoulders bowed, his limp even more pronounced. Sarah's heart ached as she followed him. She felt torn in two. How could she sail away across the sea with the man she loved, when she must leave behind her father, the dear, kind man who had worked so hard and sacrificed so much for her?

Sandy looked up and saw the love and the sorrow in her eyes. He guessed what was in her mind. He gave himself a mental shake. Sarah must never feel bound to him. Haltingly he began to tell her about the loan, and the anxiety that had gnawed at him since Lucifer's death.

'I wanted ye to have fifty-two acres of Fairlyden's best land as well as the house and steading, lassie, but I've failed ye badly. I'm sorry, Sarah,' he murmured gruffly. 'I'll ask Mr Bradshaw if he will buy Fairlyden. There should be a wee bit o' money left for ye tae take with ye.' Sandy struggled to keep his voice steady. 'If Mr Bradshaw canna - or willna - buy it, then I've lost everything. Even your Grandfather Cameron's precious savings.' He bowed his head, but Sarah ran to him and clasped her arms around his neck.

At last she understood why he had been so troubled all these months! It had not been his own injuries which had worried him, but the burden of the debt to the bank and worry for her own future. How could she leave him so alone? Her dark eyes implored William to understand.

He understood only too well. Suddenly he was afraid. He knew Sarah was fiercely loyal, and she owed a great debt to the man who had toiled for her, and watched over her, all her life. But I can't let her go! he thought frantically. Not now that I have found her again. I love her too much.

'Does that mean,' he said slowly, 'that if I can raise enough money to pay off the bank loan, I could own Fairlyden, or at least a part of it?'

Sandy and Sarah stared at him in amazement.

'Could ye do that?' Sandy asked incredulously.

'Would you do that?' Sarah asked softly.

'I think I could. Certainly I would, if it means winning you for my wife, my dearest Sarah!' A slow smile began to lighten his sombre expression.

'Ye dinna mind not returning to America, to make your fortune, William?' Sandy faltered, as new hope began to dawn.

'I cannot promise to become a good Scottish farmer but I suppose I can learn to buy and sell cattle and pigs, just as I learned to buy and sell grain on the other side of the world,' William mused.

'Maybe you could travel the stallions in Father's stead?' Sarah suggested tentatively.

'Aye! Now that wad be a good idea, if ye're willing?' Sandy agreed with enthusiasm. 'I recall ye were aye good with horses as a laddie. I wadna like to be without the Clydesdales, factor or no! And Fairlyden needs them,' he added soberly.

'So long as Sarah is my wife, I believe I could do almost anything,' William grinned. 'Besides, I often dreamt of owning a bit of Strathtod, even only a very small corner. It is the land where my ancestors trod.'

Sarah looked at him, her dark eyes glowing with love. 'I shall make Fairlyden the happiest place on earth for you, I promise!'

*

Fanny Bradshaw had brought a gift of ivory satin with matching lace and ribbons to make Sarah's wedding gown, and they had sent away for one of the new paper patterns from a ladies' magazine, so that Mistress MacFarlane could help fashion the latest style. It was even to have two skirts; the top one would be drawn back to reveal a panel of lace frills down the front, and there would be a fashionable bustle at the back, and the neatest nipped in waist imaginable. Sarah had never worn the tightly laced corsets of the fashion conscious town ladies but on this occasion Fanny insisted it was essential. Sarah knew it was going to be the most beautiful dress in the world and she could not thank Fanny enough, especially when she arrived from Yorkshire with a length of blue satin for Beatrice.

Beatrice had been reluctant to be Sarah's best maid at the wedding, because her bridegroom was a Fairly. She felt torn between her affection for Sarah and her secret loyalty to Dick O'Connor. Unknown to anyone except her grandfather, she had managed to visit Dick in Dumfries Prison. He had been pathetically pleased to see her, but was far too modest to guess he had aroused such tenderness in her young heart. It saddened him to hear that her long friendship with Sarah seemed threatened by the Fairly connection. William had always been popular with all the estate tenants in the past. Of all the Fairly sons and grandsons, he bore the closest resemblance to his grandfather, Jonathan Fairly. Even so, Dick knew in his heart that he would never return to Fairlyden with William Fairly as its new master. Nevertheless, he persuaded Beatrice to be Sarah's attendant at the wedding.

Her visit had brought him new hope and Beatrice extracted a promise that he would stay at the mill house when he was released from prison. It was a promise he gave willingly, and with relief, though next year seemed a lifetime away. Beatrice refused to consider the consequences of her invitation to Dick or her visit to the prison. She had no intention of telling anyone about them - least of all the loathsome man who called himself her father.

Sarah was grateful for Beatrice's support on her wedding day. Despite her love for William she was innocent of the ways of men, and she was nervous. She knew William had inherited none of his father's spite or his brother's cruelty, but he was proud and possessive and Sarah had seen the latent passion in his dark eyes. Even now she was half afraid happiness might be wrenched away from her.

'I really needed you today, Beattie,' she confided softly as they stood together before the long mirror which William had had sent from England as a gift. 'You have always been my dearest friend - almost like a sister.'

Sandy listened to his daughter's remark with an affectionate smile. Even as he watched the two slender figures in their lovely gowns, a shaft of sunlight came streaming through the window and burnished the golden head and the dark one with the same coppery glow. He was struck by the momentary resemblance. He saw Beatrice turn to Sarah with her gentle, reassuring smile, yet there was a wistful sadness in the depths of her blue eyes. Sandy blinked. Just for a moment he was transported back over the years. He was thirteen, at Nethertannoch, bewildered and made uncertain by the upheaval in his life. He had looked from Matthew Cameron to his mother. His own mother - yet Beatrice's smile had reminded him of her so clearly! Beatrice turned to help Sarah with her gown, and Sandy shook his head impatiently. The resemblance was no more than a fleeting fancy. He should not have drunk a glass of whisky so early in the day! Yet the sight of Beatrice's smile was to tease the edges of his memory in the months and years ahead

William had asked Crispin Bradshaw to be his best man, although the two had met only when Crispin had accompanied his sisters for short visits to the Tower House. Sarah had not met Bert Bradshaw's son at all, but she was too nervous and excited to notice anything about him except that he had the most penetrating grey eyes she had ever seen. Crispin Bradshaw was not so constrained. He stood erect, half a head taller than William, and there was little about Sarah which was not imprinted on his memory that day. Although his expression reflected none of his inner feelings he was secretly staggered by the vision of loveliness she presented. He tried to concentrate on his own plans for the future, but without his usual success. He gritted his teeth and thought of his mother.

Crispin had long since resolved that he would never marry. He would never put a woman through the agonies of childbirth such as his mother had suffered, nor love any woman as he had loved her. He had never managed to forget the grief and poverty of his childhood. He clearly remembered his early years in a cramped, damp little terraced cottage, where poverty hung around every corner and one disease after another whistled through the cracks. He remembered his sweet-faced mother, struggling to feed and clothe them on the meagre wage her husband earned in the loom shed, before he gained a precarious foothold on the first rung of the industrial ladder.

His father worked every hour of the day, and often into the night. By the time fortune had begun to peep through the stormy clouds, the Bradshaw family had expanded to three younger sisters, all born within the space of five years. Mrs Bradshaw's health had suffered accordingly. The three little girls, along with countless other children, had succumbed to the fever which swept through the town.

Bert Bradshaw had sent his wife to stay with her parents on the edge of the moors. Crispin had accompanied her and gradually a little of the bloom had returned to his mother's gentle face. When they rejoined his father they had moved to a cottage with a postage stamp garden on the outskirts of the town. Less than a year later Crispin had another sister, Fanny, and two years after that Freda had been born. His mother's health had deteriorated rapidly then; even the move to another, drier house with a larger garden could not halt her decline. Crispin had been ten when she died, Fanny three and Freda only a year old. The girls had not missed their mother as he had missed her; they did not remember the times when their father had been unable to buy enough to eat, much less silks and satins for dresses and ribbons to trim the latest creation in hats.

Now Crispin was twenty-nine years old. The Bradshaw mills were doing well, and expanding. His father had tried to convince him that even the briefest joy was better than none at all. He had urged him to visit Scotland. He had described Miss Sarah Munro in glowing terms - slender as a reed, graceful, but certainly not weak; flashing dark eyes and the fairest, clearest skin he had ever seen - just like a flower. Bert Bradshaw prided himself on being a good judge of character and he believed Miss Munro to be thrifty and intelligent. Crispin had laughed aloud.

'No woman could have so many virtues, Father!' he had scoffed. Yet, as he watched Sarah Munro in her wedding gown - already making her vows to love, honour and obey - he thought he could almost regret his stubborn refusal to humour his father.

*

On a hot afternoon towards the end of July 1882, the last load of hay had been gathered. The meadow looked shorn and brown. William was busily forking the hay through a small door into the loft above the stable where Sarah was waiting to receive and stack it. Three months had passed since the wedding but they still found pleasure in these precious, private moments, working together in harmony.

William chased the last wisps of hay around the bottom of the cart and skewered them with his two-pronged fork. As soon as he had aimed it into the loft he climbed on to the side of the cart and sprang up after it with the agility of a cat. Sarah gasped in alarm lest he should fall, but his hand grasped the frame of the narrow door and he hauled himself safely upwards and fell on to the hay beside her. They had an excellent view of the glen from their eyrie. Side by side they gazed out at the fields and the meandering burn. Beyond, the shining waters of the Solway gleamed in the sunlight, and the peaks of the Galloway and the Cumberland hills towered into the blue sky.

'The tide must be in,' William remarked. 'We could never see it from Strathtod Tower, you know.'

'I know. It is because Fairlyden slopes towards the south.' She sighed happily. William clasped her hands and pulled her firmly into his arms.

'William!' Her protest was feeble. She always thrilled to the tips of her toes when her husband had that certain look in his brown eyes, but she was far too shy to let him know. 'Louis will be bringing in the last cart'

William chuckled softly against her hair as he pulled her with him on to the soft hay in the sweet-scented darkness of the loft. 'It will be some time before Louis and the cart reach the yard, and Agnes Jamieson has gone to draw beer to celebrate the last load home.'

Sarah smiled against the roughness of his cheek. She had heard him telling Agnes to set out the beer and cakes - and not to hurry back. The hot blood surged in her veins.

Somewhere in the blue patch of sky beyond the little door, a bumble bee hummed drowsily; the warm air was redolent of the scent of new mown hay - good hay for once. What a relief that was after four near disastrous summers in a row. Sarah knew it was enough to swing the balance from failure to a safe future for them, and all connected with Fairlyden. A small sigh of pure happiness escaped her lips and she relaxed, savouring the strength of the arms that held her - giving and receiving the love that flowed between them with all the power of a river in spate.

William was filled with exultation as he sensed his wife's ultimate surrender, her triumphant response. The months of patient waiting, of care and gentleness, had brought his reward. Little by little the final barrier had begun to crumble. Sarah was his, wholly and completely.

And the minute seed of another generation was sown: to be nurtured with love and laughter; to be strengthened by the tears which must fall in every human life; to be blessed - if God was merciful.

Printed in Great Britain
by Amazon